"Brotherton and Lee masterfully cap[...] to face war's atrocities, as well as the h[...] [...]m back home. This is a winner."

Publishers Weekly starred review

"Brotherton and Lee are a narrative tour de force in their first novel together. With inspiration from true stories, the novel is an astonishing combination of gritty wartime action tempered with poignant growth and drama. A heartbreaking, resonant story with characters who effortlessly come alive makes this a must-read literary triumph."

Booklist starred review

"Brotherton lends his research prowess to Lee's suspense expertise in this gritty tale of suffering and redemption. A great read for those enthralled with real-life stories of war and survival."

Library Journal starred review

"Epic."

BookPage

"This is an unforgettable coming-of-age novel inspired by true and almost unbearably harrowing events in one of the darkest episodes of World War II. This is an important and masterful book of quality historical fiction."

Historical Novel Society

"*The Long March Home* by Tosca Lee and Marcus Brotherton is one of those books that's difficult to classify, which doesn't diminish its brilliance even a little bit. It's not a book about war so much as the strength and dignity of the human spirit. Superb in all respects."

BookTrib

"Tosca Lee and Marcus Brotherton bring to life the Pacific theater as seen through the eyes of three young enlisted men, once boyhood friends and now fellow soldiers. Packed with tension, peril, and the unimaginable horrors of a world at war, *The Long March Home* also reaches inside, bringing forth the lives lived and taken amid the turmoil . . . and a lost love that may yet be found in the ashes."

Lisa Wingate, #1 *New York Times* bestselling author of *Before We Were Yours* and *The Book of Lost Friends*

"Historically sound and deeply empathic, *The Long March Home* tells the remarkable story of three teenage boys and the girl they all adored before signing up to fight in the South Pacific during World War II. I've never read anything quite like it."

Mark Sullivan, #1 *New York Times* bestselling author of
Beneath a Scarlet Sky and *The Last Green Valley*

"*The Long March Home* is a riveting tale of friendship and war, survival and heroism. Well researched and authentic, it's a novel not to be missed by readers who find themselves spellbound by tales involving the Second World War."

Mark Greaney, #1 *New York Times* bestselling author
of *Burner: A Gray Man Novel*

"This story has such a personal feel to it that it reads more like a memoir than fiction. It has such real characters that I was rooting for them through their harrowing ordeal and weeping for those who were lost."

Rhys Bowen, *New York Times* bestselling author of *The Venice Sketchbook*

"An utterly compelling exploration of the tenacity and resilience of the human spirit. Here is an outstanding story by two master wordsmiths that honors not only those who died and those who survived the Bataan Death March but all who spent the years of World War II as prisoners."

Susan Meissner, *USA Today* bestselling author
of *The Nature of Fragile Things*

"Sometimes novelists can trump historians in bringing the past to life. That is certainly the case in Marcus Brotherton and Tosca Lee's *The Long March Home*, which re-creates the hell of the Bataan Death March in stark clarity. It's fiction—but it's truth."

Stephen Hunter, Pulitzer Prize–winning and *New York Times* bestselling author of *Point of Impact* and *Basil's War*

"*The Long March Home* is a dazzling, gripping, compelling story of friendship and war, of courage and grief, of horror and survival. Vividly painted and compassionately told, it's a story that deserves to be remembered. A must-read."

Joseph Finder, *New York Times* bestselling author of *House on Fire*

"A powerful experience, a gripping story about the strength and resilience of the human heart, and a chapter of World War II history that shouldn't be forgotten."

Edward Burns, filmmaker (*The Brothers McMullen*)
and actor (*Saving Private Ryan*)

"Not since *Once an Eagle* has a novel so thoroughly captured what it means to go to war, fight, and return home with honor. You'll cheer through your tears for the three small-town boys who must weather one of World War II's darkest moments with nothing but their unbreakable brotherhood to sustain them. Simply magnificent."

Don Bentley, *New York Times* bestselling author of *Hostile Intent*

"From Mobile to Manila, Brotherton and Lee deliver one power-punched scene after another, crafting an emotionally charged, sensory-rich story of three young soldiers and the people who love them."

Julie Cantrell, *New York Times* and *USA Today*
bestselling author of *Perennials*

"A beautiful story of youth and friendship. Inspired by true stories, this is a fascinating and visual account."

Loucas George, producer of hit TV series *Nashville*

"A story full of hope, courage, friendship, faith, and loss told in a way that only true master storytellers like Brotherton and Lee can, *The Long March Home* takes you on a wonderful and horrible journey through the eyes of characters so real they leap from the page."

Andrews and Wilson, internationally bestselling authors of the
Shepherds, Tier One, and Sons of Valor series

"*The Long March Home* is a thrilling story, excellently told. It's a tale of friendship and hope during one of history's darkest moments."

Tyrell Johnson, internationally bestselling author of
The Wolves of Winter and *The Lost Kings*

"Marcus Brotherton and Tosca Lee have crafted a well-written story of the hell soldiers of the American Army faced on Bataan and later as prisoners of the Japanese in World War II. Brotherton and Lee do a good job of weaving together details of published accounts to keep this almost forgotten story alive."

Donald Caldwell, historian and author of *Thunder on Bataan*

"Brotherton and Lee have crafted a profoundly human story set against the epic backdrop of the Pacific theater of World War II. *The Long March Home* weaves a fragile thread of hope, resilience, forgiveness, and the powerful love of friends even in the midst of the hellish conditions of war, imprisonment, and torture."

Caleb McCary, twenty-one-year Army veteran and chaplain

"*Band of Brothers* meets *Empire of the Sun*. Amid vivid scene-setting, a captivating young narrator brings us the innocence, steel, and moral choices that come from a world being turned upside down, with one thought on a girl back home and another on surviving until the end of the day. This is war-writing at the highest level."

Humphrey Hawksley, BBC correspondent and author of *Man on Ice*

"*The Long March Home* is an immersive, deeply human portrait of the horrors of war and loss. With compelling characters and vibrant prose, it is a must-read for connoisseurs of World War fiction."

Aimie K. Runyan, bestselling author of *The School for German Brides*

"Not since James Jones has anyone written so well and tellingly of the war in the Pacific and the largely untold story of the 'Battling Bastards of Bataan.' Authentic, raw, and heartbreaking, this compelling tale of love and war and friendship in the face of impossible odds is a powerful and unputdownable read. A tremendous story."

Andrew Kaplan, *New York Times* bestselling author of *Blue Madagascar*

"*The Long March Home* is a remarkable novel. It's the story of a different age—the greatest generation caught up in its hour of greatest peril and pain—beautifully and faultlessly told by authors who know their craft. Brotherton and Lee craft characters so real they grab you by the throat and draw you into the story, so much so that their survival becomes your own."

Steve Martini, *New York Times* bestselling author of *Blood Flag*

THE
LONG
MARCH
HOME

Also by Marcus Brotherton

NONFICTION

A Bright and Blinding Sun
Blaze of Light
Shifty's War
A Company of Heroes
We Who Are Alive and Remain
Call of Duty (with Lt. Buck Compton)
Voices of the Pacific (with Adam Makos)
The Nightingale of Mosul (with Col. Susan Luz)
Tough As They Come (with SSG Travis Mills)
Grateful American (with Gary Sinise)

FICTION

Feast for Thieves

Also by Tosca Lee

FICTION

A Single Light
The Line Between
Firstborn
The Progeny
The Legend of Sheba
Iscariot
Forbidden (with Ted Dekker)
Mortal (with Ted Dekker)
Sovereign (with Ted Dekker)
Havah
Demon: A Memoir

THE
LONG
MARCH
HOME

A WORLD WAR II NOVEL
of the PACIFIC

MARCUS BROTHERTON
and TOSCA LEE

Revell

a division of Baker Publishing Group
Grand Rapids, Michigan

Published by Revell
a division of Baker Publishing Group
Grand Rapids, MI
www.revellbooks.com

Paper edition published 2023
ISBN 978-0-8007-4276-8

Printed in the United States of America

The Library of Congress has cataloged the original edition as follows:
Names: Brotherton, Marcus, author. | Lee, Tosca, author.
Title: The long march home : a World War II novel of the Pacific / Marcus Brotherton and Tosca Lee.
Description: Grand Rapids, MI : Revell, a division of Baker Publishing Group, [2023] | Includes bibliographical references.
Identifiers: LCCN 2022033755 | ISBN 9780800742751 (cloth) | ISBN 9781493441266 (ebook)
Subjects: LCSH: World War, 1939–1945—Philippines—Fiction. | Bataan Death March, Philippines, 1942—Fiction. | Americans—Philippines—Fiction. | Prisoners of war—Fiction. | LCGFT: War fiction. | Historical fiction. | Novels.
Classification: LCC PS3602.R64798 L66 2023 | DDC 813/.6—dc23/eng/20220715
LC record available at https://lccn.loc.gov/2022033755

The portion of Don Bell's radio announcement on page 31 is from an actual radio broadcast as recounted in A.V. H. Hartendorp, *The Japanese Occupation of the Philippines*, vol. 1 (Manila: Bookmark, 1967), 5, 470–71.

The "Battling Bastards of Bataan" on page 102 is part of the historic and widely documented oral history of the sick, starving, and undersupplied Allied forces struggling to maintain control of the Bataan Peninsula after General MacArthur obeyed President Roosevelt's command to leave the Philippines—and its fighting men—behind.

The proclamation on pages 103–4 from the Commander-in-Chief of the Imperial Japanese Forces is an actual U.S. War Department communiqué, as recounted by 2nd Lt. John Posten, Fighter Pilot, 17th Pursuit Squadron, in Donald Knox, *Death March: The Survivors of Bataan* (New York: Harcourt Brace Jovanovich, 1981), 90–91.

This is a work of historical reconstruction; the appearances of certain historical figures are therefore inevitable. All other characters, however, are products of the author's imagination, and any resemblance to actual persons, living or dead, is coincidental.

Marcus Brotherton is represented by WordServe Literary Group, www.wordserveliterary.com.

Baker Publishing Group publications use paper produced from sustainable forestry practices and post-consumer waste whenever possible.

24 25 26 27 28 29   7 6 5 4 3

For all who are finding their way home.

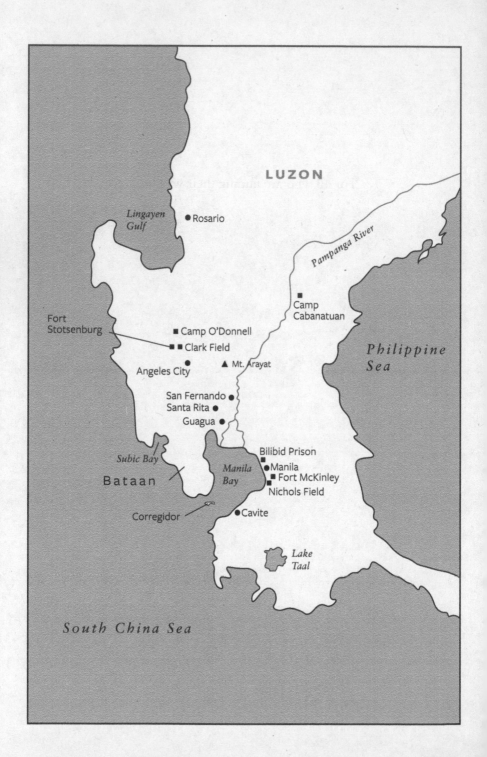

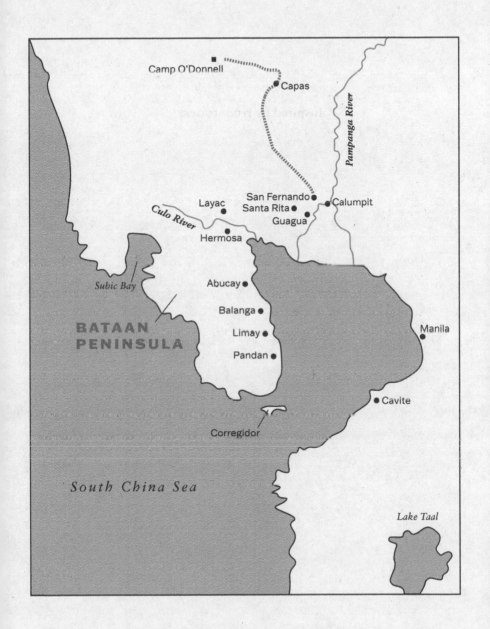

Inspired by true stories.

July 8, 1941

Dear Jimmy,

You left without a single word. How could you, James Pierce Propfield? Just three nights ago we danced and life was beautiful and almost like old times. Now you're gone and everything's different.

There are things you need to know, Jimmy. But you might as well be a ghost. I could hate you for leaving the way you did.

Then I feel guilty for thinking of myself when you're headed off to God only knows where in service to our country. I don't even have a proper address to send this yet, which means I don't know when or where these words may reach you or if they'll be lost along the way. Or if some stranger will stumble upon them and wonder who Jimmy Propfield is . . . not knowing he used to be my best friend.

Look after my little brother, please. You know very well Billy should never have been able to enlist yet. I also know he'd never have let you two go without him. I suppose you'll probably have to save Hank from himself while you're at it. You were always the responsible one.

Claire

1

DECEMBER 7, 1941
MANILA, PHILIPPINES

I admire the new cut of my khakis in the latrine mirror, flexing just enough to test the stretch of the shirt across my shoulder blades. I've filled out in the six months since we arrived as raw recruits. Grown half an inch too, I reckon. And even though I'm only a private, I got a fresh haircut and fifteen dollars left in my pocket after picking up my uniforms from the Chinese tailor, who was worth every penny.

The eighteen-year-old preacher's kid from Mobile, Alabama, is gone. A soldier of the Thirty-First Infantry stands in his place.

I tuck my tie into my shirt between the second and third buttons and straighten up tall. Raise my fingers to my brow in a perfect salute.

Not the same Jimmy "Propper" Propfield at all.

"Prop!" A lanky form rounds the corner. "Can we leave already?"

I drop my arm—too late. Even in my peripheral vision I can tell Billy's snickering. He gives a low whistle.

"Dang, we even wearin' the same uniform?" He looks down at himself. His shirt hangs from his shoulders, but at least he ain't the string bean he used to be. I wonder if his mama would recognize him with this much meat on his bones and without his freckles, which didn't fade so much as the rest of his skin just finally caught up. A state track star back home in Alabama, Billy was called "the Ginger Streak" by everyone on account of his red hair. He was so fast, that's all you'd see—a streak of ginger flying by. But the first two months here we called him the Lightning Lobster on account of his regular sunburn.

"I told you, you need to get at least one uniform cut down for parades," I say as we head out. "You wanna move up in rank, you gotta look the part."

Billy shrugs. "Don't know as I care about that. 'Sides, I think I'm still growin'."

Given that he's only sixteen and had to lie about his age to enlist, he's probably right. I also know he signed to have half his pay sent home to his mama and sisters.

I turn toward Billy as we don our caps beneath an overcast Manila sky. It's weird, him being nearly as tall as me. "Tell you what," I say. "Tomorrow afternoon we'll go down and get you fixed up. On me."

"Aw, I couldn't—"

"We're goin' and that's final. Call it an early birthday present."

"You're a good friend, Jimmy," Billy says. "I'm lucky to have you and Hank lookin' out for me."

Never mind that Hank's version of "looking out" for Billy has been to recommend he pick up a prophylactic kit with his weekend pass if he wants to avoid the clap. Ain't sure whether Hank learned that one the hard way since he got assigned to another company—a thing none of us was happy about until we found out his barracks was directly across from ours and that we could meet up any afternoon and head out together on pass.

Which we did, hitting town on payday to dance with the most beautiful girls I've ever seen at the first flashy cabaret we came to. We'd had a real good time too, first time out—before someone slipped Hank a Mickey and swiped Billy's and my wallets. We learned real fast to stay off the main strip on payday when the prices double, and to divide our money between our socks and pockets.

After waiting most of the day on my uniforms, Billy and me are the last ones we know to sign out. Everyone else—including Hank—left the Cuartel de España in the old walled city hours ago for Manila's restaurants, bars, and brothels.

There are only a few hawkers left on the cobblestone street beyond the sally port. The second we emerge they swarm us with souvenirs, candy, and postcards. Kids pull at our hands and pockets, hoping for coins.

Billy produces a pack of chewing gum with mock surprise. "Say, look what I just found in my pocket!" He asks a grinning little girl, "Did you put this here?" Kids flock to him like seagulls as he gives away the pieces.

As I wait for him, an old woman with a leathery face pushes a corsage toward me, her other hand outstretched. "For your sweetheart, Joe!"

"Ma'am, when I find her, I promise to buy them all." I press the flowers back into her palm with a ten-centavo coin. She smiles with a silent nod of thanks.

According to the news, there's tension on these islands. Here on Luzon, especially. We've been gearing up for war in the Philippines now for months—the reason General MacArthur was recalled to active duty and the Army started shipping out green recruits like us to do our basic training here.

But if there's tension, we don't feel it. And the war in Europe might as well be a world away.

A breeze blows through the park outside the old Spanish walls as I hail a brightly painted calesa. Just this morning we were out here running drills beneath pink-flowered trees. The calesa's driver brings the carriage to a stop and we climb in.

"The Metropolitan, please," I say as Billy and me climb aboard. The two-wheeled cart lurches forward and the pony clip-clops down the street. I gaze out the side of the carriage as we pass the Manila Hotel, where General MacArthur lives in a fifth-floor penthouse and officers have parties nearly every night. The portico's white columns are wound in red and green garland and I realize it's almost Christmas.

Billy starts talking about volcanoes. He's been going on and on about wanting to see one since we got here.

"We can take a bus to Lake Taal," Billy says. "There's a volcano right in the middle of the lake. Ain't that somethin'? A volcano in the middle of a lake!"

"That sounds real swell," I say before leaning forward to ask the driver, "Sir, can you take us by the Army-Navy Club?"

Billy groans. "We're gonna be late."

"No, we ain't." To the driver I say, "Is it true they got a fifty-foot-long buffet in there?"

"Buffet, yes," the man says. He's weathered and missing most of his teeth, but—like everyone else here—he smiles. "Bowling alley . . . swimming . . . restaurant . . . bar . . ."

We ride up the street, past the Army-Navy Club's tennis courts toward the university. What I ain't told anyone is that I've been looking into some courses there. Billy and Hank have already been making names for themselves on the regiment track and boxing teams since we arrived. But I was never a star athlete or fond of getting my nose broke.

So I got other plans.

Drills end at one o'clock every day on account of the heat. But while everyone else heads to the slop chute for cold beer and card playing, I'm fixing to earn me an education. By the time my tour's up, I intend to have a college degree and be lined up for a commission. I'll re-up and take out a furnished room at the Army-Navy Club. Take up tennis. Try out that fifty-foot buffet.

I glance back in time to see an officer toss the keys of his Chevy to a bellman out front of the club.

Maybe even buy me a sweet set of wheels.

But one thing I don't plan on: going back to Mobile. I was ruined for it the minute I saw the old Spanish shipwrecks in the harbor and tasted my first mango. The bells of Santo Domingo were still ringing their hellos when I swore I'd stay as long as I could. Because if this ain't paradise, I don't know what is. A place a young man like me can start fresh, prove himself, and build a future. Live like a king, even. We already eat better than we did at home and the dollar goes farther. True, there's no Crimson Tide football and I ain't seen grits or chocolate gravy. But as long as I got my two best friends, I have all I need.

The grand Metropolitan Theater looks more like a palace than a place to watch Mickey Mouse movies. *Sergeant York* just opened last night, and the line today is out the door and full of enlisted men. Billy and me get out and I pay the driver, but I don't see Hank anywhere.

"Don't tell me he ain't here," I mutter.

"Maybe he's already inside," Billy says.

I'm about to go in and look around when I hear a familiar shout farther up the street.

"Streak! Propper!" And then, with more belly, "James Pierce Propfield!"

It's the same voice that used to yell for me to pass the football, that egged me on to victory in the only fight I ever got in without him, and that announced we were enlisting back in July.

Which is how I also know its owner is drunk.

I scan the line of cabs letting passengers off at the curb and find Hank standing beside a taxi, hands cupped around his mouth like a megaphone.

"William Miles Crockett! Billyyyy!" he calls, voice going up an octave like he's calling in pigs.

Billy grimaces. "Why's he gotta carry on like that?"

"Hurry up!" I shout, waving him over as it starts to rain. "Movie starts in fifteen minutes!"

"Forget the movie!" Hank hollers. He sticks his hands in his pockets, turns sideways, and poses like some two-bit Gary Cooper. "The three of us are celebratin'. Get over here!"

Billy jogs to the curb. Next thing I know, he's whooping and slapping Hank on the back—I got no idea why . . .

Until I see the stiff new stripe on Hank's sleeve. I sigh and walk over.

At first I think it's a joke. That he must've stolen someone's uniform.

But then Hank's telling Billy thanks and grinning dimple to dimple with his chewing gum between his teeth.

Hank's been promoted to private first class.

I clap Hank on the back as we pile into the taxi, shaking my head the entire time. Because I know Hank ain't pulled half the guard duty Billy and me have. Those three days we spent marching one hundred miles to and from Subic Bay in the heat, Hank was chauffeuring officers around Manila in a car from the motor pool. Hank's the last of us three I'd have guessed would get promoted and the first I'd have predicted to land in the brig.

But I'm glad for him. He's nineteen and the oldest of us, so I guess it makes sense. Besides, Hank's the main reason we're here.

We hit the Silver Dollar Café first for fried chicken and local beer. By the time we land a table at our fourth bar, Hank and Billy have put away a dozen San Miguels and a couple jiggers of gin between them while I've nursed a series of Cokes. And because we've already toasted everyone from the company commander who approved Hank's promotion to Uncle Sam, the Crimson Tide's winning season, and Betty Grable's legs, I finally raise my glass and say, "To Private First Class Hank Wright."

Hank bows his head as we each take a drink.

"I got one," Billy says. "Remember this? To . . ." He wiggles his brows and starts gassing it up so hard the next part comes out as a squeak. "*The Lady Killers!*"

I sputter and Billy nearly falls out of his chair with a howl at the name Hank and me dubbed ourselves at the start of seventh grade.

"Boy, weren't we somethin'!" I laugh. "I got hold of my daddy's pomade and slicked back my hair and Hank thought for sure he was sprouting a Clark Gable mustache." I point my beer at Billy. "What were you in—sixth grade? How d'you even know about that? You know we can't let you live."

Hank chuckles, but he's staring at the bottle in his hand, not saying a word.

Billy and me fall quiet.

"You got one, Hank?" Billy asks after a minute.

Hank pauses and then nods, lifting his beer, if not his head.

"To . . ." He stops. Presses his lips together. The lower one trembles.

He sets down the beer, gets up, and walks off without a name.

But we all know who he meant.

2

December 8, 1941
Manila, Philippines

Hank doesn't get far. He drinks at the bar by himself for over an hour while Billy and me stay at the table and order a couple rounds—my first beers of the night—and let him be. By the time Hank leaves with a two-peso girl from the brothel upstairs, it's after two in the morning.

The cigarette smoke, so thick when we got here, is finally starting to thin when a girl in a faded dress wanders over to our table.

"You want to go upstairs? Like your friend?" she asks, smiling at me. She's got smooth skin and long dark hair and can't be a day over fifteen. The first time a girl like her ever approached me at a club, I figured she might want to talk some, maybe dance a little. When I figured out what she was truly offering, I paid her a panicked peso just to get away.

The girl leans over and murmurs in my ear, "I will make you happy." Goose bumps flare down my neck as she brushes against my arm. She smells like perfume and sin, her cheek so close I can feel the heat coming off her like a fever. Her hand slips beneath the table to my thigh. I bolt up from the chair.

22

"Sorry." I clear my throat. "We were just leaving."

She turns to Billy, who sits stock-still, his eyes darting this way and that like a caged animal's as his cheeks go up in flames. I slide her the leftover coins on the table. Rap Billy on the shoulder.

"Let's go."

"Should we maybe wait?" Billy asks, gaze following the girl to another table. "Make sure Hank gets back all right?"

"Hank can take care of himself."

A big fella at the next table—a Polar Bear of the Thirty-First like us and an old-timer by the look of it—glances up from his beer as we head out past his table.

"I'll make sure your friend stays out of trouble," he says.

We hit the road and hoof it several blocks before finding a cab, by which time it's after two thirty. Manila's streets glisten like darkened mirrors after the rain as the taxi's tires sluice through shallow puddles along the curb. The closer we get to the walled city on the bay, the breeze through the open window smells less like dank sewage and more like seawater and flowers.

"Maybe Hank'll come down with the clap and get demoted," Billy muses, his eyelids at half-mast.

I give a little laugh—not just because I've already thought that, but if there's anyone I know who could cheat VD, it's the newly minted Private First Class Wright.

We've just turned up the boulevard when the taxi driver slows, peering curiously at something through the open window. I sit up at the sight of a 1939 Chevy Master Deluxe idling on the grassy lawn outside the old Spanish walls a good twenty feet off the road. It's one of our officers.

"Sir, can you pull over?" I say, tapping the driver's seat. The cab stops and I get out and run over to the Chevy, slipping on the slick grass as a lieutenant I don't recognize throws open the driver's-side door. He waves me off like one of the bugs swarming the headlights as I salute, peering inside the car.

"Private Propfield, sir. You all right, sir?"

"Stupid car ran off the road . . ." He stands, grabbing at the door for support, misses, and falls in slow motion onto his butt. I help him up, grimacing at the reek of whiskey on him. He's lucky he didn't crash his car into one of the tall palms lining the boulevard.

"We've got a cab, sir." I motion over my shoulder. "Can we take you somewhere—maybe for some coffee?"

"No, no, no," he says. I stagger as he sways, nearly dragging me back down with him. Billy runs over and helps me guide him to the front bumper, where the lieutenant takes an unsteady seat.

"Sir, I think we ought to get you home," I say.

"Need to get to Stossenburg," he slurs, eyelids drooping. "Been trassferred."

"I'm sure you can take the morning train, sir," I say, assuming he means Fort Stotsenburg a couple hours north of here. That he's just the latest in a long list of newly appointed instructors to the local Philippine Army.

He shakes his head. "Gotta get there by morning."

The guy can barely stand.

I return to the taxi, lean through the open window, and ask the driver, "Mister, can you take us as far as Fort Stotsenburg?"

"Too far," the driver says, waving his hand.

"But that man's an officer. Someone will make sure you get paid."

"No, no." The driver points to the clock fixed to the dash. "Too late."

I walk back to the lieutenant.

"Sir, would you like us to drive you?" I ask.

Out of the corner of my eye, I can see Billy staring at me like I'm off my rocker.

The lieutenant straightens enough to dig in his pocket, and I realize he's searching for his wallet.

24

"Oh, no," I say. "Keep your money, sir—we're glad to help."

Billy shakes his head, but I figure if the lieutenant wants to pay us something, it's best for all of us if he remembers it.

"Why, thass real nice," the lieutenant says.

I flip the front seat forward, then go pay our cabdriver as Billy gets the lieutenant squared away in back. A minute later, the taxi's turning down the boulevard, heading out of sight.

"We drivin' him for real?" Billy asks, low.

I shrug. "I've only had two beers. 'Sides, what else we got to do tonight?"

"Uh, sleep?"

I glance toward the back seat of the Chevy where the lieutenant's already passed out.

"You can sleep while I drive," I say. "C'mon. It's the right thing to do."

Billy heaves a sigh. "Why you always gotta be so good, Prop?" But he gets in the car.

Truth is, I got three reasons for being willing to make the trip up to Stotsenburg and thumb it back if we have to.

One, if this officer ends up killing someone because I walked away, I reckon I'm as guilty as he is.

Two, I ain't never driven a car this nice.

Three, this man's an officer. He could put in a good word for us—especially if he knows we saved him from showing up late or not at all. He's so drunk, he might've driven into the harbor or died in a head-on collision trying to stay on the right side of the road, which is the wrong side here. For all he knows, I just saved his life.

After all, Hank got promoted for carting a lieutenant around, and that was just in Manila.

I slide onto the upholstered seat, close the door, and take a moment to appreciate the fine steering wheel in my hands before shifting into gear. When I touch the gas, the car lurches forward . . . and then rocks back, wheels spinning. I try again. Same thing.

Shift into reverse. No dice.

I put the car in neutral, get out, and go around back, where the wheels have torn through the damp grass and mired in the mud.

"Streak—"

"Yup," Billy says, sliding over to the driver's seat. He puts the car in gear and touches the gas as I shove my weight against the bumper. The wheels spin, throwing mud all over my khakis. We try again, and a third time, but this ain't a job for one person.

I go around and lean through the car's open window. Shake the lieutenant by the shoulder. He responds with a snore.

"Now what?" Billy asks. Palm fronds rustle overhead. The clouds have broken, stars crisp in the sky. I can just make out the faint sound of laughter drifting from the Manila Hotel's outdoor bar.

"Stay here," I say, figuring there's got to be a bellboy or two still on duty who'll be glad to push us out for half a peso each.

I scrape my soles off on the curb and am just striking out across the boulevard when a pair of headlights comes from the south. I hurry toward the oncoming lane, waving my arms. The car—a brightly colored taxi—slows to a stop.

The driver leans out his window. "What you need, Joe?"

"Can you help give us a push?" I gesture toward the Chevy.

The back door opens and someone gets out, shouting, "What the Sam Hill—you steal a car, Prop?"

And there's Hank—rumpled and flushed, but cleaner than me.

"How're you back already?" I squint at him.

"I try to leave before they fall in love." Hank grins. "It don't always work."

Within minutes, Hank, the taxi driver, and me are pushing the car out, yelling for Billy to keep going as he drives over the low curb and onto the road with a scrape.

"So where we goin'?" Hank asks.

I climb into the driver's seat as Billy gets in back. "Stotsenburg."

As we leave Manila, Hank's singing "Pennsylvania 6-5000," shouting it out the window until Billy's staring straight ahead, stone-faced in the rearview mirror like he's about to snap. I can't even look at him without busting out laughing.

Almost feels like old times.

Ten minutes later, Billy's asleep in the back seat with his mouth open, head bobbing with each bump in the road, and Hank's pinching the bridge of his nose like he's trying to stay awake. The next time I glance over, Hank's chin is on his chest.

Not only am I *not* tired, I'm more energized than I've felt all night. Captivated by the hum of the Chevy's engine against a silence filled with sound—the scrape of insects, the wind whispering from the forested hills, the barking dog a barrio over. The island at this hour feels wild, peaceful, and dangerous all at once. Like one of Billy's dormant volcanoes on the verge of a waking rumble.

Much as I don't miss home, I wish my mama could see this place. She'd love the big porches running along the upper floors of our barracks, the blooming vines just like the bougainvillea she grows along the back fence of our yard. I wrote her a letter just to let her know we're living better than could ever be asked—from the roast beef and Parker rolls we eat at supper to the locals we each pay a few dollars a month to work the kitchen, clean our equipment, and make our beds. That I plan to start school. That the people here are kind and friendly. I wonder if she likes the pearl I sent her wrapped in a square of silk for her birthday. She always said they were her favorite.

I don't have to wonder what my daddy would say. I bought the pearl from a Moro—a Mohammedan. The university ain't seminary. And anyone who can afford servants obviously ain't giving enough to the poor.

In the end, I never sent that letter to Mama. Only a pressed sprig of bougainvillea with a line to say all was well.

The only thing I wish I had right now is a cold drink. Especially when I pull over to let a convoy of military vehicles pass. The dust of their wake billows in through the windows. I wonder where they're headed at this hour.

When I get back on the road, the birds are singing, and by the time we reach San Fernando, the eastern sky's tinged the color of denim. I spy a small bakery with its lights on and pull in. Leaving the others asleep in the car, I get out and peer through the shop's window. Dance music drifts from a radio inside, a female figure swaying in the kitchen behind the counter as she kneads a mound of dough. I rap softly, and then wave when I catch the Filipina's attention. She wipes her hands and gestures me to come in like I'm the next-door neighbor.

"You open this early, ma'am?" I say, stepping inside. The smell of baking bread envelops me.

"For our American soldier friend, yes," she smiles, turning the radio down as the announcer comes on. She looks to be in her thirties, with wide-set eyes and a seam above her lip that hitches up her smile. It don't make her any less pretty. In fact, I think she's the most beautiful older woman I ever met. She gives me samples of buttery pastries and sweet rolls covered in dusty crumbs and others filled with cheese and sprinkled with coconut. I could stay here all morning trying everything in the shop, I'm so hungry and it all tastes so good.

I leave with a bag of warm empanadas and a six-pack of orange drinks. Guzzle the first one before reaching the edge of Angeles City. Give myself just long enough to eat an empanada and gaze out at the rice paddies reflecting the red tinge of dawn before I wake the others.

We pass the front gate of Fort Stotsenburg just before 6:00 a.m. and slowly move through the base. The lieutenant, when Billy prods him awake, is so green around the gills I wonder if he might puke in his own back seat.

"Drink, sir?" I say, offering a bottle over my shoulder.

He takes it, murmurs his thanks, chugs half of it down, and holds the back of his hand to his mouth as though to make sure it stays in.

"You boys with the Thirty-First, I gather," he says at last, leaning forward to point me past a half-empty motor pool toward the parade grounds.

"Yes, sir." I hear a bugle in the distance and pull over for reveille. We all pile out to face the music. It's the fastest I've seen the lieutenant move since we found him.

"I owe you one, fellas," he says afterward, in the front seat. "If you'll park at that post command building, I can take it from here."

Unlike the Cuartel de España in Manila's old walled city, Fort Stotsenburg looks like a boomtown with its railway station, horse stables, and hospital. The place must be bursting at the seams; in addition to the barracks and large frame houses, I note several rows of tents to the west, on the opposite end from the runways and control tower of the adjacent Clark Field.

The relaxed atmosphere I've grown accustomed to in the Philippines don't exist here. Privates hurry between bamboo buildings. Jeeps crowd Officers' Row. The sun ain't even fully crested the mountain to the east, which Billy's informed me twice is a bona fide volcano, and men are hurrying toward the officers' mess like they might run out of eggs.

I park and hand over the keys as we get out. Watch as an officer dashes from a headquarters building toward a jeep idling by the curb. A second later it speeds toward Clark Field.

"If you fellas hang tight for a bit, I'll see about getting you a ride back to Manila," the lieutenant says. He walks off, mumbling under his breath, "What's all this commotion?"

We stand there waiting while everyone rushes around us. Near the bivouac area, enlisted men come and go from a kitchen truck, mess kits in hand.

"What d'you think our chances are of getting fed?" Billy says. "I could've eaten three more of those empanadas."

I ain't exactly full myself.

"Why don't you go over there to that line and see if you can scare up some biscuits," Hank says.

Billy never argues, especially when it comes to food. A second later, he's jogging off to investigate.

As good as food sounds, the thought of sleep seems even better. I can feel the night finally catching up to me, putting lead in my limbs.

"I can't believe that lieutenant didn't offer to pay you," Hank says. "Did he even ask what happened to your trousers?"

I glance down at the mud splattered across my khakis. Start to say the lieutenant tried to pay and that I should've taken him up on it but stop as Billy comes sprinting toward us, his eyes wide.

"They bombed us!" he shouts before he's even reached us. "They bombed Pearl Harbor—America's at war!"

We stare at him like he's lost his marbles. And then Hank busts out laughing.

Billy blinks, breathing hard. "I'm tellin' the truth! Every guy in that line's sayin' so—they're about to make an announcement!"

I don't know what's more shocking: seeing the Ginger Streak out of breath or the thought of anyone taking a swing at us on American soil.

Hank stands there like he's waiting for the punch line. When it don't come, he narrows his eyes. "What're you talking about, son?"

"Japan attacked the United States!" Billy says, enunciating each word like we're dopes.

"When?" I ask. We were in Manila all night. The news would've been everywhere.

"Just now!" Billy says, throwing up his arms.

Hank snaps into gear and intercepts a sergeant coming across the parade grounds. "Is it true there's a war and we're missing it?"

"That's what they're saying," the sergeant says, not slowing. "There's a radio in the supply office where I'm headed if you want to hear for yourself."

We follow him into a bamboo building, remove our caps, and join a group of men crowded around a radio in the back room. It takes me a minute to realize they're listening to Don Bell on KZRH Radio Manila, same as we listen to. But this ain't the same bombastic Don Bell. He's breathing fast and sounds like he might be crying as he announces Imperial Japan has bombed Pearl Harbor.

Reports remain sketchy, but there is no doubt! Oh God! They hit our ships at anchor!

I try to make sense of what I'm hearing.

Hank shakes his head, jaw tight.

"How is that even possible?" someone asks, glancing around.

"I don't get it," another man says. "Why attack Hawaii when we got bombers right here, this close to their bases on Formosa?"

"I thought they only had wooden propeller planes," Billy whispers. "Like the kind wing walkers do stunts on."

I'd heard that too.

The sergeant gestures us outside.

"You fellas with the Thirty-First?" he says out on the sidewalk, nodding toward the patch on my sleeve.

"Yes, Sergeant," I say, replacing my cap. "Drove an officer in this morning."

"If you want to get back to your unit, you better go now," he says, jerking his chin toward the way we came in. He lowers his voice. "I got a buddy in the Twentieth Pursuit Squadron over there at Clark Field who wrote up his will two days ago after a briefing." He points to the airstrip. "See the pilots waiting in those Warhawks? They been on the line since the middle of the night. You know what that tells me?"

He don't need to say it. I can feel Billy looking between us as the heat leaves my face.

Formosa's less than five hundred miles to the north, and the fleet in Hawaii can't protect us.

On Clark Field's dusty runway, our first plane growls toward the sky.

3

DECEMBER 8, 1941

FORT STOTSENBURG / CLARK FIELD, PHILIPPINES

We are at war.

I try to get that thought into my head as I buzz with sleep deprivation and nerves.

It don't feel real. Someone in the supply office said it's got to be a gag like *War of the Worlds*.

A part of me might actually be disappointed if that turns out to be the case.

"We gotta find that lieutenant, figure out how we're gettin' back," Billy says, chewing his lip. He glances at the sergeant, who's rubbing his forehead like it hurts. When I peer down the street toward post command, there's no sign of the lieutenant—or the Chevy I parked out front. We're technically AWOL right now—on the verge of an attack without platoon, orders, or weapons.

"Looks like we're stayin'," Hank says, following my gaze.

"What d'you mean, 'stayin''?" Billy demands. "What are we gonna do?"

"Guess you boys are on your own," the sergeant says. He salutes a captain in a passing jeep and I notice the red, yellow, and blue tank armor patch on his sleeve. He turns toward us. "I gotta get going. We're not near ready. Best of luck."

"Sergeant," I say, stepping forward before he can leave. "How can we help?"

"Not near ready," I learn, is an understatement. From the sound of it, half the company's weapons ain't even been fired yet.

We get put to work loading machine-gun ammo by hand because somehow there's no belt loader to be found in the entire outfit.

"If I knew we'd be doin' this malarkey, I'd have hitchhiked back to Manila by now," Hank mutters.

We load belts until our thumbs are numb as the battalion's tanks get scattered in the bamboo.

At ten thirty, we help move aviation gas away from the airfield. It takes us over an hour to roll the barrels onto trucks and hide them in the brush.

By noon, we're sweating through our khakis and delirious from lack of sleep, running on adrenaline and a kind of purpose I've never felt before.

Still no sign of the enemy. Meanwhile, the B-17s that have been taking off all morning are back on the runway to refuel, their crews standing in the shade of their wings, the P-40 Warhawks getting started up and shut down, trying to stay hot.

Billy drags a sleeve across his forehead and squints down the runway. "What're we waitin' for? We coulda bombed 'em off Formosa by now!"

"I got no idea," I say as pilots cut out toward the mess hall.

"Forget this," Hank says, walking off.

"Where're you goin'?" I shout.

"To get some chow."

Billy spreads his arms and hollers, "I thought we was in a war!"

I did too.

Instead, it's a perfect day in paradise. Just a few clouds in an otherwise pristine sky as a bunch of geese glide in from the mountains in two perfect Vs.

Except no flock flies that neat.

Pistol shots fire a warning from the direction of the operations shack.

"Jimmy . . ." Billy says, following my gaze. "Jimmy, are those—"

"Attack!" I yell, my feet frozen stiff. "Attack!"

I stare for a moment, transfixed in horror, as the planes seed our sky, raining black bombs over the airfield. They shriek toward the earth.

Hank comes running back. "Get off the field!"

An air-raid siren begins to wail overhead.

I shove Billy ahead of me, sprinting hard on his heels. Three seconds later we're tumbling to the earth, hands over our ears, as the first bomb slams against the end of the runway. The ground shudders with the blast like thunder after a lightning strike. Metal whizzes through the air.

"Stay down!" Hank shouts.

We crawl through the brush, desperate to put distance between us and the runway. I glance back—then throw my arm over my eyes as one of our B-17s bursts into a ball of fire. The next bomb hits, and the next, and the next . . . exploding down the line where our flying fortresses are lined up, neat as sitting ducks.

Across the airfield, an eruption in the brush throws a column of smoke to the sky, followed by three more in quick succession, blackening the clouds.

The drums of fuel.

We scuttle along the ground, searching for cover.

"Over there!" I point to a cement latrine. "Go! Go!"

I drag Billy up with me and run. Dive through the open doorway as Hank comes skidding in after us.

We press ourselves against the walls and wait for it to end. Dust rains down on us, coating our hair with lime, mingling with the sweat running in our eyes. But it don't end. The bombs fall closer and closer.

I pray for the first time in months.

Wonder if this is how I die.

A chunk of cement crashes to the floor beside us, followed by a hail of debris.

"They ain't gonna find me buried in an outhouse!" Hank shouts. "Run between blasts. Head for those tanks!"

I push up from the floor to a runner's stance. Glance over at Billy. "Ready?"

All this time Billy's been crouched in the corner with his hands over his head. When he don't move, Hank grabs him by the shoulder and yells, "Streak! We're gonna run to those tanks! You hear me?"

Billy looks up, face ashen, as another explosion shatters the earth outside. But he nods.

Hank holds his hand up, waiting like he's counting, timing the bombs. I can't believe we ain't been blown to smithereens yet because each one sounds like it's right on the other side of the wall—until one lands so close, dirt blasts through the open doorway.

"Run!" Hank shouts.

I bolt after Hank and Billy, steps stuttering at the sight of Clark Field billowing with black smoke, Japanese fighters swarming the sky like hornets. Our Warhawks and Flying Fortresses on the ground engulfed in fire.

One of the hangars explodes across the runway. Shrapnel ruptures the air.

Another bomb hits behind us. We fall flat, cover our heads.

Machine-gun fire rakes down the field. I stagger to my feet as a Japanese fighter plane bursts from the smoke, flying so low I can see the red meatball on the fuselage.

Someone's shooting at the plane from the rice fields beyond us, thumb stuck on the trigger. The plane strafes the paddy.

The gunfire stops.

We sprint into the bamboo.

Fifty yards from the nearest tank, I trip and go sprawling. Look back to see someone's leg in the brush. Its owner lies five feet to my right, eyes open, face blackened. It's the first dead person I've ever seen that wasn't in a casket.

"Prop!" someone shouts. Billy.

"I'm comin'!"

I get to my feet as a round of tracers chews through a B-17 trying to taxi. It bursts into a fiery ball. Another, farther down the runway, gets blown to kingdom come.

By the time I make it to the tank, Hank's grabbed the machine gun mounted to the top of the turret and is yelling for Billy to hand up the ammo.

"Are you out of your mind?" I yell, climbing up. Farther upfield, someone else is firing from on top of a tank in the cogon grass.

"This is what we came here for," he says, snatching the box from Billy and pulling the pin from the mount.

But it ain't what I came for. The up-close war part never even occurred to me until today.

Billy clanks open the hatch and slides into the tank's armored belly. I follow him, and we both look up at Hank.

"Here they come!" Hank shouts. And then he's shooting, arcing up after the next fighter plane with a hail of gunfire.

"Hank, get out of there!"

"Too late—they know where we are!" he bellows, firing again.

A few seconds later, Hank pokes his head down inside. He's out of breath, his face plastered with soot and sweat. "Prop, I can't look both ways at once." An encroaching roar overhead. He mounts the top of the turret again. "Prop! I need you out here! Now!"

I climb, shaking, onto the front deck and turn my eyes to the sky.

"Incoming!" I holler, hands over my ears. "Six o'clock!" The shells fly so fast I start slipping on the casings.

Another of our P-40s explodes on the runway but it was already doomed. The airstrip's so riddled with pits and craters there's no way the Warhawk could've ever taken off. I've lost count of the enemy fighters but figure there's got to be at least fifty—all shooting at anything moving or not blown up yet, including us.

"I need more ammo!" Hank shouts.

Billy calls up, "We're out!" A second later, he's climbing up and out of the hatch.

"What're you doing?" I yell. "Get down!"

"There's another tank that way," he says, dropping to the ground.

"What? No—Billy!" But he's already disappeared into the bamboo.

I stare after him, sick. Start counting the seconds, then shout at Hank, "How could you let him go?"

"We're sitting ducks without ammo!" Hank yells back.

"Because you started shooting at them!"

"That's our job!"

But it ain't. This ain't even our outfit. Our job is to be with our company back in Manila. Where we'd be right now if I hadn't decided to be a hero and give a ride to a drunk lieutenant because I wanted a promotion.

Another fighter strafes a deadly corridor right over us, firing in Billy's wake.

Hank shouts a warning. I dive off the deck as a hail of bullets kicks the earth up around us. Wedge myself against the tank's track, screaming, "Billy, they're comin'! Billy, get down!"

The instant the fighter's past us, I push up and come around the end of the track—

Just in time to see Billy burst from the bamboo, an ammo box cradled in his arms.

Hank whoops and crows Billy's name like a madman, and I holler right alongside him.

I leap up onto the deck as Billy hands up the ammo and climbs into the tank again. Hank hooks the box on and flips the lid.

Two more Japanese fighters emerge from the smoke—one from the north, another from the east. "Hank, hurry up!" I shout.

"That ain't helpin'," he says, loading the belt.

"Incoming!" I yell. "Nine o'clock!"

Hank cocks the machine gun. "Get down!" He chases the first fighter with a stream of bullets.

"You're not leading enough," I shout, the smoke so thick I choke on the words. "You're missin' them by fifty feet—twelve o'clock!" I drop down, throwing my arm in the direction of the next fighter as it swoops in so close I can see the pilot's white scarf.

Hank screams like a banshee, chasing it across the sky. When the enemy plane abruptly banks and spirals to the earth, we roar with everything in us as it crashes. I howl until our throats go raw.

"Cowards!" Hank shouts. "Come back and fight!"

We fire until we run out of ammo, then jump off the tank and haul into the bamboo as the earth shudders around us. The hiding is more terrible than fighting. Enemy bombs give way to wave after wave of strafing for what feels like hours.

When it's finally over and the last of the Japanese planes is gone, we emerge from the scrub into a fiery hellscape, the sun blacked out, our bombers nothing but burning shells.

I've heard my daddy preach on hell my entire life.

But he ain't done it a lick of justice.

We spend the rest of the afternoon helping the wounded onto trucks and blowing black snot out of our noses. Drinking water to soothe our burned throats. Puking half of it back up. Every so often, a store of ammo goes off like a bunch of fireworks as the hangars just keep burning.

The dead litter the airfield, trenches, and smoldering remains of buildings. At the motor pool, bodies stick out from beneath cars, their torsos missing limbs . . . heads missing faces. We load their pieces into bomb carts.

At some point, I catch sight of a gaunt rider on horseback surveying the damage in the distance. He sits utterly still as the earth smolders around him.

"Who's that?" I ask a nearby private. His face is smeared with oily soot.

"Major General Wainwright," he says, low. "They brought him over to put him out to pasture, I heard. Good man."

Just before evening, we stagger past the remains of the same Chevy we drove here this morning. It's a mile from where we parked it. The windows are blown out, a piece of shrapnel lodged in the driver's neck.

We drag the lieutenant from the car. But he's been dead for hours.

Hank tries the key. The Chevy starts up.

For the second time today, we load the officer into the back seat and transport him—this time to the morgue.

We never even knew his name.

Hank says we need to take the lieutenant's Chevy, but it's got three shot-out tires and won't make it far. We got no choice but to stay put 'til morning. We stagger into the bivouac area at dusk. Bedding, woven bamboo sides of buildings, and contents of footlockers are strewn between tents. Looks like a twister blew through them. Somewhere nearby, a radio's playing Judy Garland's "Over the Rainbow."

I wonder if Manila got hit. If our barracks is intact.

My mind flashes to the sealed letter inside my footlocker. Not the one I never sent my mama but a different letter. One written to me.

I wonder if it's still there.

We wash the grime from our faces, the worst of the gore from our uniforms.

By the time night falls, the base is quiet, electricity blacked out, the twisted wreckage of planes turned to grotesque statues in the dark. Fires smolder nearby as men scatter to the brush. The base ain't safe.

Billy, Hank, and me spend the night huddled on the edge of the jungle.

I'm too afraid to sleep. Too exhausted not to.

I dream, for the first time since I got here, of home.

And her.

4

can't remember a time when Claire Crockett wasn't in my life. Our mamas were best friends, and I was barely a year old when she was born.

Being as I had no siblings, it was always Claire and me—and eventually her little brother, Billy—playing in the backyard or eating jelly sandwiches at the kitchen table of one of our houses. Sneaking caramels from the jar on the counter inside her family's gas station. Devouring blackberries straight from the patch at my papaw's farm across the bay while our mamas picked a bucket for cobbler. Making faces at each other with our berry-stained lips until Billy belly-laughed on his mama's hip. Splashing naked in a washtub together on the front porch while Billy napped and our mamas sipped sweet tea.

I only ever remember it being summer, our days filled with homemade peach ice cream and Claire's singing—in Sunday school, on the walk between our houses, and as she climbed trees. Even when she talked to Billy, she sang the words, feeding him bits of graham cracker like she was training a puppy, or carting him around the yard in a wooden wagon and pretending he, with his curly ginger hair, was a baby circus lion.

The only people she ever actually spoke to were adults and me—about the proper way to play jacks, how fireflies were really fairies, and where we ought to hide a secret treasure beneath the oak tree. How it was more fun to pee outside, which we did often . . . until the day my mama caught us with our pants down behind the shed, which landed us both spankings and me a talking-to about how it ain't decent to undo one's pants in front of a girl—not ever, until you're grown up and married.

At least she never told my daddy.

Billy, for his part, was happy to go along with whatever Claire wanted—even when she dressed him up in her clothes and put her mama's lipstick on him. There'd be Billy, with a crooked pair of bright-red lips painted across his face, in one of Claire's dresses and their mama's beads. He never stopped grinning except when he was hungry, and I only remember him ever crying as a child twice. Once when he grabbed a stem heavy with blackberries and got a fistful of thorns and the day Claire and me started school, hand in hand, and he tried to follow us up the schoolhouse steps. Billy had howled like an injured animal as his mama scooped him up and carried him home.

Just like that, summer was over.

My mama never said why she held me back. Maybe it had to do with a fever I'd had the fall before or me being born in December, which would've made me young or old for my grade, depending. Or the fact that once I started school Mama would be alone without the babies I somehow knew even then she'd lost.

But I was glad because it meant Claire and me were in first grade together. Even though I knew plenty of other kids from church, I didn't like school all that much. Not because I wasn't good at it—I was, and my teachers sent home glowing reports of my behavior—but because I became aware that these were not the things that would win me friends. I was not a jokester, athlete, or instigator, and I didn't much like being the center of attention. Unlike Claire, who became instantly popular for her fantastic stories, pert smile, and dark copper hair. Soon she had new friends to walk home with, make up new Raggedy Ann tales with, and sing her songs with. She got out the dolls I hadn't seen her play with in years and carted them to other girls' houses in Billy's old stroller while I took Billy frog hunting with me.

The one thing I had going for me was that no matter how many boys tried to get her attention, I was the only boy at school Claire Crockett cared to talk to.

The following spring, at seven years old, Claire put away her dolls. She didn't need them anymore now that her twin sisters, Betty and Margaret, had been born. For a while, things mostly went back to how they'd been: Claire, Billy, and me taking turns churning when one of our mamas made ice cream and helping pick spinach and green beans in the garden and peaches in the Crocketts' backyard. Billy and me taking turns pedaling the hand-me-down bike a family at church gave me, Claire riding on the handlebars.

But Claire's mama wasn't the same after the twins came. I saw her crying sometimes. Meanwhile, I'd never seen my mama look so content as she did when she helped tend the babies while Mrs. Crockett slept.

Hank Wright showed up halfway through third grade. He was quiet at first, taller than the other boys in our class, and rumored to already be ten. Though whether that was on account of repeating a grade, no one—at least in Mama's church sewing circle—seemed to know. What everyone did know was that he had transferred in after getting in trouble too many times at his old school—a fact that made him the object of derision to good kids and the parent-appointed charity project of a pastor's son like me.

"I want you to invite that new boy to church," Mama said one Saturday while Claire, Billy, and me sat at our kitchen table eating hot dogs.

"He didn't move here. He just switched to our school," I said, not wanting to talk to him, let alone invite him to church. Not because he was dirty, as some of Claire's friends speculated, but because I already anticipated his scorn—along with the possibility of a knuckle sandwich. "He probably already goes somewhere else."

"Don't you sass your mother!" Daddy's voice snapped from behind me. I turned, startled to find him standing in the kitchen doorway.

"I just mean—"

Claire kicked me under the table. She'd seen me taken out back for a lashing plenty of times, and more than once she'd tried to coax me out of my darkness afterward. Beside her, Billy gulped his glass of milk, eyes wide over the rim.

"Yes, sir," I said tightly.

But I didn't invite Hank. Not the next day or the day after. Not just in defiance but because Hank kept to himself, sitting at the back of the classroom and leaning against the fence with his arms crossed during recess, looking so tough even Merl Beauregard, the school bully, wouldn't go near him. I never saw Hank at lunch, and he disappeared down the street right after the bell rang at the end of each day.

"Let's follow him," Claire said a few days later.

"No." I scowled. My shoulders sagged. "Can't we do it tomorrow?" It was Thursday and I was anxious to get back to Claire's—the only one of our houses with a radio—and listen to the new *Buck Rogers in the 25th Century*, which wasn't on tomorrow.

She gave me one of her mama's looks. "We can catch the recap on

Monday. You know your daddy's gonna ask if you invited Hank to church yet, and if not, what's taking so long."

I sighed. My daddy would also have a fit if he knew I listened to the shows he called "trash"—the reason we didn't own a radio and, I suspect, why Mama was always helping out at the Crocketts' whenever *Betty and Bob* was on, which Mrs. Crockett never missed.

The minute school got out, we grabbed Billy from the second-grade hall and took off after Hank as he headed up the street. He walked with his head down, hands shoved in his pockets, pausing only long enough to kick an old can as he cut to Old Shell Road.

Twice I said we ought to turn back around, that our mamas were going to be wondering after us when we didn't show up at the Crocketts' in time to turn on the radio. We'd gone at least a mile by then—maybe two.

But Hank kept walking, and we kept following, hanging back a block or more until he turned down a street of small houses. When he reached one with peeling paint, a small, sparse yard, and a rickety-looking front porch, he leapt up the steps and let himself in through a creaky screen door that slapped shut behind him.

For a minute we just stood there. I could tell by Claire's expression that she was having second thoughts. Not out of fear, like me, but because she'd always been sensitive to the pride of others.

Neither of our families was rich. My mama sewed our clothes, and my daddy joked that he'd become a pastor to support his farming habit. I wasn't sure why this was funny, but I'd heard him talk about falling crop prices my entire life. And while we lived on what the congregants could spare, I'd always had shoes to grow into and toys—even if most of them were hand-me-downs from another family. We ate Sunday dinner at a different house every week after church, the invitations marked on the wall calendar a month in advance. And Daddy regularly came home with green tomatoes, canned peaches, pickled beets, jars of jelly, or any number of things that got dropped off at the church office throughout the year and especially during Christmas.

After the Crockett twins were born, Claire's daddy added a garage to the gas station and turned his hobby of tinkering with cars into an auto service to help make ends meet. None of them ever went without, either.

"Well, let's go say hi," Billy said with a shrug.

Claire chewed her lip. "I don't know . . ."

"What d'you mean?" Billy said, spreading his scrawny arms. "We came all this way, didn't we?"

I could lie to my daddy. Say that we invited Hank and that I was right—his family already went to a different church. Which, of course, would never be good enough if it was Methodist, Lutheran, Presbyterian, or any church that wasn't ours. But I wasn't a good liar. The truth would come out and I'd be in even bigger trouble than if I'd never come here at all.

"All right," I said. "Come on."

I marched up the steps of the front porch, Claire and Billy in tow, and rapped on the screen door before I could lose my courage.

A boy's voice sounded from within: "Hank! Get the door!"

A few seconds later, footsteps jumbled down the wooden staircase in the hallway, a pair of trouser-clad legs coming into view through the screen. And then there was Hank, stock-still at the bottom of the stairs.

"What do you want?" he said, coming to stare at us through the wire mesh.

"We, uh . . ." I shifted on my feet. "I'm Jimmy and this is Claire and Billy."

Hank's eyes darted to Claire and then dropped.

"I recognize you from school," he murmured. He glanced up, brows quirking. "How did you find me?"

Billy grinned. "We followed you."

Hank gave him a weird look but before he could say anything, a woman's voice called from somewhere above.

"Hank, honey? Who's there?"

"It's okay, Mama," Hank called back. "Just some . . . friends from school."

"Well, invite them in." Her voice was sweet but weak.

He looked away, scratching the back of his neck, then opened the door and gestured us in as a woman appeared in a dressing gown at the top of the stairs.

"Welcome. Come on in," she said with a small wave. "Hank, make your guests at home."

"I will, Mama," Hank said.

He led us back toward the small kitchen where an older boy in a pair of overalls was spreading peanut butter from a big tin on a slice of bread. He had Hank's square jaw and dirty-brown hair—or rather, Hank had his. It was hard to tell which of them was older at first, except that the boy making the sandwiches was taller by an inch.

"Who're your friends?" the older boy asked with a friendly smile.

"Um, that's . . ." Hank looked at me.

"Jimmy," I said. "And Billy and—"

"Claire," Hank finished, not looking at her. "This is my brother, Roy. Everyone calls him Cowboy."

"Are you twins?" Billy asked, glancing between them.

"He's ten months older," Hank murmured, like he'd answered this question a lot.

"Ten and a half. Want a peanut butter sandwich?" Cowboy asked.

I shrugged. "Sure."

Over peanut butter and apple-slice sandwiches, we learned that Hank and Cowboy's mama was ailing and their daddy worked long hours at the lumber mill, where Cowboy was headed now that school was out.

"Our daddy took care of her while he was out of a job most of last year," Hank said, mouth full.

I looked around the kitchen with new eyes at the dishes drying in the washtub, the one remaining apple on the windowsill, the beans soaking in a shallow pot. The way Cowboy carefully returned the bread to the box and the peanut butter to the cupboard and Hank wolfed down his sandwich like he hadn't eaten lunch.

"Nice to meet you," Cowboy said, taking his sandwich with him out the back door. I could hear him whistling down the drive.

"Who does your laundry?" Claire asked, nodding to a sheet billowing like a sail on a clothesline in the backyard.

"Neighbor lady," Hank said. "My daddy's making her a set of chairs like ours."

"Who cooks for you and your mama?" Claire whispered, glancing at the stove.

Hank shrugged. "I do, most days."

We learned Hank and Cowboy went to the Delchamps supermarket every weekend with four dollars from their daddy and a list from their mama. That Cowboy took their groceries home and started dinner while Hank stuck around to carry groceries home for little old ladies who paid him a nickel, maybe even a dime.

We gulped down the sandwiches that I now felt guilty for accepting, not daring to stay too long given the walk we had back to Claire's. As we said goodbye at the door, I turned back and blurted, "Do you go to church? We wanted to invite you—your whole family—to ours."

"Not so much no more," Hank said. "My brother and daddy work on furniture or fixin' porches or any odd jobs they can get most weekends."

"Come this weekend," Claire said. "It's the church potluck after and there'll be banana pudding and sweet-potato pie and there's always leftovers, so you can bring a plate back for your mama. And you can't say no, or else Jimmy's gonna get in trouble on account that his daddy's the pastor, so we'll see you Sunday morning, you hear?"

"I'll try," Hank said, meeting her eyes at last.

"Don't be late," Claire said.

Claire got her way with Hank, as she so often did with us. That Sunday, he showed up for church in a too-big but clean button-up shirt, and I don't think I ever saw a boy eat as much as he did that afternoon. Afterward, Mr. Crockett drove Hank home with an entire box of food for the family.

The next day at lunchtime, Claire handed Hank the extra banana sandwich her mama had packed in her pail, and I invited Hank to come play with us after school.

"Okay," he said, his face brightening, but then he lowered his head. "I probably shouldn't."

"Sure you can," I said. "I know! You can borrow my bike. You'll get home faster, which means you can stay a little while before you have to leave."

"Really?" Hank said, looking at me like he was waiting for some kind of catch.

"Sure. You can ride it back in the morning and we'll walk to school together. You know how to ride, right?"

Hank nodded. "My brother used to let me ride his, but it's got a busted rim."

All afternoon, I had big plans for us to play catch until *Buck Rogers in the 25th Century* came on the radio. Maybe even kick the can.

But that day after school, Merl Beauregard and his gang—which included two fourth graders—finally called Hank out.

The last time Merl came for us, Billy put up his seven-year-old dukes and I resigned myself to the two of us getting beat up good, until Claire ran for one of the teachers, who sent Merl home.

This time, we were halfway to the Crocketts' before we realized Merl and his goons were following us.

"Who's your new friend, Jimmy Propfield?" Merl called. "I heard he's stupid. You slow, new kid? You stupid like a fence post?"

"Just ignore them," Claire said. We walked faster. Which only seemed to make Merl madder.

But the minute he started cussing us, Hank spun around and said, "You got five seconds to get lost."

"Or what?" Merl sneered. "You're gonna get puny *Billy Crockett* to defend you?"

"Merl Beauregard, you leave my brother out of your filthy mouth!" Claire hollered.

"Make me," Merl said, stalking toward her.

Hank didn't say a word. Just walked over and pasted Merl right across the jaw and sent him sprawling on his butt. Galvanized, I launched myself at fourth-grade Cecil Spikes with a roar. We were all in it then, Billy's fists flying beside me, Claire swinging her lunch pail. It was our first after-school fight, and we sent them all home with bloody noses.

That fight changed my friendship with Claire. Because it didn't just send Merl Beauregard packing but brought Hank Wright permanently into our lives.

Hank, Billy, and me dominated the chin-up bar at recess and played football every Saturday, soon as Hank finished hustling for dimes at the grocery store. He fixed up Cowboy's bike and started staying longer on weekends to fish past twilight. Sometimes we'd let other boys from school come along. Hank had that effect on others—they wanted to follow him, if only out of curiosity. As though being around him they'd become as fearless or tough as he was. Within weeks, most every kid in our class was rolling the short sleeves of their button-up shirts over their biceps like Hank and petitioning their parents, God, and Santa for a bike so they could pop wheelies and ride down the street with their arms wide the way he did.

The only one immune to Hank was Claire, who didn't like the chin-up bar and came with us fishing less and less as more boys tagged along. Though we'd fought off Merl and his goons together, I knew Claire resented Hank for the way he took Billy and me away from her after that.

Two and a half years later, at the start of sixth grade, Billy, Claire, and me stood next to Hank and Cowboy on the day of their mama's funeral. At the sight of Hank struggling to help carry his mama's casket, Claire cried and, I believe, forgave him completely.

It was almost like old times after that. First, on account of Claire's new peace with Hank. She never liked baseball much, but she would even play shortstop then in order to spend more time with us. Second, on account of Hank discovering girls, who found his bad-boy ways irresistible. Which meant he had less time to play ball because he was too busy chasing skirts. Though he always had time for cars and had begun helping Mr. Crockett in his repair shop.

Three years later, Claire and Billy's mama had another baby girl, Dorothy Jean. She was a beautiful child, everybody said. Sweet peach of a mouth. Tiny wisps of strawberry hair. But Mrs. Crockett wasn't healthy afterward and spent weeks in and out of the hospital.

A month after the baby's birth, during one of Mrs. Crockett's spells, Mr. Crockett was driving home from the hospital after visiting her when a truck coming the other way veered into his lane and hit him head-on. According to the police report, the driver was passed-out drunk at the wheel. The truck driver survived. Claire and Billy's daddy went to heaven.

It was August 1938, just before the start of our ninth-grade—and Billy's eighth-grade—year. My daddy did the funeral. We sang, "Shall we gather at the river, where bright angel feet have trod; with its crystal tide forever." But for all the time we'd been friends with the Crocketts, his voice never quavered once.

I hated him for that.

Claire turned inward, consumed with caring for Dorothy Jean, the twins, and her mama. My mama split time between our house and the Crocketts'. Billy and me took over the gas station. Hank, who already knew more about fixing cars than any of us, rolled up his sleeves to keep the garage part going. He was ready to quit school to do it too, until Cowboy and Claire talked him out of it.

Bad boy or not, Hank had the best grades of all of us. School, like so many things, came easy to him. What's more, he and Cowboy were on track to be the first boys in his family to graduate high school.

On the day he offered to drop out to help her family, Claire hugged Hank for the first time I ever saw, holding him so hard I could see her fingers digging into his shoulder. She was thinner than I'd ever remembered her being, and she shook as she asked Hank to stay in school and help look after Billy.

He promised, arms folded carefully around her, fingers reverent against her skin.

5

DECEMBER 9, 1941
MANILA, PHILIPPINES

The next morning, Billy, Hank, and me catch a ride from Fort Stotsenburg with one of the trucks carrying wounded to Sternberg Hospital in Manila.

The closer we get to the capital, the more cars, taxis, buses—even pony-drawn calesas—we pass full of people fleeing the city. By the time we reach the new Pasig River checkpoint, I can already see the black plumes of oily smoke wafting toward us from the direction of Nichols Field to the south.

"Looks like we got thrashed good," Hank murmurs.

"Every airfield on the island's taken a licking, is what I've heard," the private driving the truck says.

Beside me, Billy stares out the window at a long line outside a bank.

By the time we reach the hospital a quarter mile east of the old walled city, I can just make out Japanese planes swarming through the smoke. Machine-gun fire crackles in the distance.

Hank points to the squad patrolling a nearby roof, the gunners positioned on the mossy walls. The exotic allure of the island that seduced me on my arrival is gone—along with the antique Spanish and modern charm I wished so many times I could show my mama. Under siege by unrelenting Japanese fighters, my new home feels alien and surreal.

With all the smoke in the air, it don't even smell the same.

I barely register helping unload the wounded or crossing the grassy park where soldiers are busy digging in against the old city walls. I can't get to our barracks fast enough, impatient at the gate as I Iank hands the corporal of the guard a note from an officer at Fort Stotsenburg.

The corporal of the guard looks up and down at the soot and gore-stained mess of our uniforms, the grime in our hair and ears. He reads the note, brows raised. Says nothing about the caps we lost during the attack and lets us pass without a word.

The instant Billy and me get to our barracks I rush to my bunk, relieved to find it intact. Surprised, too, to find several men napping as though bombs ain't exploding a few short miles away.

"Where you two been?" Stacey asks. He's a private from Jacksonville, Florida, everyone calls Moose. His finger's folded in a comic book. "You both look like crap." He sniffs the air. "Smell like it too."

"Stotsenburg," Billy murmurs, shucking off his ruined khakis.

Moose sits up straighter. "You there when Clark Field got bombed?"

This time Billy don't answer. But a few more heads lift up from bunks.

I throw open my footlocker and pull out the top tray with its shoe-shine and shaving kits. Dig past socks, towels, and underwear until I find the unopened letter buried at the bottom. Holding it inside the locker out of view of anyone else, I stare at the sealed envelope. The handwriting I watched evolve in school is so familiar to me, it's like I can hear her speaking the words in my mind:

James P. Propfield
31st Infantry
Manila, P.I.

My gaze follows the curve of the elegant Cs in the name above the return address.

Claire Crockett

I turn it over, the envelope thin between my fingers—far too fragile for the payload of anger I assume to be inside it. I tell myself I don't care. That if anyone's got a right to be angry, it's me. Even if that's a lie.

"Crockett! Propfield!" Staff Sergeant Knox barks from the end of the barracks.

I tuck the letter inside my Bible and straighten up. I'll read it someday when I can quiet my mind enough to bear her words. If that day ever comes. Billy snaps to in his skivvies.

"Sounds like you boys had quite a day yesterday," Knox says. He frowns, the scar on his cheek pulling the corner of his eye downward as he takes in the sight of my khakis, his gaze lingering on the bloodstain down the front of my shirt. His brow wrinkles. "You need to visit the infirmary, son?"

"Ain't my blood, Sergeant," I hear myself say.

"What'd we miss, Sergeant?" Billy asks.

"A whole lot of loading ammo belts by hand since no one can find a loader," Knox says. "You two get cleaned up, grab your helmets and packs, and get downstairs. You'll be issued your pistol and gas mask."

I soap up three times in the shower but can't shake the smell of smoke, the copper tang of blood.

We're allotted two clips of ammo each, along with our pistols, and rotated out on duty. We spend the rest of the day on the hot rooftop of the National Hotel with another fella from our outfit—a Texan named Guy Skinner.

"They let the bunk and mess boys go," Guy says. "Don't know why—

they still need jobs and I still need my uniform washed. Otherwise, you ain't missed much. Though some folks say that's only what we're *supposed* to think. That there's enemy spies hiding out all over, waiting for the signal to take action. People been sayin' they seen weird flares too. That right before Nichols Field got hit in the middle of the night, an old car exploded and lit the place up. Led them right in."

A courier I recognize as the company bugler shows up with our supper. Rumor has it he's only fifteen.

That one I believe.

At night, the city sounds almost normal. The *clip-clop* of a pony pulls a carriage down the street. A baby's cries drift out an open window. But the cars motoring to and from the hotel ain't got their lights on. Even the moon is shrouded, the darkness around us broken only by the glow of Guy's cigarette.

I hope my mama ain't too worried. I'd write to let her know we're okay, but the mail closed down with the shipping lanes.

I try to stay awake. Jerk alert at the rumble of distant thunder, heart pounding in my chest. The clouds drift, sending shadows scampering across buildings. Billy starts, hand on his pistol, as jittery as me.

At dawn, loudspeakers on top of the post office play Kate Smith singing "God Bless America." A courier delivers coffee and rolls and, a few hours later, pressed ham sandwiches.

"Not much of a war," Guy says around a mouthful of food. It's just past noon and I'm ready to get off this roof, get me a cool shower. Maybe some sleep.

An air-raid siren sounds from across the bay. Billy, Guy, and me leap to our feet as three formations of planes sail just west of us out over the water toward Cavite Navy Yard.

Next thing I know, I'm yelling every obscenity I can think of as ice grips my nape in the midday heat.

Because I recognize the planes the airmen at Clark Field called Zeros.

As they pepper the sky, I ain't shouting at the enemy anymore, but for the Cavite-based Marines—God, anyone—to shoot those fighters down.

"Those leaflets they're dropping?" Guy asks, a weird tremor in his throat.

"No!" Billy says, hands going to his head. "They're bombs!"

They barrage the base long past the time we're relieved and rotated back to the barracks. When the attack is finally over, I don't know how that piece of land ain't been knocked clean into the bay. The only way we know it's still even there is the fact that it's on fire, plumes of smoke rising to high heaven, torpedo warheads exploding in the flames through the night, lighting up the black surface of the water.

The next day, as bulldozers rumble toward the burning naval yard to begin collecting the dead, we learn Japanese troops have landed on the northern coast of the island.

Two nights later we move out under cover of darkness, not knowing where we're headed or when we'll return. Only that there's a .30-caliber machine gun poked through a hole cut in our bus's roof that ain't likely to protect us from anything but highway robbers.

We inch along, vying for road space with civilian vehicles fleeing the city, blue lenses over their headlights. Outside Manila, we pass a long string of evacuees. Some in wagons pulled by carabao. Others pushing carts loaded with kids, elderly, and crated chickens. All of them heading *to* the capital. Everyone seeming to assume that the safest place to be is somewhere else.

Just before dawn, we get stuck in a traffic jam at Calumpit Bridge, separated from our lead element. That's how stealthy this entire operation is. Because we ain't just stalled at daybreak out in the open, but in commandeered local buses painted bright orange and yellow with the names of girls on them. I close my eyes and try to nap aboard "Henrietta" and jolt awake when someone outside the open window screams, "Hapon! Hapon!" *Japan!*

Commotion on the bus. The approaching drone of fighter planes grows louder by the instant. I grab Billy by the shoulder with one hand, my newly issued pistol with the other, already anticipating bombs and gunfire as we shove our way off the vehicle. Outside, we dive to the dirt and crawl beneath the undercarriage, packing ourselves like sardines. And all I can think of is the bodies we hauled out from under the cars at Fort Stotsenburg . . . and that I regret not reading Claire's letter tucked inside my pack on the seat we just abandoned.

And then they're over us, the roar of fighter engines drowning out the hammering pulse in my ears. I cover my head—didn't even think to put on my helmet—and hope I've been good enough and believed in Jesus hard enough to save me. Which I thought I did, but now I ain't so sure. So I start praying fast as I can, glad for every spare second I got left.

But the bombs don't come. Three waves of Zeros—enough to take out our entire outfit—pass overhead like they got somewhere more important to be.

Which ain't a settling thought.

Someone shouts the all clear. It takes a minute before any of us move, before our shaking limbs obey. By the time we crawl out from under the bus, others are just beginning to emerge from a bamboo thicket on the side of the road.

"Maybe they didn't see us," Billy says. But dawn's already dappled the surface of the Pampanga River and turned Mount Arayat—a darkness devoid of stars at night—into a ghostly shadow.

"Heck with this," I say, my knees watery. "I ain't getting back on 'til we're ready to go."

We wander up the road, trying to shake the jitters, and catch sight of Hank's unit crossing the bridge ahead of us as things finally start to move.

It's eerie getting back on that bus, and first thing I do is put my helmet on. Just as we start rolling, Hank leaps aboard.

"Hey! Ain't you supposed to be with your outfit?" I say as he comes down the aisle, handing out cigarettes like they're cigars and he's running for office.

"Forget that," Hank says, as we slide over. He perches on the edge of our seat and lights up, blows out a stream of smoke. "If I'm gonna die, I'm doin' it with you boneheads."

"You don't really think we're gonna die?" Billy asks.

Hank makes a face like that's the stupidest thing he's ever heard. "No, we ain't gonna die!" But I also know he smokes when he's nervous.

"Wonder where those Zeros were headed?" Billy says, chewing his lip.

"Hopefully to hell," Hank mutters.

What I think but don't say is, *anywhere they want*. Because we've lost control of the air—the sea too, I'm guessing, after the naval yard went up in flames. But they've got to know we'll never let them take control of the land.

By the time we reach San Fernando, the big Spanish cathedral is blushing in the morning sun. Civilians wave at us as our convoy goes by, their fingers raised in the *V* signal for victory, kids running alongside the bus. Gazing out the window, I search for the bakeshop where I bought the drinks and empanadas four mornings ago. Catch just a glimpse of it—enough to see the shop's lights are on and for me to imagine the woman inside it swaying to the radio as she slides a tray of fresh sugar-dusted pastries into the display case.

We leave the city and wind southwest, skirting the swamp. I'm just starting to get antsy that the Zeros that passed us over might come back and finish the job when we finally pull off and hide the vehicles beneath a mango grove. There, we set to work smearing mud over Henrietta's orange paint, fastening brush and palm fronds to her roof.

We camp the rest of the day, eat the last of the sandwiches the mess hall provided. Sip warm water from our canteens.

Sometime after noon, when Hank and Billy are asleep, I pull out the Bible my mama gave me the day I left. There's an inscription inside the front cover.

July 7, 1941

My beloved son,

May the Lord bless you and keep you safe until the day you return home. I love you and pray for you constantly.

Mother

Reading it, I feel guilty that I've only written to her once—twice, if you count the gift I sent with just one line for a note.

I flip to the unopened letter tucked into the Psalms. It's stamped August 31—just long enough for us to have arrived in Manila and for Billy's mama and sisters to have received word from him of our safe arrival and our mailing address. Which means Billy, dutiful son and brother, paid fifty cents to send his letter via the China Clipper, which only takes a week to reach the States.

And now I feel bad that my mama got the news from Mrs. Crockett and had to wait three more weeks to hear from her own son.

But Mama also knows it wasn't her I was avoiding.

I snick the envelope open with my pocketknife, take out the letter . . . and then hesitate.

A moment later, I unfold the paper.

July 8, 1941

Dear Jimmy,

You left without a single word. How could you, James Pierce Propfield? Just three nights ago we danced and life was beautiful and almost like old times. Now you're gone and everything's different.

There are things you need to know, Jimmy. But you might as well be a ghost. I could hate you for leaving the way you did.

Then I feel guilty for thinking of myself when you're headed off to God only knows where in service to our country. I don't even have a proper address to send this yet, which means I don't know when or where these words may reach you or if they'll be lost along the way. Or if some stranger will stumble upon them and wonder who Jimmy Propfield is . . . not knowing he used to be my best friend.

Look after my little brother, please. You know very well Billy should never have been able to enlist yet. I also know he'd never have let you two go without him. I suppose you'll probably have to save Hank from himself while you're at it. You were always the responsible one.

Claire

I read the whole letter again with rising frustration—and then anger.

Not one word about what happened. The entire letter is practically a lie. I wad it up and pull my arm back to chuck it . . . and then stop. The last thing I want is anyone else finding it and knowing my business—or worse yet, learning Billy's real age.

I shove the crumpled ball to the bottom of my pack and then prop the pack beneath my head. Close my eyes. Pretend to sleep.

I wonder if she'd tell me the truth if I were still home.

But I ain't, and none of it matters now anyway. The only reason I'm glad I read the letter is so I don't have to think about it—or her—the next time I think I'm about to die.

I sleep some, but not well.

We load up at sunset as the mosquitoes come out in force.

"Where you think we're headed?" I ask Hank on board Henrietta.

"Depending how many come ashore," Hank says, low enough that Billy can't hear, "either to the coast to fight or somewhere we can hold 'em 'til reinforcements come."

We move out after dark, wending along backcountry roads beneath the waning moon.

Toward the foothills of Bataan.

6

DECEMBER 13, 1941
BATAAN PENINSULA, PHILIPPINES

Our convoy creeps along narrow dirt roads in the darkness, gaining only a few miles before dawn threatens the eastern sky. The next night we're delayed hours by a flat tire and a broken-down civilian vehicle blocking the road, and we end up camped a second day in the same location. Wherever we're headed, we ain't seen our lead element for days. I assume they're deep in the peninsula; rumor has it our commander, Colonel Steel, is in the hospital, sick, on the southern tip of Bataan.

We load up at twilight, start well after dark. Stop hours before sunrise to camp beneath the jungle canopy, out of sight from the daily Japanese air reconnaissance we nickname Foto Joe. Firing on the low-flying planes would only give away our whereabouts.

But it's tempting.

Despite commandeering enough vehicles to get us to Bataan, half the trucks that are supposed to be carrying food are empty. Meals get cut to canned meat and fruit with rice twice a day.

"No more roast beef for us, boys!" Hank says, rolling his neck and shoulders. "I was just thinkin' it's time I got back to my fightin' weight anyway."

The mosquitoes attack us in force as we load up at dusk and again at dawn as we bed down in the jungle, blankets pulled over our heads.

Our fifth night, as Henrietta scrapes past some branches, something falls through the open window of the seat in front of us where a sergeant named Yancy is sitting. Next thing I know, Yancy's flying over the guy next to him, cussing and slapping his clothes.

"What the—?" Billy says, and then leaps to his feet about the same time I feel like I've just been stung by a wasp—and then another, and another. Hank flicks his lighter on and finds a giant nest rolled under the seat two rows in front of us. We end up having to stop for the night; the bus is full of fire ants.

"We could walk wherever we're going faster than this," Hank gripes the next day.

He ain't wrong; I figure us to be somewhere east of Subic Bay. Which puts us closer to Manila than we were when Billy and me marched from the bay back to our barracks. We did that in three days.

But we got other problems: water, for one—to drink and to bathe. We're all ripe, our uniforms stiff from sweat, rubbing our skin raw. And our canteens have been empty since yesterday.

Finally, the next morning, we camp near a shallow stream beneath the jungle canopy. The water's crisp and cool, shimmering with light from tiny windows in the shade above, and I don't see how the garden of Eden itself could've been any prettier.

We wade in, fill our canteens, and drink deep. Soak our mosquito-bitten flesh and wash out our uniforms. Brushing my teeth has never felt so good.

Yancy lies nearby on his stomach, a thick layer of mud coating the rash of pus-filled ant bites across his back, neck, and arms. Billy sits down beside him, outstretched arms resting on his knees.

"I ever tell you 'bout the sweet V-8 I got at home?" Billy asks.

"I don't think so," Yancy says, his words muffled against the blanket beneath him.

"This fella brought this Ford V-8 to my daddy's repair shop in such bad shape, it was gonna cost more to fix than the guy could pay," Billy says. "He ended up selling it to my daddy instead. Soon as I get back, I plan to fix it up, paint it real slick."

"Oh yeah?" Yancy murmurs. "What color you thinkin'?"

"Well," Billy says, "that's the thing; I ain't sure. Thought I'd ask your opinion."

It's the first time I've heard Billy talk about the roadster he and his daddy were working on before Mr. Crockett died. I glance at Hank. His back's toward us. But he's gone still, and I know he's listening.

Pretty soon Billy and Yancy—who's got his nose in car magazines more than Hank does in girly ones—are talking flathead V-8 engines and specialty paint, and Yancy seems a little less miserable.

I doze for a while. But not knowing where we're going and never getting there—while hungry and on edge for the sound of Japanese planes—makes it hard to sleep. When I get up to relieve my bladder, I notice Yancy, at least, is mercifully asleep, but Hank and Billy are missing. On my way back, I see them sitting with Sergeant Knox and a few other men and go join them.

Hank rests a forearm on my shoulder and lifts his cigarette toward a guy I recognize as one of the regiment's radiomen. "He's saying there's about four thousand of 'em ashore right now," he says.

"Then why're we here instead of shootin' 'em on the beach?" Billy asks, looking around.

"'Cause it might be a feint to draw forces away from a bigger landing," the radioman—a boy from Omaha everyone calls Buggy—says.

"Boys, no one's confided in me, but far as I can tell, we're here on a contingency," Knox says. "If need be, we can hold this peninsula and

Corregidor Island at the entrance of the bay 'til the fleet in Hawaii gets fixed up enough to get here."

"How're we supposed to do that without food, Sergeant?" I ask. In the past, I might have expected a rebuff; Knox, a weathered soldier in his thirties, was always aloof toward Billy and me. But things seem different ever since we got back from Fort Stotsenburg.

"Don't know. From what I hear, supplies are still in Manila," Knox says. "No one organized how to get them here from Port Area, the idiots."

When the other men go off to catch a few winks, Hank strides after Knox.

"What's he up to?" I murmur as Billy and me follow.

"Sergeant," Hank's saying. "If you give Propper, Crockett, and me a truck, we'll be back in a day with a load of supplies."

Knox squints at him. "Son, are you even in my unit?"

"We all serve the same great nation, Sergeant," Hank says, straight-faced.

Knox looks at us. "He always this full of it?"

"Yes, Sergeant." I nod. "But he also shot down a Zero at Clark Field."

"We," Hank says. "We shot down a Zero. Sergeant."

Knox looks between us like he's waiting for the punch line to a joke.

"Something happens to us, you can say we went AWOL," Hank says. "But when we get back with the loot, you'll look like a genius."

Knox sucks on a tooth for a minute. Looking away, he says, "We never talked about this. I never saw you. Stay sharp."

That night, Knox rotates out the drivers of one of the empty trucks near the rear. We wait until the convoy begins rolling south, then jump in the truck with our packs and pull onto the road in the opposite direction.

The moon is barely a sliver in the sky, the blackout lights little help on the narrow jungle road. Our progress ain't fast, but compared to what we're used to, it feels like we're flying.

"Woo-wee!" Hank crows. "Holy smokes, this feels good."

It does feel good just to be in motion.

Every now and then we pass a motorbike abandoned on the shoulder. A family traveling in the darkness. A small military convoy headed the opposite way.

But it's peaceful.

A few hours later, we reach San Fernando. Silver stars glimmer faintly in the windows of shops. Giant tinsel pinwheels that weren't there the last time we passed through hang from eaves. No sign of war other than the darkened streetlights, the lanterns hovering like ghosts beneath the splintered moon.

I seek out the bakery. But the shop, like the entire street, is cloaked in shadow.

It's my birthday tomorrow. When we pass back through town before dawn, I'll stop in for orange drinks and sweet rolls to celebrate. I wonder if the lady will remember me.

"I'm hungry," Billy says softly in the darkness.

"I got us covered," Hank says, pulling into the Pikes Hotel. The entrance lights are off, but there's a glow through the main door from within. Stepping inside, I wish—as I have so many times since arriving in the Philippines—that my mama could see this. From the unlit chandelier in the lobby to the broad staircase sweeping up to the second floor, it's the grandest building I've ever been in.

When we get to the dimly lit bar, I'm surprised to find we ain't the only military men here. Hank orders us sandwiches and gin. I start to say I just want a Coke but then leave be.

The tender pours until Hank signals him to stop.

"Where you boys coming from?" a private at the end of the bar asks.

"Bataan," I say. "You?"

He chuckles, but the sound ain't merry. "Everywhere. The two of us," he nods toward the guy sitting beside him, "were with the 200th Coast Artillery at Clark. Now we're driving for the 228th Signal Operations Company." He points his drink toward a lieutenant sitting at a cloth-covered table, talking up a pretty Filipina. "That man there is an Air Force officer without a plane. He's a courier now."

"We even got any planes left?" Billy asks.

"The last B-17s were ordered to Australia just a few days ago," the guy beside the first fella says. I blink at his answer, unable to fathom why they'd be sent away, leaving us with none.

"What's happening at Stotsenburg?" Hank asks.

"Nothin'. We blew the place."

I stare. "*What?*"

"Why would we do a thing like that?" Billy says, his voice cracking.

"How long you been on Bataan, kid?" the private says, words slurring. "The enemy's comin'! I don't mean them ones the Philippine infantry are busy running from up north neither. I mean the ones that've been fighting the last three years in China. Which is why anything that can't get moved—food, ammo, bases—is getting blown up so they can't use it." He tilts his head and squints at Billy. "How old're you anyway, son? If you got any reason to not be here when they come, I say take it and get off this island fast as you can."

Billy straightens.

"He's old enough," Hank says, clapping Billy on the back.

We down our drinks and I try not to choke; stuff tastes like aftershave. First time in my life I've ever had hard liquor, and I can already feel it settling in the back of my neck and swirling up toward my head. When we try to pay, the bartender says it's on the house.

Five minutes later we're headed out the door with a buzz and a bag of sandwiches.

7

DECEMBER 18, 1941
MANILA, PHILIPPINES

If Manila seemed different before, it's unrecognizable to me now. The Pearl of the Orient is a ghost town, her streets bleak, her buildings abandoned, pale shadows like phantoms moving in her windows. The perfume of flowers and seawater is gone. Even the stench of fish, car exhaust, and sewage has been replaced by the lingering reek of smoke.

Manila's still standing, but I wonder how many times Nichols Field just south of the city and Cavite across the bay have been bombed. One of the men at the Pikes Hotel said he'd heard there were a thousand dead at the naval yard that first day alone.

No moon tonight. Hank drives slowly, navigating by starlight reflected in the bay. We're on edge, but don't see a single soul until the Port Area checkpoint. The guard's a Polar Bear from the Thirty-First—one of our own.

"You guys come from Bataan?" he asks, his cigarette butt just one more ember in a city that smells like a pyre.

"We did," Hank says. "And the fellas are hungry."

"Thirsty too, I bet," the private says, opening the gate. "If there's any booze left, you'll find it three rows down."

We drive toward the customs house and my eyes go wide at the aisles of crates and boxes piled around us. They just keep going.

"Sweet Moses," Billy breathes as Hank gives a low whistle. We drive down one way and up another, straining to read the crates in the darkness. We finally give up and just start loading. We work out a system where Hank and me lug a few crates to the truck, jump up, and slide them in back while Billy drives a little further. Soon as he stops, we hop out and grab a few more—over and over until we're out of room.

"You heard any news?" I ask the private at the gate on our way out.

"Heard we'll be setting up lines north and south of Manila 'til we can get everyone to Bataan. Roosevelt should be sending ships out any day."

It's eerie leaving; Port Area lies right along the western side of the old walled city. I wonder if there's anyone left in the Cuartel de España.

Day breaks as we reach San Fernando. No time for the bakery. We turn west and pull beneath a grove of palm trees a quarter mile off the main road in Guagua and get out.

"Well boys, I don't know 'bout you, but I'm ready for some chow," Hank says. "Let's see what's on the menu." He grins dimple to dimple, grabs the axe off the truck, goes around, and opens the back. Leaping up on the tailgate, he pries open the closest crate and sets the axe aside to sift through a layer of paper. And then stops cold.

"What the . . ." He lifts up a handful of floral fabric.

Billy blinks, stock-still. And then busts out laughing. I do too, if only at the look on Hank's face.

Hank turns to the next crate and pries it open. Setting aside the axe, he digs through a bunch of shredded paper and pulls out what looks like a small wooden house with Roman numerals on the front and a little door on top.

A cuckoo clock.

"You kidding me?" he shouts.

Billy and me grab a screwdriver and hammer from the toolbox in back, leap up into the back of the truck, and start prying open crates.

It takes a few tries but we find food at last—cans of roast beef, pears, peas, and carrots, as well as C rations and two cases of Canadian Club whiskey.

"What do we do with those?" Billy says, nodding toward the clocks and calico.

"Leave 'em," I say. We even show up with that stuff, we'll get laughed off the peninsula.

"I got an idea," Hank says.

We take turns sleeping through the rest of the day, then climb into the truck at dusk. That night, we head to the nearest barrio and spend an hour bartering—drinking too as Hank and Billy toast my nineteenth birthday. By the time we load up for Bataan, the clocks and fabric have been replaced by bottles of gin and cases of Piedmont cigarettes.

We catch up with our outfit the next morning at a cane plantation near Abucay Hacienda.

I search for Sergeant Knox and find him digging trenches with our squad.

"Nice you could join us," Moose mutters, his face covered with sweaty grime.

"Propper," Knox says, sounding surprised to see me. I don't know when or how he picked up my nickname from home, but it rankles. "What happened? You get stuck somewhere?" He looks at me real funny then, sniffing the air between us.

"Got something to show you, Sergeant," I say, trying to act more sober than I am. Knox tosses his shovel aside and climbs out to follow me.

We get to the truck and as we go around back, Hank and Billy are just finishing the gin we shared on the drive here, an empty can of stew between them. Billy hands Knox a bottle of whiskey.

"Well, well. Looks like I'm a genius after all." Knox grins, cracking the seal and taking a long, thirsty swig.

We make a second run to Port Area the next night and a third two nights after that. Each time, we stop at the Pikes Hotel. Each time, the trip gets harder. Whatever reason the Zeros had for ignoring us before is gone. Several times a day, they strafe the glut of military and civilian traffic along Route 7 from San Fernando to the Bataan Peninsula. Vehicles litter the road, many of them riddled with bullet holes, some nothing more than burned-out shells.

We haul back flour, cans of turkey, beans, and tomatoes. We also bring fuel and ammunition.

Most important, we bring news: that forty-three thousand Japanese troops have landed in Lingayen Gulf due north of here. That a plan to defend the beaches didn't last the day, as the untrained Philippine infantry—who were still drilling with wooden rifles the day Pearl Harbor was bombed—fled. That the mounted Philippine Scouts and tank group from Fort Stotsenburg are among those fighting a delaying action against the Japanese advance, covering the retreat to Bataan.

On Christmas Eve we make a final run to Port Area. We don't say it's our last; far as anyone in our outfit's concerned, there's no reason we can't make these trips anytime we need. Running supplies has made us minor celebrities with our unit, and now Knox is talking about organizing a second and third truck to go with us. But word has it fifty thousand Imperial soldiers are crashing their way to Manila. When we insist a convoy's too dangerous, Knox cusses us out as glory mongers and tells us to pick our men.

Instead, we leave without saying a word.

It takes us two hours longer than normal to reach San Fernando. The bartender, a local named Ernesto, sets out three glasses the moment we walk in.

"I worried I would not see you, friends," he says, pouring the gin.

Hank grins. "Here we are!" He throws out his arms like he just performed a magic trick.

It's close to midnight and there's maybe fifteen men in the bar, all of them military. A couple of them chat up a local girl at a corner table.

"Well," Hank says, lifting his drink, "let's learn the news." He pulls the pack of cigarettes from his pocket and joins a group at the end of the bar. Billy disappears to the men's room—the only bona fide toilets we got access to anymore. I swear that kid spends an hour on the crapper every time we're here.

"Hey, Ernesto," I say, low, as the barkeep returns from the kitchen.

"Cook says the bread is all gone," he says, tossing the towel he's been drying glasses with over his shoulder. I figure him to be about forty and, like most folks here, he's got a relaxed way about him. "So we have special Christmas hotcakes tonight instead!" He grins, a silver-rimmed tooth glinting in the bar's low light.

My mouth practically waters; we haven't had real breakfast for nearly two weeks. "That sounds real swell. Say, Ernesto, I wondered if you could tell me who owns the bakery on the corner?"

"Old Renaldo Reyes," he says, wiping down the bar.

I wonder if we're thinking of the same place, because Renaldo don't seem like a girl's name, and this woman's not old. "The one just before the corner—with the lady?"

"Ah!" he says softly, the silver tooth winking as he smiles. "Marisol! His daughter."

Marisol. It's as beautiful as she is, and I know the minute he says the name that it's her. I want to ask more but also don't want to sound like some sap.

"Ah, Marisol," Ernesto sighs, hand over his heart. "Every man who sees Marisol wants to eat what she bakes." He lifts a finger. "And every man who eats what she bakes—even the smallest crumb!—falls in love with her."

I feel the heat rush to my cheeks.

"You too." Ernesto chuckles. "It is okay, my friend. Half the men on Luzon have lost their hearts to her."

He goes off to check on the kitchen and returns a few moments later with plates of thin, yellow hotcakes sprinkled with sugar.

That night as we leave town, we pass a church with open doors. Candlelight glows from within, tambourines sparking the air as the faint chorus of "Gloria in Excelsis Deo" drifts out to the street, the melody following us to our truck.

"Everyone's been ordered to Bataan," the Port Area guard says when we show up. "Word has it MacArthur's gonna declare Manila an open city."

"What's that?" I ask.

"A gentleman's agreement that MacArthur won't defend the city, and Japan won't destroy it."

The return trip is our longest yet, the route choked by vehicles and foot traffic. Military outfits wait for stragglers by the side of the road, their members strung out for miles. Families trudge through the dust, carrying sleepy children in their arms, weary elderly on their backs.

Day breaks and we've barely reached San Fernando. This time the bakery's windows ain't just dark; the place is boarded up. I wonder where Marisol and her daddy have gone.

We keep going, trying to reach Guagua and our usual stopping point away from the highway near the home of several locals who let us refill our canteens at the barrio well.

Morning light creeps across the sky. I get more antsy with each passing minute.

"We gotta pull off," I say.

"It's Christmas," Billy says. "They gonna strafe us on Baby Jesus's birthday?"

Hank snorts. "I bet this highway gets raked ten times today instead of five. We'll cut off there," he says, pointing to a dirt trail ahead.

We're maybe a hundred yards from the turn when the familiar drone of aircraft in the distance turns the back of my neck to ice. Those on foot dive for the cover of abandoned vehicles in the ditches. Others sprint into roadside thickets—and keep on running.

"Go, go!" I shout, as Hank lays on the horn, yelling out the window for people to move.

Further ahead, three denim-clad Filipino soldiers leap out of their truck like fleas off a wet dog. The entire lane stops at a dead halt.

"*What're you doin'?*" Hank bellows at the windshield, cords standing out from his neck.

Billy's staring at the Zeros in the side-view mirror, eyes wide. "Here they come!"

"Get down!" We duck, helmets crashing together as the bullets punch a murderous tattoo through traffic.

Shouts—a pained shriek nearby. Further on, a woman starts screaming as the planes roar away. I lift my head to hazard a glance at the mirror. Somewhere through that haze of dust, the sky behind us is bluer than it's got a right to be. But it's empty, at least, for the moment.

I lean out the passenger-side window and holler at those ahead of us to get a move on as Hank punches the horn, cussing out the other side.

But nothing's moving and now I see why: The engine of the abandoned truck is on fire.

"You gotta be joking!" Hank pounds the wheel.

I glance at Hank. "How much you reckon that truck weighs?"

Five seconds later, the three of us are shouldering our way up the road to the burning vehicle.

One of the Filipino soldiers—a skinny kid maybe a year younger than me—comes to stand by my side. He stares at the truck like he don't know what to do, and I feel a little sorry for him. I imagine he might have been in school before he enlisted, just like us.

"What do we do now, Joe?" he asks.

"Hey, you—get over here!" Hank calls over to a couple one-stripers trudging along the shoulder. "Let's clear this road!"

Next thing I know, the six of us are grunting against the side of that two-and-a-half-ton truck as Hank says, "Heave!" More men rush over to help. Ten seconds later, we've tipped the truck into the ditch with a lumbering crash. Cheers sound from behind us as traffic starts up again. We jog back to our vehicle, and I'm just climbing in when I notice the Filipino kid standing in the road like he's lost. Hank follows my gaze, sighs, and then waves him over.

"Well? You comin'?" Hank says.

The kid slides into the truck beside me with a grin and I notice he ain't even got a weapon. Right after he closes the door, a couple guys from his truck show up. They peer in at us as though to gauge if we got room.

"We're full," I say. It ain't a lie.

"Okay, Joe," one of them says, holding up two fingers. "V for victory."

As the truck resumes its slow crawl forward, I learn that the Filipino soldier's name is Andres and that he worked at his daddy's tailor shop in Rosario until he enlisted fifteen days ago.

"I came to do my duty," Andres says. "But the Japanese are so many, and I am so scared."

I can't fault the kid for his honesty. Wonder if he's ever fired a gun. He ain't even wearing boots—just a pair of dirty tennis shoes.

"You're safe with us, little buddy," Hank says, offering him the rum bottle he's been nursing since the strafing. The kid takes a long, hard swig as an explosion rumbles in the distance.

"What'd they have you doin' since you enlisted?" I ask, not understanding how green recruits like him got sent to meet war-hardened Japanese forces on the beaches.

He sighs. "Translating. Many soldiers do not speak English. And American officers do not speak Tagalog. I hoped to become a famous Philippine Scout," he says, a twinge of mourning in his voice. "But now I do not think that will happen. We will fight, and the Japanese will win, and then who knows what will become of us."

Hank shoots him a dirty look. "We ain't gonna lose."

Our usual spot is occupied by several others by the time we get there: men from Cavite Navy Yard, Fort McKinley, and Nichols Field, who've been bombed nearly every day since the war here started over two weeks ago. Also, a private from the Twenty-Seventh Bombardment Group and a fighter pilot of the Seventeenth Pursuit Squadron from Clark Field trying to catch up to his unit.

"Locals brought those," the pilot says, gesturing to a big bunch of bananas. "After the half-rotten meat we been living on, I swear they're the best thing I've ever tasted."

"Well then, it's a good thing we brought the main course," Hank says, opening a bottle of rum. We loaded half the truck with booze at his insistence.

"Never been so glad to see the 'Thirsty-First' live up to its reputation," one of the other men says with a grin.

We crack open crates of canned chicken and creamed corn, toss the tins to the men like candy in a parade, and spend the morning swapping news. The men from McKinley say more Japanese troops have landed south of Manila and that MacArthur moved his headquarters from the top floor of the Manila Hotel to Corregidor Island in the bay. The pilot from Clark Field says the 192nd and 194th tank groups have been fighting north of us for three days.

No one can agree how fast Roosevelt's ships will get here.

But everyone agrees there's more enemy soldiers coming.

"How long you reckon it takes to fix a fleet?" the fighter pilot asks.

"Six weeks," Hank says. "Two months, tops."

"As if you know," I snort.

Hank lowers his cigarette and stares at me. "Am I hallucinatin', or ain't the three of us lived five miles from the shipyard all our lives?"

"A few ships ain't the same as a fleet."

"Two months then," Hank says, leaning back on an elbow. "And a month to get here."

A few minutes later, when the others are arguing about whether we should even be retreating to Bataan or fighting on the beaches, Hank mutters, "What kind of rock you got stuck in your craw?"

I shrug. "Nothing."

"Then take a load off."

Billy turns to Andres, who's been following our exchange like a tennis match. "I tell you yet about the Ford V-8 I got at home?"

We nap through the day as dust from the highway rises to high heaven in the distance. Wake each time fighters roar from the clouds to strafe that winding column. Load up after dark.

No matter how many times we make this trip, the road is never quite the same. Tonight the traffic is thicker, more obstacles on the shoulders.

More than one body too.

I try not to stare. Try not to wonder who that person was before they became a shadow in a blackout headlamp, like one more thing thrown away on the side of the road.

Explosions shatter the darkness. We got no way of knowing if it's enemy attacks or our own men blowing up whatever gasoline, equipment, or ammo they can't carry. But it sounds like it's happening just over the next hill.

Billy starts humming "Silent Night." Andres joins in.

Billy eventually stops humming when Andres starts singing the actual words. He's got a voice like a choirboy. After a while, I realize he ain't singing in English. But I heard it the same in my head.

The wind picks up, carrying the smell of gunpowder and smoke. Twice, when the clouds roll in, we drive off the road. The second time it happens, our truck keeps going and rolls off the shoulder. None of us is hurt, but when we climb out and survey the damage, half our cargo has toppled into the ditch.

Hank kicks the truck's fender in frustration.

We take stock of the situation best we can, but it don't look good. Just when we think we're gonna have to abandon the truck, the brush begins to rustle. We draw our weapons. A second later, a band of Philippine Scouts emerges from the darkness, their mounts snorting.

"Need some help, Joe?" one of them says, and I exhale in relief, just able to make out the carabao patch on their sleeves. Unlike Andres's fellow recruits who don't know their backsides from the shooting end of a rifle, the Scouts are famous Filipino fighters who, according to Andres, sign on for life.

"Salamat sa Diyos!" *Thank God!* Andres says, as though the cavalry just showed up. And I suppose they did.

Thirty minutes later, we've got the truck upright and the supplies reloaded, and the Scouts have offered to get Andres back to his unit. Hank gives them a case of whiskey.

"You better get going, Joe," one of them says. "Keep an eye out for patrols."

Just before we reach Hermosa, the moon emerges from the clouds. My eyes are beginning to droop when Hank slows almost to a stop. A curse escapes with his breath. Billy sits upright, .45 instantly in hand. There, farther up the road: a beam of light. It flickers away and back, seems to float in the darkness.

"What is it?" I ask, voice low.

"Enemy scouts," Hank whispers.

"How can you tell?"

"Look. They ain't headed to Bataan. They're checkin' the area."

The light floats our way. Billy and me drop down in the seat.

Hank hits the gas.

"What're you doin'?" I holler. But Hank's already accelerating, hunched over the wheel. He flips on the headlights and sure enough, five Japanese soldiers spring to stark life. Next thing I know, we're taking fire. Billy shoots out the open passenger window as Hank floors it. I grab my pistol but got nowhere to fire, stuck between Hank and Billy like I am. A Japanese soldier flies up onto the hood of the truck, and for an instant, that's all I see—the man suspended in midair like a comic book frame—until his head shatters the windshield.

Hank swerves to the right. Another enemy soldier hits the truck. We roll over him in a series of hard thuds and are half a mile down the road when Billy whoops and hollers, "Drove through them like it was nothin'!" Hank howls like a wolf beneath a full moon.

But I'm in shock. That we've come such a long way from Alabama.

That we just encountered real, live enemy soldiers—not in planes, but on the road.

That we might've killed them.

That we're alive.

Hank shuts the headlights off and keeps driving while Billy and me kick the windshield out.

We get back to camp just before dawn. Enough of our boys are still up to help us unload.

"Ho, ho, ho, Merry Christmas!" Hank says, as we hand down crates of tinned ham, green beans, and canned fruitcake.

But it's the booze that turns us into heroes.

When a group of guys from our unit offers to make a supply run two days later, Knox gives them our truck. They leave that night.

We never see them again.

8

MOBILE, ALABAMA
SEPTEMBER 1938

I couldn't get it out of my mind, the way Claire had clung to Hank.

Hank's arms wrapped around her.

He'd always been deferential toward her, though I thought it was just him kowtowing to the fact she was used to getting her way. I'd chalked up his willingness to jump in and help out with the Crocketts' car repair shop to Mr. Crockett taking Hank under his wing, acting like an uncle with Hank's daddy so busy all the time, and teaching him so much before he passed.

The sight of them jarred something in me. Not just because I'd never seen Hank full of anything but swagger around girls or seen Claire hold on to anyone that tight . . .

But because I wished the arms around her were mine.

Until that moment, Claire had only ever been . . . Claire. Mrs. Crockett's daughter and Billy's bossy, copper-haired big sister. Who stood on the back of my tricycle and dictated what direction to go as I pedaled, made me dig holes in the yard for our homemade treasure maps and time capsules, and told me I'd never have a girlfriend if I kept chewing with my mouth open.

But as Hank's head bowed over hers, Claire engulfed in his arms, something shifted.

Walking to school the first day of ninth grade—eighth grade for Billy—I watched her out of the corner of my eye, trying to reconcile the person I saw with the girl who sang as she hopscotched down the driveway and claimed that the radishes we pulled from her mama's garden were really trolls with long, leafy hair. But she wasn't even shaped like a girl anymore. At some point the magic that surrounded her had turned to mystery—from the cryptic tilt of her head to the secrets beneath her lowered lashes. I had never noticed, let alone been distracted by, the way her hem brushed against her knees . . .

And her dress stretched across her chest.

"Where's Hank this morning?" she finally said, looking at me.

Heat sprang to my face as I dropped my gaze.

"Well?"

I made a show of shrugging. "Who knows. It's Hank."

"Maybe he's walking Anna to school," Billy mumbled. "She keeps coming by the shop to buy caramels but never leaves."

Anna Knight was one of the girls Claire played dolls with growing up. Her daddy managed the Woolworth's on Dauphin Street, where Mama bought Daddy's shoe polish and collar stays. I never minded having to accompany Mama there because I could read comic books while she gazed wistfully at dress patterns. And because she might treat me to ice cream.

"Why would he walk Anna to school?" Claire said, looking from him to me, her expression appalled. Not just because Anna had turned on Claire when she couldn't meet Anna's need for constant attention but because Anna was known for being a gossip.

"It's Hank," I said again, not adding that there was a reason they called her Any Night Anna Knight.

Claire huffed and chewed a nail—a thing I'd never seen her do before.

I found myself wanting to take her hand away from her mouth and clasp it as I had the first day of grade school. To twine my fingers through hers. Considering how many times we'd held hands the first half of our lives, I told myself it'd be the most natural thing to do.

Except that it wouldn't be—not anymore. Which is what made the thought all the more tantalizing. I imagined her looking at me with surprise and a small, pleased smile. Seeing me with new eyes too.

And I might have done it except that I was stopped in my tracks by an unwelcome question.

Was Claire *jealous* of Anna?

Was it possible Claire *liked* Hank?

Billy trudged along beside Claire, dark circles like bruises beneath his eyes. It had barely been four weeks since Mr. Crockett's funeral, and Mrs. Crockett had hardly left her bed. Come to think of it, today was the first day since her daddy's passing that Claire wasn't tending her sisters, and Billy, Hank, and me weren't working the gas station or garage. Nor would we be, except after school and on weekends, now that Mrs. Crockett's brother-in-law had taken over the shop and hired a part-time mechanic.

It seemed a shame to waste our first day of freedom in weeks on school.

"Let's ditch," I blurted. It was a perfect September day in a week of record-high swelters.

Billy lifted his head, and Claire turned to stare at me as though crawfish had just wriggled out my ears.

In all my life I'd hardly ever missed school—and made a point of us never being late. But this was different. We were grown up now. Ditching was rebellious . . .

Something Hank would do.

I lifted my chin. "I say we get ice cream sodas. Spend the day swimming."

"I'm in!" Billy whooped, grinning for the first time in weeks.

"And what'll we tell our mamas?" Claire demanded.

"Leave it to me."

Claire spun at the whir of a bike flying down the street. I reluctantly slowed as Hank came cruising toward us.

"We're ditchin'!" Billy yelled.

"Best news I've heard all day," Hank called, skidding to a stop.

Claire wrinkled her brow. "It's only seven thirty."

"See?" Hank grinned. "Just keeps gettin' better."

Mama was at the Crocketts' by the time we got back to Claire and Billy's house. Her brows arched at the sight of us coming in through the door, but she sighed when I pulled her aside, Baby Dorothy Jean hanging over her shoulder.

"Please, Mama," I said. "Claire and Billy, they ain't had a real day of summer since July. Not since Mr. Crockett . . . not since Dorothy Jean was born." None of us had.

My mama sighed; she'd been exhausted too, running the Crocketts' household and getting supper on the table at our house by the time Daddy got home. But there was color in her cheeks, and even though she wore her hair in a kerchief almost every day now, she'd never looked prettier.

"You're probably right," she said as Dorothy Jean let out a belch far too big for her tiny body. "I'll take care of it."

This was code for "Daddy doesn't need to know."

We piled into Mr. Crockett's truck with Cokes from the gas station's icebox and drove to Chickasabogue Creek, Hank behind the wheel. He was sixteen already and maintained Mr. Crockett's truck, but we both drove it regularly to pick up parts or supplies since his death, and

I chided myself for not getting to the driver's side first. At least sitting on the other side of the cab gave me the chance to see if Claire, sitting between me and Billy, was looking at Hank any different.

But if she did, I couldn't tell.

Hank, for his part, drove with his eyes straight ahead, one hand dangling over the wheel, the other holding a cigarette out the open window. He'd taken up smoking since Mr. Crockett's death and also knew his way around a bottle of beer—which I could only assume my daddy knew nothing about or else he'd have told me to stay away from "that Wright boy." No longer the new kid from the other side of town carrying groceries for little old ladies on the weekend, Hank was the tallest of us—taller than my daddy, even, which might have irked him, had he known. But Hank wasn't one for church these days, and whenever he did slip into service with his daddy or brother, he disappeared quickly after.

Claire made a face, waving at the air in front of her nose.

"Wasn't me," Billy murmured.

"He who smelt it dealt it," Hank said.

"Hank Wright, could you not smoke in my daddy's truck?" Claire said. "Or at least when I'm around?"

Hank held up the pack of Lucky Strikes on the dash. "Physician tested, doctor approved," he said in a fake radio voice before flicking the butt out the cab without even taking a last drag.

Meanwhile, crammed together as we were, I became acutely aware of Claire's thigh against mine as the truck jostled toward the creek.

"Here," I said, taking the lunch pail from her and pulling it onto my lap. "I'll—carry this." A crumpled mass I recognized as her bathing suit dangled from the open top of the pail in which we'd all stashed our sandwiches. I wanted to touch it.

Instead, I thought about baseball. About fish guts and my mamaw making sandwiches when we were kids. About her wrinkly arms and liver spots on the back of her hands and the smell of talcum powder that followed her everywhere.

Hank parked and I bolted out, dropping down to retie my shoe.

By the time I caught up to them I felt foolish for feeling jealous. That is, until Claire slipped, her saddle shoes sliding against the dewy grass. Without even hesitating, Hank caught her hand—then leaned down at the waist and pulled her onto his back.

"Mush!" Claire laughed, slapping him on the shoulder, skirt bunched around her knees. Hank howled like a dog and took off at a run.

"I remember when she could hardly stand him," Billy said beside me, Claire shrieking, "Hank Wright, don't you dare!" as he veered toward the water.

"Girls," I said.

"I'd offer you a piggyback ride too, but I got these beauties," Billy said, gesturing to the two Cokes in each of his hands.

By the time we caught up to them at the big tree that hung out over the water and had a fresh rope at the start of every summer, Claire was disappearing through the trees with her bathing suit and Hank was stripping down to his skivvies. Next thing I knew, Billy had torn off his clothes and was diving for the rope, swinging out over the water and howling like a banshee.

"We playin' chicken?" Hank said, squinting at me. We'd spent half of last summer lunging for the rope at the same time, the victor getting to fly out over the water. The loser plopping unceremoniously into the marshy weeds.

I opened my mouth to challenge him. Closed it at the sound of a rustle: Claire returning in her bathing suit, her dress and shoes in one hand.

"Say, what's going on between you and Anna Knight?" I asked instead.

Hank squinted at me. "Come again?"

"Billy thought you might be walking her to school this mornin'."

Hank rolled his eyes. "She wants me to take her to the back-to-school dance."

"What? She said that?" Claire asked with a too-quick frown.

"No. She just asked if I was taking someone and why wasn't I going and if I liked anyone."

"So you *were* walking her to school?" I pressed, unable to help myself.

"No." Hank scowled. "'Sides, she lives the other direction."

I lifted my brows.

A blur shot past us as Claire sprinted and then leapt out for the rope, her laughter trailing behind her.

If Hank was spending time with Anna, she wasn't troubled.

Neither would I be.

But I didn't miss the way Hank's gaze followed her as she sailed over the water.

"So, what's it going to be?" Claire asked later as we sat on the knoll eating peanut butter sandwiches and drinking warm Cokes. "You gonna ask Anna to the dance?"

Hank didn't even look at her. "No."

"Why not? She clearly wants you to."

"Because."

"Because what?"

Hank dropped his shoulders and rolled his head around to look at her. "I don't know! I got things to take care of."

"You don't wanna get cheek to cheek with a girl?" Billy ogled.

"Don't need a dance to do that," Hank drawled.

"I'm goin'," Claire said.

Our heads swiveled in unison.

"With who?" Billy laughed, and then schooled his features. "I'll beat 'im up."

"Paul Harrington. And you'll do no such thing."

"The *dentist's* kid?" Hank said, making a face.

"He asked me Sunday at church and I said yes." Claire licked the peanut butter off a finger.

"Harrington? He used to eat paste!" I said.

"You used to eat boogers," she shot back.

"Everyone ate boogers," Hank said.

Billy wrinkled his nose. "Y'all are disgusting."

"You ate your own earwax," Claire said.

Billy grinned.

I dropped my chin to my chest. Now I'd not only have to see Claire dancing with squeaky Paul Harrington, but I'd also have to go through the awkward trouble of asking another girl.

That thought was the only cloud in an otherwise perfect day—the best of the entire summer.

At least until the rope, worn down by sun and water all season, snapped with Hank holding tight upside down. He crashed to the bank and broke his collarbone. I never saw him get so much attention from girls as he did in his sling, and I swear he wore it a week longer than he needed to.

The night of the back-to-school dance, my mama drove me to Helen Humphrey's house, where I, decked out in my Sunday suit, presented her with a corsage my mama made.

And while Helen, whose daddy was a deacon at our church, looked real pretty in her yellow dress, she wasn't who I was going to the dance to see.

That night as we pulled up at the school, I watched Paul open the passenger door of his family's Chrysler. Claire took his hand as she stepped out, looking like a princess.

I knew I was being a heel, but I hated Paul Harrington in that moment. For thinking faster than me. For his family's nice car. For the fancy store-bought corsage pinned on Claire's shoulder.

Until halfway through the night, when Paul politely asked Helen to dance and Claire and I found ourselves side by side at the punch bowl. I poured one for me and one for her, then blurted, "You don't really like him, do you?"

"Jimmy Propfield, what a thing to ask!"

I couldn't take my eyes from her mouth, even as she chided me—it was the first time I'd ever seen her wear lipstick. "Well?"

Her shoulders slumped and she took a sip of punch. Even the white corsage with the pink ribbon looked deflated.

"Mama said it was bad manners to say no to him and yes to someone else. That I had to say yes or not go at all. And I didn't want to miss out on my first high school dance," she said, lifting her chin.

The words tumbled out in a tangle. "Go to me with the next one," I said.

"What? James Propfield, have you been drinking?"

"No! I meant, go with me to the next one. Please." I took her hand. "I would've asked you to this one, but *Paul* beat me to it." This new truth sounded strange to me, even as I said it.

She tilted her head, regarding me with a look I couldn't decipher.

"What about Helen?" she asked, arching a brow.

"She's swell," I said. I gazed full into her face, having never wanted to kiss a girl more in my life. "But she ain't you."

She lowered her lashes, red lips pursed. "You haven't even told me I look pretty tonight."

"You look *so* pretty," I said with a soft laugh.

She gave a small smile. "Then I'll think on it. Now, are you going to ask me to dance or not?"

9

JANUARY 2, 1942
BATAAN PENINSULA, PHILIPPINES

Manila is on fire. Black smoke blots out the sun rising over the bay. The Japanese bombed the capital the same day it was declared an open city, blasting Port Area and all the supplies left in it.

They've bombed it every day since.

Having established our main defense near Abucay, we move north to set up a delay line at Layac Junction, where all the roads to Bataan converge.

We string barbed wire and dig foxholes. Dive into trenches when the planes come to rake us by the hour.

Our Christmas haul is long gone, including the bean stew Cook made with the last of the ham. We eat a single hot meal after dark. C rations during the day.

Tonight, Hank waves Buggy the radioman over, offers him a swig of gin, and asks for news.

The ex-linebacker drinks deep and passes the bottle back. "Heard the last of the Asiatic Fleet left for Australia a couple days ago," he says.

I stare at him in the darkness. "That don't make sense!"

"Just like the planes," Billy murmurs.

I wonder what they're hearing about this at home.

"Could Roosevelt be launching the rescue from Australia?" Hank asks.

"Possible. I'll keep my ear to the ground," Buggy says.

The next morning we learn Buggy and two other men drove into an ambush while laying communications wire in the middle of the night. No one survived.

Hank takes it hard. We all do. Buggy's the first man we knew personally to die in the war.

"It's weird to think he'll never go home," Billy says quietly the next day. It's Billy's birthday; he's seventeen. This morning Hank gave him a can of franks and beans he held back from one of our runs and a pack of C ration chewing gum. I gave him a roll of toilet paper I filched from our last stop at the Pikes Hotel.

"Who'd want to go back to Nebraska anyway?" Hank says, mussing Billy's hair. And I know he's just trying to lift Billy's spirits. "Ain't you heard? It freezes there in winter. Besides. Buggy don't care no more. He's walkin' those golden streets."

But it does something to me, thinking of that. Of Buggy being separated from his family here, alone, permanently. Of them never visiting his grave. Maybe not even knowing exactly where he's been laid. My daddy would say it don't matter; that if he believed right and toed the line, he's already in the presence of the Almighty. But the thought works on me. Maybe because even though I had no plans to go back to Alabama, it was always, at least, an option.

The Japanese advance, closing the lines of battle between us. No one's worried—word has it there's over eighty thousand American and Filipino troops on the peninsula. Enough to hold it until kingdom come.

Only problem is there ain't enough food.

Within days, General MacArthur orders everyone onto half rations.

We string barbed wire. Dig foxholes. Sleep in rat-infested bamboo thickets and scratch mosquito bites, which is about the highlight of my day anymore.

And we talk about food.

Barbecue. Corn bread. Fried chicken. MoonPies and Mallo Cups. Pork chops, biscuits, and red-eye gravy.

When a couple Filipinos show up with a washtub full of ice and San Miguel beers, we pay a peso each without complaint, only too glad to relax with a cold drink.

The last Philippine Scout unit arrives in Bataan sometime after midnight, followed by the 192nd and 194th Tank Battalions. Engineers blow the Culo River Bridge behind them, cutting us off from the Japanese advance, even if not for long.

The next morning, I wake with a start. I've barely slept since coming off guard duty but am instantly alert inside the foxhole I share with Billy, Moose, and Yancy. I try to listen over the sound of Moose's snores for what woke me, but don't hear it.

I don't hear anything. We're dug in on a slope overlooking the main road. The birdsong that starts long before the katydids have turned in for the night, and that should be coming from the brush around us, ain't there.

I grab my rifle, picked off a body of someone I didn't know. Shake Billy and the others awake.

"What is it?" Yancy says.

Before I can answer, artillery fire shatters the air as the Japanese open up on us.

Moose ducks down with a curse as Yancy calls to the next trench over. And all I can think is, I wish Hank was here right now, but he's holed up with his squad.

"What do we do?" Billy asks, hunched down low.

"Stay down and hold tight!" I yell, wishing we'd dug the trench deeper. A Philippine Scout battery opens up from behind our position, crossfire flying over our heads.

It goes on forever, explosions erupting in the direction of the Scout Howitzers. I see all over again the bombs blasting down the runway at Clark, shattering the earth as they fall closer and closer: *Poom, poom, poom!*

Sometime late morning, Knox comes crawling through a cloud of smoky dust and drops into our trench.

"We're gonna retake that right flank!" he says, pointing toward a cane field alive with Japanese soldiers. "Show them cowards who's who. You hear me?"

I don't know what happened to the right flank or why we have to retake it. I just know that if Knox is scared, he don't look it. In fact, I've never seen him so alive.

The instant the Japanese let up, Knox leaps up with a yell.

It goes against everything inside me to leave the safety of that trench. But I do, running hard on Billy's heels, firing at the enemy streaming toward the Culo River. Yelling like a madman as Zeros roar overhead.

We advance a few more paces, fall flat as mortars slam to the earth around us, deafening our ears. Then Knox is up, waving us forward with his .45 into the storm of debris. We dash after him, shooting across the field. Drop as shells explode around us. Run again, firing—over and over until the Japanese scatter back to a mango grove as an ammunition dump goes off in the distance.

By late afternoon, we've managed to retake the right flank. Dusk falls. Machine-gun fire bursts through the night.

"I wonder where Hank is," Billy whispers.

I do too. Word has it the Seventy-First—Andres's division—is in pieces. I hope the kid's okay.

Sometime before midnight, Colonel Steel—back from the hospital—gives the order to withdraw.

"Why we pullin' back?" Moose hisses soon as Knox is out of earshot. "We could take 'em right here, right now!"

We withdraw up the road, covering the Seventy-First's retreat. Hike several miles in the darkness beneath a half-moon bright as a new nickel. Finally meet up with a convoy of trucks and buses well after midnight.

"I don't know 'bout you fellas," Hank says, appearing from the shadows, "but these buses make me jumpy anymore." He grins, teeth white against his soot-stained face as we clap him on the shoulder and slap his helmet. I don't know that I've ever been so relieved to see him.

"Where you been?" Billy says.

"Chasing skirts," Hank drawls, poking a cigarette between his lips as we climb aboard. "You fellas?"

"Had myself a nice steak dinner," I say, realizing I ain't felt hungry all day.

"Just woke up from a nap," Billy says as we drop into the nearest seats. "I miss anything?"

Hank's just lit his cigarette when gunfire erupts somewhere behind us.

We're off the bus quicker than we loaded, trying to make sense of the chaos in the dark.

Enemy fire advances up the road. Men scatter to the trees. We leap into the ditch as a group of U.S. soldiers comes running, carrying a wounded man between them. The instant they're past us, we open up on the pursuing Japanese, the beehive shape of their helmets unmistakable in the moonlight. Two of them drop. Three. One of them screams. The rest run for cover but I don't stop firing until the empty clip pings from my rifle.

"Prop!" Hank grabs me by the shoulder. "C'mon!"

The Japanese are regrouping. More of them coming all the time. We plunge backward into the thicket and spend the night picking our way through the jungle. We keep sight of the road and stay quiet. There ain't much to say anyway. Layac was the gateway to the peninsula, and it's been taken.

We gotta hold this peninsula at all costs. If reinforcements don't come soon, there won't be anywhere left for us to go.

10

February 15, 1942

Bataan Peninsula, Philippines

We dive into ditches when we hear the Zeros coming. Watch the horizon as village after village goes up in smoke.

By now we've been all up and down the eastern half of the peninsula. Sometimes forward a few steps. Most of the time backward. Pandan. Balanga. Abucay. We held the line there for a week before being ordered to withdraw east to the beach and then south to Limay.

We've charged across cane fields mowed down by machine guns, marched through the night without sleep, waded through carabao wallows, fought delaying actions, picked off Japanese snipers in the jungle canopy, been pinned down by enemy fire in ravines crawling with biting ants, and pulled leeches off our butts.

I've seen men sit down hard with bullet wounds, talk for a little while like they were only stunned, and die two minutes later. Soldiers blown to more pieces than can be scraped together in a box. Barrios of civilians bombed to nothing just because they were in the way.

Most of the time when we arrive somewhere, the place is already on fire and we're too exhausted to care. We sleep to the sound of artillery shells. Spend the night on patrol. Anything comes at us without the right response after dark, we light them up like the Fourth of July.

Or we try. Half the time our rifles jam. More than one man in our outfit has swapped his shiny M-1 for an old Springfield from the locals because at least he knows it'll fire.

Walkie-talkies ain't worth a spit neither. The batteries don't last in these tropics and there ain't enough replacements. Most companies rely on runners, which is what Billy and me find out Hank was doing during the fighting at Layac Junction.

Meanwhile, the Japanese don't stop. We shoot until our fingers cramp up, but they don't surrender. They'd rather die, drown, or kill themselves than do that.

You shoot them or you die.

The first Japanese soldier I encountered up close was in the jungle. Billy, Hank, Yancy, and me were scouting trails and went off into some underbrush, and Billy practically stepped on him. The soldier sprang to his feet. Seeing as how he was outnumbered, I expected him to throw his weapon down, get on his knees, and beg for his life. Instead, he reached for his rifle. Before he could lift it, Hank shot him in the neck. He fell down with a sneer as the blood spurted from the wound and spat at us before he died.

Hank took his weapon and searched him, coming away with some rations—oyster crackers, sticks of dry fish soup, and some little balls of sugar—that he split between us.

But I was unnerved. I don't know how any man summons up hate like that on the threshold of hell. The image haunted me for days, as though he took a part of me with him. I did finally throw the stick of fish soup into a canteen of water and eat the crackers and sugar.

These days we don't ask where our portion of meat comes from because there's a good chance it's one of the Scouts' horses. Rumor has it General Wainwright was the first man in his outfit to sacrifice his mount.

"I heard that horse cost *twenty-five thousand dollars*," Hank said when he told us about it.

"That can't be right," I said, unable to even fathom that amount of money. "Ain't no horse worth that much."

"What about Seabiscuit?" Billy asked.

"Nobody's eating Seabiscuit."

Sometimes the fighting's so thick, we don't get anything at all. Last time that happened, Billy was so hungry he ate a bunch of raw roots and spent the next three days crapping all over our foxhole.

By the end of February, we've all taken turns with malaria, no quinine to be had. One night I watched as Hank, shivering with fever, took off his shirt, wrung the sweat out, and put it back on, if only to protect himself from the mosquitoes. Yancy's down with a fever now. No sense in trying to get him to the hospital—first off, because the hospital ain't nothing but a row of cots out in the open, and second because if every sick soldier left his trench, there'd be no one left to fight.

"You gonna p-preach like your daddy when this is all over, P-Prop?" Yancy asks, teeth chattering in the heat.

I glance up but say nothing.

"Prop knows better than to try to save the unsavable," Hank says, clapping me on the back.

"I'm here, ain't I?" I murmur.

Hank looks at me sidelong, but before he can say anything, shells start to explode farther down the line.

By mid-March there's no more carabao or horses on the peninsula to butcher and we're so hungry we'll eat anything. One day Hank shoots a monkey.

"I can't eat that," Billy says.

"It's meat," I tell him.

But I make sure to cut off the hands before we cook it. Something about the little hands just don't sit right.

Billy rigs up a snare and catches a fat lizard. We eat it that night, and a bony cat the next day.

Meanwhile, rumors keep us going. Someone tells us they heard a ship of colored troops just landed in Manila. That we're going to get out, sent back directly to the States. We hold out another day. Then two, and three. We trade rumors with the other foxholes in a giant game of "Telephone," our eyes turned toward the island of Corregidor, where MacArthur is holed up.

It can't be long now.

A few days later, Billy comes back from the log over the trench we've been using as a latrine, his expression baffled.

"What's eating you?" Hank says.

"They're gone," he says, blinking.

For a minute I think he means the Japanese. That our reinforcements have come in, that they saw the fleet and fled.

But the Japanese don't flee.

"Who's gone?" I say.

"General MacArthur. Word is he left yesterday for Australia with his family and a bunch of officers. They're all gone! Wainwright's in charge now—the old guy."

Hank stares at him blankly and then turns away and punches the earthen side of our trench.

I sit back hard and pull off my helmet. Gaze up at the sky.

No fleet. No troops.

We don't need to speculate on what that means.

We're on our own.

"That can't be true," Yancy says. "If that's true, we're screwed. We're dead!"

"Don't say that," I say, glaring at him. I can feel Billy's eyes on me. But the truth is I don't know where or how we go on from here.

Maybe I was more right than I knew in thinking I was never going home.

That none of us will.

For a moment, Hank sits very still, jaw hard. Then he leaps up and out of the trench, paces away and then comes stalking back, chanting,

We're the battling bastards of Bataan!
No mama, no papa, no Uncle Sam!

His voice cracks. He beats his chest and starts over, spittle flying from his lips:

We're the battling bastards of Bataan!
No mamá, no papa, no Uncle Sam!
No aunts, no uncles, no cousins, no nieces,
No pills, no planes, no artillery pieces!
And nobody gives a damn!

He starts over, louder this time. Billy and me pick up the refrain, and by the end, all the men in our unit are on their feet shouting the words, fists in the air.

Defiant, and alive.

11

April 3, 1942

Bataan Peninsula, Philippines

mperial Japanese Forces have poured twenty-two thousand fresh troops and sixty new bombers onto the island in the last month. They hit us without ceasing, thousands of rounds an hour. They take out foxholes, command posts. Even the white cross on the hill beside the hospital gets shellacked.

Billy manages to get hold of one of the leaflets the planes dropped:

PROCLAMATION

Bataan Peninsula is about swept away . . . Manila Bay is under complete control of the Japanese Navy. Hopes for the arrival of reinforcements are quite in vain.

If you continue to resist, the Japanese Forces will by every possible means destroy and annihilate your forces relentlessly to the last man.

This is your final chance to cease resistance. Further resistance is completely useless.

Your commander will sacrifice every man and in the end will surrender in order to save his life.

You, dear soldiers, take it into consideration and give up your arms and stop resistance at once.

Commander-in-Chief of the

Imperial Japanese Forces

"Gimme that," Hank says.

He shoves down his trousers and squats right there—the dysentery's back—wads up the proclamation, and uses it for the only thing it's good for.

We retreat again, this time to Mount Samat. Every time we form a new line, it breaks. Someone says our command post is gone, along with our commanding officer. Haven't seen him in days. There's only chaos and fighting to survive.

We inch through the foothills. Japanese snipers across the valley shoot at anything that moves. Bombers swarm like hornets overhead. We've spent the better part of the day trying to catch up to what's left of our unit. Just before we get there, a round drops right on top of them. It blows us back. We get up and run, ears ringing, as gunfire erupts from a ridge above us.

"Get down!" I shout.

"I see 'im!" Yancy says, raising his rifle.

He fires once as a new burst opens up on us. Yancy's arms fly back, shoulders jerking as bullets riddle his torso.

Ten yards behind him, Billy drops to the ground.

"Billy!" Hank screams as my breath leaves me all at once. And then I'm clawing my way through the brush, legs churning before I'm even aware I'm running. I skid to the ground, drag him behind the sprawling roots of a giant tree.

"I'm all right," Billy says.

I yank him up by a fistful of his shirt, looking for blood, wounds.

"I'm okay," Billy says, and then shoves me away. "I said I'm fine!"

Hank comes skidding after me. He takes one look at Billy, slaps him in the shoulder and me on the helmet, and then peers around the edge of the tree. A shot whizzes by and he jerks back.

"Hey, Yance," Hank calls. "Yance! You hang tight. We're gonna get you out. Okay, buddy?"

A soft clicking sound, like the start of a snore comes from Yancy's position. And then, "I . . . I—"

His words choke off, replaced by a gurgle.

Hank cusses. Billy lowers his head to his palms, fingers clasped tight over his eyes.

I look up at the sunlight fading through the leafy canopy. We got maybe an hour of daylight left. But Yancy can't wait that long.

"You cover me, I'll go for him," I say. Hank grabs me by the arm, silently shakes his head.

The gurgling has stopped.

Billy rocks in the darkness beside me. He's mouthing the words to the Lord's Prayer.

I wonder if God even hears him.

Just before dusk, the Scouts move in and open up on the snipers. I actually see one of them fall dead from his perch only to dangle by the ankle from the rope he'd tied himself up with.

We retrieve Yancy's body during a lull, struggle to carry him between us. Bury him the next day.

The island tremors after dark. No mortar or anti-tank gun fire. Just the jostle of the ground beneath us.

Hank sits up straight. "What the—?"

Billy's eyes are white in the darkness.

And for a minute I think this is the end—not just of us, but the world. That not even the earth can stand what's been carried out on its soil.

It goes on for what feels like minutes and I don't know what I'm waiting for.

"It's an earthquake," Billy says, voice incredulous.

It stops a few seconds later and all is still. Too still.

And then, a light in the sky! A bright, burning star. But it ain't no star. It's a flare. The first of dozens, arcing toward the ground. They drop in the darkness over our supply point.

Where the ammunition is.

The sky explodes in an orange flash. The roar, when it comes, deafens my ears, followed by ammo crackling and popping like a bunch of fireworks.

Smoke billows into the sky.

All night long explosions shatter the darkness, one ammo dump going up after another, as we creep along looking for a safe trail. If anyone else from our company is alive, we ain't seen them.

"Screw this," Hank says, as the sun rises on one more desolate day. The cogon grass is burning, trees in the distance like giant torches. "I tell you what we're gonna do. We're finding ourselves a boat to Corregidor."

Our canteens are nearly empty and the familiar rumble is back in my bowels. Didn't know that could happen when you ain't had anything to eat.

"We'll get to Corregidor"—he pauses to catch his breath—"and chat us up some good-lookin' nurses. That's the plan."

"After we get some chow," Billy says, voice dull. "Some waffles or chicken 'n' dumplings . . ." He stares ahead, unblinking.

I'd be happier than a clam just to have an entire C ration. I'm still fantasizing about canned ham and graham crackers when machine-gun fire erupts from the jungle.

We drop into the nearest ditch, scaring up a swarm of flies and a terrible stench, and I realize I'm lying on a corpse. I search the body and come up with nothing but some Japanese money, which I shove in my pocket. We scramble into the bamboo and startle five other soldiers already hiding there. One of them's so jumpy, he don't even look twice before taking a wild shot at Hank. He misses, and the second we catch up to them Hank slugs him hard in the shoulder.

Howitzers ring from the mountains—the shot's given away our position. Shell fragments cut through the thicket. We crawl behind some rocks and wait. We ain't got the strength to run.

But the next round doesn't come.

Trucks rumble down the road toward us.

One of the other men rises up to peer through the brush.

"Get down," I grit out, sure he's about to get one between the eyes.

"White flag," he says, voice cracking. "They got a white flag!"

"What d'you mean?" Billy says.

"Made out of a sheet or somethin' . . ."

"You're sayin' they surrendered?" Hank says incredulously.

"No," the fella says, shaking his head. "We did."

We stumble onto the road to stare after the truck. A couple minutes later, a few Filipino soldiers come marching in its wake. Farther on, someone's blowing a whistle and I can't believe what I'm hearing.

"Cease fire! Cease fire!"

It don't seem possible that after the horror of all we've been through, a war can end with a whistle and two words.

Hank sits down hard by the side of the road.

"Is it true? Is it really true?" Billy asks, staggering where he stands.

I drop my rifle like it's a two-ton boulder.

The bombers let up over the mountain and turn away from us. The sky goes eerily quiet, the smoke starting to drift so that I actually see a tiny patch of blue.

It's over, and we're alive.

12

After the back-to-school dance, everything seemed the same on the surface: Billy, Hank, and me working the Crocketts' gas station and garage. Fishing Three Mile Creek behind the old Augusta Evans house after dark as gators rumbled nearby. Helping at the farm when Daddy complained he'd lost his best help to the Crocketts.

But unlike before, I was keenly aware of Claire anytime she was near. And looking for chances to be alone with her—which had become harder than ever now that her twin sisters were old enough to tag along everywhere.

I'd long quit replaying the image of her and Hank in my head, as new scenarios of Claire and me together became more active in my imagination than any movie, distracting me by day, haunting my sleep at night.

The first time I held her hand—really held it—we'd spent the afternoon picking apples for our church harvest festival. We dragged the last bushel into the back of Daddy's old truck and shared a thermos of lemonade as the crickets began to twitch and the frogs started to sing. Claire laid back to gaze up at the first stars winking to life in the sky, and I stretched out beside her and lifted her hand between us, twining my fingers through hers.

"Jimmy Propfield, I can't figure you out." She sighed beside me, gaze tracing the constellations.

"What d'you mean?"

"You tell me I'm pretty—"

"You're beautiful."

"—but you won't ask me on a date."

"I asked you to the winter dance."

"That's two months away."

"Well, *I've* been thinking about somethin' else," I said.

"What's that?"

"The fact we've never kissed."

Her mouth curved in a smile.

I leaned up on an elbow and gazed down at her, but when I leaned in, her other hand flattened against my chest.

"What kind of girl would I be if I kissed before the first date?" She laughed.

"C'mon, Claire—I've known you your entire life!" I said. "We grew up in a washtub naked together, for Pete's sake."

She leaned up, kissed me swiftly on the cheek, and made to slide off the tailgate, sing-songing, "That didn't count . . ."

I tightened my fingers around hers before she could move away. Lifted them slowly to my lips, then gently let her go.

That was the moment I saw our entire future: Claire and me getting married and moving into our first house. Vacationing in Ocean City, where Mr. Crockett had taken Claire's mama on their honeymoon, or driving Route 66 all the way to California just for kicks. Seeing the world outside Mobile—a world bigger than the safe bubble my daddy lived and preached in. I'd never been sophisticated or brave, but I felt both of those things when I was with her.

The next night at the church harvest festival, I drew her aside in the darkness beside the hay bales to caress her wrist and touch my forefinger to her lips. Her smile teased and her eyes invited, even as she pulled away again.

I knew she was waiting, if only so she could tell herself she hadn't kissed me before our first date. Not because she was accountable to anyone—with her daddy gone and mama barely managing the girls—or being watched by an entire congregation, like me. Claire never acted out of fear of punishment. She did what she deemed right simply because it pleased her.

But I was waiting too. For just the right moment. When Hank worked late at the garage on weekends, he was right there at the Crocketts'. And Billy still tagged along with Claire and me for ice cream, Cokes, and movies. I didn't want to make things awkward with him or between the four of us. Far as I could tell, the winter dance seemed the best way for Claire and me to formally step out as a couple.

I saved up for a new tie. Asked my mama to make me a dress shirt for my birthday. The dance was less than a week before my sixteenth birthday. I wanted to look good.

More than that, I wanted to make Claire proud to be seen with me.

The night of December 12, I came downstairs in my new shirt and tie, hair freshly cut and slicked back except for the unruly curl that kept breaking loose to fall over my temple.

"I don't mind it one bit," Mama said, before her voice dropped to a whisper. "I think it makes you look like Errol Flynn." She smiled like a girl, her eyes sparkling.

"What? He's old!" I said, secretly pleased.

"Shush! He's younger than I am."

Mama handed me Claire's corsage and went to get her purse. I looked down at the pink flower wrapped up with green leaves and white ribbon. It was beautiful, and I could already imagine it pinned on her dress.

Daddy came into the foyer, hands in his pockets, and arched a brow as he looked me over.

"New tie?"

I straightened. "Yes, sir."

"I would've been happy to lend you one."

"Figured it'd be good to have one of my own."

"Seems foolish to me. Especially when you ought to be saving up for seminary."

Mama came from the kitchen with her purse over her wrist, camera in one hand and keys to the truck in the other.

"Are you sure you don't want to come to the Crocketts' for pictures?" she asked him.

Daddy never went out on Saturday nights except for church emergencies. Hardly even came out of the small office that doubled as the guest room except for supper. Sometimes I could hear him practicing his sermon through the closed door late into the night, roaring through Jude and straight on into Revelation. Calling down damnation on the nations and galloping into hell with the apocalypse's four horsemen.

"I need to finish tomorrow's sermon." He walked down the hall and shut the door behind him.

I'd never been jittery on the way to the Crocketts' before. Never so conscious of the dampness in the armpits of my undershirt as I followed Mama up the steps of the Crocketts' front porch, my dress Oxfords—a pair of Daddy's hand-me-downs—clomping across the worn boards.

Mama didn't bother to knock but just opened the front door, announcing, "We're here!" The twins sprang up from the living room floor where they'd been playing with Baby Dorothy Jean.

"Claire, Jimmy's here!" Margaret shouted, running toward the stairs. "He's all dressed up!"

Mrs. Crockett came from the kitchen wiping her hands on a dish towel.

"Jimmy, don't you look handsome!" She was wearing a housedress, her hair styled for the first time that I could remember since summer.

I meant to tell her thank you. To say that she looked really nice—which was just how she used to look before she had the baby and Mr. Crockett died—but the words died on my lips when Claire came down the stairs.

I'd thought she looked pretty the night of the back-to-school dance. And I suppose in my mind I expected her to even be wearing the same dress. But it wasn't the same dress.

Or the same Claire.

She wore a blue dress, white gloves, and high heels. Her hair was up, showing off the earrings dangling from her ears.

She looked like a movie star.

"Oh Claire. You're just lovely!" Mama breathed. Claire beamed and twirled around in the dress as Mrs. Crockett talked about altering it to fit her.

"I was never that tiny—I must've taken in two whole inches off that waist!" she said, smiling for the first time in months. "Course, I was two years older and engaged to Claire's daddy at the time." They exchanged a look and Mrs. Crockett turned away.

"Here," I said, holding out the corsage.

"It's beautiful," Claire said, looking up through her lashes at me. "You gonna pin it on me, Jimmy Propfield?"

I glanced down at her dress, at the fabric perfectly fitted over her shoulders and chest. There was nowhere to land without my hand brushing against something it shouldn't. A solitary drop of sweat rolled down the side of my ribs inside my shirt.

Claire laughed.

My mama snapped photographs as Mrs. Crockett pinned the corsage on Claire and a boutonniere with a little white flower on my lapel. It smelled like Claire's perfume.

"It's my favorite," Claire whispered with a smile.

Billy was coming from the direction of the shop as we stepped outside for pictures, his shirt sweaty, face smudged with grease.

"Woo-wee!" he crowed upon seeing us, grinning as he yelled, "Hank! Hank! You gotta see this!"

"Billy Crockett, you keep ten feet away from us," Claire said.

I rolled my eyes, relieved when Hank failed to respond as the sputter of an engine issued from the garage.

I stood awkwardly for photos with Claire on the front porch in the setting sun, trying to ignore Billy mimicking our poses from the yard below. And then I was helping Claire into Daddy's truck, wishing we owned something nicer.

I'd never felt so proud entering any building as I did walking into the school gymnasium that night, Claire's hand through the crook of my arm.

The dance floor was empty, so we drank punch to Glenn Miller and Tommy Dorsey as more kids filtered through the door and Claire's friends came over so they could admire one another's dresses. Mama had insisted on getting us here "on time," but I wished now I'd had the foresight to suggest we go out for Cokes first so it'd be busier when we arrived.

Truth is, I wasn't much for dancing—half our church frowned on it and Mama only danced in the kitchen when she thought no one was looking. The only moves I knew were what Claire taught me the times she'd made me practice with her when Billy—her usual victim—was doing chores.

Claire leaned closer as her friends drifted off to greet a group of new arrivals.

"Next time you take me out, James Propfield, I'll let you kiss me."

Her words, so warm against my ear, sent my pulse racing.

I turned to gaze at her. "What are you doing tomorrow?"

"Tomorrow's Sunday." She laughed, laying her cheek against my shoulder.

"Monday."

"We have school."

"After school."

"You're working and I'm looking after my sisters."

I groaned. She laughed again—and then lifted her head. We both straightened at the sight of an upperclassman named Dewey Lowell cutting across the gymnasium toward us. I let go of Claire's hand.

"Where's Hank?" Dewey asked, not smiling.

"I dunno," I said. "Why?"

Dewey glanced over his shoulder. Now I noticed a commotion near the door where another kid from the class ahead of us was talking to several guys in casual clothes, his arm out as though to keep them from coming in. And though we couldn't hear them, it was obvious that the words they were spitting at one another weren't compliments.

"Who're they?" I asked, but the minute the words came out of my mouth, I knew if I didn't recognize them from school or church, they must be students from the Catholic school.

"That's McGill's quarterback sayin' Hank's been foolin' around with his girl," Dewey said as a couple more fellas joined the conversation at the door. Mrs. Crawley, who taught English and was the chaperone closest to the scuffle, started toward the group, the boys from our school parting like the Red Sea before her.

Claire looked at me. "Did he?"

"How would I know?" I said, relieved to see the boys from McGill leaving, eager to get back to the conversation Claire and me were having before Dewey showed up. Until Dewey's friend Cal Perkins came jogging toward us.

"They're spoilin' for a fight, all right," Cal said. "That quarterback, John Pugh, he's got it out for Hank."

"Well, they're gone now," I said.

Cal shook his head. "They ain't givin' up."

"What does that mean?" Claire demanded.

"Does Hank usually work late on weekends?" Dewey asked her.

"He was working with Billy when we left . . ." Claire said. Her words faded off and her gaze shot to me.

"Either of you got a car here?" I asked.

Cal shook his head. "I can ask Sid—"

"Find some help. I'll go," I said, backing up a step and then starting across the floor.

"Not without me, James Propfield!" Claire said, instantly at my side. I grabbed her by the hand.

We hurried past the first couples starting to dance, out into the hall-way, where Claire stopped just long enough to tug off her high heels.

And then we ran, shoving our way out the entrance to the street just in time to see the McGill boys drive off—in the direction of the Crocketts'.

We bolted across Dauphin Street past Old Shell Road in the twi-light, Claire's stockinged feet silent on the pavement. My dress shoes slipped on the grass as we cut through the next neighborhood toward the church, leaping hedges and gnarled tree roots, ducking beneath branches and clotheslines, to emerge between two houses the next block over.

When we reached the sidewalk, Claire started to lag. I hesitated and she waved me on, high heels clasped in one hand.

"Go!" she shouted, darting up a gravel driveway where a couple kids were playing.

A block from the Crocketts', she whirred by on a rusty Schwinn, wheels squeaking as she pedaled straight for the house, shoes hooked by the heels in the front basket.

The Model-A Ford was haphazardly parked next to the gas pump by the time I reached the shop. I could hear voices coming from inside the garage the closer I got to the big open bay. Someone—the quarterback, I was guessing—making loud accusations. Someone else—Billy—saying we didn't know any fancy Catholic schoolgirls.

Someone else—Hank—saying they sure were pretty.

I cussed Hank out in my head.

If he was going to ruin my night with Claire, he could've at least denied it.

I paused in the darkness near the pump, the McGill boys silhouetted in the entrance of the open garage, blocking any escape for Hank and Billy inside. There were five of them. Three of us.

"Then you admit it!" the quarterback shouted.

"No, he don't admit it," Billy said.

"I ain't talkin' to you, chum!"

Hank scratched the back of his head. "What'd you say her name was again?"

Billy scowled, straightening to his full five-and-a-half-foot height—which still made him shorter than anyone else there by at least four inches. "Hank ain't foolin' with your girl. He's foolin' with Anna Knight!"

"*What?*" One of the other boys gaped. "That's *my* girl!"

Dadgummit, Billy!

"Billy—put a lid on it," Hank said, not unkindly. His gaze flicked to the McGill boys, assessing, and found me in the darkness. I held a finger to my lips.

"Maybe—maybe it was a different Anna," Billy said quickly. "Anna Wright."

Hank looked at Billy funny.

"I mean White! New girl—from Birmingham." Billy shook his head. "No relation to Hank."

"You're dead meat!" Quarterback John growled, hands clenching into fists. "No one messes with our girls."

Hank hung his head, nodded. And then looked up with a smirk.

"You sure 'bout that?" He grinned.

John roared and Hank lowered his shoulder and barreled into the quarterback's midsection, the two of them staggering out into the darkness like rams locked together. Another boy piled on, punching at Hank's ribs before grabbing him around the middle and tearing him away. Hank flailed, fists flying, catching the second boy in the nose before John got a punch in.

I dropped my head, blew out a breath, and launched myself onto the back of the closest football player. Toppling him to the ground, I pummeled him as hard and fast as I could before trying to get up—only to have him grab my pant leg. I heard a rip, felt a seam give somewhere in my good pants . . . and saw in a flash the grief I'd get from my daddy for getting drawn into a fight—on the night before church, no less.

I fell back on the football player, kicking and punching until another boy grabbed me around the neck and hauled me off. I thrashed and twisted, leg twining with his, and sent us both sprawling into the dirt. When I rolled away, I saw that his shoe had come off in the scuffle and snatched it up. This time when he came at me, I smacked him hard across the face with it then lobbed the shoe up onto the garage roof as the kid reeled away.

I got to my feet and staggered into the shop just in time to see Billy roll beneath the car with its hood propped open and land a square kick to the jaw of the McGill kid who got down on a knee to see where he'd gone.

"You ain't too smart, are you?" Billy said, before rolling out the other side—and getting stomped in the ribs by Anna Knight's beau.

I ripped off my jacket as I ran around the car and threw it over Lover Boy's head. Pulling the arms tight, I yanked him down hard against the fender of the car before swinging him into the kid Billy kicked in the face as he came around the bumper.

Out in the yard, John and two others were pummeling Hank good. Hank was down, still fighting, blood running from his nose to his chin. I threw myself at the McGill kids like a bowling ball at a trio of pins, grabbing at faces and hair. In my peripheral vision, I saw one of the boys in the garage pin Billy's arms behind him as the other kid made a show of winding up a punch.

"You let 'im be!" I shouted, not sure which of my friends I was talking about.

A horn honked down the street. A second later, an engine rumbled toward us so fast I thought for sure we were about to get run over. One of the boys let Hank go and skittered back as a car stopped five feet from us, gravel crunching under its tires.

Not a car—a rusty Model TT. I knew that truck.

The doors opened. Hank's brother, Cowboy, stepped out.

For the first time in my life since I met him, he wasn't smiling. Eugene Gafford, one of Cowboy's friends, got out the other side.

John Pugh straightened, the color draining from his face.

"Roy Wright?"

Hank lifted his head, looked John square in the eye.

And winked.

I realized right then that John hadn't put together that Hank's brother was Murphy High's star quarterback. The same one who led Murphy High to victory over McGill the last two years, thrashing them last season 20–0.

Cowboy rolled up the sleeves of his dress shirt. He must have come from the dance.

"You got a problem with my brother, you got a problem with me."

"And me," Eugene—who played left tackle—said, walking toward them.

"Hey now," John said, palm lifted.

Anna Knight's boyfriend looked from Cowboy to Eugene and took off running down the street.

John's friends shifted uneasily as Hank climbed up on the hood of the McGill boys' Ford to watch.

John narrowed his eyes. "You gonna let your brother fight your battles?"

"Sure." Hank leaned back with a lazy smile. But I knew he was just evening the odds. Hank liked to stir trouble, but he never fought dirty.

John snorted and put up his dukes. "Coward."

"Wow. You really are a dip," Cowboy said, waving him in.

John gave a wild yell and rushed him. The rest of us jumped in the fray.

I ain't never had so much fun fighting in my life. Ain't never thrown so many punches or chased anyone so many times around a garage.

By the time Mrs. Crockett and Claire came running, Hank was giving the play-by-play like a radio commentator as Billy yelled like Tarzan in the ruckus.

"Stop!" Mrs. Crockett shouted, waving her arms. "You boys stop it right now!"

No one listened.

It ended when Cowboy threw John up onto the hood of his own car, sending Hank skittering out of the way.

"Oh, that one's gonna hurt—the car, not John Pugh's noggin," Hank called through cupped hands. "The Ford takes a dent to the hood thanks to Pugh's thick skull . . ."

John climbed in the car, the other three boys diving in after him. Ten seconds later, they were speeding away as we hollered in their wake.

Claire threw her arms around me. "You hurt? You okay?" she asked.

I hugged her against me, breathing hard. "I'm fine."

Mrs. Crockett looked Billy over and then patted Hank's cheek, calling him a good boy, saying loudly enough for Billy to hear that she was glad someone, at least, had the good sense to sit on the sidelines.

"You sure look pretty tonight, Mrs. Crockett," Hank replied as Billy rolled his eyes.

As we walked to the house, I realized two things in quick succession:

That this might be the greatest night of my life . . .

And the crotch of my slacks was torn clean apart and my underpants were showing.

We sat on the porch that night, me in a pair of Mr. Crockett's trousers while Mrs. Crockett fixed my pants, cool cloths held to bloody noses and swollen eyes as we sipped sweet tea and yukked it up. Cowboy and Eugene told us how Cal and Dewey had intercepted them the minute they got to the dance saying the three of us were in trouble.

"Hank was the one in trouble," Claire said, giving him a pointed look. She'd kicked off her ruined stockings and unclipped her earrings. Even now, with her hairdo mussed, she looked like a dream.

I wasn't the only one who thought so. I noted the way Hank, Cowboy, and Eugene all glanced at her when she wasn't looking.

But she'd gone to the dance with me.

"I was with Hank," Billy said, raising his hand.

"That's trouble by association," Cowboy chuckled.

Hank started laughing. "And then Propper comes flying onto that knucklehead's back like a flying squirrel—"

"You mean like Superman," I said.

"No . . . it was definitely a flying squirrel," Hank said.

Billy nodded. "It kind of was."

Eugene leaned his chair back against the porch railing. "So who's this girlfriend you been foolin' around with then?"

Beside him, Claire muttered, "Which one?"

Hank shrugged. "I'm guessin' he means Mary Jo Graham. And we ain't been."

"Ain't been what?" Eugene asked.

"Messin' around. She comes by the shop sometimes, wants to chat, and won't leave."

"What?" Claire said. "All this over nothin'? Why didn't you *say* so?"

"'Cause it was more fun not to?" Hank grinned.

Eugene chortled and Cowboy shook his head.

"And Anna Knight?" Claire asked.

"Yeah, we mess around some," Hank said with a sly smile.

Howls of laughter.

"I will never understand you boys!" Claire said.

Cowboy winked. "That's because we're simpleminded and not nearly as complex as you girls give us credit for."

Claire arched a brow. "Oh, trust me, I don't give any of you that much credit."

"You might just be the smartest woman I've ever met." Cowboy chuckled and got to his feet. "Well, I suppose we ought to get back before our dates leave with someone else."

"Thanks, Roy," Hank said, reaching up to clasp Cowboy's arm. "Pugh had it comin'."

By the time Mrs. Crockett called Mama to let her know we were at her house, Hank had headed home—or maybe to Anna's—and Billy had gone in to find something to eat. Which left just Claire and me on the porch. We sat on the swing and watched the moonlight through the branches of the trees, fingers intertwined. Me stealing glances at Claire out of the corner of my eye.

"I don't know if I told you how beautiful you look tonight," I said at last.

"You did. But you can say it again."

"You're beautiful."

She leaned in toward me. "I don't think I can wait 'til Monday. Let's go on a picnic after church tomorrow. Just you and me. Somewhere we can be alone for a spell."

"You sure? I feel like I owe you a better first date."

She nodded. "I'm sure. And if you see Hank before I do, you tell him he owes me a pair of stockings."

That night I lay awake, willing the hours to go faster, my sheets unusually hot.

13

APRIL 9, 1942

BATAAN PENINSULA, PHILIPPINES

The first group of Japanese soldiers to march past us looks nearly as hungry as we do. We sit by the side of the road and watch them pass.

The second group stops and hollers at us. They toss our rifles in a pile, separate the Filipinos from the Americans, and put us in rows where we turn out our packs and pockets. They work their way down the line, sorting through possessions, helping themselves to whatever they want. Yelling and punching.

I stare at the meager pile of possessions on the ground in front of me. It don't amount to much. The things could belong to anyone, except for the Bible, which has my name in it. But it's the letter folded back inside it that makes me feel laid bare. I don't want them knowing Claire's name, seeing her address, or learning the truth of Billy's age.

Before they get to me, I slip the letter from the Bible's pages, fold it up real small, and tuck it between the binding and the leather cover.

And then I notice, on the ground between my canteen and my toothbrush, the ten-yen note I got off the dead soldier—telltale evidence I shook down one of their own, even if he was already dead.

The soldiers are only three men away from Billy. Close enough to spot the money if they look over. I start to cough, the sound rattling up through my lungs. I fall forward coughing as one of the Japanese infantrymen slams the butt of his rifle into the head of a U.S. soldier.

"Prop," Hank grits out. "Get up."

I push back, hand over my mouth, and fall quiet again. Billy looks at me nervously. The American two men down from him sags on his knees, blood running into the dirt.

One of the guards is holding a bag, collecting watches and rings. They kick through our things—including the Bible—take my matches and toothbrush. When one of them snags my canteen, I look up in alarm but don't dare open my mouth.

"Go you to hell!" he shouts in my face.

When they get to the man on the other side of Hank, one of the guards barks an order. A few seconds later, he's yelling nonstop. I glance over to see the American spitting and tugging on his finger, trying to get his wedding ring off.

In an instant, two Japanese soldiers are on him. The one in charge cuts off the ring, finger and all. The fella's still screaming when one of the soldiers grabs something from his belongings and holds it in front of the man's face. Japanese money.

They shoot him point-blank in the head. My throat convulses as I try to summon the spit to swallow, ten yen stuck to the back of my throat.

They march us northward in the afternoon heat, up the Bataan Peninsula, four abreast in a long column. When we crest the hill, I note another column of prisoners in front of us, and another in front of them. Units and ranks all mixed together like they don't exist.

I glance back, and there's a string of columns behind us, stretching as far as I can see.

"When you reckon they're gonna feed us?" Billy asks.

An old sergeant hobbling on a pair of crutches on the other side of Hank says, "Trust me, boys. Feeding us is the last thing on their minds." He's got a tattered towel soaked through with blood wrapped around his thigh.

The sun beats down. Sweat trickles down my sides. The stiff grime of my filthy uniform rubs my crotch and armpits raw.

I'd give just about anything for a cool sip of water from one of the barrio's artesian wells. To bathe in a carabao wallow with the leeches.

Hank unscrews the top of his canteen and holds it toward me.

"Go on," he says.

I allow myself a single hot, metallic swallow before giving it back.

Billy takes a swig from his own canteen and offers it.

I take a tiny sip from his.

"Drink, Sergeant?" Billy says when I'm done. The sergeant stares at it for a minute.

"Nah. I don't want your water," he says, and looks away.

A military truck comes up the road and speeds past us. Japanese soldiers hang off the back, rifles slung over their shoulders. The dust chokes us as they pass.

A hundred yards ahead, the truck slows at a dip in the road. One of the soldiers leans out the back of the truck, rifle held backward. He swings at the column of prisoners like a batter at spring practice. *Crack.* The butt connects with the back of a prisoner's neck. The prisoner topples over, out cold.

I stagger as the Japanese soldiers laugh and the truck catches its gearing and roars away.

"Stay in line," Hank hisses.

A taller prisoner heaves the fallen man to his feet. But the instant he lets go of him, the man collapses. When he tries to drag him out of harm's way, one of the guards marching alongside his column runs toward them—I assume to yell at them. Instead, he kicks the wounded man to the ground, lifts his rifle, and blasts the Good Samaritan in the head.

Every man in line tenses. The guard jabbers but no one can understand a thing he's saying. A minute later he swings his rifle around and bayonets the wounded prisoner in the neck.

New fear rises inside me, turning my skin cold in the heat of the day.

Another truck roars up from behind us but doesn't stop. Three tanks follow behind.

By the time we pass the fallen men, there's nothing left of either one of them except their Army greens pressed into the dirt.

The next truck that approaches downshifts and slows, moves parallel to us for some time. Billy's marching closest to the road. The cords on his neck stand out, his gaze fixed straight ahead.

The truck eventually speeds on, and Billy's posture relaxes.

"Streak, switch places with me," I say.

"I'm fine," Billy says, not looking at me.

I glance at Hank.

"We'll take turns," Hank says. "Switch out every few hours."

We come up on a mess of bodies—all Filipino soldiers, their bellies swollen.

I turn away at the smell, but the old sergeant chucks one of his crutches under his other arm and gimps over to the nearest body and swiftly searches it.

"Halt!" a Japanese guard ahead of us yells. He's looking out over our column like he don't know exactly what he saw or who did what. "Halt!" He slugs the closest prisoner in the shoulder with the butt of his rifle. We halt. The guard strides down the column.

"Better hurry up, Sergeant," Hank bites out.

The sergeant searches a second body and straightens, a small fabric package in his fingers. He tosses it my direction and I catch it one-handed.

"I want that back when they're done with me," he says, hobbling back into line as the guard comes stalking toward us.

In one quick motion the guard whips the rifle hanging from his neck behind his back and then kicks the crutches away from the old sergeant. He yanks him to the side of the road by the collar and shouts, "What you take, Joe?" The guard doesn't wait for an answer but pastes him across the jaw with the other fist.

I hold the package against my opposite thigh, heart pounding. Soon as the guard's shoulders are turned, I shove it in my pocket.

The sergeant tumbles in a heap, tries to rise, and spits. Blood trickles down his chin.

"You are dog! Traitor to your country!" the guard yells.

The old sergeant says nothing but looks the guard full in the face. Goes so far as to prop himself up on an elbow as though he might say something. But before he can, the guard shouts, "Coward!" and jumps forward, landing with both feet on the sergeant's bandaged leg. The sergeant twists in pain, eyes squeezed shut, but refuses to scream.

The guard goes berserk. He whips his rifle around and plunges his bayonet into the sergeant's gut and rips the blade to the side.

The old soldier gasps and lays back. Blood bubbles out of his mouth.

I tell myself to look away and then watch as his eyelids flutter. The guard stabs him again and again and then kicks him for good measure. The sergeant's gaze rolls away.

The guard ain't finished. He turns on us, stares straight at me. I look forward and then at the dirt.

"You!" he yells. "Gimme water!"

"I got no canteen, sir," I say.

"Where canteen?"

"The guard took it, sir."

He turns to Hank.

"You—gimme water!"

Hank stares ahead.

"Gimme water!"

The butt of the guard's rifle smashes against Hank's cheekbone. Hank staggers to a knee. Billy starts to turn. I give him a sharp, tight-lipped glance at which he straightens and stares ahead, blinking hard.

The guard crouches, his face level with Hank's. He's younger than I thought, with close-cropped hair. His neck muscles bulge as he slices Hank's canteen from its strap. It topples to the dirt and the guard scoops it up, unscrews the cap, mashes his lips against the rim and tilts back his head. One swallow. Two. Three. Four.

The guard straightens and grins. He pours water on his wrists and forearms and all over the back of his neck. After one more swig, he turns the canteen over. The last of the water trickles into the dirt before he flings the canteen into the bushes.

"You march, Joe! Speedo!"

Hank jumps to his feet, the hard look in his eyes made murderous by the blood pouring down his face, his cheek split to the bone.

Our column starts up again, leaving the old sergeant by the side of the road.

"You okay, Hank?" Billy whispers, with a swift glance at him.

"I will be the day I kill him," Hank murmurs.

"We got to stop that blood," I say.

"I got my kit," Billy says, pulling his pack open as the guard starts in on someone farther back in line.

"Do it," Hank says.

"Right now?" I ask.

"Unless you wanna ask for a chair."

Billy hands me his kit. I fumble around for a needle and make sure not to drop it. Get the thread, put the rest in my pocket. I don't know how many tries it takes but I finally get the needle threaded and knot the end.

"You ain't gonna be pretty after this," I say. I wish we had some whiskey.

"Folks might finally think we're brothers."

I lock arms with Hank to match his gait. Reach up with the needle, hold it as close as I can to the gash. It stretches all the way up to his eye.

"Wait. Your mama sews, right?" Hank asks.

"It ain't genetic."

I hesitate, and then plunge the needle into the right side of the gash, push it through the flesh on the other side, and pull the first stitch tight. I repeat the stitch but stumble on the edge of a pothole—and accidentally jab Hank in the eye.

"Propfield!"

"Sorry."

Tears run from the corner of his eye as I stab in a third stitch, pull it tight, and quickly add a fourth and a fifth as we hit a rocky patch. Hank stumbles and I let go, needle dangling from his face. It's a bloody disaster, but at least it's mostly closed.

I grab the thread, tie and break it off. Angry red has already begun to pool in the white of his eye.

"Can you still see?" Billy asks.

Hank blinks, opens his eyes wide, and squints against the sun.

"For now," he mutters.

I reassemble the kit, hand it back to Billy.

We switch positions, trudge the next quarter mile in silence, sweat dripping in our eyes. Our tight formation stretches long and thin as stragglers fall behind. Every so often, we hear a gunshot from near the back.

"You reckon they're takin' us somewhere just to kill us?" Billy says.

"Too many troops to shoot." Hank says.

I want to think he's right. But I also know that a lot of men means a lot of mouths to feed. And after seeing the shape some of their own men are in, I wonder how much they're willing to spare.

"We didn't come through hell just to die when it's over," I say. "If we have to run—if we have to swim off this island—we're gettin' through this. The three of us—all home alive. That's our only aim from here on out."

"All home alive," Billy repeats, quieter.

"Unless Prop has to stitch anyone else up," Hank says. "Then we're all dead. But yeah, I agree. That's the pact."

"Long as I don't have to sew any more of you yahoos up, Billy'll be fixin' up his hot rod by fall, and Hank'll be scarin' girls with his new face."

A half mile later a soldier ahead of us drops to the road. When he don't get up, a guard marches over and shoots him in the back.

The earth is a smolder of decay. Trees charred to skeletal fingers. Bamboo burned to matchsticks. It's been so long since I haven't had the stink of smoke or dead bodies in my nose, I can't remember what clean air smells like.

I count my steps. One. Two. One thousand. Two thousand. Five thousand. Six. I might have skipped four thousand, so I start again but lose my way when our column veers, winding down a bank and through a shallow lagoon. It's stagnant and swarming with blowflies.

Some meatball a few rows ahead reaches down to palm the warm water. The next minute the guard is sloshing toward him, yelling, "No drink!" But the soldier doesn't stop, crazed with thirst. The guard's bayonet slashes out, catching the sun. The prisoner screams and sinks to his knees. A red ring blooms across the scummy surface as another guard bayonets him in the back. He falls over, all the water he could ever want flooding his open mouth.

We reach a manufacturing area on the outskirts of Orani after dark. A wrecked jeep lies in the ditch.

The guards start shouting, waving us off the road. They march us down a gravel drive toward a corrugated-metal warehouse where they order us inside.

As darkness closes around us, I fight the urge to panic.

"Stay together," Hank says. "Keep close to the walls."

We hook arms and he pushes his way to one side. Men collapse and moan around us, cramped and too many in this space. The door scrapes shut and a beam thuds into place against it.

It's pitch-black. Some fella groans and someone else yells, "Shud-dup!"

"Where are we supposed to crap?" someone asks.

A voice calls out, "In your pants, fathead."

I lean back against the metal wall. Wish it was cool.

A rasp near my shoulder: "You boys got water?" I feel Billy shift—and then Hank seize the canteen from him before he can hand it over. It's nearly dry and all we got.

Within an hour the warehouse stinks of diarrhea.

In the darkness I pull out the package from my pocket. Turn it over in my hands. I feel a few small, hard bumps through the fabric but can't be sure of what they are and don't dare risk dropping one in the darkness.

I close my eyes and imagine my bed at home with the crisp cotton sheets, the smell of fresh-cut grass drifting through my window. And clean, cold water from the faucet.

And then, despite my best efforts not to, I think of Claire.

About how the day after the winter dance, my eye still throbbing with a shiner, we laid on a blanket beneath a big oak along the riverfront, the picnic basket forgotten as I held Claire close and kissed her for the first time, my heart hammering in my ears.

"Why James Propfield," she'd said, breathless.

She kissed me back then, and I spent the rest of the afternoon reveling in the softness of her lips as I caressed her with trembling fingers.

I had thought, when we finally went home as the frogs started singing just before twilight, that maybe I'd gotten the distraction of her out of my system. Instead, it had the opposite effect, so that all I wanted was anything to do with her.

14

April 10, 1942

Bataan Peninsula, Philippines

Twenty guards barge into the warehouse at dawn.

"Speedo! Speedo!" It's the one English word every Japanese soldier knows.

We scramble to our feet. A few men, including the one who asked for water last night, lie where they are, unmoving.

We hike back to the road and form up in rows. The first American gets bayoneted fifteen minutes later for falling out of line.

A Filipino soldier gets bayoneted an hour later for stopping to take a crap.

A short while later, a prisoner ahead of us limps to the side of the road and lies down in the brush, facedown, hands over his head. His sides heave, and he doesn't rise even after a bunch of prisoners shout at him to get up and keep going. A guard rolls him over, sticks his bayonet in his belly, and tears it open, gutting him like a dog.

When I'm sure that the guards are too far down the line to notice, I pull the packet from my pocket. Carefully peel it open.

Chlorine pills. Six of them.

Billy flicks a glance my way. Hank grins as I lift one between my fingers, low between us.

Now all we need is water.

Three hours later my tongue is so thick in my mouth, I imagine it's choking me. Billy passes his canteen to us midmorning and again at noon. One small swallow each and our water's gone.

By early afternoon I'm stupid from thirst and hunger and fatigue. We've made forced marches plenty of times—day and night. But never without food or water, crapping our guts out, and sweating through our clothes.

I walk in a daze, imagining my legs moving on their own, the rest of me floating above them . . . and then startle alert when I notice a couple dozen men break from the column for a sugarcane field.

The guards halt everything, chase the men down, shoot two, bayonet four, and herd the rest back. Sorry as I am for them, a part of me is just glad to catch my breath.

There's a mango tree on the edge of the field. It's bent in half from mortar fire, green fruit still dangling from its branches. I stare at it, wishing for one of those mangos so hard, it's all I can do to tear my gaze from the tree as a guard passes alongside us.

Soon as he's gone, Hank says, "We're gonna need to try for food soon."

"You crazy?" I grit out.

"Right after we find water."

But Hank's right. We have a more immediate danger than getting bayoneted: collapsing from thirst or hunger.

And then getting bayoneted.

The air is stifling. They march us through a slimy buffalo wallow.

Billy loosens the cap on his canteen and lets it down by the strap, drags it through the water.

I hand him a chlorine pill and he pops it in the opening. Swishes it around 'til the pill dissolves.

We all get a drink.

It tastes like mud, manure, and rotting weeds.

And I still want more.

We march the rest of the day. Spend the night in a field ringed in by guards, crammed as tight together as they can shove us.

Around midnight a lieutenant gangs together some soldiers and gets them to dig a shallow slit trench with their hands. When they're finished, everybody takes turns crapping in it until even the guards are grumbling at the smell. Those lucky enough to sleep spend half the night getting stepped on by those fumbling their way to the makeshift latrine. It's full by morning.

As we form up at dawn, a truck stops on the edge of the field, motor idling. The guards order us into columns and herd us toward the truck. One by one, a small ball of rice gets squished into each man's hand.

I never much liked rice back home, but I wolf mine down, thinking of the way my mamaw used to put butter and sugar on hers as it slides down my throat.

"Oosh!" a guard shouts.

We move out.

The first bayoneting happens less than twenty minutes later when a gaunt soldier falls out of line and collapses.

It ain't until we walk past him that we recognize the lifeless form of my squad leader, Sergeant Knox.

Shortly before noon an old colonel carrying a large pack falls by the side of the road. The nearest guard runs him through, spilling the colonel's pack open. An extra pair of shoes topples out with four cans of food. When a soldier ahead of us swoops down for a can, he gets bayoneted in the back.

We walk right by the food, our eyes fixed ahead.

Soldiers have been dropping their belongings by the side of the road—everything from extra uniforms to tents, pistol belts, and books. Anything to lighten the load. We regularly see locals picking through the things as we pass by.

I don't have much load to lighten, but the next time I see a group of locals foraging by the road, I take out my Bible. I know I should feel guilty, but it weighs a couple pounds and I got most of it crammed in my head anyway. I hold it out as we pass. "Take it," I whisper to a boy with a dirty face. When he don't, the girl with him darts forward and grabs it from my hands.

Only afterward, as I watch the pair hurry away, do I remember that Claire's letter and picture are tucked inside.

That afternoon we cross a shallow creek. "No drink!" a guard hollers, but a couple of prisoners fall to their knees and splash water into their mouths.

When we reach the other bank, the guards call a halt. They order all prisoners with wet shirts forward—about a dozen men—to line up there on the bank. The guards shoot them all.

We camp that night in the ditch. The next morning, about ten soldiers along our stretch of road never get up.

Just before noon, our column passes a sweet-potato field. A pack of men spring from line and run for it.

"Go!" Hank says. "Go now!"

No time to think. We sprint into the field. Rifle shots crack the air. A man to my left arches his back and drops flat. I dive headlong into the weeds and try to scoop up a plant. Something. Anything. The guards fire on three more men and bayonet two slower ones while we scramble to our column in the confusion, sneaking back in line. It takes us two miles before the three of us manage to form up together in the same row.

"I got nothing," Billy says. His expression is beleaguered, eyes blank.

"Fistful of dirt," I say, staggering from the exertion. "Sorry fellas."

Hank unbuttons the lowest button on his shirt, looks around, and pulls out two sweet potatoes.

My mouth remembers how to water.

"Good thing it's such a hot day. They've been cooking against my gut." He looks around, chomps the end off of it, and hands it to me. I take a bite and pass it to Billy. The potatoes are gone within a mile.

"You fellas remember that time we snuck out and spent the whole night crabbin' behind the old Augusta Evans house?" Billy says, his eyes half-lidded. Those bits of sweet potato must've found their way straight to his brain. He keeps talking as though lost in thought. "And Hank was pulling in a big, old blue crab when that gator showed up . . ."

I half listen, my plodding steps having turned to a stagger. Hank trudges beside me, swatting at the flies drawn to his wound.

"And Hank was ready to fight him but the gator came up and took his sandwich instead—"

A truck rumbles in the distance, growing louder as it comes down the road behind us.

"Billy," I say. He's on the outside of our row again, the most exposed position.

"You fellas remember that? How that gator just leapt up out of the creek—"

I glance back. The truck is fifty yards and closing, nearly upon us. I should say something, but my tongue feels stuck to the roof of my mouth. It all happens in a rush. A Japanese soldier leans out the back. He shouts to the driver and the truck accelerates. And then he raises his rifle.

"Streak!" Hank yells.

I grab Billy by the arm, but I'm too late. The bayonet catches him in the back. Rips across his shoulder. Blood blooms across the tattered fabric of his shirt.

As the truck roars away, Billy collapses without a sound.

15

the sight of Billy bleeding is the most awful yet. I must have
screamed his name; the echo of it rings in my ears.

APRIL 12, 1942

NEAR LAYAC, PHILIPPINES

Of all the terrible things I've seen since the start of the war, the sight of Billy bleeding is the most awful yet. I must have screamed his name; the echo of it rings in my ears.

"Sling him between us!" Hank says as our column marches around and past us, not daring to let up.

We haul Billy to his feet. His eyes flutter and his breath comes in gasps.

We fling his arms over our shoulders, grab him round the torso. He groans, head hanging to one side.

"Prop, can you stitch it?" Hank asks, breathing hard.

I glance back at the wound, shake my head. "Gotta stop the bleeding somehow."

"I'll carry. You fix him up."

I shift Billy onto Hank piggyback style. Hank staggers and then bears up with a grimace. Not five months ago he could've run a mile carrying Billy. Now the cords stand out on his neck as fresh blood trickles from the stitches on his cheek.

I lift my knee, hop on one foot while snaking the shoelace out of my right boot. I do the same with the other then tie the ends together. After unbuttoning my Army greens, I shrug out of my shirt, tie the sleeves around my waist, and pull my undershirt over my head. It's sweat-, blood-, and mud-stained, stinks, and ain't been completely dry in months. But it's all I got. I roll it up and pad it inside Billy's shirt over the gash. Lash it snug against him with my bootlaces tied round his chest.

"Billy. Billy!" I shrug into my shirt. "We're gonna get you somewhere you can rest. Just hang tough."

He sags between us as I take his arm from Hank's shoulder and sling it over my neck.

"Ain't gonna make it," Billy murmurs, eyes closed.

"Sure you are," I say. "You've skinned your knees worse than this."

"Gotta leave me . . ."

"Quit talkin' crazy," Hank says. "We ain't leavin' you. All home alive, remember?"

"Leave me . . ."

"No way. Now shut up."

We stagger like drunks for a mile. Two. My boots flop around my ankles. Sweat pours from our bodies. Billy's breath comes in a shallow rasp as the toes of his boots drag furrows in the road between us.

We stumble another mile. And then another, and Billy's still breathing. I know because I'm listening, afraid he might stop even as I tell myself God won't let that happen.

But after all I've seen, I ain't so sure. All I know is this world don't work without Billy in it. He's the only little brother I ever had, the glue holding the three of us together.

The best of all of us.

My tongue's so swollen in my dry mouth, I don't make the effort to talk. There's just the prayer running over and over in my head:

Don't take Billy.

It becomes a silent chant—a word, a step at a time.

The shadows lengthen. We drag him through tiny barrios of burned-down nipa huts. Filipino refugees lug burlap sacks of belongings along the sides of the road. We pass by an artesian well where some of them fill their buckets and drink, water dripping from their chins. It's twenty yards away—so close I can smell the crispness of that water—and there's nothing we can do. The guards made it clear we ain't allowed to leave the road.

Oosh!

The road by the next well we come to is so congested our column slows to a crawl and loses formation. The guards holler over the bustle. Some prod prisoners with the points of their bayonets.

Speedo!

I don't know how much longer Hank and me can keep this up. Billy's gotten heavier by the minute, in and out of consciousness as he is.

I stagger forward, not sure I got another step in me. And then take one more. Not knowing if I can do it again. Only knowing I have to.

A woman and an elderly man jostle onto the road beside us. The man is gaunt, leathery skin taut over his skull, and for a second I think she must be leading and holding him up, until I see him push several others out of the woman's way.

Next thing I know she's right next to me. I can't help staring. Her face is dirty, thin, her hair the color of the road dust clinging to it, but as I take in the seam above her lip, I know her.

Marisol. The woman from the bakery. I glance at the old man, assume he must be her father. We must've marched to the outskirts of San Fernando.

She leans toward me, brushing against my side. She smells like sweat and smoke. I shirk away, ashamed. I smell fifty times worse.

"Open the canteen, Joe," she whispers, glancing at me.

"Do you remember me?" I ask softly.

"The boy's canteen," she says again, looking nervously around as the old man says something and reaches for her shoulder.

I blink and stare straight ahead as I fumble for the cap of the canteen dangling at Billy's hip. Without looking at me, the woman passes me a coconut shell filled with water. I glance down long enough to pour it into the mouth of the canteen and hand it back.

When I do, she presses a greasy packet against my palm and squeezes my hand.

"Thank you," I whisper, but she's gone, already falling back into another group of soldiers, murmuring to one of them while the old man keeps a lookout.

I slip the packet into my pocket. Wait several steps and finally look down to find a small, wilted white bloom cradled in my callused palm. I recognize it as the same flower the locals make into garlands and give to visitors as a sign of friendship.

It reminds me of the one Claire gave me in a boutonniere for the school winter ball. The one that smelled like her perfume.

I'm pretty sure the guards wouldn't take well to seeing us with one of these, so I crush the flower in my hand and let it fall. But when I bring my palm to my face, I can smell its heady scent stronger than ever. And for a moment, I ain't here at all, but standing by the punch bowl at the winter dance, gazing at Claire. Breathing her perfume as I kiss her a day later on the bank of the river.

We march on, saving the precious little bit of water, unwilling to risk it until we're alone.

I stare down the street, seeking the bakery. The city's been burned, windows broken out of storefronts. The Pikes Hotel is reduced to shambles. I wonder what happened to Ernesto, the bartender.

The guards march us to a large wood-framed building on the edge of town. There's an opening on each end, like a shed, with wooden bleachers on one side. I realize we're in a cockfighting arena.

Inside, we find an area between one of the entrances and the bleachers where we'll at least have some fresh air. That wide entrance seems so close, the idea of escape—just a sprint around that corner—seems so within reach, I'd be tempted to say we should make a run for it tonight if Billy weren't in such a bad way. As things are now, the guards would hunt us down in minutes, if not seconds.

We lay Billy on his stomach and I fumble the canteen open as Hank turns Billy's face enough to drink. He groans and sputters but manages a few swallows before we lay him flat again.

I pass the canteen to Hank and slide out the packet Marisol gave me: a banana leaf filled with rice and beans, a chocolate bar from a K ration, and a piece of bread. Much humbler food than the pastries for sale in her bakery, but a far more costly gift.

We poke little bits of rice, bread, and chocolate into Billy's mouth in the darkness, and he manages to swallow a bite or two of everything before he turns his head. Hank and I split the rest between us. It feels like a feast.

After eating, I check Billy's wound and repack it, folding the cleanest side of my undershirt against the wound.

I lay down and listen to the sound of his breath. Lean close when I don't hear it, holding my own until I do.

Hank's gone when I wake the next morning. I check that Billy's still breathing then scan the mass of men penned inside with us. Outside the entrance, a guard yawns and scratches his armpit as he chats with someone beyond my line of vision. They seem to be waiting for some order to move.

"Here," Hank says, appearing by my side. He's cradling his helmet in the crook of his arm like a bowl and it might as well be; there's a spare canteen, a banana leaf filled with rice, and a lump of what looks like brown sugar inside it. I blink at the windfall—and instinctively move to block the gazes of anyone else.

"Where'd you get this?" I hiss as we kneel down and prop Billy up to feed him.

"Did some hunting before sunup," he says. "Found a stiff with half a canteen full of water on him. Go ahead." He nods toward it. I drink deep, mentally preparing to haul Billy between us for ten, twenty, or a hundred more miles.

We get some food in Billy and even more in ourselves before we're ordered up and out.

Oosh!

This time we ain't marched to the road, but to a nearby railway station where we're put into groups and made to sit still on the ground with our hands on our knees. We wedge Billy between us and hold him fast. The sun beats down and we don't move. Those who fidget are slapped or kicked. It feels shameful, like grown men put back in kindergarten, but I'll sit like this all day if it don't mean marching.

"How you doin', Streak?" I murmur. Billy's lips move, but he don't say nothing.

We sit motionless for hours until a train chugs into the station and squeals to a lazy stop. Guards order us to the cars. Hank and I drag Billy with us toward the nearest one. A guard slides the boxcar's door open. Heat blasts out. Men elbow their way past us.

Hank grabs my shoulder. "Stay as close to the door as you can."

Once inside, he muscles us to the front side of the car where a little light filters through a notch in the wall.

"C'mon, Streak," he says, holding Billy up so his nose is in the light.

"Keep him breathin'," he says to me.

More men crowd in around us. And then more still, until we're crammed shoulder to shoulder, belly to back. I reckon the cars, which normally carry cattle, might hold thirty-five people comfortably. I count ninety in ours.

The door closes and we wait as other cars finish loading. The heat suffocates. Men pound on the wood sides of the car and beg to be let out.

By the time the train rolls forward, more than one man's already screaming like a loony. A guy just a few men down from us throws up all over the back of another. Those with dysentery crap down their pants to the floor.

We keep Billy's nose propped against the vent, do our best to shield him from getting jostled. I count the minutes, trying to guess where we might be going and then give up. Close my eyes until there's just the heat and stench of diarrhea and the rancid breath of the man behind me against my neck.

By the time the train stops and the door to our boxcar finally slides open, my legs are so stiff from standing I don't know if they'll even move. Billy's still breathing but others ain't been so lucky. Four bodies crumple to the car floor as we stumble out, doing our best not to fall and slam Billy to the ground.

The guards form us up into columns. The sign on the station portico reads CAPAS. The sun's high overhead and, despite the water we had last night and this morning, I'm thirstier than ever. My feet are raw with blisters, and the thought of marching makes me want to scream like the loonies on the railcar.

Oosh!

I hold tight to Billy. We move out.

A mile in, my knees wobble.

Can't go down.

Three miles in, Hank stumbles, Billy's arms heavy around our necks. We stagger, and the ground looms. It takes all the strength we have to find our rhythm again, put one foot in front of another.

We go five, maybe six miles. Just when I think I can't go any further, that I ain't got anything left, we arrive at what I reckon might be our final destination.

Camp O'Donnell.

16

MOBILE, ALABAMA
JANUARY 1939

On New Year's Day our family ate dinner at the Humphreys', which I didn't expect to be awkward given that Helen had dated increasingly popular boys in quick succession since the back-to-school dance. Far too many to mind that a square like me never asked her on a second date.

Or so I thought.

"I heard you escorted Claire Crockett to the winter ball, Jimmy," Mrs. Humphrey said, passing the bowl of greens for a second round.

"Yes, ma'am," I said.

Helen, sitting between her two little brothers, tilted her head. "You were there?" she asked, a little too loudly.

"Mostly in the corner—I ain't much of a dancer," I said, aware of my daddy's gaze, the corn bread in his fingers poised over the hog jowl and black-eyed peas on his plate.

Mrs. Humphrey leaned forward to look at me. "That was kind of you, Jimmy. I'm glad to hear Claire's enjoying some of these rites of passage with a good boy like you and not running around wild like some of those girls." She lowered her voice to a whisper. "You know when they don't have daddies, they get *promiscuous*."

Daddy glanced up. "My Evelyn's been at their house nearly every day. The Crockett children seem to be getting along just fine."

"Evelyn, you are a saint," Mrs. Humphrey said, reaching for Mama's hand.

Helen frowned. "That's funny. I don't recall seeing Claire at the dance either." She gave a small laugh. "It's easy to overlook a boy, but you can't miss Claire Crockett."

I felt trapped, not sure why she wouldn't drop it. Maybe Helen was sore after all that I never asked for a second date.

My mother dabbed her mouth with her napkin and smiled. "There was a bit of a ruckus at the Crocketts' garage. Claire and Jimmy got word of it and left the dance to help smooth things out."

"That how you got your shiner?" Helen asked.

"I'm afraid that's my fault," Mama said with a chuckle. "I pulled up right as everyone was going inside for sweet tea. Jimmy waved at me and then turned around just in time to walk right into the doorjamb." She glanced at Daddy. "Like I told you."

Daddy set down his corn bread. "You never mentioned a ruckus, Evelyn."

Mama waved it off. "Turns out it was all a misunderstanding. Jimmy went over and the boys . . . discussed it and ironed it all out."

"Well. Jimmy's always been a peacemaker," Daddy said, frowning slightly.

"Like father, like son," Mrs. Humphrey said.

Deacon Humphrey glanced up from his plate, where he'd been chasing the last black-eyed peas onto the tines of his fork. "I hear you're planning to attend Southern?"

It took me a moment to realize he was talking to me and that he meant Southern Baptist Theological Seminary—the same school my father attended in Kentucky.

"Yes, sir. That's the plan so far," I said, grateful when talk finally shifted from me to the Louisville flood two years ago.

On the way home from the Humphreys', Mama hummed under her breath as she did when things got too quiet.

"Is there a reason you never mentioned a ruckus the night of the dance?" Daddy asked at last.

Mama, sitting between us, glanced at him as though surprised by the question.

"Why, you were working so hard I didn't want to bother you with it. By the next morning, it had already slipped my mind," Mama said. "It truly was nothing."

"What was the cause of it?" Daddy asked.

"Just some boys from another school bothering Hank because they heard he was tough," I said.

Daddy's mouth flattened into a tight line. "I knew it would be something to do with that boy. Jimmy, you are not to spend time with him anymore."

I blinked. *What?*

"But—"

Daddy pulled over and stopped the car so abruptly, Mama and I grabbed the dash. He turned in his seat to stare at me. I averted my gaze.

"James . . ." Mama laid a hand on his arm.

"I didn't quite hear you, son," he said, ignoring her.

My nostrils flared.

"Yes, sir," I managed at last.

Daddy put me to work at the farm the rest of the afternoon. I cleaned ditches until dark, jaw tight, without a word.

The next morning, with school out of session for the holiday, I got ready to head to the Crocketts' to work. But mostly, I needed to talk to Claire and Billy.

My daddy was reading the paper at the table as I grabbed a piece of toast on my way out the side door.

"I assume you'll be putting in your two weeks," Daddy said from behind the *Mobile Register*.

I stopped. "Sir?"

He lowered the paper.

"If you want to call on Claire or take her on a date, that's fine—as long as Billy or one of his other sisters is with you. You heard what Mrs. Humphrey said. You're a young man headed to seminary who can't afford any question of impropriety. You don't need to be loitering on the property of the young lady you're courting."

"I ain't loiterin'—I work the gas shop," I said, panic rising inside me.

"You can find a new job. Until then, you can work for me at the farm."

Even as I heard myself say, "Yes, sir," I felt my world closing around me.

I don't remember striding down the street. Only the way it blurred before me, helpless anger tightening my chest.

Two weeks earlier, I'd celebrated my sixteenth birthday by borrowing Daddy's truck and taking Claire to the movies. We'd sat at the back of the theater in the dark and necked the whole time, her fingertips sending electric jolts through my body. I'd felt alive. More than that, I'd been excited to ring in 1939, sure this was going to be the best year of my life.

I found Claire hanging laundry in the backyard and pulled her behind the curtain of a damp sheet swaying in the brisk morning breeze and kissed her on the lips.

"Well, good morning," she said, throwing a glance to her mama's bedroom window to make sure it was empty before twining her arms around my neck and kissing me back.

"Come with me," I said urgently, unlacing her arms.

"What's eatin' you?" she said, searching my face.

"Where's Billy?"

"He and Hank left with a piece of old chicken, so I suspect they went crabbin'. Jimmy, you're making me nervous. What happened?"

"My daddy. That's what." I raked back my hair and told her about dinner at the Humphreys', Helen's questions, and all that was said.

"That little fink!" Claire said. "You know Helen's had it bad for you since sixth grade."

"*What?*"

"She's jealous, pure and simple. The rest, I suppose, was just a matter of time. I'm surprised your daddy let you run around with Hank as long as he did. Though it's strange to think of anyone looking cross-eyed at you or me. I mean, what does he think we're gonna do?"

"All the things I wanna do," I said, catching her fingertips, twining them with mine.

I kissed her once more for good measure, this time defiantly. As deep and long as she'd let me.

"What're you gonna do for a job?" Claire asked as we took off, skirting through backyards and beneath giant, gnarled oaks to the creek.

"I don't know."

Neither did I know what I was going to tell Hank.

"I guess I ain't even supposed to be walkin' alone with you," she said.

"My daddy don't make the rules for you."

"If I can walk alone with you but you can't with me, then in a way he does."

"Well, Billy will be there and we won't be alone."

But so would Hank.

It wasn't fair. The four of us was all I'd known since third grade.

We heard Hank and Billy before we saw them, Hank hooting and hollering, Billy howling with laughter. Claire glanced at me and we jogged over to find them staring at something in the middle of the canal.

"What're you two goin' on about?" Claire asked.

"Hank had two big crabs on his string but before he could pull them in, that gator out there nabbed 'em!" Billy said, and then pointed. "That's the end of the string right there!"

"'Bout took my hand off!" Hank grinned, glancing from Claire to me. His expression faded. "Who died?"

"Me," I muttered.

"Helen Humphrey flapped her gums about the fight, and now Jimmy's daddy says he can't be friends with you," Claire said, hands on her hips.

I noticed she left out the part about the two of us.

Hank's gaze snapped to me and right then, I saw the look in his eyes. I'd seen it when he was new to school without any friends. And again the day his mama died.

"But he don't get to dictate who I'm friends with," I said. I spat on my palm and held it out. Hank slowly nodded, spat on his palm, and clasped mine.

Billy spat on his and smashed his hand down on top of ours. Claire gagged and turned away.

"We ain't friends anyway," I said. "We're brothers. All of us. That ain't changin'. He don't need to know."

"I dunno. Your daddy has lots of eyes keepin' watch for him," Hank said as we wiped our hands on our trousers.

"But he don't have brothers like I do."

Later that day, I walked Claire down the bank to talk to her alone. "So I'm thinkin' that if we have to have a chaperone, we really must be dating."

"Except we've only been on one date," she said, squinting into the sun.

I turned toward her. "Every date I go on from here on out is only ever gonna be with you."

"Oh really?" she said.

I hesitated. "Do you want to date anyone else?"

She seemed to consider.

"You really have to think about it?"

"No." She grinned.

"'Bout made my heart stop."

She laughed and I realized how much I enjoyed that sound.

"Then you'll be my steady?" I asked.

"Kind of thought I already was."

"You were. You are. It's only ever been you, Claire," I said. And I was telling the truth.

That spring, I got a job as a paperboy on a route half a mile away. On Saturdays, I collected twelve cents from each subscriber for the previous week's papers. Some Saturday afternoons, I'd take Claire and the twins to a matinee, drop them off at home afterward, go hang out with Billy and Hank at the garage while Daddy was holed up in his office, catch a quick nap in the back seat of whatever car Hank was working on, then wake at daybreak to fold papers for delivery early Sunday morning. I drank enough coffee to stay awake during Daddy's sermon and slept most of Sunday afternoon.

The route didn't pay a lot, but given that I had only been working a few hours at the Crocketts' lately, it worked out about the same.

Most importantly, it gave me an excuse to leave that was never questioned and, on occasion, a chance to be with Claire, who waited up late Saturday night or got up early to walk the route with me. Especially when school got out for summer. Mrs. Crockett had, by then, taken over running her own household, though my mama still made excuses to visit—boiling poke sallet, canning dilly beans and green tomato relish—whenever she could.

I guess Mama and I had that in common.

That summer when I wasn't working at our farm, I took Claire and her sisters fishing and Claire and Billy swimming or on picnics—at least as far as Daddy knew. Hank often met up with us as we left our old haunts behind. We abandoned Three Mile Creek for Dog River or the pier, crossing the bay for Cokes in Spanish Fort when our parents let us borrow a vehicle. In one way, nothing had changed. In another, everything had—from the way the four of us snuck off together to Billy and Hank discreetly disappearing upriver to give Claire and me an hour or two of privacy, alone and hidden among the trees.

Still, I saw less of Hank that summer. He was dating a girl from McGill—I swear, just to teach John Pugh a lesson—and working a lot too. And though he and Leona met up with Claire and me once at the movies, he'd become harder to pin down.

One sticky, predawn morning in August, I'd just thrown my first three papers when I heard a phone ringing inside a house on my route. Too early for a social call—had to be an emergency, I thought.

Until I heard a dinner bell clang in the darkness, carried from the east—the direction of the bay. I coasted toward the house with the ringing phone as a light went on downstairs, trying to remember how full the moon had been before it had dropped behind the oaks. I stopped, my bag over my shoulder, bike between my legs. A few seconds later, a towheaded boy about eight years old came tearing out the front door toward the house across the street.

"Hey, kid," I called. "What's the news?"

"Jubilee!" he yelled. "The fish are comin' in!"

I turned in the street and pedaled for all I was worth toward the Crocketts'. Reaching the back door, I dropped my bike and my papers, let myself in, and hurried up the stairs to Billy's room, not even trying to be quiet.

Within five minutes, Billy, Claire, and me were running out back, loading the truck with gigs, nets, and baskets.

"You go on," Mrs. Crockett said. "I'll send Betty to the Wrights'. Betty, hurry up!"

"Tell her to take my bike," I said. I'd taught her to ride it myself.

We hopped in, Billy dopey, Claire bright-eyed, practically bouncing on the truck seat as I drove south to the bay.

We stopped near Dog River Point as dawn broke, the surface of the water unusually calm as pelicans and gulls swooped and dove, feasting on the fish fleeing the sluggish deep to gasp for air.

Billy whooped, awake at last. We threw off our shoes and ran through the sand to the shallows swarming with sea life. Claire squealed as she stepped on an eel—the shore was crawling with them—gig pole in one hand, basket in another. Several cars pulled off on the side of the road, excited voices suspended in the still morning air. Families lugged washtubs and buckets toward the beach, telling one another to hurry. Farther down shore, two men knee-deep in the water had already filled the front of a skiff with fish.

A few minutes later, a truck pulled up next to ours. "Breakfast time!" Hank proclaimed, as he and Cowboy got out and grabbed their gear.

"An' lunch and dinner!" I called back.

"Mornin' boys." Cowboy grinned as they waded into the shallows. "Claire."

For one glorious half hour, we speared flounder and scooped up shrimp, sidestepping stingrays and collecting the crabs that crawled up old pilings and tree trunks and anything else sticking out of the water.

That morning, we ate crab-stuffed flounder for breakfast at the Crocketts' and spent the rest of the day cleaning fish, Claire and me slipping out back more than once to kiss. We both stank of salt water, sweat, and guts, but her mouth tasted like the lemonade she'd been sipping, sweet as the last sun of summer.

One week later, on September 1, Germany invaded Poland.

17

CAMP O'DONNELL, PHILIPPINES

Camp O'Donnell sits like a prison on a dry plain of cogon grass. Hot wind blows through the rusty barbed-wire fence strung between gun towers, gusting dirt onto the thatched huts inside.

We ain't the first to arrive; hundreds—maybe thousands—of Allied POWs mill behind the fence, their eyes hollow as corpses'.

Just past the gate, we're ordered forward one at a time, shaken down by a guard who pokes through our remaining possessions. They take everything except our canteens and mess kits, including as many cigarettes as they can scrounge.

We're marched to an open area in front of what looks like the main building. The Japanese flag blazes overhead. We're ordered to sit beneath the burning sun. Dust coats our faces. An hour later, we're ordered to stand. We stand, supporting Billy between us, struggling not to sway. Two men drop into the dirt. We sit again . . . until it's time to stand.

A man could go crazy like this, and I wonder if that's what they're after.

Finally, a door bangs open on the main building and three Japanese march out. The one in the middle has a cropped mustache and a chest full of ribbons. He stands with his hands on his hips as one of his men jogs off and comes back with a wooden crate and turns it over on the ground. The commander steps up and stares out at us, his features chiseled into a frown. I wait for him to bark at us in Japanese.

To my surprise, he addresses us in meticulous English.

"Know that you are here as guests of divine Emperor Hirohito and his infinite generosity," he says, his voice carrying out over our heads. "To disobey any order by a guard on this Japanese soil is to disrespect the holy emperor himself.

"Your country is large, but weak. Japan is small, but strong. Your survival is proof of your cowardice. You shall note that Japan never ratified the Geneva Convention. For that reason, you are not prisoners of war. You are dogs and lower than dogs, living by the mercy of our benevolent emperor. That the emperor has seen fit to spare you is better than you deserve. You are traitors, worthy of nothing but contempt. To surrender is nothing less than a criminal act. To not die honorably by suicide but choose to live in dishonor makes you fools and pigs."

I glance over at Billy, slumped between us, and then at Hank. His chin is straight, eyes squinted, his jaw working.

"You, pigs, will salute every soldier of the Imperial Army. You will bow whenever you see one of your superiors. You will not speak except to answer 'Hai!' when spoken to. You will not leave camp except to work in service to the emperor. You will not wish to leave at all, as there is no place for you to go. You are a disgrace to your country and government, a dishonor to your families, reviled by anyone who sees you, and an abomination to us. We allow you to live in the shame you have chosen as a fate worse than death. If you do not obey or prove yourself of service, you will be shot. If you disrespect the benign hand of the emperor, you will be shot. If you fail to express gratitude that our divine emperor has chosen to allow you the full extent of your humiliation, you will be shot."

He turns, steps off the crate, and walks back into the main building, followed by his entourage.

"That was upliftin'," Billy murmurs. They're the first real words he's spoken since getting bayoneted, and the best thing I've heard all day.

We're assigned to a nipa hut with sixteen bunks along with thirty-nine other men. The three of us stake our claim on a lower bunk and lay Billy down.

Guards walk around outside, but prisoners seem to be coming and going at will, so I leave in search of water.

There's a line leading to the center of camp. Hundreds of men stand ahead of me, all waiting, shifting their weight in the heat. But I ain't here just for water. I'm also hoping for news.

"Hey there, I ain't taken a crap in a week," a corporal ahead of me says by way of introduction, a dopey pucker in his cheek. "How d'you do?"

"James Propfield." We shake hands. I lower my voice and glance around. "What do you know about this place?"

The corporal's smile stays stuck to his face like glue. "They feed us. Had a real nice wormy rice soup this morning. Fella next to me wouldn't eat his. A real blue-blood lieutenant. Said the food wasn't fit for human consumption. So I ate it for him. You gotta stay alive, buddy."

Another twenty men are lined up behind me by now, canteens in their hands. The line just keeps getting longer.

"What about news?"

The corporal lifts his brows.

"You know. *Rescue*." I whisper the word.

He snorts. "Ain't no Army coming to save us. The war's all turned to the Nazis now. President's clean forgotten us. You and I don't even exist."

"That can't be right. Germans or no Germans, everyone knows we're here."

Commotion, from farther up front. The line begins to break up amid shouts.

"Look sharp, buddy," the corporal says sidelong to me. "Water's been turned off for the day. Clear out. Fight'll break out soon."

"What about the water?" I ask.

"Tomorrow," he says, already walking away.

Hank's gone when I get back. I lie down on the hardwood bunk beside Billy, who's sound asleep. My feet burn. My gut twists and cramps. But even though I'm too worn out to get back up, I can't sleep when I close my eyes.

A weight on the bunk. "Chow time," Hank says, elbowing me. My eyes flutter open. He opens his hands to reveal two rice balls, two candy bars, a tin of canned tuna, and some roasted meat on a stick that's still hot.

"Where'd you get all this?" I ask, incredulous.

Hank breaks off a piece of the meat and pushes it between Billy's lips. Billy slowly chews. I pinch off a piece, shove it into my mouth with dirty fingers, and wish there was more.

"Traded it for some cigarettes I found. Some of them boys'll trade anything for smokes."

"Where'd you find the cigarettes?"

"Same place I get all our food. Searching stiffs."

We eat in silence. When it's all gone, Hank lets out a belch.

"I do declare," Hank says, laying back on the bunk, arm behind his head. "That's the best-tasting rat I ever ate."

"Hank," I say, low enough that no one else can hear. "You think the president's forgotten us?"

He gazes up toward the rafters. "Old Man Wainwright's still holding Corregidor Island. Turns out he's tougher than anyone figured. Means someone's gotta be comin' soon."

We sleep, our shrunken bellies full.

18

April 14, 1942
Camp O'Donnell, Philippines

We wake to the sound of a board slammed against our hut. Shouted orders. Jostling inside the hut. Through the gap between the wall and the thatched roof I can see the dark ridgeline of the hills far away on the other side of the barbed wire.

We line up and stand for an hour beneath the eye of a bored-looking guard, rifle dangling from his fingers.

Finally, the guard says something I don't understand, but the others start for a building, so we follow. Turns out it's a mess area and the closest thing to heaven I seen in a while. They plunk down a ball of rice and ladle of soup in our kits. Hank and I push Billy through the line ahead of us. While we're eating, we learn that sick call is allowed here. I breathe easier than I have for days when we return Billy to our bunk before hustling outside to report for work.

An American officer comes down the line, separating us into groups as Japanese guards look on. Hank goes one way. I go another.

A skinny American sergeant named Jenson elbows me in the ribs. "New kid, huh? You ain't gonna believe the detail you just pulled."

He's almost laughing. But he ain't smiling. I doubt Jenson's been in camp more than a day or two ahead of me, but already he's a big shot.

Jenson hands out shovels with no explanation and barks at us to follow him. Two guards yawn and trail us at a distance. We hike past the barbed wire, out of camp, toward some patches of tall grass. Mounds of dirt stretch in every direction.

The man next to me is a thick-necked corporal. "Make your hole at least three deep," he says.

I ain't sure what he means and so just start digging, watching the others out the corner of one eye. Half an hour later, another group of prisoners shuffles into view. They walk in twos, carrying a blanket slung from two poles between them. The first pair sets down their load and tugs up one end of the blanket. A man's body rolls out at our feet, naked.

I've pulled grave detail.

Another pair of fellas shows up and another two after them. The line is impossibly steady, an endless parade of death. We can't keep up. In an hour the bodies are stacked like cordwood, waiting for graves. Stinking to high heaven.

By now I've struck water. We all have. It sloshes against our shovels, murky and black. We throw our backs into it, each shovelful heavier than the last, knee deep in the swamp. It takes an hour to finish our hole.

"All right," the corporal I'm digging with says. "Give me a hand."

I drop my shovel, wipe my arm across my brow, and shuffle after him to the pile of bodies. He gestures to the closest one. It ain't hard to figure he died of the runs; filth covers the dead man's buttocks all the way down his legs. I grimace and grasp him by the feet as the corporal takes his wrists. We carry and then drop him in the water.

The corporal jerks his thumb back to the pile. We grab another, lug him to the hole, and sling him on top of the first.

"One more," he says.

I refuse to look beyond the next corpse, to take in the pile of bodies.

"Grab a pole," the corporal says, pointing to a pile of bamboo. I go over, eyes averted, and bring one back. "Give it here. Shovel while I hold the stiffs down. Be quick."

He sets the end of the rod against the chest of the body on top and leans his weight on it. The bodies hiss and bubble down in the water.

I shovel blindly, frantic to get them covered.

Soon as they're buried, there's just the pole sticking up out of the mound. I stare at it.

"Should we say something?" I ask.

"Any of them friends?"

I shake my head.

"Then get back to digging."

Dig graves, cover bodies. As quickly as we drag one from the pile, another takes its place, startling the swarm of flies.

By the time we finish in early evening, my palms are a welter of blistered, raw skin and I am covered in the filth of decomposing bodies, maggots, and mud.

As we form up to head back, I make the mistake of glancing back. One poor stiff's hand sticks up from a mound of dirt, waving from the grave.

Hank comes back, practically splashed clean after lugging fifty-gallon drums of water all day, and collapses on our bunk. But I returned too late to wash up, contaminated by death and afraid to be near Billy, who's sweating through his shirt. I sleep on the floor as he moans and kicks in his sleep, thrashing against whatever dark spirit is trying to carry him away.

I dig graves the next day and the next, until my palms are bloody. We bury sixty, eighty, and then a hundred corpses a day. Death is in my nostrils, on my hands, my clothes, my skin. The flies are incessant. As the rest of us starve, they feast.

I collapse every night covered in filth, with no chance to wash before the spigot's turned off.

"We gotta get you off your detail," Hank says. "Before you work yourself to death or die of whatever those stiffs died of."

I nod, but when I ask around, there's nothing anybody can do. Nothing for me to do but keep going.

When Hank and me compare notes a few nights later, he pulls at his hair.

"I've given away everything I can get my hands on, made friends with one of the medics, and hustled cigarettes for one of the guards who don't seem to hate Americans as much as the others." He's got a fresh bruise on his good cheek that makes me wonder if he threatened someone too.

He takes me by the shoulders like a corner man in a fight. "You hang in there, Prop. I'm gonna figure somethin' out."

I learn the nicknames of the guards from the soldiers who arrived before us: Snake, Bull, the One-Armed Bandit, and Big Crumb. We learn which ones are okay and which ones to watch out for.

And then there's the Crate, the man in charge of them all.

"You still here?" the corporal says at the start of my second week.

"What d'you mean?" I ask.

He don't answer.

I carry the stench of decay with me everywhere I go. For Billy's sake, I've started sleeping outside our hut, huddled like a calf in the dirt. I don't want death anywhere near him. Hank brings me food and a tattered blanket. Tries to coax me back inside. But death clings to me.

By the third week, I now know what the corporal's question meant. Our detail is filled with all new faces except for him and me. The work killed everyone else. Jenson, the skinny sergeant who bossed our crew my first day, collapsed and died four days ago.

"What's the secret?" I ask the corporal. "How do you get off this detail?" It ain't the first time I've asked him and he ain't given me a straight answer yet.

He stares at me good in the eye. "You want to know how to end this job? For real, kid?"

I nod.

"Stop eating." His gaze is ringed with darkness.

Two days later, one of the bodies I bury is his.

That night, the Crate gathers us for a special announcement. I hang near the back, away from the others.

"You will be informed that Corregidor has surrendered to the supreme strength of the emperor," he says. "You have no more stronghold. You have no more foothold. You have no hope. Your weakness has betrayed you. Your own countrymen have betrayed you. Your government has abandoned you. We are your utter masters."

I stare without seeing, unable to make sense of it.

Old Man Wainwright finally caved to the pressure. He surrendered. The reinforcements we waited for never came.

I wonder if they ever intended to rescue us at all.

I finish four weeks on grave detail. But the work is finishing me.

"We just gotta hold out a little longer," Hank says to me outside our hut one morning as he brings me a ball of rice for breakfast. "You hear me, Prop? You gotta hang on."

I look away.

"They're comin' to rescue us soon as they can," Hank says. "I got it on good authority."

"You're lyin'."

"No, I ain't."

I turn and squint at him. "How do you know?"

"Because," he says, something desperate in his eyes. "There's too many of us to forget."

I nod, finally, for his sake. Because I know how much he wants—needs—to believe that it's true.

Two nights later, I lie on the dirt beside our hut and decide to give my rice to Hank and Billy from now on. Billy's started sitting up and walking around a little. He needs the food. So does Hank, if he's going to keep Billy alive.

I close my eyes beneath the indifferent moon, hearing voices.

Claire's. Billy's.

"Propper." A hand on my shoulder.

I shrink away.

"Prop, can you sit up?"

I skitter back in the dust. "Don't touch me. I'm dirty."

"That's why I'm here." His voice is stronger than I've heard it in weeks.

I open my eyes to find Billy squatting on his heels like a local, his forehead dry, his eyes clear.

He holds out a small, square cake. Of what, I ain't sure in the darkness.

"Take it," he says.

I shake my head.

"C'mon, Jimmy."

He presses it into my palm, which is caked with blood and muck. And I think what a shame it is to defile whatever he's just put there.

"Chuck off your clothes. You ain't gonna need those rags no more."

I don't know what he means, but when he tugs me to my feet, I get up and start to strip them off. They tear and fall away.

Then I recognize the texture of the thing in my hand. And its scent. Soap.

I ain't seen soap in months.

Billy straightens, a canteen in his hands, another near his feet. He begins to pour fresh water over my head. It sluices down my back and between my eyes.

I squeeze my eyes shut and feel my mouth, my entire face twist with shame.

"Don't. You need this to drink," I say.

"We got plenty. Hank's standin' watch, but we ain't got all night. Get to washin'."

I have no strength to argue and just start sliding the soap over my chest. Pretty soon I'm scrubbing at my armpits, my legs, groin, hair, and then—in a fever—my hands. Billy pours water on me again and again, washing the death from me—mud, morbid juices, and decay running from my naked body until I stand completely clean.

"Here," he says, handing me a folded uniform. It's worn but clean, stripped and boiled from the latest batch of corpses. "Too bad we ain't got that Chinese tailor to cut 'em down, huh? Could've got two uniforms out of it, skinny as we are these days." He grins, the Billy I know back in his eyes.

Hank steals back into our hut a short time later and pulls us aside.

"New plan," he whispers. "We're gettin' out of here."

"How?" Billy asks.

Hank shakes his head. "Don't know yet. But we're doin' it."

"What happened to waiting for rescue?" I ask.

"Screw waiting! We wait any longer and you ain't makin' it out of here," he hisses. "Billy and me'll keep our eyes sharp, ears open. We'll find a way."

"What do I do?" I ask.

"Stay above ground."

"All home alive," Billy whispers.

My heart hammers in my chest as I nod.

Tonight, as Hank snores on the floor beside us, hope returns to me for the first time in weeks. I lay on the bunk without fear of infecting Billy, both of us back from the dead.

19

May 10, 1942
Camp O'Donnell, Philippines

When I wake, I am almost happy in this place of horror. There's promise in the vivid blue of the sky showing beneath our thatched roof, even as thunder rumbles in the distance.

Hank sits up and fumbles for a cigarette, as if on habit. He ain't kept a smoke for himself in weeks. But I close my eyes, unable to think of anything better than a good, old-fashioned rainstorm.

Shouts outside. And then I realize what I'm hearing ain't thunder but a band of guards marching to our hut. They rush up the steps and stride across the floor, kicking bunks and yelling what I've learned are Japanese obscenities.

"Look sharp, boys," Hank says, rapping Billy on the chest and me on the shoulder. "We're in for it now."

I have no idea what he means but get to my feet—only to fall against the bunk when something cracks me in the back of the head. A bamboo stick clatters to the floor beside me as a guard grabs me from behind. He drags me outside, my heels thumping down the steps of our hut, and throws me in the dirt. Hank goes sprawling beside me.

A pair of shiny boots steps into view.

"Did you think we would not investigate your theft?" their owner enunciates in perfect English.

The Crate.

A guard kicks me in the gut. I curl into a ball, sucking air, forehead on the ground. In my peripheral vision, Hank arches back from a kick in the kidney.

I shove up on my hands and knees. Try to force my lungs to expand.

That's when I notice two guards dragging Billy across the yard toward a stubbly field.

"Where're you takin' him? Leave him alone!" I shout. A boot connects with my back, which begins to spasm.

And all I can think is *Why? Why are they singling us out?*

"What do we do with dogs?" the Crate says above me. "We find out which of them is weakest."

He says something in clipped Japanese.

Guards seize Hank and me from behind, haul us to our feet, square us off against one another, and shove us forward. We bounce off of each other and stagger back. I glance over at the field in time to see two guards chaining Billy to a series of spikes in the ground.

Panic rises ice-cold inside me.

"Prop!" Hank says, breathing hard. Blood runs from a cut in his chin.

"What?"

He raises his fists. "They want us to fight."

"I ain't fightin' you!"

"We got to. Now c'mon!"

The guards close around us. I raise my fists.

Hank starts weaving, heavy on his feet. He throws a loose jab. I dodge and pretend to punch. It wouldn't break through a paper bag.

Hank jabs toward my chin but pulls it at the last instant. He's holding back, and I ain't the only one to see it. One of the guards smacks him in the back with a bamboo pole. Hank goes sprawling. The guards jeer. Beyond their immediate circle, a crowd of prisoners has gathered to stare. Some with a flicker of more life than I've seen in any of them since arriving here.

"Prop." Hank's breath comes in short pants as he pushes to his feet. "Don't take this wrong, but these guys hate cowards. If we don't put some fire into this, we're gonna be here all day."

"You callin' me a coward?"

"Yeah. If that's what it takes, I am."

My fist connects with his jaw, catching him off guard. He staggers back, clearly surprised. The guards hoot and holler. Hank licks the corner of his mouth and smiles. His gums are bloody.

We circle, and I'm aware of money being exchanged between the guards, who start to shout and wave us on. Of Billy sprawled on the ground. Of Hank, waving me in, and the Crate poised behind him with his unforgiving glare.

Hank feints. This time when I duck, he uppercuts my chin. My head snaps and I careen into several guards, who curse and shove me back into the makeshift ring.

Hank comes at me, pastes me across the jaw. My knees buckle and I fall to my hands in the dirt.

Hank circles above me. "C'mon, Prop! Get up. I know that ain't all you got!"

I scramble up and barrel forward with a yell, plowing my shoulder into Hank's chest. He pounds my back with both fists like a gorilla and I pelt him in the kidney, right where he got kicked. He doubles over and I swing for his face, aiming for the jagged scar I sewed up on the march. He goes down and I'm on him with a fury.

The crowd roars as I pummel his body and head.

Hank rolls, shoves me off of him. And then he's up on a knee and punching me in the face. I try to grab his arms, clinch him tight, but he hits me again and again, connecting with my nose.

Blood spurts between us. For a minute, I think I've gone deaf, but it's the guards, roaring at fever pitch.

"Get up!" Hank shouts, spitting droplets of blood. He pulls me up by the front of my shirt, and I hook my leg around his, drag him down again like a wrestler, fists flying as my vision goes white.

The next thing I know, I'm getting pulled away. I flail, still swinging, until one of the guards punches me in the jaw and sends me back to the dirt.

This time I have the sense to stay down as blood drips from my nose, splattering the earth with dark crimson circles.

"Enough!" the Crate says.

Guards haul us to our feet, yank our arms behind us, and push us toward the commander's building. Hank turns to stare at me with an unreadable expression, blood dripping from his chin. The gash on his cheek has reopened.

A blast of air from a swamp cooler hits us the instant we step inside. The guards march us down a hall, throw us in a windowless room with three chairs and a desk, and lock the door behind us.

I sag against the wall, feeling like I might throw up.

"Geez, Prop," Hank says, swiping at his chin and working his jaw. "Almost believed you had it out for me."

I turn slowly, eyes fixed on him.

"Is this about the soap?" I ask.

"Probably. Though I ain't the one who swiped it. Not originally, anyway. Your new crew boss stole it from a guard. Traded it to me for four cans of Spam."

"*What?*" Four cans of Spam is a fortune.

"Must've sold us out. There's no way the Crate could've known otherwise."

"Did you ever think that maybe you should've tried to actually obey the rules for once?" I hear myself say, afraid of what Hank's wheeling

174

ng—even on my behalf—has cost us all. "That this ain't a
be screwin' around?"

Hank stares at me. "Take a look, son. There ain't no rules here except stayin' alive!"

A key turns in the door lock.

"Look sharp," Hank says, and I straighten from the wall, leaving behind a bloody smear.

The Crate enters the room with two guards. He walks behind the desk, sits, and retrieves something from one of the drawers.

A pistol.

All this time we been standing here, there was a pistol in that desk.

Not that there's any chance that pistol's loaded. Or that we'd get away with helping ourselves to it; if this is the punishment for a cake of soap, it don't take much imagination to figure the consequences of stealing a weapon.

The Crate lays the old .38 on the desk in front of him, leans back in the chair, and waves the guards off. They exit and he nods toward the chairs. "Sit."

We sit.

He folds his hands and regards us for what feels like a long time, his face drawn in its perpetual frown as though this place—this entire assignment—is as distasteful as the smell of the prisoners in it and the corpses in the makeshift mortuary outside.

"You may wonder how I have come to speak English so proficiently," he says at last. "For six years of my youth I studied at the University of Washington. Business. Literature. Economics. I also learned your weaknesses. The ways of your cowardice. Your ignorance of war."

My eyes stay focused on the desk. I try not to look at the gun. For all I know, it really is loaded and he's about to shoot us. Or it ain't and he's about to accuse us of trying to steal it. Or it's got a single bullet and he's about to make us play Russian roulette.

Because Hank's right: There are no rules.

"Your friend, Private William Crockett, is the weakest of yo̶
Hence, he is staked in the field. He has neither food nor water ñ
shelter from the sun. No one will tend him, and he will soon die if you̶
do not do exactly as I say."

My gaze snaps up to find the Crate gazing directly at me.

"What do you want us to do?" Hank asks.

The Crate folds his hands. "There is a town called Santa Rita. You
will travel to Santa Rita and carry out a task for me. As a courtesy, I will
provide Private Crockett one half canteen of water. Enough to survive
five . . . perhaps six days at the stake if he is judicious with it. When you
return with the job accomplished, I will remove your friend from his unfortunate position. If you return quickly enough, he may even be alive."

"Sir, we'll come back," I say. "I promise. You don't need to keep him
staked outside."

The commander pauses, and for a minute I think he might actually
agree.

Instead, he says, "You will locate the mayor of Santa Rita and give
him a message." He turns the revolver and holds it toward me.

I don't move.

He waves the handle at me.

I reach for it slowly. Take the pistol in my hands. And then I understand.

He wants us to kill someone.

"The guards will escort you outside the camp," he says. "There they
will give you the rest of what you need." He holds out his hand for me
to return the revolver. I lay it in his palm. "Including this."

He pauses to consider the weapon in his hand.

"If this is loaded, you might have easily killed me," he says. "Or I,
you. You, however, were too cowardly to check. And now . . ." he shrugs.
"You will never know, will you?"

and dealis a clipped command. The door swings open and two guards place to. We get to our feet.

"What about our friend?" Hank demands.

"Bring me the head of the mayor of Santa Rita in a burlap sack and your friend will live," the Crate says. "Flee, and he will suffer to his death knowing you abandoned him. Take too long, and he will die."

20

T he headlines were all about Europe: the annexation of Danzig
to Nazi Germany. British and French declarations of war.
U.S. neutrality.

I read the papers before I delivered them, consulting the map in
Daddy's office when he was gone or asleep, trying to make sense of the
numbers, imagine the bombs and warships, the swift German advance.
I hadn't read about much of the world except what was required for
history class, but now I was hungry to know more.

Meanwhile, Claire and her sisters had been dying to see *The Wizard
of Oz*. Mrs. Crockett decided to take the entire family and invited
Mama and me. I tagged along just for the newsreel but became en-
grossed in the movie, amazed when Dorothy from Kansas opened the
door on a fantastical, Technicolor Oz, as Claire gasped beside me.

The next night over supper, Mama and Daddy got in the first argu-
ment I ever remembered them having when Mama recounted the moment in the movie to Daddy.

"Why in tarnation would you go to a movie about a wizard?" he
asked, staring at her.

"It wasn't a real wizard," Mama said gently. "It was a man pretending to be a great wizard. And the main characters find out he's a fraud."

I sat stock-still in my chair, glad no one told him the movie had witches in it.

"This fantastical nonsense isn't good for young people," Daddy said. "Or adults. It's worse than the garbage on the radio. Or novels."

"Oh, calm down, James. It's just a children's story," Mama said, her voice flat. She set down her napkin, pushed back from the table, and got to her feet.

"Where are you going?" Daddy demanded.

"Seeing how it isn't Sunday, I'm in no mood for a sermon." She walked back to the bedroom and closed the door behind her.

I stared at her empty place at the table in shock. Waited for Daddy to stride down the hall after her. To storm out and drive to the church to work. Instead, he quietly finished the chicken divan on his plate.

He folded his napkin. "Go do your homework. I'll clean up."

"Yes, sir," I said.

I fled to my room, even though I didn't have any homework, and listened to the sounds of Daddy doing the dishes. Twenty minutes later, he walked down the hallway to his office and closed the door.

The next afternoon, Daddy came home early with several plant cuttings wrapped in a wet cloth that he handed to Mama before announcing we were going to the Dew Drop Inn. That day, we ate hot dogs and banana pudding, and the next morning Mama was out planting the cuttings along the fence by the time I left for school.

That winter, Daddy's sermons, usually filled with enough exhortation to last two weeks in case anyone missed a Sunday, turned to dire warning. God's wrath had fallen on Europe for their godlessness.

He preached about wars and rumors of wars—things that were supposed to mean the end of the world, like the terrible economy and joblessness that people had been talking about for years.

And though lots of people nodded during his sermon, I hoped the world wasn't ending and that the war would be over soon. One day I hoped to see the places I'd only begun to read about in the news.

One Sunday after the Russian invasion of Finland, we ate dinner at the Boyingtons', who had seven kids and lived in a fancy house on Dauphin Street. Mr. Boyington was some kind of bigwig at the waterfront Alcoa plant that sold aluminum to Japan, and he was one of the few men Daddy deferred to. He and Mr. Boyington talked about the Bankhead Tunnel project and football and made predictions about the Tennessee game while Mama and Mrs. Boyington talked about the cookware sale at Woolworth's, canning brown-sugar sweet potatoes, and Opal Boyington's boyfriend, who was Cowboy's friend Eugene.

"Opal says with all this talk of war that Eugene's thinkin' about enlisting," Mrs. Boyington said.

"Really," Mama replied, sounding only mildly surprised.

Eugene, like Cowboy, was one year ahead of us in eleventh grade, the last year of school at Murphy High, and about to graduate in May.

"I thought I heard he had a shot at playing for the university." Daddy frowned.

I knew for a fact that he'd heard it. I'd told him so when he'd quizzed me about the Boyington kids on the way to their house.

"You know how it is," Mr. Boyington said. "Young men these days are looking for excitement and jobs where there aren't enough of either. He'll probably eat better than any of us. What about Jimmy?" Mr. Boyington nodded in my direction without looking at me. "Any future plans?"

"Jimmy's fixin' to go to Southern," Daddy said in the humble-but-proud tone he used whenever answering this question. It sounded a lot like his preaching voice.

"Gettin' into the family business, very good." Mr. Boyington nodded before asking about the farm and corn prices.

As I sat there picking at the food in front of me, I felt the color drain out of the room, everything around me gray, as though Technicolor hues existed only in the world outside mine. A place so fantastical, it might as well be Oz.

Two days before my seventeenth birthday, which fell on a Monday, Mama and Mrs. Crockett bought Claire and me sundaes at Woolworth's while they pored over a magazine featuring the new *Gone with the Wind* movie everyone was talking about.

I did a double take, seeing the picture on the inside spread. I wasn't the only one.

"Why Claire," Mama said, holding it up next to Claire's face. She covered the actress's dark hair with her hand. "You and Vivien Leigh could be sisters!"

"She looks like a grown-up Dorothy Jean," Claire mused, looking at it.

"She looks like you right now," I said.

"I'd give my left arm to have a waist that tiny," Mrs. Crockett sighed, as Mama paged through the pictures. She stopped on a Chesterfield cigarette ad with a girl about our age.

"That's Patricia Donnelly, the new Miss America," Claire said.

"Why don't you try out for Miss America?" I asked. "You're prettier than she is."

Claire just laughed. "It ain't that simple."

"Why not?"

"It just ain't."

We got ready to leave and Mama put the magazine back.

"Bring it along," Mrs. Crockett said.

"Why bother? James'll just throw it in the trash," Mama said.

Mrs. Crockett snatched the magazine and put it on the counter with her purchases. "Then it can live at my house."

We left Woolworth's and Mrs. Crockett said, "Let's go see the window display at Gayfer's!"

"I say we should go look for mistletoe," I murmured in Claire's ear. She swatted me on the shoulder, but I saw the way she smiled—as though there were two new secrets for every one I learned about her, from the smell of her skin to the ticklish spot on her nape . . .

And the other behind her knees.

We'd been careful—not just to avoid getting caught, but to not go too far. Wanting her drove me crazy until I could hardly think straight and, truth be told, I would've pushed the limits if she had let me. But Claire was more levelheaded and aware of all the potential consequences—the same ones that flew out of my mind the instant we were alone.

We walked down Dauphin Street to the department store I'd seen all my life but never entered and admired the *Christmas Carol*–inspired scene in the window, complete with a hobbling Tiny Tim mannequin.

Daddy always said that looking at places like this only got one's "wanter" up. And Mama always said there was no reason to look at things we couldn't afford.

"I should go home and get supper started," Mama said.

But I saw the wistful way she gazed through the open doors as though into another world, her eyes soaking in the sights from there.

We trailed our mamas as we walked back to the Crocketts' truck, Claire's hand tucked through the crook in my arm.

"You ever think you would want to—model, I mean?" I asked her.

"And how would that work, Jimmy, with you in seminary? I doubt it would be well looked upon."

"Who says?"

She glanced at me, one fine brow arched higher than the other. "Folks."

"Not all folks. Not everywhere. You ever think of goin' somewhere else, Claire?"

"Louisville is somewhere else," she said.

"Yes, but Louisville is just three years."

"It'll be lovely. We'll be poor, and I'll have to find a job caring for someone's children, but . . . it's something different, isn't it?"

But it wasn't—not really. Only the location would be different. And I didn't want Claire working to put me through school. Not if she could live a bigger life—not just for me, but for herself. I hadn't even applied to seminary yet and I already dreaded the idea of returning from it. Of coming home to work with Daddy—which had been his plan for me for as long as I could remember. The two of us working together. Living in the same house, probably, if we couldn't afford our own. And with the way things were these days, there's no way we'd be able to.

"What if I don't wanna go?" I blurted.

Claire stopped in her tracks and spun toward me. We were, by now, half a block behind our mamas, who walked with their heads together, talking intently about something.

"You don't want to be a preacher?"

"I—I don't know!" I said. "Do you have your heart set on bein' a pastor's wife?" The thought of Claire living like my mama—holding her tongue, hiding her desires, taking criticism from all the cowards too chicken to talk to Daddy directly, pretending not to want things she gave up dreaming about years ago—was unimaginable to me.

And I didn't want to be like my daddy.

"No!" Claire said. "This is all just really sudden. Jimmy, what's gotten into you?"

"Did you know Eugene Gafford is thinking of enlistin'? Maybe I could do that."

The words were out of my mouth before I knew what I meant to say. But now that I'd said them, I realized how envious I'd felt hearing Eugene's plans, the thought of him heading out on some adventure—and getting paid for it, even. One of the last newsreels I'd seen had included a bit about American military men shipping out to Puerto Rico to defend the Caribbean—from what, I wasn't sure. But it didn't sound bad to me.

"Maybe you could do *what*—enlist?"

"Sure, why not?"

"Your daddy would have a fit," she said, eyes wide.

"My daddy don't get to say what I do for the rest of my life." I took her hands. "Claire, don't you just sometimes wanna *go*? Be anywhere but here?"

"Jimmy," Claire said, searching my face. "This is where my family is. And they need me. It's one thing for me to be gone a few years while you're at seminary. But I couldn't leave them indefinitely. It ain't the same for me as it is for you. It's just you and your parents. But my sisters don't have a daddy, and some days they don't have a mama either. One day they may only have Billy and me."

"What about when they're all grown up and have families of their own—what then?"

She gave a soft laugh. "Dorothy Jean ain't even a year and a half old. The twins are nine. By the time they're all grown enough for families of their own . . . I'll be in my midthirties."

She'd already done the math. Had already rejected any dreams of a life bigger than Mobile in favor of a reality with no room for pageants or careers or escape other than through a movie screen.

Mama bought a bottle of Coty perfume for me to give Claire for Christmas. When I asked why, saying we had never given each other gifts before, Mama smiled as she wrapped the small box on the kitchen table.

"Well, I'd say that's about to change," she said, eyes bright. "When a young man and young lady date for a certain amount of time and have serious intentions, a gift is appropriate."

"What if she didn't get me anything?" I murmured against the rim of a mug filled with lukewarm cocoa.

Mama lifted her chin as she tied a ribbon around the box in a glossy red bow. "I have it on good authority that she did. And that she picked it out herself."

I liked the idea of her picking something for me. Or should have. Instead, I found myself wishing this Christmas would just be like the last one—like all the ones we'd had before.

"I assume you and Claire have talked about your future," Daddy said from where he sat in his chair reading the paper.

"Sure," I said.

"When are you planning to propose?"

"I don't know," I said.

Daddy laid down his paper. "You only have a year and a half of high school left. You'll be eighteen by then—the same age I was when I proposed to your mama. Christmas next year would be a fine time for an engagement. Six months to plan a summer wedding, plenty of time to get settled in Louisville before fall."

"Why do we have to get married?" I asked.

He looked at me with surprise. "Because you'll need the support. Marriage provides a stable foundation and removes the temptations in a dating relationship."

I glanced down, my cheeks burning.

"It's a valuable time for Claire as well," Daddy went on. "She'll make friends with women she has something in common with."

"I still keep in touch with some of the ladies I met in Louisville," Mama said, putting away the wrapping paper.

I wondered what Claire would think of that. She'd had few real female friends. The ones she'd had in school had one by one turned against her when she didn't have enough time for them—or so I long thought. I saw now that they betrayed her the older and prettier she got, as she refused to seek their approval.

And the more it became apparent that boys like Hank would drop anything at a word from her.

"Jimmy," Daddy said. I glanced up. "Answer your mother."

"Yes, ma'am," I said, not remembering what she'd said.

On Christmas Eve, I gave Claire the bottle of Coty perfume, and she gave me a pocketknife from Fulbright's hardware store.

She tried on three occasions that evening to get me to slip out behind the house. But somehow, it didn't feel right. *I* didn't feel right.

We rang in the New Year glued to the Crocketts' radio as the Finns fought back the Russians and the Germans bombed France.

That February, the 1940 Olympics were canceled due to the war. I took Claire and her sisters to *Pinocchio* since Mrs. Crockett, who usually let Claire do whatever she wanted, drew the line when it came to the new Mae West film.

And though Claire and I spent the rest of the school year together like normal, things were different. She was quieter, like she was waiting for me to say something. But I didn't know what that might be. I still wanted her—more than ever. I just didn't know where we were headed anymore, or how to make her part of a future I wasn't sure I even wanted or she wouldn't grow to resent. And no matter how much I tried to figure it out, the whole situation felt more and more like a knot that just pulled tighter the more I fiddled with it.

I'd never known Claire to not speak her mind or hesitate to boss any of us in her life and tell us what to do. But now, she wasn't directing me at all.

And so I did nothing, stuck in limbo as the world exploded an ocean away.

The first week of August 1940, Mrs. Crockett threw a birthday party for Hank. She'd done it the last couple years with sandwiches and lemonade. This year, we all took turns churning the handle of the ice cream maker I remembered from childhood, sweating in the swelter of a particularly hot Alabama summer. All the talk was of the war—France had fallen and Britain was fighting for its life—and the fact that President Roosevelt had been nominated for an unprecedented third term.

Cowboy was there, and his and Hank's daddy, Mr. Wright, even came by long enough to eat a sandwich before leaving to deliver a load of lumber to the new Brookley Army Air Field, which had just begun construction at the old Bates Field south of town. When Cowboy got up to leave with him, Mr. Wright waved him back.

"The mill will still be there tomorrow. You stay and keep your brother out of trouble." He'd always been a tall, hard-looking man, with leathery skin and a roundness to his neck, as though, having put his shoulder to the wheel, he'd never quite straightened again. He turned to Mrs. Crockett.

"Thank you for bein' so good to my boy," he said. "You're the closest thing to a mama he's had since . . ." He lowered his head and didn't finish. Just put his hat back on and quietly left.

"What's goin' on at Brookley anyway?" I asked. Hank had split his summer between the mill and the Crocketts' garage, putting in more and more hours working with Cowboy and his daddy in the last week alone.

"Gonna be quite the place," Cowboy said. "I deliver so much lumber there, I ain't sure whether I work for the mill or the U.S. government."

"Forget Brookley." Hank grinned, leaning his chair back. "Let's talk football."

Unlike Eugene, who had no guarantees that he'd get to play and no way to pay for college without a scholarship, Cowboy had been offered a full ride to play for the Crimson Tide. I wasn't at the Wrights' the day Cowboy got the news, but Hank told us later he had hugged his brother and cried like a baby.

"Don't know if it was pride or jealousy," Hank joked to Billy and me, though his eyes were shining when he said it.

But when we tried to talk about Cowboy's training schedule and the season's first game against Spring Hill, Cowboy shifted in his chair.

"It's just hard to think about football when there's gonna be a war," he said.

"I hate to break it to you, but there already is. A war, I mean," Claire said, lemonade balanced on her knee. "But there's nothing you can do about it, so you might as well make us all proud."

Cowboy grinned, dimples winking from both cheeks. He and Hank could pass for twins when they smiled. "I aim to do just that. Still, I think we might be involved sooner than we think."

"Oh pshaw," Claire said. "President Roosevelt promised we'd never fight in foreign lands again."

"That was before Germany conquered France. They're talkin' about a peacetime draft."

"Roy Wright," Claire said, sitting up straighter. "Are you thinkin' of joining the military?"

My pulse quickened—from excitement or nerves, I wasn't sure.

"I figure the day'll come," he said somberly.

"If there's gonna be a draft, why rush?" I asked. I knew my reasons for considering it, but Cowboy had more promising prospects here.

"After spendin' so much time at Brookley, I'm thinkin' I might like to learn to fly." He gave Claire a lazy smile. "Don't you think that sounds like fun—learnin' to fly?"

"I think standing on solid ground sounds better," she quipped as Hank came trotting through the yard, pulling Dorothy Jean behind him in a Radio Flyer wagon. A second later, Billy jumped out from the corner of the house with a G-Man tommy gun and opened *rat-tat-tat* fire on them until Hank fell over, playing dead.

Dorothy Jean threw her head back with a loud yowl and Claire got up from the porch with an exasperated huff.

"'Scuse me," she said, striding across the porch and down the steps to give Billy and Hank each the what for.

"I better help myself to another sandwich before I get in trouble too," Cowboy chuckled, getting to his feet.

From the other side of the porch, Mama and Mrs. Crockett's laughter lifted into the air where they sat with Claire's uncle, who had come up from the shop for lunch and to relieve Betty and Margaret at the ice cream crank for a spell.

It was the perfect end-of-summer day, but I was unsettled, feeling like it was going too fast, like I was speeding toward seminary in Louisville with no way to stop or change my path. Knowing if I did, I risked a future with Claire.

I watched her take the tommy gun from Billy only to turn it on him and Hank, sending them both running.

I never wanted this day to end, for anything between us to change.

Mrs. Crockett had just emerged from the house carrying the cake when a familiar truck turned down the road.

I got to my feet, pulse racing.

"Mama," I said urgently. "Mama!"

Mama looked at me and then around, confused, before finally spying Daddy's truck.

Touching her hair, she got to her feet, but then sat back down as Daddy pulled over in front of the house and got out. She waved to him from the porch.

"You're just in time!" she called brightly as Mrs. Crockett set the cake down on the small side table.

Daddy removed his hat as he came up the steps. His gaze paused on Cowboy, who rose from his chair beside me. Just then, Billy and Claire came running around the side of the house chased by Hank, who had the tommy gun now.

I had never seen my daddy show up at the Crocketts' unexpected. He'd never cared for the chaos when Mrs. Crockett invited us for dinner, and I knew he felt his family spent too much time here as it was.

"James," Mama said, rising again. "What a surprise."

"You're just in time for some ice cream and cake," Mrs. Crockett said.

Hank, I noticed, had already disappeared.

Daddy's brow furrowed as he took in the scene on the porch. "I was actually on my way to the shop to see if your brother-in-law could take a look at my tire."

Claire's uncle got to his feet and gestured Daddy to follow. "Sure thing, we can get you taken care of, Pastor."

I watched them go as Mama busied herself helping Mrs. Crockett scoop ice cream.

That night, Mama made small talk over supper. About the Jell-O recipe she planned to submit for the church cookbook. The ham on sale at Delchamps.

She glanced between us, lingering, until she finally had to leave to play piano for choir practice.

The minute the truck pulled out of the driveway, Daddy set down his fork and folded his napkin.

"I was disappointed to find you at the Crocketts' while the Wright boy was there today," he said at last.

"Which Wright boy?" I asked dully, having dreaded this conversation all afternoon.

"You know exactly which one. Moreover, I understand the event was a party for Hank's birthday. I thought I made myself clear that you were not to be around that boy," Daddy said.

I exploded. "What am I supposed to do? You put me in impossible situations!"

"Son, you put yourself in that situation."

"Claire is my girlfriend. Hank works for her mama. It's not my business who she invites to her house!"

"It is your business when you choose to be there!" He slammed his hand on the table. "You have to think about how others view the company you keep. The movies you attend. Who you date and when you marry and how you conduct yourself before—and after! Not just for you, but for Claire. Trust me, you don't want Claire around a boy like that either!"

I got to my feet. "I ain't gonna tell Claire what to do!"

"You will need to," he said.

"Like you do with Mama?"

In a flash, he was on his feet, grabbing me by the front of my shirt, shoving me against the wall.

"You are not a child anymore!" he said, his face inches from mine. "You're nearly a seminarian!"

"What if I don't want to be?" I demanded, my chin trembling. "What if I don't wanna go to seminary or live here after?"

"Of course you do," he said, letting me go. He backed up a step, looking at me like I was a stranger.

"How do you know? *I* don't even know! There's a war going on. They're sayin' there's about to be a draft!"

He shook his head. "Seminarians are exempt."

"Maybe I don't wanna be!"

He waved it aside like so much nonsense. "You don't know what you're saying."

I opened my mouth to protest but he clasped my arms with his hands, his gaze intent.

"There's time. Time to decide. If the U.S. enters the war and the world breaks apart around us . . . you'll be grateful for the exemption. Trust me, son."

I saw it then, in his expression: fear.

He let me go and I burst out of the house and ran all the way to Claire's, where I found her taking out the trash.

"Jimmy, what's wrong?" she demanded.

But how could I say it? Telling her I didn't want to stay or come back to Mobile meant I didn't want a future with her.

No matter what, I couldn't win.

Five weeks later, the president signed the Selective Training and Service Act into law, making it the first peacetime conscription in U.S. history. All men between the ages of twenty-one and thirty-five were required to register.

"By the time you're twenty-one, the war will be over," Daddy said.

I wasn't sure if he said it to comfort me or him.

On Sunday night before the start of our final year of school, I went to Claire and Billy's for supper—at least as far as Daddy knew. The real reason I went over was because *The Shadow* was on—a show Daddy would've disapproved of from the opening line: *"Who knows what evil lurks in the hearts of men?"*

Especially if he knew Claire played the theme song on the piano at church when we helped clean.

That night after the episode, Billy asked if I wanted to play catch, but Claire told him she and I needed some time alone to talk.

Billy wiggled his eyebrows. "Have a good chat," he called after us, as Claire led me out to the porch.

We sat down together on the old, creaky swing Hank and me had fixed at least three times between us.

"Jimmy," she said, turning toward me and taking my hand.

"This sounds serious," I said, brushing the backs of her fingers.

"It is. I want you to know everything I say, I'm sayin' out of friendship and love. Okay?"

"Okay," I said slowly, not sure I liked the sound of this.

"I know you're hungry for the world. Not in a bad way like something your daddy would preach about, but for your own life, away from him. I know you, Jimmy, and I know you are chafing at the idea of seminary and comin' back to Mobile when you're done. I know you're jealous of boys like Eugene gettin' to go off and see the world, even if the world is ugly right now . . ."

She glanced down, and a tear rolled down her cheek.

I swiped at it with a finger. "Claire—"

She looked up at me, her lashes wet.

"And I want that for you. To be able to make your own way, even if you ain't sure what way that is yet."

"Claire, what're you sayin'?"

"I'm sayin' I ain't gonna hold you back."

"But you ain't!"

"I am. I want all that for you. But my heart's here, with my family."

She started to cry then, her words breaking. "And I know you'd come back and try your best to make me happy 'cause that's who you are, Jimmy. You're good. You're my best friend. But I'd hate myself just a little bit more every day if that happened. Because you'd just be trading pleasing one person for another."

I panicked. "Forget all that stuff I've been sayin'—"

"No. I won't. You ain't your dad. He's tryin' to make you in his image, but you ain't anything like him. You need a chance to be your own man."

"We'll figure something out," I said. "We could get a big house and bring your family to live with us. Billy too."

Her shoulders slumped. "How would that ever work? The gas station is here. The garage is here. It's what we live on."

"We'd sell it and start a new one!"

She looked down and shook her head. "I appreciate the sentiment, Jimmy, really. But even if all that were possible, you can't take my mama away from yours. Or vice versa. They wouldn't survive without one another. I think you know that."

"We could live across the bay in Daphne or Fairhope. Somewhere close enough to your family and far enough from—"

"It would never be far enough." She gave a bitter laugh. "That's the same county your daddy's farm's in. You'd live with people asking you 'bout your daddy all the time. Knowing he could show up on your front porch any day."

"I could do it," I said.

"It's not what you want and I know it."

I glanced down at our hands. Felt a tear slip from my lashes and drop onto my knuckles.

"And the truth is, Jimmy, I'd rather be friends with fond memories than have you learn to resent me."

"I wouldn't," I said, my mouth twisting. "I swear!"

"You would. And I'd hate you for the way it'd make me feel."

"Just gimme some time to figure it out," I said.

"No," she said gently. "It'll just make it hurt more." She gave a sad smile and started to cry.

The sound tore my heart in two.

"Claire, don't cry," I said, pulling her close. She hitched a sob and I held her tight, not knowing what else to do.

21

The guards march us past Billy on the way to the gate. They've stripped him of his shirt, the ugly red scar across his back exposed to the climbing sun. We kneel down beside him, and I hand him the half-full canteen I was given at the Crate's command.

"Listen," Hank says. We've only got a few seconds. "We gotta run an errand for the Crate. Soon as we get back, they're lettin' you go. We'll be fast as we can."

Billy flicks a glance to the guards and then locks eyes with each of us in turn. He shakes his head.

"Don't come back," he whispers.

"We ain't leavin' you!" I hiss through gritted teeth.

"He's just talkin' crazy again," Hank says to me.

"No, I ain't," Billy says, gaze intent. "This is what we talked about. It's the best chance any of us is ever gonna get and the only way Jimmy stays alive. You gotta take it."

"And what're we supposed to tell your mama?" Hank says.

"For all you know, the Crate's gonna kill me the minute you leave and you'll have come back for nothin'!"

He's right—it's possible. But right now, us leaving is the only chance he's got.

Hank pats him on the shoulder as the guards prod us to our feet. "See you in a couple days."

"No!" Billy says, pulling on his chains. "Don't!"

"We're comin' back!" I say firmly—for the Crate's benefit as much as Billy's.

"You hang in there, Streak!" Hank says, as we follow the guards to the entrance.

It takes everything in me to walk away, and all I can tell myself is the faster we leave, the sooner we'll return.

But when I look back, I find Billy's gaze following us and know he's saying goodbye.

Out past the gate, one of the guards escorting us from the compound hands me a lumpy knapsack. He pulls out the .38 and hands it over. Hank takes it and cracks open the cylinder.

"Where's the bullets?" he says angrily. "We need bullets!"

The guard points to the knapsack, turns on his heel, and returns to camp.

It's strange, being out in the open like this.

Free.

For a minute, I think, *It's true. We could run for it. Never return. For all we know, Billy's as good as dead no matter what we do.*

That's when I realize why the Crate singled Billy out: because there ain't three friends like us. And he knows as long as there's a chance Billy's alive, there's no way we'll leave him behind.

He might call us traitors to our country, but he knows we'll never betray each other.

I bet he's never had a real friend in his whole life. The thought scares me, because it makes me think he might have it out for Billy from sheer spite.

I open the knapsack, rummage through the contents, pull out a battered old map, and unfold it.

Santa Rita lies southwest of San Fernando and north of Guagua, where we used to stop for the day during our supply runs to Manila. Far as I can tell, we got over twenty-five miles to go just to get there.

We've marched as many miles in a day before, but we ain't in near the same condition as we were then.

Hank leads the way as we hike across a field, wade through a stream, and head into the forest. The temperature dips in the shade, and on any other occasion I'd stop and eat whatever's in the knapsack and do nothing but welcome the rest.

But Billy's got six days. And I can't find any relief in the shade knowing that by tomorrow the sun will blister the skin from his back.

Even so, we have to pause every hundred paces or so to huff and catch our breath.

Sometime after noon, we stop long enough to rummage through the rest of the pack. I find a hunk of old bread, some rice wrapped in a banana leaf, and a rag wrapped with twine.

I hand the rice to Hank and unwrap the old rag. Blink at the single bullet nestled inside.

"You kiddin' me?" I shout.

"Figures." Hank hands me the rice and takes the bullet, slips it into the chamber.

"If he's so worried 'bout us goin' rogue, why not send his own men?"

"Whatever his beef is with the mayor, he obviously don't want to be tied to it," Hank says. "We get caught, a couple Americans get blamed. Maybe that's the real plan. Either way, his hands are clean. Which makes me think his superiors ain't in on it."

"So it's personal?"

He shrugs. "Who knows?"

We pick our way through the edge of the forest toward a patch of grassland.

"Maybe we should have followed the road," I say.

"You think a Japanese patrol's gonna take kindly to two Americans walking around with a loaded .38? I say we walk another hour, get a few hours' sleep, and cover some miles in the dark."

An hour later we find an old tree trunk that's fallen over, add some more cover to it, and lie down against it, practically hidden from sight.

It's hard to sleep. But worn as we are, even harder to stay awake.

I jolt from sleep at a nudge—no, a boot—in my side. It's light out, the grass around me wet with dew.

I shove up in a panic, realizing we slept through the entire night . . .

And then start again, realizing we ain't alone.

Three Japanese soldiers stand over us, bayoneted rifles pointed at our heads.

I glance at Hank. He's got his hands up.

"Get up, Joe," one of the soldiers says. Another one kicks the sole of my boot.

The third soldier don't make a sound. He's skinny and when he scowls, I can see he's missing one of his front teeth. I sit up, but before I can get to my feet, Tooth lunges at me. I twist away, and his bayonet catches flesh and fabric both just above my hip.

I fall back with a grunt.

Hank springs to his feet. "Why'd you do that?" he yells at the soldier.

In answer, the soldier swings his rifle at Hank. Hank ducks and uppercuts him, landing a hard crack to the soldier's jaw that sends him reeling.

To my surprise the others start to laugh, guffawing long and loud. One of them slings his rifle over his shoulder and crosses his arms. The second one grins, lifts his chin, and hollers something to Tooth, rifle pointed at us.

Tooth squares off and lunges at Hank with his rifle. Hank dodges and jukes behind the soldier's back and grabs him in a headlock.

"Fight, Joe!" one of the soldiers shouts. The other yells in Japanese, laughing.

I press the knapsack to my side where I lie, trying to stop the bleeding. The cut don't seem to be deep, but it hurts so bad my vision blurs.

Tooth struggles in Hank's headlock, but Hank don't give an inch—until the Japanese soldier hooks Hank's leg and shoves his weight backward. Hank falls hard on his back and the soldier scrambles from his grasp. Back on his feet, Tooth stabs his bayonet at Hank's chest but finds only earth as Hank rolls away. Before he can pull the blade free, Hank grabs the soldier's legs out from under him. The instant he's down, Hank's on him, pinning him to the dirt. He blasts him with a left hook, follows with a right, punching him over and over.

I glance at the guards, who've all but forgotten me, fixated on the struggle in the grass as Hank twists, reaching for something along the ground. An instant later, Hank rears up and smashes a rock down on Tooth's face. Once. Twice. The man goes still.

I look up to find myself staring down the barrel of a rifle. The soldier holding it blinks, glances at the other, and says something as if asking for clarification. His companion responds by unslinging his rifle and fumbling with the safety.

In a flash, Hank springs for the second man's throat. The soldier goes down beneath him. The soldier above me swivels and takes aim directly at Hank's back.

A shot rings out.

The man above me pitches to the ground, a bloody hole in the back of his head.

Punched by a bullet from the .38 in my hand.

Hank grapples the other soldier to the ground, hands wound around his neck. The soldier claws at Hank's face and arms and finally convulses in the dirt and goes still.

We've killed all three.

Hank staggers to his feet, breathing hard, his face spattered with blood.

"Can you still walk?" he asks.

"Yeah." The Crate's .38 dangles from my fingers.

I shove it into my belt as Hank slings two of the soldiers' rifles over his shoulder, then searches their packs, grabbing food and an extra clip of ammo. He adds them to our pack and pulls me to my feet.

Shouts issue nearby. Japanese. Close enough to have heard the gunshot.

Hank sets his shoulder under my arm and we start off, hobbling down a ravine and across a muddy creek. On the other side he glances back, panting, his forehead creased.

"How many?" I say.

"Thirty. Maybe forty."

Blood oozes through my fingers. My vision begins to prickle.

"Can't go . . . much further."

"No. They're almost on us. We gotta run, buddy. Say a prayer and kick it into gear. For Billy." His face is red.

Billy's name brings me back. I grit my teeth and plunge forward through the scrub—only for the ground to break and for me to tumble down a bank in a landslide of shale. I roll to my knees as Hank flails head over heels after me. When he skids to a stop, the rifles are gone.

I try to get to my feet. Hank tugs me back down.

Voices, somewhere above us. The familiar staccato of guttural Japanese.

"Sorry, buddy," Hank pants. "I think this is it for us."

It can't be. Not like this. We die now, and we drag Billy to the afterlife with us. Can't let that happen.

Darkening.

Darkening.

Everything around me goes black.

22

MAY 11, 1942

UNKNOWN LOCATION, PHILIPPINES

I can't breathe. But I know I'm dying or dead because I can see a
skinny funnel of light ahead of me.

Down near my feet.

And that just don't make sense. The light is supposed to come from
above, not below. Unless, of course, something is horribly wrong.

Sounds of struggle. Of breath, labored and uneven.

Mine.

"Shhh." Hank.

He presses his hand tighter over my mouth. We're wedged together
in some kind of pipe, my feet pointing to an opening.

Scuffling of boots. A grunted "Hai."

We lay like that for hours. The stench of the two of us in such a
confined space is nearly overpowering.

The funnel of light is gone by the time he lets me go and wriggles
away from me. A minute later, he grabs me by the ankles and pulls me
out, my back scraping the inside of the hollow log.

It's dark, and I realize with alarm that it's already the second day.

"They're gone," he says. "We lost the canteen."

"The pack?"

"Gone too."

I still got the revolver but a lot of good that'll do now that I used our only bullet.

"Think you can walk?" he says.

"Yeah. Help me up."

"I saw smoke coming from the other side of that hill." He points. "I think there's a village."

I squint in the darkness. "How do we know it's friendly?"

"We don't."

The moon's overhead by the time we reach the ridge. We crouch down in the brush. The valley below is aflame with burning huts, sparks like lightning bugs drifting into the sky. I see shadows and silhouettes, Japanese soldiers rounding up villagers, herding them like sheep.

Bodies dot the ground.

I make out the bent back and lined face of an old Filipino. He's holding on to the hand of a little boy. A few old women huddle together.

Hank juts his chin in the direction of a lone Imperial sentry standing about fifty yards from the nearest fire, rifle in hand, his back to us.

"Why would they burn the village?" I say. "It's just kids, old men, and women!"

"Probably figure they're helping escaped American soldiers."

A shot rings out. The Japanese sentry ahead of us collapses to the ground.

We drop flat as gunfire issues from the hillside.

"If the enemy's down there, who's shooting up here?" I hiss, hand over my head.

"I don't know!"

A grenade sends three Japanese soldiers hurtling into the air. Another explodes somewhere beyond the ring of burning huts. Screams. More shots. One of the soldiers herding villagers jerks and goes down.

A group of men in army fatigues emerges from the darkness around us, Thompson submachine guns trained on our heads. Some Filipino. A few Caucasian.

We raise our hands. I toss the .38 to the ground.

"We're Americans," Hank says. "We escaped from Camp O'Donnell."

They don't talk—they don't need to. They're the ones holding the guns. One of them comes over and pats us down. I grimace and groan.

"They're clean," the man says. "Stupid, but clean. That one's wounded." He's got a long beard and a dark bandanna tied around his forehead. He retrieves the .38. Checks the barrel.

"Not even loaded."

"I don't like it," another man says.

"Take 'em to the commander," Bandanna says, sending a younger soldier on ahead. I struggle to my feet.

They march us down to the village where the little boy is staring at the body of a dead Japanese soldier. My head's woozy. Each step harder to take.

"My friend needs water," Hank says.

"We need answers," Bandanna says. He shoves us toward a large hut on the edge of the clearing with the point of his rifle. I lurch up the steps and follow Hank inside.

There's an armed guard to the right. Three others bend over a cot, working on a body by the light of a torch, their sleeves rolled up, hands bloody. I'm so fixed on the sight of them, trying to figure out who or what they are, that I fail to notice the figure standing in the darkness.

"On your knees. Hands behind your heads. Cross your legs behind you." Snap of fingers. "Steady that one."

I sink down, kept from falling on my face by a hand gripping my shoulder.

It ain't the lowest voice I've ever heard from a man, and a second later, I learn why: The person who steps into the orange glow of the torch ain't a man at all but a woman in military fatigues with a .45 pointed at our heads.

I squint, thinking that can't be right. But sure as my name's Jimmy Propfield, those are bosoms staring me in the face.

She's taller than any Filipina I've seen, thickset and muscular, the sleeves of her fatigues ripped from the seams, leaving her shoulders bare. She ain't young neither. And though I wouldn't call her handsome, she's as striking as an Amazon. No man in his right mind would want to mess with a woman like this.

She flicks a finger toward me. "Give that one some water."

A guard brings me a canteen and I drink greedily before passing it to Hank.

"Now," she says. "What were you doing so close to this village?"

"Ma'am," Hank says. "If we could speak to the commander—"

She crosses her arms. Regards him in silence.

Hank glances at Bandanna, who hasn't moved a muscle, and back at her.

"*You're* the commander?" Hank says, before adding, "Ma'am?"

She lifts her chin. "I am Felipa Culala. If you've heard of me, the rumors are all true. Some of my resistance fighters are Filipino. Some are American and once belonged to your Army. Now they fight for me."

"Who, but—who are . . ." I hesitate, not even sure what I'm asking.

"We are the Hukbo ng Bayan Laban sa Hapon," she says. "The People's Army against the Japanese. Now, who are you?"

"I'm Hank Wright and this is my friend Jimmy Propfield." Hank gestures to me. "We're privates with the Thirty-First Infantry. Ma'am."

She frowns. "You escaped the Japanese?" Her gaze goes to my wound.

"Ma'am," I say, "we're on a mission from the commander of Camp O'Donnell. He wants the mayor of Santa Rita dead in six days or our friend'll die, and that's God's honest truth."

Hank gives me a swift, pointed look to *shut up*. But we need food, water, and ammo. We also need help. And we need it quick.

She lifts a brow.

"Well, little man, that's quite a story." She points to the soldiers bent over the cot. "You see this woman they're working on?"

I glance toward the figure and nod.

"One of the men recognized her as the wife of this village's leader. The Japanese cut off her nipples. Her husband is in O'Donnell. She was left in charge. Many women in charge these days. And this woman knows things. That's why we need her to live. I like it when people know things. In fact, I believe the two of you know things. Perhaps things of value to me. Tell me: Why does the commander at O'Donnell want this mayor dead?"

"We don't know, ma'am," Hank says.

"You're not very useful, are you?"

She jerks her chin toward one of the guards.

"We can be useful!" I say. "Please! We need to live—not just for our sakes."

Her guards drag us to our feet.

"Please!"

But she's already turned away.

To my surprise, they don't take us out and shoot us. In fact, one of them throws a quick patch on my gut.

They move out a half hour later and take us with them.

It's a ten-minute hike to the trucks they've hidden in a thicket near the road. Hank and I struggle to keep up, his shoulder beneath my arm, and I find myself waiting for a bayonet in the back every time we start to lag.

Oosh!

Soon as we reach the trucks, we load up and roar down the road in the dark, headlights off. The man next to me offers us each a cigarette. I refuse as Hank lights up.

We travel up a mountain road and onto a goat path as the moon breaks through the clouds. Jostle through the jungle in low gear, branches scraping the sides of the truck. I'm close to nodding off by the time we stop and get out to hike the rest of the way on foot. We pass several guards on the trail. A couple on the ground, more calling down from the trees.

I smell roasting meat before we even reach the cave.

Inside, Bandanna points to a place on the ground and orders us to sit. Another man brings us a mess kit piled with broiled pork and hunks of pineapple and sets it down between us.

"It's fresh. She was running in the forest this morning," he says.

It's so delicious I have to steel myself between bites to keep from eating too fast and making myself sick. Hank seems to be doing the same, nothing but the sound of chewing and licking fingers from either one of us.

"Please, can you help us?" I ask Bandanna when Hank and me finish eating. "We need to get to Santa Rita."

And we've lost too much time.

"That's up to the commander. You ain't in any condition to travel, anyway."

He comes over with a lantern and some supplies to doctor my wound for good.

"It's gonna hurt," he says, handing me a bottle. I take a long pull. It burns all the way down. I hand it back and Bandanna pours a trickle on my wound. It might as well be fire, and I ain't got enough pride left to keep from groaning.

"You okay holding him?" the man murmurs above me.

"Might as well be me," Hank says.

"Just stitch it up, I don't need no hand-holding," I say, words already starting to slur.

"We ain't gonna stitch you," Bandanna says to me. Then to Hank: "I best get a couple others, just to be safe." He comes back a few minutes later with two other guerillas who kneel down as the bearded man disappears again.

"What's goin' on?" I demand, looking at Hank.

"Gonna fix you up right, Prop. It'll be over in a minute," Hank says.

Bandanna returns and Hank and the others grab on to me.

"What're you doin'? Hank!" My heart pounds loud in my ears. I twist beneath their weight.

And then I see the red-hot knife.

23

MAY 12, 1942
THE HUKS CAMP, PHILIPPINES

A warm palm checks my forehead for fever. Backs of fingers press against my cheek.

My eyes flutter open on the scarred face of the commander.

"Good. You're awake. Drink," she says, lifting my head. She hands me a canteen. I take it with stupid fingers, dribble water down the side of my mouth.

She helps me sit up and my vision swims. Pain sears my side and I think I might puke.

Hank stands in the entrance of the cave smoking a cigarette in the light through the leafy canopy outside.

It's daytime.

"How long have I been out?" I ask, panicked. Hank tosses the butt away and comes over to peer down at me. His hair is damp, his face clean. His uniform looks cleaner too.

"All night," he says, mouth set in a grim line.

"No," I groan.

"So," Felipa says, straightening. "If I choose to believe your story, your friend has three days to live. A hike to Santa Rita will take two days.

210

It is another three back to O'Donnell, assuming you are not waylaid. By then, your friend will be dead."

"Maybe we don't gotta go all the way to Santa Rita," I say. "We just need someone's head. Someone who could be mistaken for the mayor. God knows there's enough corpses on this island—"

Hank shakes his head. "Even if we managed to pass some stiff's head off as the mayor's, what d'you think the Crate's gonna do to Billy—to all of us—once he finds out the mayor's still alive? We need to find this guy and kill him. It's the only way."

I see it then: the worry around his eyes. I can't remember ever seeing Hank frantic. In any other circumstance, I'd marvel at the sight.

Instead, it fills me with dread.

It never occurred to me that we'd have to actually murder a fella who might be innocent. Kill him in cold blood.

It ain't the same as shooting someone in battle, not knowing if they live or die. That kind of killing is an order, and justified. A responsibility borne by someone else to be answered for in the life to come.

But murder . . . how could I live with a sully like that on my soul? I could never look anyone I loved in the eye. Would never feel clean again.

Another awful thought spikes through me then. What if refusing to kill the mayor is as good as killing Billy?

Panic prickles my nape. Makes it hard to breathe.

Hank turns toward Felipa. "Can you get me to Santa Rita?"

"I can," she says. "I'm no friend of the commander of Camp O'Donnell, but I don't like the mayor either. My men can drive you there in four hours and get you back to O'Donnell in just over six. I will do this for you. But I need something in return."

"Ma'am?"

"A convoy of Japanese supply trucks is coming from Manila this afternoon. They must never reach their destination. Many of my men are away on another mission, which leaves me only ten to strike the

convoy. I can use two more soldiers who know how to handle a rifle."
She glances from him to me.

"How many trucks?" Hank says.

"Six. With perhaps four armed men on each."

"And you give your word you'll get me to Santa Rita and back,"
Hank says.

"You mean 'us,'" I say, wondering what he plans to do.

"You're injured and we ain't got time, Prop," Hank says. "Billy's
dying—right now, this second!" He turns to Felipa. "We'll do it. Just
get me to Santa Rita and back."

I shove painfully to my feet. I can't let him do this. There's got to
be another way.

"He ain't goin' alone," I say.

"I can't be worrying 'bout you," Hank says.

"Worrying 'bout me? I'm here because of you!"

"What're you talkin' about?"

Felipa silences him with a hand on his chest. "I will take you both
to Santa Rita. In the meantime, you"—she looks at Hank—"help my
men gather supplies."

"Yes, ma'am," Hank says, glaring at me as he leaves.

"Come," Felipa says. "We need to soak your wound so you are stronger for the task."

Felipa leads me through the jungle, two drums of ammo slung over her
shoulders. She pushes branches and giant leaves out of the way with
one hand, her Thompson steadied with the other. And even though
she's armed, I feel naked without a weapon and under the protection
of a lady.

"You have not been in the Army long," she says. It ain't a question.

"No, ma'am," I say.

"You are eighteen?"

"Nineteen."

"Such youth. What does your father do in America?"

"He's a preacher, ma'am."

I'm used to impressed, raised brows accompanied by straighter posture, sage nods, and "Ahhh!" in response to this answer.

Instead, she clucks her tongue.

"We are all Catholic here. I feel sorry you do not have the sacrament of confession."

I don't know what to say about that, having never grown up with sacraments—or much to confess. Instead, this is the first time in my life that the faith and my daddy's vocation that I've been taught to brandish like a shiny badge has ever been treated as less preferable or even unfortunate.

I hear the cascade of water before we reach it. As we get closer, I notice that the stony outcrop ahead drops away into a natural hollow fed by a narrow waterfall about twenty feet above. It's one of the best swimming holes I've ever seen.

I glance at Felipa and she juts her chin toward the water. "Wash the stink from your skin. I will be here with the rifle."

I hesitate. It don't seem right, knowing that Billy's baking in the sun.

"If you do not stay clean, you will become sick," she says, lighting up a cigarette. "And what help will you be to anyone then?"

I unlace and toe out of my boots, peel off my socks. Moving down toward the water and out of her direct line of sight, I shuck off my shirt and pants, dog tags jingling. It feels strange stripping down to my skivvies with her so close by, but the pool below me is blue, deep, and cool as I gingerly wade in.

It feels like heaven. Smells like rainfall and moss. Felipa sits on the rocks, the Thompson across her knees. Her jaw juts as she blows smoke rings in the air. With her head canted like that, I can almost make out the younger woman she once was, before the scars and guns.

I slip below the surface. Stay under as long as I can. I've forgotten what it feels like to be submerged in water, so fresh and alive. Couldn't even fathom it those days on the march, the weeks of grave detail since arriving at O'Donnell.

I think of Billy pouring water over my head. The closest thing to this, and best gift he could've given me.

And look what it's costing him.

It feels wrong to enjoy the water after that. I surface and grab my shirt and trousers, squeeze the blood from them in the water. Wring them out and slap them up on a rock to dry before climbing out in my soaking wet drawers, shivering in the sun.

When I get back to Felipa, her hair's loose and she's kicking off her boots.

"Here, little man," she says and hands me the submachine gun. "Watch the eastern hill for me. That's the only flank exposed."

She shimmies out of her fatigues. I turn away but can't help noticing she's in my peripheral vision. She unstraps a large bolo knife from her calf, sets it on a rock beside the extra ammunition, and unbuttons her shirt. The woman looks as though she was built to lead armies. To march through the forest for days on end. To carry a rifle in her hands.

"The eastern hill," she says.

"Yes—yes, ma'am," I say, fumbling with the Thompson as she dives in.

I sit awkwardly, pointed toward unseen enemies, not even seeing the hill. I can feel the sun shrinking the moisture on my skin. Hear the music of waterdrops falling like rain as she climbs out of the pool some time later.

"You are a virgin," she says, sitting down nearby. It ain't a question.

"Ma'am?" My voice cracks.

She leans back on her elbows. "I was seventeen when I married.

214

My husband was twenty-four and two inches shorter than me." She chuckles. "He managed his own textile plant. I gave birth to my son when I was eighteen."

"Where are they now?" I ask, staring fixedly at the waterfall. My own toes. Anything but the naked woman mere feet from me.

Felipa sighs and sits up, drapes her arms around her knees. "They are with God. I am a soldier today, in part, because of the misfortune of their deaths. I have had and lost much wealth, many friends, and countless dreams." I sense more than see her squint up at the sun.

"I lived for a time in Naples with an artist. He painted landscapes and studied Holy Scripture exhaustively, every day. Not because he was religious, but because he was agnostic and wanting to be convinced. Though he embraced neither church nor creed, he longed for the divine. Every painting he created was a prayer he did not know the words of. When he died in an accident, I wondered if God had taken him directly to heaven. I had no such surety for myself. I felt cheated—angry, even. And very alone.

"When I returned to Luzon, I chose to become a soldier and fight for the only thing left that I loved: my country. I find great purpose in soldiering. Much good. You do not understand this, because you are not fighting for your country the same way I am fighting for mine," she says. "Not as I am. Perhaps you do not even know why you are here. Does your tall friend know why you are so angry with him, what you are blaming him for?"

I glance at her, startled.

She ain't asking me to explain. And I wouldn't, even if she was.

"No," I say.

We sit in silence for a moment before I ask, "Would you take an innocent life to save a friend?"

She laughs. "Innocent? Who is innocent? Not the mayor . . . and not the friend you are trying to save. None of our hands are clean."

She pauses. "The mayor of Santa Rita claims that he wants to help his country . . . and then aids the Japanese military and executes a young boy for helping the resistance. That I know for sure. I am happy to have him killed. But what you must ask yourself is why the Japanese commander would also want this man dead."

She reaches over and pats my leg, then starts putting on her clothes.

"Soak for a while longer if you like, little man," she says, taking the Thompson from me. "We won't see real action until this afternoon."

24

We walked together the first day of the new school year, trying to act normal as Billy's gaze flew between me and Claire like a nervous bat.

"Billy, stop that. Everything's fine," Claire said.

Billy glanced at me. "Guess this means we won't be brothers."

"We'll always be brothers," I said.

"Brothers for life!" Hank called, turning a lazy circle in the street beside us on his bike.

"Well, I guess I'm out," Claire muttered.

"You're my sister for life," Billy said somberly.

Claire punched him in the shoulder.

"Mine too, apparently," I said under my breath.

I told myself what was done was done. But I didn't breathe any easier now that the pressure of an engagement was off my shoulders. Now that the only thing I had to worry about was how to inform my daddy I wasn't going to seminary—or coming back home to live with them or preach.

I was miserable. And though I knew Claire and me could still talk, I missed the feel of her lips against mine and her skin beneath my fingers. Not getting to touch her—even to hold her hand—made me feel sick, like something was missing, cut from my torso where she used to lie against me, or my shoulder where she would rest her chin to whisper in my ear.

Turned out, I didn't have to tell Mama that Claire and me broke up because Mrs. Crockett told her. That day, Mama pulled me aside before Daddy got home.

"You don't let someone like that just slip away," she said, hazel eyes stark.

"Just . . . We want different things." Any excuse sounded flimsy.

"Different than what? She doesn't want to go to Louisville?"

I sighed. "Mama, Claire ain't like you. And I ain't like Daddy." I didn't know how else to explain it.

She blew out a breath and wiped her hands on her apron before pulling me over to sit at the kitchen table.

"That is true," she said. "Claire's younger and she's far more responsible than I was at her age. And you're far more impetuous than your daddy."

I didn't know what *impetuous* meant, but I had a feeling it wasn't good.

"Listen," she said, leaning forward to clasp my hand. "Ups and downs are part of relationships. Are you sure you've thought this through? Who broke it off?"

I peeled my eyes from the enamel surface of the table to hazard a glance at her. "Mrs. Crockett didn't say?"

"No. She said Claire was very mysterious about it. Which is why I'm asking you."

"Claire needs to stay with her family," I said. "To help take care of them."

"Of course she does. And she will when you get back. Until then, you know Louise and the girls have me. And their big brother, and the neighbors, and everyone at church to look after them."

"Mama, I really don't want to talk about this."

"Well, that's too bad. Because I need to know what's going on with my son and my best friend's daughter!"

I lowered my head, fingers digging into my hair.

"Claire wants to stay. And I—I ain't sure I wanna go to seminary. Or even live in Mobile." It was the closest I could come to saying I didn't want either of those things without fear that she'd tell Daddy or that I might hurt her feelings. "And I don't wanna talk about it 'cause I don't have any answers. And I definitely don't wanna talk to Daddy about it."

She sat back in the vinyl-covered chair. When she didn't say anything, I glanced up at her.

"All right," she said at last. "Maybe I understand. You will need to tell your daddy at some point. Because I will not be accused of keeping something from him again."

I nodded, head in my hands.

"Son, just know that I'm fine with you taking the time you need to make decisions. And know, too, that if you aren't ready to start seminary next fall . . . there's nothing to say you can't defer a year. Lots of students do that. Lord knows, there's enough noise in the world for a person to want to seek a little stillness here and there. And a lot can happen in twelve short months."

I skipped the back-to-school dance. Claire did too. I spent all night wondering what she was doing, thinking maybe I ought to just go over to her house so we could listen to the radio together, at least . . . and then thinking that was stupid because we might as well have gone to the dance then.

Which we couldn't, because we weren't dating.

I didn't know the right thing to do. I only knew that I missed her, even though I saw her every school day and sometimes for a while after.

Billy was the only one of us who went to the dance, and only because Claire informed him two weeks before that she'd asked the girl he secretly liked on his behalf, that her favorite flowers were roses, and to pick her up at seven.

The day she told him this, Billy—the Murphy High track star known as the Ginger Streak—practically fainted on the way home from school, he was hyperventilating so bad.

On September 26, five days after the dance, President Roosevelt ordered a complete scrap metal embargo against Japan after its invasion of French Indochina. On the twenty-seventh, Japan, Italy, and Germany signed a pact formalizing their alliance.

That night, Cowboy's first college football game against Spring Hill took place at our high school stadium. It was the first night game in the university's history. I slipped out of the house that evening without saying where I was headed. There was no way I was missing that game and no way I wasn't watching it with Hank.

The Crimson Tide crushed Spring Hill 26–0, and even though Cowboy was a freshman, Alabama was so far ahead by the fourth quarter, he got to play.

Hank, Billy, and me went crazy.

Everyone did.

We didn't get to the next games against Mercer and Howard on account of them being played in Tuscaloosa. But Alabama shut out both those teams too, and Cowboy played in the fourth quarter of each one.

I saved a copy of the newspaper every morning after one of Cowboy's games. Reading his name in the article, seeing him praised as an up-and-coming young quarterback and "player with great potential" made me feel like I was rubbing elbows with someone famous, and I wanted to shout to everyone I saw that I knew him.

Hank became more popular than ever despite having turned down our high school football coach's efforts to recruit him. But Hank wasn't one for regular practices, and there was too much work at the mill—especially with Cowboy in college.

That October, registration for the draft began. On October 29, the first number was drawn at noon: 158.

The next day, Hank and me had to stay late after school for getting caught shooting spitballs in algebra. Which no one usually minded, except that Frances Purdue just happened to get one in the ear that the nurse had to dig out with tweezers. Not only had Claire and Billy not waited for us, but they'd left a note on the rack where our bikes should be.

Got tired of waiting.

"What d'you make of all this draft business?" I asked Hank on our way home. He was older than me and Billy and would be the first one of us to register for the draft if it was still going on in two years.

"I dunno."

"What if you get drafted?"

"I'll look real good in uniform." Hank licked his fingers and smoothed back his hair.

I chuckled. "Private Wright."

"What, I don't strike you as military material?"

"I know how much you love rules."

"What? I'd be a good soldier!"

"You ain't thinkin' of enlistin'?"

"What? Nah. The mill's doing good. An' Cowboy's havin' a great season with an even better one comin' next year. I don't want a draft or a war to ruin that for him. My big brother's a star, you know that?"

"Oh, I know." The only one busting his buttons more than me was Hank himself. And maybe his daddy.

"Things are lookin' up, Prop! Our family's doin' better than it has since my mama got sick." He glanced at me. "You know?"

"Yeah," I said. "I can see that."

"Why, you thinkin' of enlistin'? I heard you weren't so keen on seminary." It's the closest he'd ever come to asking about me and Claire.

I shrugged.

"Say . . ." Hank kicked a rock along the curb. "If all you want is to get away from home, you know you can come live at our house if you ever need to."

I shook my head, imagining just how well *that* would go over.

"I mean it. We're brothers."

"I know. Thanks, Hank."

He squinted up at the sun like he might say more, but then shook his head as though deciding against it.

I spent that fall fishing and crabbing with Billy and Hank. Claire, too, sometimes, though those occasions became more and more rare. Daddy hadn't talked about seminary lately, even after I told him Claire and me broke up. He didn't ask questions, which made me wonder if Mama told him something, and he didn't ask if we could still work it out, which made me wonder if he'd never thought Claire was good enough.

Which made me miss her that much more.

I still went over to the Crocketts' on Sunday nights to listen to *The Shadow*, and sometimes after school. More than once while we were sitting on the living room floor, I nearly took her hand. And every time I saw her, I wished I could kiss her. Even wondered a few times what she'd do if I tried.

But I didn't, not knowing if her feelings for me had changed.

The thought sent me into a panic.

Claire was all I knew. I could be brave enough to go anywhere with her by my side. Try anything. Do anything.

But without her . . . Did I even want to leave Mobile, if it meant leaving her?

The Crimson Tide didn't have a perfect season—they lost to Tennessee and ended a winning season with a 13–0 loss to undefeated Mississippi State. But Cowboy had proven himself in four shutout wins. I never saw Hank grin as much as he did that season or carry his head so high. Even the McGill players, when they drove by our school or we saw them at the Woolworth's soda fountain, clapped Hank on the shoulder and talked about Cowboy.

Billy asked Nora Sue to the winter ball. It would be their second date but the first one he asked her out on himself, and I was shocked when he didn't break out in hives. But even more surprised when I learned Hank had asked Ginny Pruitt—one of the most popular cheerleaders—to the ball. I snickered every time I thought of Hank trying to cut a rug at the dance. Would've gone just to see it too. Only problem was that every time I thought of asking someone, I remembered Claire in her blue dress, looking like Vivien Leigh. Riding down the street on some kid's bike, her high heels in the basket.

Throwing herself into my arms at the end of the fight.

No girl would ever compare. I knew that for sure.

And sure as I knew that, I knew I couldn't let her go.

I spent all night awake, finally sleeping a few fitful minutes before it was time to get up for my Saturday morning route. I staggered through the rest of the day like a dummy, almost dozing off at supper as Mama talked about some new restaurant on the causeway.

"Lola Penington said they have the best fried oysters she's had in years," Mama said. "Palmer's, I think it's called."

"Well, I happen to know someone who has a birthday coming up," Daddy said.

He didn't mean me; Mama's birthday was December 16, two days before mine. It was the reason, she told me once, that she made sure I always had separate presents for my birthday and Christmas. "None of this 'this is your birthday and your Christmas present too' baloney," she'd said, even though Daddy accused her every year of spoiling me.

"We'll take Jimmy and celebrate both our birthdays," Mama said cheerfully.

"It's fine. I don't wanna go," I said.

If Claire and me were still together, I could've taken her there for my birthday—or hers in January. Or for Valentine's Day.

In fact, there was nothing I wanted more.

I went stock-still.

There was *nothing* I wanted more.

Claire had said moving across the bay wouldn't be far enough away for me. But she was wrong. Living anywhere other than where she was would be too far away for me.

Daddy used to preach something about a man gaining the world but losing his soul.

And I felt like I was on the verge of losing mine.

I leapt to my feet, heart pounding. "Can I be excused?"

I left the table without waiting for an answer, ran out the door, and grabbed my bike.

All the way to the Crocketts' house, I felt new, invigorated, the cool December air slapping me in the face as though to say, "Wake up, knucklehead!"

And I had been—a knucklehead. Afraid of standing up to Daddy and holding my own. The only option to flee.

But I was more afraid of being without her.

Which is why I'd settle down across the bay if it meant keeping her in my life. Stay right here in Mobile. Heck, we could move in with her family, even, if she wanted. Why not? She'd be with her mama and sisters, and Billy and me would be brothers just like he wanted. I'd go to work for Alcoa or the Alabama Drydock and Shipbuilding Company or anyplace that would pay me to work. Whatever it was, whatever came, no matter how many times I had to go toe to toe with Daddy, it would all be okay because Claire would be beside me.

And she was wrong about me growing to resent her. The only thing I'd ever resent is three more months without her.

I flew up the left strip of the Crocketts' double-track driveway, surprised to see the mill truck parked by the shop. Hank was working later than usual.

I leaned my bike against the side of the house and let myself in through the kitchen door, where I found Claire opening a Coke.

She looked so beautiful in her pale-pink sweater, her hair done up in a ribbon.

"Jimmy!" she said, looking startled as I took the Coke from her and set it beside a second one on the table. "What are you doin' here?"

I took her by the arms. "I came to talk to you. I need to talk to you," I said, out of breath.

"Who's here?" someone called from the living room. Claire pulled away as Cowboy appeared in the archway to the kitchen, his face splitting into a grin. "Hey, Jimmy!"

"Cowboy!" I exclaimed. I grinned and moved to shake his hand, surprised to see him but feeling lucky to have bumped into him. This night just kept getting better and better. "You back for Christmas?"

"Yup. Finished the semester a little early and thought I'd put my feet up, but they've been workin' me like a dog at the mill." He gave a lopsided smile. I noticed he wasn't wearing dungarees, though. He was dressed nicer than I was used to seeing him, in a button-up shirt and sweater-vest. But then again, all eyes were on him these days.

"Wow, that sure is some season you just came off of."

"Except for that last game. I have to say, that one stung." He chuckled.

"Care to join us for a Coke?" Claire asked.

"Sure, why not?" I said, thirsty after sprinting here so fast.

I started to go out to the shop to get one, but Claire said, "I've got an extra in the Frigidaire."

"Oh, swell," I said as she got it out. She opened it and handed it to me. "Thanks."

She sat down at the kitchen table and I moved to join her, Cowboy leaning in the archway.

But as I guzzled my Coke over small talk, something didn't seem right.

The Crocketts never kept Cokes in the refrigerator, except when they were expecting company. But if they knew Cowboy was coming, then where was Billy? He should've been here hanging on every word Cowboy had to say about the Alabama football season, demanding the play-by-play of every game. For that matter, where were Claire's sisters? All three of 'em had a crush on Cowboy the size of Texas.

I got to my feet. "You know—I just . . . is Hank in the shop?" I gestured over my shoulder.

"No," Cowboy said, scratching the back of his neck. "I ain't exactly sure what he's up to tonight. Probably safe to say, getting in trouble somewhere."

Mrs. Crockett came down the stairs into the living room with a basket of sewing and, on seeing me, made straight for the kitchen.

"Jimmy!" she said, a little too brightly.

"Hi, Mrs. Crockett."

"Are you looking for Billy?"

"I—" No. "Yeah, actually, he around?"

"He's out in the shop putting up some new shelves. Let's see if we can find him." She put down her basket and steered me outside.

Now I knew something was terribly wrong. I glanced back through the kitchen door on my way out in time to see Claire head to the living room with her Coke, Cowboy in her wake.

Out on the driveway, Mrs. Crockett turned toward me in the twilight.

"Jimmy, honey, I don't know how to say this . . ." she said, her expression tight.

"What's Cowboy doing here?"

"He came to call on Claire."

"Call on . . ."

"Honey," she said gently. "They're dating."

Just then Cowboy emerged from the back door, the screen door slapping behind him as he crossed to where we stood, hands in his pockets.

"Ma'am, d'you mind if I talk to Jimmy for a minute, man to man?"

She lifted her palms. "You two go ahead," she said, looking relieved as she went on to the shop.

I studied the ground between us as it fell away beneath me.

"Jimmy, listen. Claire just told me you probably didn't know that she and I've been seein' one another."

"No," I heard myself say. "I didn't. How, uh . . . how long have you two . . ."

"Just a few weeks. I was real sorry to hear you two broke up and thought for sure you and her were gonna get back together. But, well, seein' as you hadn't, I gotta be honest with you. When I came home for Thanksgiving, I took a chance and asked her out. We've written once or twice since then and, well, I'd be lyin' if I said she wasn't the reason I came back for Christmas early."

I couldn't believe this was happening. He was looking down at his feet and kicking dirt as he explained. Cowboy Wright, the Murphy High golden boy.

And me—what could I do?

"I know you and Claire've been best friends all your lives," he said. "And that you truly care for her. I also know she thinks the world of you. Which is why I'm tellin' you I came over tonight to ask her to go steady. I hope I have your blessin'."

My blessing.

I couldn't compete with Cowboy.

Got tired of waiting.

"You don't need my blessin'," I said. "It's not like you're gettin' married."

"All the same, thanks, Jimmy. I respect you. You know that."

I nodded, stupidly, as he shook my hand. Mumbled something about it being mutual.

I don't remember what I said to Mrs. Crockett as I stumbled toward my bike.

I took off down the street. Rode aimlessly for an hour.

When I finally got home, my mama asked what was wrong as I strode through the living room.

"Nothin'," I said.

"Jimmy!"

I didn't stop or answer. I just shut my bedroom door and climbed into my bed, shoes and all.

The next afternoon Billy came to see me.

"Why didn't you tell me?" I asked, not looking at him. He sighed and leaned back against the wall where he sat across from me on my bedroom floor.

"I didn't know for sure 'til last night, and Claire didn't say."

"Don't matter. We broke up. She can do what she wants. You probably like having Cowboy around anyway."

"So would you," he said.

That was true. Just not like this.

"So now what?" Billy asked.

I'd spent all night thinking of the "now what." Tortured at the idea of Cowboy holding Claire's hand. Kissing her. Doing everything with her that we had done. Maybe more.

In the end, I only knew a few things.

Cowboy was in college. He might not have time for a high school girl—especially with so many girls throwing themselves at him, as I'm sure they were already doing. And in a year he could get drafted.

I felt like a heel thinking each of these things, but they were all true.

I promised God if I was ever lucky enough to get a second chance with Claire, I wouldn't lose her twice.

For now, I'd pray and wait.

25

MAY 12, 1942

UNKNOWN LOCATION, PHILIPPINES

The familiar weight of a loaded Springfield is back in my hands as we bounce along with ten other soldiers in the back of the truck. My belly's rounded from two meals in the same day. My wound hurts, but it's closed and clean.

Hank sits behind the cab, rifle across his knees, a pistol and three grenades on his belt, cigarette glowing between his fingers.

He up-nods to Bandanna, who's sitting beside me. "Prop, this is Walt from Beaumont, Texas. His daddy's an oil man."

I nod and reach out to shake Walt's hand.

"Jimmy," I say.

"You from Mobile too?"

"Same town, same school, ever since third grade," Hank says. "Practically brothers."

The truck abruptly turns off the road, rumbles down a shallow embankment.

We follow the other men out the back as Felipa emerges from the cab, rifle under her arm. She gestures toward the truck and the men set to work hacking at a thicket. Within minutes they've scrubbed out our tracks and camouflaged the truck.

230

Felipa signals for two groups. Walt gestures us over to him. He cradles a grenade launcher over his shoulder as we crouch in the brush, ears trained up the road.

If all goes straight, we'll take care of the convoy and arrive in Santa Rita by midnight.

And then . . .

I can't think about that. I imagine Billy scorching in this afternoon heat. His days ticking away.

A rumble of vehicles in the distance. Walt, closest to the road, lifts a hand. I flick the safety off my rifle.

He holds up four fingers. His signal is mirrored by Felipa across the road.

Four trucks, not six.

The engines grow louder, downshift as they approach the bend. I can see them now, the driver and armed man in each cab. Two guards riding on the back of each load.

Walt shoves through the bushes, grenade launcher on his shoulder. He marches straight to the center of the road in full view of the oncoming trucks. Another man follows him with a rifle. I expect the Japanese to shoot, wonder what's supposed to happen if Walt goes down. Instead, the trucks speed up, come right at them, bearing down.

A hundred yards. Seventy-five. Fifty.

With a snap and a hiss, the grenade springs from Walt's launcher and slams into the first truck's grill.

It explodes in a ball of fire, sends the truck swerving, engine ablaze. "Now!" another man yells.

We open fire. Brakes squeal as the first vehicle goes rolling. The second truck flips over in its wake, follows it into the ditch. The two behind it skid to a stop at an angle. Guards jump off the back, take cover, and open fire. We blast back, aiming for their foreheads.

An enemy soldier flies back. Another falls to the road, screaming.

It's over in less than five minutes.

"Get those trucks started!" Felipa orders. "Unload the two in the ditch!"

We scramble from the brush onto the road. One of the guerillas is limping, blood pouring down his pant leg, but everyone else seems fine. Walt moves from body to body, kicking and shooting the dead just to be sure. Another man climbs into the closest truck and tries to start it, but the engine won't turn over.

"C'mon," Hank says, waving me toward the vehicle, weapon drawn.

Weak as we are, it takes both of us to tug the driver's body from the cab. I'm about to climb inside the truck when Hank says, "What now?" and strides off toward the vehicle on the road in front of us, where one of the guerillas has propped open the hood to fumble in the engine compartment.

Someone shouts.

The man stands frozen near the hood, a wire in his hand.

"Ambush!" Walt bellows, mouth stretched wide.

He's barely gotten the word out when the fella in front of the hood explodes in a stew of body parts.

The blast sends me flying into the ditch. I cover my head, ears ringing. Machine-gun fire pelts the road above me, but I can't make sense of where it's coming from.

"Hank!" I yell, twisting around to search for him.

A mortar shell flies onto the road and explodes. A man's torso lands right in front of me. I search that face, terrified of what—who—I might see.

It's Walt.

"Hank!" I shout.

I rise up but can't see where the fire's coming from—can't see anything through the smoke.

"Prop!" From across the road. Hank.

Bullets *ting* off axle wells.

A convoy of trucks roars toward us, stops at the blaze on the road, brakes squealing.

I lurch away from the ditch, ready to hightail it into the forest. But as I turn, three Japanese soldiers appear like ghosts from the brush, rifles trained on me. I glance back at the road as more jump out of the new trucks—six of 'em apiece.

There's nowhere to run.

"Hands up!" one of them barks.

I look frantically for Hank. For Felipa, any of the guerillas.

"Hands up! Now!"

I slowly set my rifle down and back up the ditch toward the road, hands in the air.

26

A rifle butt wallops me in the back and I go down. Gravel bites my cheek. And then they're on me, kicking me in the ribs and face, jumping on my legs and hips.

Jabbering above me. A string of guttural orders. The beating ends with a hard kick to the kidney.

Someone hauls me to my feet and ties my hands behind my back so tightly my fingers feel like sausages. They bind my ankles and then lug me into the back of a truck. My head hits the metal side. The enemy climbs in around me so close I can smell the mud and dried blood on their boots, cigarette smoke and whatever they ate for lunch on rancid breath.

The motor starts and I close my eyes tight.

This can't happen. I have to find Hank. Get to Santa Rita.

Back to O'Donnell.

If I don't make it, Billy's dead. If Hank returns without me, I got no faith that the Crate will let Billy go even if Hank carries out the mission.

The engine shifts gears. Tires hum on packed-dirt road. I try to keep track of the distance. Count the seconds—three hundred. One thousand. Five thousand. Six.

But I lose track as the numbers fall away into a refrain in my head: *Not like this. Can't go like this. Not now.*

I can't do this to my mama. Can't do this to Billy's—or his sisters.

The truck slows to a stop. Doors slam and the tailgate opens. I get shoved out of the truck and fall to the ground. Grimace as rough hands drag me to the shade of a thatched roof, boots scraping the dirt.

I land on my knees before a squat wooden desk. The figure behind it barks an order.

"Hai!" The soldier behind me bows and disappears. He returns a moment later with two other men, one of whom is wearing glasses.

"Hello," the one in the glasses says. "My commander demands to know where your leader is. The woman they call Felipa Culala. Where is she?"

"I don't know," I say.

He translates and the man behind the desk snarls a response.

"So you admit you were . . . fighting for her? This woman, Felipa Culala?" Glasses asks.

"No. I—no."

Glasses gives a curt nod. The one who dragged me in here punches me in the mouth. I sag, head spinning.

"The commander demands your answer. Where is Felipa Culala?" he says lightly, almost polite.

I shake my head slightly, working my jaw. "I don't know."

Another fist, this time to the gut.

"If you do not answer the commander's questions, your punishment will be . . . severe."

"I'm tellin' the truth! I don't know!"

I brace for another blow. Instead, I'm forced backward onto a board and rough-tied to it. I kick and twist as a strap tightens around my throat and another around my head. Around my legs and ankles, arms and wrists. Cinched tight. I can't move.

I'm hefted, board and all, onto the edge of something with a jarring thud.

The first gush of water hits me like the splash by the edge of a pool. Cool and shocking, but not unwelcome.

Except it keeps coming, gushing over my nose and mouth. I sputter and twist against the ropes, haul in a breath that's nothing but water and gulp for air. Except there ain't any—just water and more water until my limbs jerk and my vision starts to go black.

Next thing I know, I'm upright and puking like a geyser.

"Where is the woman?" the translator asks. "Tell us now."

I haul in a wheezing breath. "I don't know."

They lower the board.

And then I'm choking again, struggling to turn my head, straining against the straps.

They stop and I gasp painfully, try to suck in air. Again with the question.

"I—told you . . ."

They lower the board. Pour the water.

They raise me up, ask the question.

Again, and then again, and again.

Near the end, I can't help thinking how upside down it is that I'm about to drown when I've been thirsty so long.

It takes some time for me to realize that I've been unstrapped. I squint up at the sun as I'm dragged across the compound to a smaller hut.

It smells like diarrhea, a scent I know all too well.

One of the guards cinches a heavy belt around my waist. I'm forced to kneel, a bamboo pole shoved behind my knees. Another guard threads a second belt through the binding at my ankles, fastens it to the one around my waist.

They loop a rope through the binding of my wrists, hoist my arms up behind me until I start to come off the ground, legs folded beneath me. I think my shoulders might rip from the sockets.

It takes everything I got not to scream.

Lastly, one of them ties a heavy stone around my waist, resting on my thighs.

A final kick sends me swaying, pain blazing like lightning behind my eyes.

The bamboo door slaps shut. I am alone.

I push up against the stone, try to relieve the agony in my shoulders until my thighs begin to shake . . . and then to burn. I drop down an inch. Pain shoots down my arms. The bamboo pole behind my knees feels like it's prying them apart.

"Come back," I say hoarsely.

The muscles of my neck have begun to spasm. I push up a few inches once more, sputter, and hold it as long as I can . . . until I drop back down with a gasp.

I try to count, but every second feels like an hour. Every minute a lifetime. I try to recite the pledge of allegiance. Find myself rushing through the words, the syllables jumbling together.

My breath is shallow, serrated as a knife.

And all I can think is that if I'd gone to seminary, I'd be home asleep right now in bed.

Instead, for all I know Hank's dead and I'm about to die alone.

I try to pray the Lord's Prayer.

Finally, I just pray for this to end.

I'm so sorry, Billy.

Somewhere in the darkness, I dream of blackberries . . . the sticky ripe scent of them, the grit of seeds stuck in my teeth. Blackberries staining Claire's lips, which was the best way I liked to taste them.

She thought it was funny when she turned my mouth purple too, and she'd laugh as I pulled away.

This time, I kiss her until it's gone.

I scream when they untie my arms. Again when they throw me to the ground outside.

"The commander demands to know what is your association with Felipa Culala?"

I don't answer. What's the point?

A boot slams into my chest. I topple backward, my back seizing.

And then they're tying me to another board, my arms spread wide. I think I'm gonna get crucified for real this time.

I'm left alone again, this time in the middle of the compound, staring at the sky.

The sun blazes overhead. I wish I had a mouthful of the water they nearly drowned me with. I think of Billy chained to the stake. Has it been three days now? Four?

It seems only right that I should be here, suffering the same.

I close my eyes but can't block out the bright red light through my eyelids. The skin on my face has tightened.

At some point a shadow looms above me, blocking out the sun. I peel open my eyes. It's the same man who strung me up in the hut. No translator this time.

He holds up a small bucket of water. Dumps it in my face. It ain't cold, but it's wet. I open my mouth.

But it ain't water.

I sputter and spit urine to the sound of his laughter.

He leaves me alone in the middle of the compound. Insects buzz in my ears. Settle on my nose, crawl across my face.

The sun beats down.

No one comes, except the flies.

By the time the sun slants low in the sky, my skin is blistered raw. The shadows lengthen and the heat abates, but only a little.

This is my punishment for leaving home. For not believing in God better.

For believing in God at all.

Dusk comes, too late. My body retains the heat of the day, a broiling welter of pain.

Let me die.

27

May 13, 1942
Unknown Location, Philippines

By nightfall, I'm shivering—from the heat in my skin, the cool of the air. From pain. Thirst.

In the last hour alone, I have pleaded with and spat on God. Affirmed and renounced my faith. Cursed my father and cried for my mama. Wished I'd told Claire goodbye.

That I'd never left.

By the time I feel a rap on my shoulder, I don't know anything for sure anymore.

It comes again. Not a blow, just tapping. The interpreter and a soldier stand over me, the soldier's rifle leveled at my head.

I wait for him to pull the trigger.

Instead, he bends down and unties me.

I try to move, but my arms ain't my own.

"You must eat this," the interpreter says, holding up a bowl as the guard bends down and pushes me upright.

I cry out, and then grimace. Refuse to open my mouth as the interpreter attempts to spoon rice into it. I don't know why they'd feed me except to keep me alive for another round of torture.

I won't let that happen.

"As you wish," he says, setting the bowl aside. "You must stand now."

The interpreter snaps something in Japanese and the guard pulls me to my feet.

I hobble forward, ready to lunge for the one with the rifle. To make sure he puts a bullet in my brain.

"Come with me," the interpreter says. He leads me toward the gates.

I know what's outside. After a month of grave detail, I know the drill.

The thought fills me with relief until I think of the rice. Japanese captors ain't in the habit of offering dead men last meals.

A truck idles on the drive outside the gate. A guard waits by the lowered tailgate. I hesitate and am pushed forward by the rifle at my back.

"Get in," the interpreter says. I climb in slowly, but of my own accord.

The guard gets in after me, thumps the side of the truck. It lurches and rumbles down the road.

"Where we goin'?" I rasp.

He grunts something in Japanese.

We drive for an hour, maybe two, jostling along dirt roads.

Finally, the brakes squeal and we come to a stop. The truck door opens and slams shut. A soldier comes around, drops the tailgate. The guard nudges me with his rifle. I climb out and he follows me into the night air.

So this is it.

I tell myself my mamaw is waiting for me. Maybe Billy too. For all I know, Hank died in the ambush, and they're both cussing me from the other side for taking so long.

I wonder how they'll do it: here on the road, or somewhere off in the brush, where no one but animals will find my body.

But the soldiers don't seem in any hurry. We just stand there, the truck idling.

Five minutes go by. The blood is flowing in my hands and fingers again, pin-prickling to painful life. It hurts to breathe; I reckon I got at least one cracked rib.

A motor rumbles toward us in the dark. A few minutes later, a truck swings up the road, headlights out, and stops some fifty feet away.

Someone gets out in the darkness. I can't see his face. He goes around back and pulls something from the truck—a gunnysack. He hauls it half the distance between us, leaves it on the ground, and goes back to the truck. Gears grind. The truck turns and heads back the direction it came, rounds the corner, and is gone.

The first driver says something to the guard beside me. The guard answers, and the driver pulls out a pistol, shoves it in my face. I don't move as the guard strides over to the gunnysack and unties the string. He flicks his lighter to life and peers inside the sack. A second later the light flicks off and he carries the sack back to the truck. He opens the cab, slings it inside, and gets in after it, slamming the door shut.

The driver pushes me to my knees. He mumbles something, and I cross my legs at the ankles. Bow my head.

Our Father, who art in heaven . . .

The revolver clicks. I wait for the boom to deafen my ears. To silence my senses.

Instead, I hear footsteps.

I crack open an eye and see the driver hurrying back to the truck. He gets in.

The truck roars into gear, swings around, and heads away.

An owl hoots from the trees. Crickets chirp in the ditch.

I am alone in the dark.

The gravel digs into my knees. I uncross my ankles, sit back on my butt. And then lie down in the middle of the road. Alone.

28

Cowboy came to church with Claire every Sunday he was home that winter. For the first time in my life, I was glad to be seated in the front row with Mama. At least that way I couldn't see the two of them sitting together.

Meanwhile, I'd never seen Daddy in such form, on fire at the pulpit. It was January 12, the first Sunday after the president's State of the Union address. I hadn't heard it, but I'd watched my daddy making notes in the margins of the following morning's paper about the president's remarks on freedom of speech, freedom of worship, freedom from want, and freedom from fear.

Daddy had a lot to say about what God thought of each of those things and preached well past noon. I sat through the sermon, stomach growling, plagued by the thought of Cowboy and Claire together. I wondered if they had kissed yet and, if so, how many times. If the sighs that haunted my sleep were the same with him . . . or sweeter.

Cowboy left that afternoon to go back to college and I breathed a little easier. But even though Claire and I still walked to and from school like usual, things were anything but normal, the conversation superficial and strained. I sensed her looking at me when we spoke but had a hard time meeting her gaze. Because even though she'd been my best friend since childhood, she was something else now.

She was Cowboy's girlfriend.

Hank made a point of meeting me when work was slow and the weather was warm to toss the football around. I wondered if he understood a sliver of what I was going through; I hadn't forgotten the way he'd held her in his arms after her daddy died.

That February, Hank, Billy, and me snuck off to see the Mardi Gras parade—a thing forbidden by Daddy and frowned upon by our church as an all-too-easy opportunity to give in to the lusts of the flesh.

Never mind that everyone in the church knew of members who gave in to such desires on a regular basis without a parade.

I marveled at the crowds, the elaborate floats, like mythical beasts and royal courts. The fantastic costumes that must have taken a year to make: knights and jesters, kings and queens. We ended up at a party near Spring Hill College with a bunch of boys from McGill, who Hank had become popular with on account of him being Cowboy's brother. I drank my first beer that night. But the effects, like the fun, were far too short-lived.

It was our last semester of high school and even though it felt like everything should be changing, so much felt the same. President Roosevelt had begun a third term in office. I'd sent off my application to Southern, if only to buy myself more time. And Claire rushed home after school to check the mail and disappeared completely the weekends Cowboy managed to get a ride back from Tuscaloosa.

I was miserable those weekends but held out hope. A future without Claire was unfathomable. So I waited. For Cowboy to meet another girl in college—maybe a cheerleader. For Claire to get fed up with the long-distance relationship.

A week later my hopes were realized when, on the way to school, it dawned on me that neither Claire nor Hank had said a single word, while Billy rambled on about the new *Captain America* comic.

"He's got a buddy named Bucky and he's punching Hitler on the cover. Captain America is, not Bucky . . ."

"Cowboy's gonna enlist," Hank blurted.

I stopped in my tracks, trying to parse what he just said, and then took several long strides to catch up.

"For real?"

Hank nodded.

I remembered Cowboy talking about it, but that was before his first Alabama football season made him a minor celebrity. And though plenty of boys tossed around the idea, Eugene was the only one of our friends who had actually enlisted so far.

"But what about college? What about football?" I asked.

What about Claire?

I glanced at her, but she looked away.

Hank shrugged. "He's dropping out."

"He's not dropping out. He's taking a leave," Claire murmured, still not looking at us.

"I don't get it," Billy said, staring at the ground in front of his feet. "Why not just wait to get drafted?"

"He don't want to wait. Says this way he'll be able to choose," Hank said.

"Choose—what?" I asked.

"Air Corps. All he can talk about is planes. How there's gonna be more than ever and they're gonna decide this war. I just found out he's been takin' flyin' lessons up in Tuscaloosa as part of some new program."

My mind was spinning with the implications—for him. For Claire. For me.

"Well, he'll do you real proud," I said at last. "All of us. He always does."

Hank just nodded, looking miserable.

I didn't know what it felt like to have a sibling leave. But I imagined it would feel like having Billy or Hank enlist without me.

In which case I'd be miserable too.

"When does he ship out?" I asked.

"He promised to be here for prom," Claire said, squinting against the sun, her eyes puffy.

I wanted to put my arms around her. Tell her I was here and that I wasn't going anywhere.

I couldn't, of course—not yet. But dang if my shoulders didn't feel lighter as I inhaled what felt like the first full breath I'd taken in months.

I couldn't concentrate in school, already thinking about Claire's lips against mine. About when I'd tell Daddy I wasn't going to Southern after all, no longer afraid of how he'd react. I'd have Claire, and that was all that mattered. We'd start a new life together.

And then a thought struck me in the middle of class that sent a cold spike through my spine.

What if she couldn't feel the same for me as before? She was upset Cowboy was leaving. But she'd only been with him because she thought our futures were incompatible.

Right?

Or did she like being with Alabama's up-and-coming all-American quarterback? Cowboy wasn't just the first boy in his family to graduate high school but the first to go to college. The kind of boy who would always be successful—not just because he was smart but because he had an easy way about him that made people like him.

I'd never had that.

But most of all, I would never have the kind of conviction driving him to leave everything he had going for him behind in order to enlist. I did not own that kind of courage and wondered if I ever would.

Still, when Cowboy was gone, if Claire would have me, I'd do my best to make her happy.

"I heard Opal Boyington and that Eugene fella broke up before he shipped out," Daddy said over supper that night. He never expressed interest in what was going on with the kids we knew. But then again, Opal's daddy was a deacon.

Daddy looked up from his plate when Mama failed to respond with her usual "Oh really?" the way she so often did, her voice rising and falling in gentle surprise, when she was really just being polite. I wondered if she'd heard about Cowboy.

"If you feel you simply must attend prom, why not ask Opal?" Daddy said, poking at his chicken and dumplings. "I'll even pay for the tickets."

I opened my mouth, on the cusp of saying I'd already asked someone else or didn't plan to go—I wasn't sure which—but then shrugged.

"Okay," I said. Because it didn't make any difference. And I wasn't above one small gesture to make Daddy happy with me, maybe for the last time.

He nodded. "Good."

I asked Opal the next day at school. She politely accepted. But I knew I wasn't who she really wanted to go with any more than she was who I wanted to take, and I felt bad for her.

That March, the U.S. started sending planes, tanks, ships, and food to Britain. Meanwhile, Billy had given me a new reason to flip past the headlines to the local news, as the Ginger Streak ran off with win after win in the first track meet of the season. Hank, Claire, and me practically flew off the bleachers, we cheered so hard.

It was almost like old times.

The first Saturday in April, Daddy loaned me one of his ties and insisted on driving Mama and me both to the Boyingtons', where I gave Opal a corsage and her mama pinned a boutonniere on my jacket, and Daddy and Mr. Boyington made small talk over sweet tea and fancy little sandwiches while Mama and Mrs. Boyington took pictures. And though Opal looked nice in her lavender dress and her mama's pearls, I was anxious to get tonight over with . . . and the next six after that.

Cowboy was shipping out in a week, and I couldn't wait to tell Claire all the things I'd meant to say the night I found him at her house.

That night, Daddy dropped Opal and me off at the high school just as Billy pulled into the parking lot in the Crocketts' truck with Lola Maine, whom he'd asked out after Nora Sue started dating someone else and broke his heart.

The gym had been transformed by streamers and decorations, a big OVER THE RAINBOW banner painted in bright colors, a long table set with a big punch bowl and platter piled with cookies, and a band playing on a makeshift stage at the other end.

I smoothed back my hair, self-conscious. I didn't have Cowboy's dimples, which were the same ones Hank deployed like a secret weapon whenever he talked to girls. I wasn't as tall as him or as muscular.

But I loved Claire Crockett with all my heart. And that night when she walked in on Cowboy's arm in her long dress and bare shoulders, she took my breath away.

"Well, the gang's all here," Hank said, coming over to observe the spectacle as Claire and Cowboy were waylaid by members of the football team, Cowboy hailed as returning hero.

I'd never seen Hank—who'd come with popular girl Arlene Banks—dressed up before. Neither, apparently, had Opal, who couldn't take her eyes off him.

I'd seen that look on girls' eyes around him most of my life.

When they finally made it over, Cowboy shook my hand and slapped Billy on the shoulder, grinning.

"It's a good night, boys!" he said. And I couldn't help but smile back.

"We don't have to stay for the whole thing," Claire said.

"Are you kidding?" he said, sweeping her toward the dance floor. "This is my last prom. No way I'm leavin' early."

We danced more that night than I had at all the dances combined, Billy and me guffawing and then shaking our heads in amazement as Hank bebopped with his date across the floor. They were nearly as smooth as Cowboy and Claire—who was the only reason I knew any moves at all.

At the end of the night, we hooted and hollered as Hank and Helen Humphrey were announced prom king and queen. Arlene looked jealous enough to spit as Hank led Helen out to dance like they were at some royal court, Billy and me gassing it up as he glanced back and wiggled his brows.

At some point during the dance, Cowboy strolled to the edge of the stage to make a request as the rest of the prom court joined Hank and Helen on the floor. I thought about going over to Claire where she was fidgeting with her glove. All night, I thought she'd looked both radiant and fragile at once. And oh so beautiful. I wanted to tell her. There'd be no harm in telling her, would there?

But before I could work up the courage, the song ended and the court returned to their dates—some of them looking uncomfortable and others flat-out jealous.

As the music died, the band fell quiet.

Heads turned in the silence, kids looking toward the stage to see what was up.

That's when I noticed Cowboy stepping into the clearing where Hank and the court had just been, hands in his pockets.

"What's he doing?" Billy whispered.

"Now, I don't have a microphone, so I'll just have to speak up," Cowboy started. "I promise y'all can go back to dancin' in a minute.

Those of you working on your second set of blisters already from your fancy shoes can thank me later."

Chuckles all around. Across the gathering, I spotted Hank watching his brother, brows drawn together.

"Some of you might've heard I've enlisted and am fixin' to ship out—next week, in fact . . . But there's one thing I need to do before I go." He held out a hand. "Claire Crockett, would you come here?"

Ahead of me, Claire raised a gloved hand to her heart, obviously startled. Looking down, she lifted her hem with one hand and moved to join him in the center of the gym.

"Just what is this about?" she said with a nervous laugh.

Cowboy took her hand, gently pulled the glove from it, and dropped to a knee.

Gasps all around. A few girls squealed.

"Claire Crockett . . ." Cowboy pulled his other hand from his pocket, something small clasped between his fingers.

A ring.

"Would you do me the honor of becoming my wife?"

The air went out of the room.

"Yes!" Claire exhaled with a joyous laugh as the gym erupted.

29

He's dead," a voice mutters above me.

"Roll him over. Make sure."

"Look what they done to him."

"Wait, he's still breathing."

They grab me by the shoulders. I hear myself groan—whether in pain or at the prospect of breathing one hour more, I ain't sure.

"Help me get him in the cab." And then, to me: "I got you, buddy."

They lift me up, slide me onto the seat of the truck until my head bumps into the ample hip of the driver. In the moonlight through the open window, I recognize the jawline above me.

"Hello, little man," Felipa says and pats me on the shoulder.

Hank swings in after me, tugs me upright, and closes the door. And I can't help the tears that run from the corners of my eyes as we rumble down the road.

Felipa murmurs something to him about one of my wounds. The one they cauterized is oozing.

"We're gonna get you somewhere safe, Prop. You hear me? Where you can heal up while I go take care of the mayor."

I try to wrap my brain around his words. If Hank's talking about the mayor, it ain't too late.

Hank unscrews a canteen and holds it to my lips.

I drink so greedily I start to choke. Feel like I'm drowning again and sputter. I been to so many extremes in the space of the last few hours, I don't even know which way is up. But one thing I do know.

"How long?" I ask, sucking in a breath.

"We left O'Donnell four days ago," Hank says, his mouth flattening into a tight line.

"Your friend will inform the commander that you died along the journey," Felipa says. "You're far too valuable to return to O'Donnell now."

"What? No—I gotta." Even as I say it, the thought of returning to that place fills me with dread.

But I can't let Hank go back alone. We can't split up.

All home alive.

"We lost a lot of men on the road yesterday," Felipa says. "I need more soldiers in my army."

I swallow hard. "Whatever you gave 'em, I promise I'll find a way to pay you back," I say, my voice raw.

Felipa laughs and pats my shoulder. "You have already paid me by not disclosing my whereabouts. Had you told them how to find me, we would not be here now. Nor would Alfonso"—she jerks her thumb toward the back of the truck—"have had the opportunity to negotiate as your 'uncle' for your release on behalf of your banker father in America."

"Banker? My daddy ain't a banker . . ." But then I understand.

"For as much as they would like to kill me, they liked the idea of money more. Your loyalty is greater than theirs, little man."

But that ain't true. I knew where her camp was but assumed everyone scattered after the hit on the convoy. If I'd known where she was, I would've told them just to make it all stop.

252

"How'd you find me?" I ask as Felipa slips a cigarette between her lips and lights up.

"One of the guards at the compound up north is on the commander's take," Hank says. "Word got out they were roughing up an American soldier. Figured it had to be you."

Felipa gestures to a duffel on the floor and Hank takes out a packet of banana leaves, feeds me bits of chicken and melon as we bump along. When he pulls out the whiskey to doctor my side, I grab the bottle from him long enough to drink a quarter of it down.

Dawn is spreading over the eastern hills like a bruise by the time we stop on the outskirts of town. I sit up painfully as Hank goes around back. I want nothing more than to lie down and never get up. Then I think again of Billy.

It's the fifth day.

As though reading my mind, Felipa turns toward me.

"You will not hear me, but I will say this anyway: You would be better off fighting with me. Your friend is likely dead. If you succeed in this mission, you will have carried out the wishes of your enemy and what will you have gained? You will die at O'Donnell. Fight with me, and at least you will die free. You are loyal. If your friend is as loyal to you, ask yourself if he would want you to lose your life for him. If the answer is no, the commander of O'Donnell has no leverage over you. You are free."

I picture Billy the day we left, telling us to go and not come back.

I squint at the rising sun. "We still gotta go."

Felipa sighs at the steering wheel. "So now listen. The Japanese garrison headquarters stands next to the public square. The mayor's house is across from the public-square park. The mayor is a fat man who lives alone with his housekeeper. You need not concern yourself with her. But be on guard—Japanese soldiers patrol the city at all hours. My man will meet you at the railroad bridge on the far side of town. If you are not at the bridge by dusk, he will leave without you. As for you and I, we will not see one another again." She leans over and kisses me on the mouth. "Go with God, little man."

I slowly slide out of the truck, will my legs to support me as I shut the door.

"Thank you," I say to Felipa through the open window. "For everything."

I move around back, where the bearded man I know now as Alfonso is loading Hank up with a rifle, the .38 pistol, a sheathed machete, and a short coil of rope in a gunnysack. Hank buckles on the machete, adds the pistol and rope to his pack. Slings it and the rifle over his shoulder.

"Let me carry somethin'," I say.

"You can barely walk," Hank says. "I still think you ought to let Alfonso here drop you off at the bridge to wait for me."

"Nothin' doin'," I say.

We nod our thanks as Alfonso climbs into the passenger's seat. Head out as they drive away.

At first, I think Hank might be right. My legs want nothing to do with holding me upright, let alone walking. My knees ache with every step, and pain shoots down my arms whenever I move them even to scratch my nose.

We make our way through a stubby field to a one-lane road and I worry I'm holding Hank up, but he don't say nothing.

It's light out by the time we come to a few rickety farmhouses and bamboo-walled shops with shaggy thatched roofs. An old man on a broken-down-looking motorbike putters by as the road widens, black smoke puffing out the tailpipe. We pass a schoolyard fenced in by a squat stone wall, a nipa roofing factory, and a row of little houses with laundry lines strung between them.

A sign stretches above the road ahead: SANTA RITA.

In town, we cut our way through a fenceless backyard, past telltale craters and the debris of several houses.

Up a narrow side road, we pass a tiny blue chapel. Two girls walk ahead of us in frayed school uniforms. Neither one of them wears shoes. A bare-legged boy trails after them in only a T-shirt.

Hank points to the park ahead. We duck down behind a stone wall. He peers over the top. "That's the garrison headquarters. Two guards out front."

"You see the house?"

He glances again and nods. "That must be it, over there."

We move from tree to tree through the park. The guards are out of view by the time we reach the walk in front of the mayor's house. There's a two-tone 1939 Buick parked out front, and we crouch in front of its sweeping fender.

Hank retrieves the pistol and snaps the safety off.

"Ready?"

I nod. But just as he takes my arm to help me stand, two figures—Americans, judging by their threadbare uniforms—come around the side of the house and rush up the path to the mayor's door.

"What the—" Hank pulls me down as one of the men raps on the door with what sounds like the butt of a revolver. A moment later, the door opens, and though I can't hear what the men are saying, from the timbre of their voices it sounds like official business. I push up just enough to see an older woman standing in the open crack of a door held fast by a chain lock, apparently refusing to let them in.

"Ma'am, stand aside!" one of the men orders.

The woman inside starts yelling, "No! You go away! You go!" until she's braying like a donkey.

She tries to close the door only to have it pop back open as far as the chain will allow as the men drive their shoulders against it.

"Do we help 'em?" I ask. If they're here to kill him, maybe they'll let us have his head.

An upstairs window shatters. Glass rains down into the yard. A gunshot cracks through the still morning air.

"Help!" a man shouts through the broken window. "Please! Somebody help me!"

The front door gives with a crack. The woman screams.

Another gunshot from above. "Help!" the man shouts, followed by a plea in Japanese.

A second later, the two Americans burst onto the lawn.

"Split up!" one of them shouts, veering up the street as the other heads into the park.

Hank drags me to my feet. "C'mon. The guards'll be swarming this place in seconds."

We hustle around the corner of the yard toward an old shed. Glance back in time to see the old woman run from the house for the Buick, a fat man in her wake.

"What just happened?" I ask, breathing hard.

"Not sure. But I bet that's the mayor."

Hank pushes me ahead of him toward an alley. I hobble along, my side and limbs on fire. We duck behind a brick wall and Hank pushes up just enough to peer over the top of it.

"They stopped in front of City Hall. He's surrounded by Japanese guards."

"Now what?" I ask.

Hank drops back down to lean against the wall. "I dunno. But apparently we ain't the only ones who want him dead."

30

MAY 14, 1942
SANTA RITA, PHILIPPINES

Y ou think those other Americans were on the same mission as us?" I ask as the sun rises overhead. We've waited three hours for things to die down after the mayor's flight across the square to garrison headquarters. "Maybe the Crate's hedging his bets?"

The thought fills me with equal parts panic and anger. Panic that two other assassins tried to rob us of the one thing we need to buy Billy's life. Anger because that seems just like something the Crate would do: pit prisoners against each other to get what he wants.

"Those fellas weren't nearly as skinny as anyone at O'Donnell. Nor nearly as filthy neither. And they were armed. They might be working for the Crate. But I bet they're workin' for someone else."

"Another guerilla outfit?"

"That's my best guess."

"So then it's true that the mayor killed that boy."

I want—I need—this to be true.

"Who knows." Hank pushes up to squint over the wall. "Just a couple guards patrolling the place now. C'mon."

We move down the block, cross the street, and turn back up an alley behind a row of buildings. The mayor's Buick is parked ahead of us in an open shed behind the City Hall building. No one in sight.

"His office has to be one of those." I point to a string of windows above a long balcony on the second floor.

We wait as a guard passes by. The instant he disappears around the corner, we hurry to the Buick and crouch down against the fender.

"See that back entrance?" Hank says, unslinging the pack and laying it at my feet. "If I don't walk out that door with the mayor in the next five minutes, you hightail it out of here."

I shake my head. "I'm comin' in with you."

"No, you ain't. You wait here out of sight. I mean it, Prop—if you don't see me in five minutes, you get to the bridge and tell Alfonso you're joining up with Felipa. 'Cause there won't be any point in goin' back to O'Donnell."

I stare at him for a hard minute, unable to fathom going on without him or Billy.

"Screw that," I say. "You got four minutes or I'm leavin' without you."

Hank hands me the rifle and pats my cheek with a grin. "That's the spirit."

With a swift look around, he springs onto the car's bumper and hoists himself to the top of the shed. Through the metal roof I hear him back up. And then he's thundering overhead in three quick strides. I glance up in time to see him silhouetted against the sun as he leaps for the balcony's railing.

He dangles several seconds, struggling to pull himself up. Six months ago, he would've vaulted right past it. Now, forty pounds thinner, he searches for a toehold, grappling to get an arm over.

Movement along the edge of the building—the guard, coming around the corner.

I search around me. Spying a stone on the ground beside me, I lean out just far enough to chuck it out past the building, in the opposite direction.

The guard's head swivels at the sound as Hank pulls himself up and over. He glances toward me. I gesture to him: *Get down!*

He flattens himself against the balcony floor as the guard passes underneath. I give him the all clear the minute the guard rounds the far corner. Hank springs to his feet, pistol drawn, and peers in through the window. Then he moves down the balcony to the next, and then to the very last window of the far corner office. He glances in at an angle, pulls back enough to nod toward me, and then steps into full view. He taps the window with his pistol and levels it. A second later, he grabs the sill, shoves the window open, and dives through the opening.

I see his head and torso as he straightens, pistol raised. I can't hear what he's saying as he moves out of my line of sight. All I know is I'm counting the seconds. Counting, and watching for guards.

My knees are numb. Sweat drips into my eyes.

I get to sixty and don't know if it's really been a minute or if I'm counting as fast as my heart is beating.

I listen for sounds of alarm. Shouts.

One hundred six. One hundred seven . . .

Gunshots.

Two hundred forty-one. Two hundred forty-two.

The back door opens. The mayor emerges—

Right as the guard rounds the corner.

Hidden, I lift the rifle. Prop it on the fender. Thumb off the safety and stare down the barrel at the approaching guard.

The mayor halts, the door not quite open. With stunted movements, he reaches into his pocket and takes out a pack of cigarettes. Pokes one between his lips. Fumbling for his lighter, his hands shake as he flicks it open and he drops it.

The guard angles toward him. My heart stops. Without a word, the guard bends and retrieves the lighter, flicks it on, and offers the light to the mayor, who murmurs his thanks around the cigarette as he leans in, puffing the end to glowing life. After accepting the lighter with a nod, the mayor pockets it as the guard continues down the building and away. He's still only halfway out the door.

A moment later, the mayor murmurs something with a nod. He emerges awkwardly, Hank—and his pistol—at his back.

I straighten, painfully, the rifle raised as he drops his cigarette and Hank hurries him to the Buick.

"Open it," Hank says.

"Please," the mayor says, unlocking the door. "Why are you doing this?" He's sweating.

"Get in," Hank says, pistol leveled at the mayor's head. He slides in after the mayor and I climb in last. "Drive. That way—out of town."

The mayor starts the engine. We duck low as he pulls from the shed and turns down the alley.

"Who do you work for?" the mayor asks. "I can pay twice as much."

"I seriously doubt that," I murmur.

"You are American. We are your friends!"

"Why were two Americans trying to kill you first thing this morning?" I ask.

"That—is a terrible misunderstanding. I am a simple politician. But there is nothing simple in these times."

We duck down as a truck roars by, Japanese soldiers hanging off the back. The mayor wipes his brow with the sleeve of his suit jacket. It looks expensive. Probably custom made.

"What about the boy you got killed?" Hank says. "Was he your friend too?"

"You are here because of the boy?" the mayor sounds incredulous. "Then you know there was nothing I could do! He was caught helping the guerillas. They executed him publicly as a message to the people. If I had tried to stop them, they would have killed ten more of my people. By not interfering, I saved lives!"

"Now you're gonna get to save another," Hank says, his expression grim. "Head toward the railroad bridge."

"You're going to kill me," the mayor says. It ain't really a question. Neither one of us answers.

"At least tell me why." He turns and gazes not at Hank, but me. I look away.

After a moment, Hank asks, "You know the commander of Camp O'Donnell? He's the one who wants you dead."

"I do not even know who that is," he says, his voice rising.

"He seems to know who you are."

"Please," the mayor says. "I—I will disappear. You can say you killed me."

"Yeah," Hank says with a sigh. "Turns out that's not gonna work."

"This commander—he won't know. Many people are missing because of war. Unless . . . unless . . ." It dawns then, across his expression. "I see. He requires . . . proof."

Hank doesn't answer.

"So, this is what we will do. There are many dead. We can find what you need—"

"Sir, he has our best friend. And he's gonna kill him if we don't return with . . . proof."

The mayor drives in silence for several moments. He seems to be churning, working a hard idea through his mind.

"You say my death will free your friend," he says at last.

"Yes," Hank says quietly. In all this time, he hasn't lowered his pistol.

"There is a chapel not far from here. I would like to give my last confession."

"Sorry," Hank says. "No can do."

"Please." The mayor's voice falters. "My eternity is at stake. You are taking my life. Please—at least let me confess to the priest. Please!"

I glance at Hank. I don't like this. Not one bit.

I remind myself that Felipa doesn't trust the mayor. Picture again the way the guard retrieved his lighter and lit his cigarette for him like they were friends.

Hank blows out a breath.

"Try anything, and you meet your maker with every bit of dirt on your soul," Hank says at last. "Once we arrive, you got five minutes."

"I understand. Thank you." The mayor's hands tremble on the wheel as he turns at the end of a lane. We bump down a road toward a small chapel that I wouldn't be able to tell from a shack if not for the cross on top of it.

The place appears to be empty.

"Stop here," Hank says.

"The priest lives in the house behind. Please. It is not far."

"Then we'll walk. Park here and keep your hands where I can see them," Hank says.

Tall grass sways in a rare afternoon breeze as we get out of the car. Hank walks behind the mayor, the revolver pointed at his back.

A tiny thatched hut squats behind the chapel.

"Father!" the mayor cries, stumbling forward. "Father, please!"

The door to the hut creaks open. There are no windows.

A voice comes from the darkness. "What is the meaning of this?"

The mayor calls out, "Father Bartholomew . . . it is me. I have come to see you at last."

An old man in a long, rough robe with frayed hems shuffles out from the hut. A small wooden cross dangles from a chain around his neck. The priest, seeing us, lifts his palms.

"Who are you to come to this sacred site with guns?" he says, in a stronger voice than I anticipated. "In the name of God, put them away!"

"Can't do that, Father," Hank says.

The priest spreads his arms. They're lean, dark, and scarred. A laborer's arms. "At least allow this man the privacy of the confessional!"

"Sorry, Father. This is as private as it's gonna get."

"Please, Father," the mayor says, clasping his hands together. He falls to his knees right there.

The priest looks from us to the mayor and finally places his hand on the mayor's bald head, his own wrinkling.

"Bless me, Father, for I have sinned . . ." the mayor begins as the priest makes the sign of the cross. "It has been twenty years . . . maybe twenty-five since my last confession. I'm not sure."

"If I'd known that . . ." Hank mutters, taking a deep breath.

The mayor bows his head.

"I did not treat my wife kindly. I was harsh with her. I did not appreciate her kindness to me. She died of consumption three years ago, but—" his voice cracks. "I did not protect her. I did not honor her. I have no right to miss her." He begins to sob.

I gaze at him without seeing him. Listen without hearing. I ain't comfortable seeing a grown man—even one facing death—cry. Even after months of war, of hearing men beg for their mamas as they died, because that's different.

But this . . .

"I have entertained lustful thoughts about my secretary," the mayor says. "I wanted to use my position to have her. I have lied. I have envied those more powerful than me. I have been greedy. I have eaten when others have gone hungry. I have forgotten our Lord. I have not prayed for forgiveness—at first because I did not think I needed it, and then because I thought I did not deserve it."

The mayor falls forward onto his hands, shaking. "I do not know that I made the right choices . . . I have turned away from God. I have killed—not with my own hands, but by my silence. How will I enter the kingdom of heaven? What reassurance is there for me?"

The priest is quiet for a moment before he makes the sign of the cross.

"The blood of Christ cleanses you and forgives you from all sin.

There is no separation between you and God. Neither will what you have confessed result in eternal damnation. Go in peace. There is no penance. In the name of the Father, the Son, and the Holy Spirit. Amen."

The mayor looks up, bewildered. As though that couldn't possibly be the end after all he's just confessed. And I think that we ought to feel better, having heard everything he's just said.

Except I don't.

Finally, the mayor gets to his feet. He exhales a long breath, wipes his nose on his sleeve, and turns.

"All right," he says to us.

"You will wait," the priest says, raising a hand and taking two steps toward us. "In the wilderness a feast is set, and all are welcomed to eat at God's table." He looks from Hank to me. "What do you have to confess?"

"We—we ain't Catholic," I stutter, caught off guard.

"God is for all people," the priest says.

I want to say my daddy's a pastor. That I've spent my entire life in church. That we don't confess to priests, and even if we did, I've got the shortest list of sins of anyone I know.

I glance at Hank.

"We ain't got a confession," Hank says.

The priest steps even closer.

"Every man has a confession," he says.

He lingers as if waiting for a reply. I stare at Hank. At the pistol aimed at the mayor. Finally at my own two feet.

Hank grabs the mayor by the back of his collar and hauls him upright. Confession is over.

The mayor is no longer sweating as we drive away. He rolls down the window in the silence and sits back as though enjoying the breeze.

We stop near the railroad bridge and get out. The mayor lifts his hands and clasps them in prayer as he follows us to a clearing half ringed by trees.

"I loved this country," he says, staring up through the leaves.

Without a word, he sinks down to his knees, facing away from us. He should be sweating. Should be straining to run away. But instead, he breathes in like lilacs have just come in bloom all around him, when all I smell is the dump outside town.

Hank steps over, raises the .38 to the back of his head.

I make myself watch. Refuse to look away. At the last second, the mayor twists around.

"What is your friend's name?" he asks.

Some kind of bird jabbers in the trees. An instant later, the noise dies away and all I hear is the pounding in my chest.

"Billy." Hank's voice cracks at last.

"My name is Emmanuel. I would like it if you told him my name. I will remember him to God. All of you."

I shake my head, turn, and walk away. Wait for the sound of pistol fire, wanting this over. When it don't come, I turn on my heel just in time to see Hank staring at the revolver.

"What're you doin'?" I say.

He shoves the revolver into his belt and turns away, fingers laced on top of his head.

"This ain't right."

"Ain't none of this right," I say.

"I can't do this."

"What d'you mean? We have to!"

"No we don't. We don't gotta do anythin'."

"We made a promise to Billy!" I say, with rising panic.

"Yeah. To survive."

I point to the mayor. "He's playing us. Countin' on our good graces."

265

"He's on his knees, Prop!" Hank says. "Does he look like he's trying to get away?"

"Felipa said he was a snake," I say. "And you saw how he was with that guard!"

"Felipa—Culala?" the mayor says, turning to look at us. "You know where she is?"

"See?" I say, gesturing to him.

Hank walks over to me and says, low, "What d'you think Billy's gonna say, knowing me and you killed an innocent man for him? Billy told us to run. And now we're gonna go back and put this on him?"

I don't bother to lower my voice. "No one's innocent! This is war. People die in war. And I think Billy's gonna be glad to be alive, that's what I think. For his mama and sisters!"

"His sisters?" Hank narrows his eyes. "So this ain't about the mayor then, is it? This ain't even about Billy. This is about Claire!"

"No, it ain't."

"It is! You still ain't got her out of your system!"

"You jealous traitor," I say. "You always wanted her."

"*I'm* the jealous one?" Hank says, pointing at his chest before stabbing his finger toward me. "How long you been going round trying to be me? Condemning everything I do but wishing in your *heart of hearts* you was just like me? If you loved Claire, you'd have never let her go. But you were always more scared of your own daddy than you were in love with Claire. And she knew it."

"You shut your mouth," I say, low.

"You know what I bet? I bet you tried for her just because you didn't want me to have her. That was the whole thing, wasn't it? Well, I got news for you, Propper. You ain't any better than me. Never have been. The only thing you've ever been is scared."

I grab the pistol from Hank's belt. Cock it, and level it on him. And then swing around and pull the trigger.

The shot rattles up through the trees, sends a spray of green flitting to the earth.

The mayor slumps over, the side of his head blown out.

I stare at his lifeless form and then at the pistol in my hand as Hank spins away with a curse.

I lower my arm, shaking.

Move, on unsteady legs.

To fetch the machete.

31

May 14, 1942

Santa Rita, Philippines

Alfonso arrives at dusk. We don't talk, and he don't ask questions when we get in the truck and set the bloody gunnysack on the floor between us.

Two minutes later, we're rumbling away from Santa Rita in the darkness.

I stare out at the night, swaying with the truck as we creep along burned-out and cratered roads, our headlights off.

Hank escapes into sleep. But I can't get the image of the mayor on his knees out of my mind. Not because he was begging for his life, but because he wasn't.

I close my eyes, but he's still there.

What have I done?

Billy can never know.

I drift off at last, the mayor's face before me.

Sometime later, Alfonso jostles me awake.

"We're here," he says. "The camp is two kilometers down this road."

It's nearly dawn. The start of Billy's sixth day on the stake.

Hank climbs out of the cab without a word, the gunnysack hanging from his fist. I return the rifle, ammo, and machete to Alfonso.

A minute later, the truck rumbles back into the darkness.

Hank and I start down the road.

The long walk to hell is filled with silence.

32

MOBILE, ALABAMA

APRIL 1941

Everyone cheered as the band played Bing Crosby's "Only Forever" and the newly engaged couple began to dance.

I found Hank and grabbed him by the shoulder. "Did you know Cowboy was gonna do that?"

"What? No." His brows furrowed. "Sorry, Jimmy. I know how you feel—how you felt about her."

But he didn't. No one did . . .

Including her.

I could tell her, lay it out plain and simple—give her the choice between Cowboy and me.

But it was already too late. Tomorrow everyone would be talking about Murphy High's prom and Cowboy Wright's engagement to Claire Crockett. Going back on it would be a disgrace. Would ruin her.

"How's that gonna work?" I asked when I finally found her coming out of the restroom after she and Cowboy had spent the last half hour getting mobbed by everyone in the gym. "I thought you didn't want to move away." I hated the accusatory tone in my own voice.

I could smell her perfume—not the Coty I'd given her, but the one she'd worn before.

"I'm not moving," she said, looking at her hand as though that ring had a gravity of its own. "I'm staying and he'll come back when he can. At least that's the plan for now." She glanced up, meeting my gaze at last. Her words felt like a sucker punch.

All the while I had been hoping they might break up, they had been planning for the future.

"But you'll be alone, Claire."

"No. I won't. I'll have my family." She paused. "And you'll be free," she added quietly, before one more girl who probably never paid attention to Claire before came over to hug her with a squeal and demand to see the ring.

As jealous as I was of Cowboy, I couldn't hate him. I couldn't even claim to be the better man because I wasn't. Except in one way.

I'd known Claire—the tilt of her head and cast of her gaze, the lilt of her voice that spoke so much more than any of her words—all my life. I'd loved her as a friend before I ever noticed she'd become a woman. And the only thing I wanted more than her touch and soft sighs was just her, always, in my life.

Claire and Cowboy's prom engagement made the local section of the paper.

I resigned my paper route the next day and spent the following week in a daze, skipping school with Hank to work on cars and drink beer. I never had more than a couple, too afraid of staggering home or Daddy smelling it on me. Never mind that a drop was a drop too much when it came to my soul.

But my soul was untethered, adrift.

"Now what?" I asked one night. Hank and Billy had been looking at the broken-down V-8 someone had sold to Mr. Crockett after being unable to afford the repairs, making a list of all the things it would need.

Despite spending long days in the Crocketts' garage, I had yet to catch a glimpse of Claire coming or going. I assumed she must be spending every day and hour that she could with Cowboy before he left and wondered why I tortured myself by being close enough to the house to notice.

"What d'you mean, 'Now what?'" Hank, sitting on a dolly, spun around to look at me.

"We enlistin'?" I said. "'Cause I can't stay here." Merl Beauregard, the grade-school bully, was the latest of the boys we knew to join up. He hadn't even waited to graduate.

Billy squinted. "I thought you was goin' to seminary."

"It ain't for me." Even though it was a ticket out of here.

Hank sighed, arms dangling on his knees. "Things are busy at the mill, especially with Cowboy fixin' to leave. And Billy's gotta finish school."

"Why?" Billy asked.

Hank swiveled toward him. "'Cause you ain't old enough to enlist."

"I'm almost as tall as Jimmy. 'Sides, I hate school."

"No, you don't," I said.

"I hate it without you two there. Who am I gonna walk with?"

"I'll loan you my bike," Hank said, before getting to his feet. "So here's the plan. Billy graduates, then we decide."

"What am I supposed to do 'til then?" I demanded. "Or maybe I could help out at the mill. You're shorthanded without Cowboy—"

Hank leveled a gaze at me. "And how's that gonna go over with your daddy?"

"Like a lead balloon," Billy murmured.

"I don't care!"

Hank scratched the back of his neck, let out a slow breath. "Prop, why not go to seminary after all, get a year under your belt. Give yourself something to come back to."

But that was just it; I didn't want to come back.

A few days later, Cowboy shipped out. Hank hung his head, and even an afternoon battling on the rope swing at Chickasabogue couldn't lift his spirits.

The second week in May, Hank, Claire, and me walked across the stage to collect our diplomas. Mrs. Crockett cried and Mr. Wright, who openly wept at Cowboy's graduation, beamed with tears in his eyes at the sight of Hank following in his big brother's footsteps.

"Happy graduation, Jimmy," Claire said, after posing for a picture with her mama. "I hope you'll come by the house sometime. The twins and Dorothy Jean miss you, and you're behind on *The Shadow*."

I'd meant to for a while now. But in the weeks since prom, I hadn't made it closer than the shop.

I told her I would.

That night, Daddy took Mama and me to Palmer's to celebrate. Over fried oysters he announced that he'd arranged for me to stay in Louisville with a seminary friend, his wife, and their three children still at home.

"You'll have to share a room with one of the boys, but you'll have home-cooked meals and a good family to attend church with," Daddy said, looking pleased.

And someone to report on my comings and goings.

I stared at my plate, seeing not the buttered roll and last remaining hush puppy but my entire future fading before my eyes.

"Jimmy," Mama prompted.

"Thank you," I mumbled. But my heart was racing.

I felt more than saw Daddy exchange a glance with her before folding his napkin.

"I thought you'd be grateful," Daddy said. "Or maybe I shouldn't have bothered calling in a personal favor that will save you hundreds of dollars."

I waited for him to slam his hand down on the table. But we were in public.

I should tell him. I'd graduated. I was a man now, ready to make my own choices. And what could he do here, in this crowded restaurant where people at no less than three tables had greeted him on the way in?

"I really appreciate it," I said tightly, cursing myself as a coward. "Sir."

Near the end of May, President Roosevelt announced a state of unlimited national emergency against Nazi world domination. He pledged to build U.S. defenses in preparation to defend American workers from Teutonic enslavement.

Daddy's sermons intensified.

"When this war is over and Hitler has been defeated, the world is going to need more—not fewer—pastors," Daddy said to me more than once. The last time he said it, he added under his breath, "Assuming the world doesn't end first."

For once, I understood what he meant. The headlines were a jumble of Soviet and German fighting, of Finland joining the Reich, and of British bombs smashing Nazi-occupied France. Of the Navy secretary urging that it was time to clear Hitler from the Atlantic and the president ordering nine hundred thousand more men inducted into the Army.

That June, I paid a visit to the Crocketts' with my mama. In part because avoiding Claire's house had become nearly as awkward as showing up would be. But also because I didn't know what to do with myself. I'd spent the first weeks of summer working at the farm and my free time loitering in the garage with Hank and fishing or frog gigging with Billy. But half my life had been spent in front of the Crocketts' radio, in their backyard, at their kitchen table, and on their porch.

The minute I showed up, the twins and Dorothy Jean launched themselves at me, and Mrs. Crockett added two places for us at the dinner table. It was strange eating there, something I'd done hundreds—maybe thousands—of times before. But for as much as it looked the same, everything was different. Even the conversation that used to center on movies, radio shows, and school and church gossip was all about the war and the question of when Claire and Cowboy would be able to plan their wedding.

"Oh, it might just have to be a spur-of-the-moment thing," Claire said, waving it off for my benefit, I knew.

At least in that case it might be a judge officiating instead of my daddy.

A few nights later, after working past supper in the garage, I went up to the house to ask for coffee for Hank and me. I found Claire sipping tea at the kitchen table, her eyes puffy. When I asked what was wrong, she shrugged it off. I figured she must've gotten a letter from Cowboy. Even so, my arms ached to comfort her.

"Stay for a game of checkers?" she asked, managing a small smile as I put the coffee on.

I hesitated. "I dunno, Claire."

"Please."

"Why?" I asked, the question pulling at something inside my chest.

"Because it's a game for friends."

The word gutted me. *Friends.*

I played checkers with her that night, but it didn't feel anything like before.

"You know Americans are already fighting," I told my parents over dinner. It was the day before the Fourth of July, and pilots with the American Eagle Squadron in England had just shot down three Nazi fighters.

"God willing, this doesn't become a shooting war," Daddy said.

"Didn't you hear me?" I said. "It already is! Why ain't you glad? If Nazis are heretics, ain't it our duty to help the Brits fight them off? Ain't that the Christian thing to do?"

I hadn't meant to say all that and braced myself the moment it was all out of my mouth.

Mama, sitting across the table from me, didn't even look up. To my surprise, neither did Daddy.

"Son," Daddy said, stabbing at the mess of green beans on his plate, "your mama tells me you might be a little blue about Cowboy and Miss Crockett's engagement."

I shoved my napkin onto the table. "May I be excused?"

He went on as though I hadn't spoken. "I have no doubt one day soon you'll find a fine young woman you'll be able to build a future with. The fact that you've been so emotional about Miss Crockett tells me it would never have been a happy or stable arrangement—for either of you."

I looked up then at the face I had known all my life, the stern lines and graying hair but otherwise forgettable features, and wondered what my mama had seen in him. How he had ever wooed her. How she subsisted on what he called love. And I realized I despised him and the God he preached. There was no point in pretending anymore; I didn't want to devote my life to pursuing a God just like my father, or even one more minute trying to know either one of them.

"I need a job," I told Hank that night.

"You thinkin' 'bout the mill?" Hank asked, leaning in the doorway of his kitchen. I sat at the wooden table that Billy, Claire, and me had eaten peanut butter sandwiches at the first time we showed up here, now with a beer from the Wrights' icebox sweating in front of me.

"Actually, I was thinkin' I'd go see Mr. Boyington first thing Monday morning. See about gettin' a job at Alcoa," I said. "But I'll probably need a place to stay."

"Cowboy's room's available," Hank said, bottle dangling from his fingers. "His job too, if you decide you want it."

"Thanks, Hank," I said. "You're a good friend."

"We're brothers," he said.

On July 5, I rode with Hank and Mr. Wright to the Haggerts' annual barn dance west of town. My daddy, who thought I was tagging along with the Crocketts, wouldn't be any the wiser; he'd never be seen alive at an affair known for jitterbugging and gin.

Claire found me at the punch bowl and pulled me aside.

"I need you to do me a favor," she said, looking around.

"Sure," I said, hating the way my heart still leapt around her.

"Nora Sue's here and chasin' Billy again," she said. "I'm so mad I could spit."

"Why don't you?" Hank said, coming up behind us to drape an arm over both our shoulders. I could smell booze on his breath. "Good way to shine your shoes."

"It took him a month to get over her and if she thinks I'm lettin' her get near him—well." She shrugged out from under Hank's arm and turned to point at him. "You. Go dance with her. Every girl you dance with becomes infatuated with you."

He gave her a lazy grin. "It's a hard cross to bear."

Hank strolled off to find Nora Sue as Claire watched, arms folded across her chest.

"I thought you wanted my help?" I said, feigning hurt feelings.

"There they are," she said, grabbing my arm and hauling me toward the dancers.

"Wait. What're we—"

"I want her to know I'm watchin'. C'mon."

She dragged me to the hay-dusted floor, and I was suddenly aware of my sweaty armpits and clammy hands.

"Claire . . ."

"Don't you dare step on my foot."

I couldn't help a small laugh—whether at the fit she was in or just the feeling of dancing with her like old times, her hand both familiar and strange in mine. I twirled her around the way she'd made me practice so many times growing up, and after a few minutes she was smiling.

We shed our shoes and sang along with "The Woodpecker Song" and danced until we were out of breath.

"I think it's time for punch," I said.

"C'mon, Jimmy. Just one more," Claire said, her cheeks flushed.

"We better wait," I said as a fiddle started up "I'll Keep on Loving You." I noticed a couple girls whispering off to the side.

"Why, what's eatin' you?" she said, her expression petulant—no, defiant.

I glanced around. "I just—I think people are gonna talk if we keep dancin'." That's when I noticed Mr. Chavers from church, who managed the Western Union office, pulling Mr. Wright aside near the table of refreshments. Mr. Chavers wasn't here socially—I knew that much on account of him being as strict on dancing as my daddy. And because of the envelope in his hand. Sometimes when a telegram came in after regular hours he'd been known to hand deliver.

"Let 'em talk," she said bitterly. "C'mon."

I hardly heard her as Hank strode over to the two men, looking far more sober than he had all afternoon.

"Wait," I said. "Somethin's wrong."

Claire followed my gaze as the three men headed out back.

"C'mon," I said, grabbing her hand and going after them.

Outside, we found Hank and his daddy staring down at a paper in Mr. Wright's hands, Mr. Wright's expression pale and stark.

Before we'd even reached them, Hank reeled away, heels of his hands over his eyes.

Beside me, Claire stopped as though struck.

"What?" she cried, her voice shrill. "What is it?"

Mr. Wright staggered, the telegram dangling from his fingers.

"You tell me what that is right now!" Claire demanded, starting to cry.

But we already knew.

The rest was a blur. Mr. Chavers consoling Hank's daddy. The awful telegram trembling in Claire's hand as Mrs. Crockett found us and Billy came running.

It is with deep regret that I inform you that your son, Sergeant Roy C. Wright, died in service of his country as a result of injuries received in an aircraft accident . . .

People drifted out from the dance. Others gathered in the barn's broad doorway, talking behind their hands.

"Jimmy, find some of that lemonade," Mrs. Crockett said, leading Claire over to a tree as she started retching.

I jogged back inside, my mind in a whirl. Searched blindly for the pitchers of lemonade beside the punch bowl, belatedly realizing that the music had stopped. Mr. Haggert, who owned this farm, was trying to make an announcement, hat in his hand.

"I'm sorry to have to say this, but given that the Wright family just received some awful news, it don't seem right to continue . . ."

"Who died?" someone shouted, words slurred. I looked around, ready to punch whoever it was in the jaw.

"Mobile has lost one of its shining sons. Y'all know Roy Wright, Bernard Wright's boy, though I guess most of us call him Cowboy . . ."

Gasps and stifled cries.

Even after reading the telegram, I still couldn't believe what I was hearing.

I grabbed a pitcher of lemonade and got out of there as fast as I could before realizing I hadn't brought a glass. I found Claire kneeling at a nearby water pump, her mama splashing the back of her neck and her cheeks as Billy worked the handle.

"Where's Hank?" I asked Billy, shoving the pitcher at one of the kids standing there staring.

He wiped his face on his sleeve, squinting against the setting sun. "Must've left with his daddy."

We helped Claire to her feet and into the Crocketts' truck, where she buried her face against her mama's shoulder.

"We should go look for Hank," Billy said when he dropped me off at my house.

"I reckon he'll show up when he's ready," I said, realizing—too late—

that I'd left my shoes at the dance and would have to borrow a pair of Daddy's for church.

None of the Crocketts were in attendance the next morning, by which time the entire congregation was buzzing with the news. After Sunday dinner at the Lipfords', where all the talk was about Cowboy and "that poor Claire Crockett"—until Daddy diverted the conversation to me attending seminary—Mama took the truck to the Crocketts'. I tried to go with her, but she warned me off in private.

"It won't look good, Jimmy. Especially if you and Claire ever decide to get back together now that Cowboy's . . ."

She didn't finish, and I didn't know whether to feel ashamed or a little better that I wasn't the only one thinking it.

I didn't want Cowboy dead—not for anything. But if Claire and me did get back together, this time I wouldn't let her go. Not out of uncertainty or vacillation about the future or worry about my daddy, or any detail about where or how we'd live. I didn't have all the answers, but I did know this: I would not lose her twice.

Mama came back with the truck just in time to make supper, which meant it was twilight by the time I drove west of town to the Haggerts' to pick up my shoes.

"Ah, yes, Jimmy," Mrs. Haggert said and then hesitated. "There's another pair here—a lady's shoe. I wondered if they belonged to Claire. I thought I might have seen the two of you dancing . . ."

Heat sprang to my face.

"I'd be glad to take them home for my mama to give her," I said.

"Very well," Mrs. Haggert said. But I saw the sideways glance she gave me as I said goodbye.

Driving home, I looked over at the pair of Claire's shoes sitting on the seat next to me in the dark.

I thought about what my mama had said about being seen at the Crocketts', and I understood. And I was willing to bide my time.

But how was I supposed to show—to prove—that I'd be here for Claire no matter what, if I wasn't around? Was it so wrong for me to be there for her while she mourned Cowboy? I mourned him too. I'd admired him—heck, I'd wanted to *be* him. I grieved him for Hank, and Hank's daddy too.

I turned down the road toward the Crocketts'.

I'd only stay long enough to return her shoes. That's all.

Not wanting to give the neighbors anything to talk about, I stopped along the road half a block from her house, plucked up her shoes, and headed up toward the Crocketts'.

I was just coming up on the gas station when I noticed a light on in back, glowing into the adjacent garage. My first thought was that Billy or his uncle had forgotten to turn the lights off for the night.

My second was Hank, who no one had seen since he disappeared during the dance.

I headed up the drive, tried the shop door, and found it unlocked. Inside, I set Claire's shoes on the counter, then walked back to where the light was on and passed through to the garage.

"Hank?" I said quietly, stepping into the dim work bay. I'd just about decided that someone had forgotten to lock up when I heard a muffled murmur, a groan in the darkness. It came from inside the broken-down Ford permanently parked in the second bay. The door was ajar, a boot I recognized as Hank's sticking out past the seat. On any other day, I would've been tempted to prank or scare the bejeezus out of him and whatever girl was in there with him.

I moved silently back the way I came as the two forms rustled inside the Roadster, but then froze at the sound of a female voice I would've recognized anywhere.

"You know you look just like him?"

My breath left me all at once.

I retreated to the shadows on the garage side of the open doorway, heart pounding in my ears. But even as I told myself to leave, to get out, I had to know.

A hitched sob, and Hank's voice broke.

"I'm in love with you, Claire."

I stumbled into the shop, pushed my way out the door and into the night before fleeing down the block to the truck.

At home, I shut myself in my room and paced the floor. I wanted to rant, to shout curses. But instead I crawled into bed and buried my face in my pillow with a groan, trying to sleep if only to turn off my mind.

Unbidden images dogged me through the night.

I was staring, wide awake, at the ceiling, when a pebble clattered against my bedroom window just before dawn. Rustling out of bed, I opened it to find Hank in our front yard, looking drawn and rumpled.

Hank, who'd just been with Claire. My Claire. In ways I'd only dreamed of for years.

Had he come to gloat? To confess? To tell me what I'd always known—that he'd been in love with her ever since we were kids?

"What're you doin' here?" I hissed. I wanted to shout at him. Accuse him. Leap out the window and strangle him.

"You still wanna enlist?"

"What?"

"We're leavin', Prop. Billy and me. Driving over to Pascagoula where nobody knows us. Enlistin' the minute the recruitment office opens."

I squinted at him in the early morning darkness. He'd just been with Claire. How could he be talking—let alone thinking—about enlisting right now?

But I couldn't bear for him to know that I knew. Couldn't stand it any more than I could stomach the thought of staying here one minute longer. Of running into Claire and knowing—remembering—what I had heard.

Claire had made her choice. Twice. There was no way for us now.

Hank waited, not even blinking as he stared at me.

I shook my head at the sight of him. His stupid face. My two best friends were enlisting. About to leave me behind.

"Go suck an egg," I said.

I met him down on the road and the two of us drove over to Billy's. The Ginger Streak was already waiting by the mailbox. He climbed in and held a folded paper up between two fingers. I recognized his clean, clear cursive.

"A letter from my recently departed mama," he said with a dramatic sigh and then grinned.

Recruiters weren't going to check. Not in Mississippi.

That night, after the three of us had signed our names and taken our oaths, I returned home, if only for a moment. My mama cried as I informed her and Daddy what I'd done, no longer afraid of how he'd react. Far as I was concerned, I was already gone.

"When do you leave?" Mama asked, hand over her mouth.

"Tomorrow."

Daddy slowly shook his head, gaze steely. "After all we've done for you."

"It's my life. And I can't live it here anymore," I said.

He got to his feet. I braced for him to start shouting. To come at me.

"Once you leave, don't bother coming back," he said, before disappearing into the office and slamming the door behind him.

"I'm sorry, Mama," I said in the silence that followed. "I'll stay at Hank's tonight."

She swiped at her eyes and then lifted her chin. "Promise me you won't go 'til I get back."

I nodded and she grabbed her pocketbook and went out the door. A minute later, I heard the truck pulling from the driveway.

I went into my room and packed my canvas newspaper bag. Emptied the shoebox I kept my money in and folded eight dollars into my wallet first. Out in the kitchen, I tied another ten dollars into a cloth napkin and tucked it inside the canister of sugar, where I knew Mama would be sure to find it.

When she returned, she handed me a Bible I recognized as one from church.

"Since I don't have time to get you a new one, this'll have to do," she said, pressing it into my hands. Her eyes were puffy, but she'd stopped crying.

I tucked the Bible into my bag and told Mama that I loved her.

She stood in the doorway as I slung the bag across my torso and took off on my bike for Hank's house one last time.

The three of us shipped out on the 6:00 a.m. train to Atlanta the next morning, bound for San Francisco.

33

MAY 15, 1942
CAMP O'DONNELL, PHILIPPINES

We smell the camp before we see it. The stench carries on the early morning breeze: feces and death.

Shouts from the tower as we approach the gate.

Hank tosses the gunnysack and .38 to the ground in front of us.

The guard outside the fence raises his rifle. We both raise our hands.

"Let us in," Hank says.

The guard kicks the weapon aside, gestures for us to stay put.

"Let us in," Hank repeats. "We're prisoners here."

The guard glances at the gunnysack and gestures for me to open it. When I do, he takes one look inside and turns his head in disgust. Waves the sack away.

He shouts something to another guard on the other side of the fence, who jogs toward the command building.

We wait, minutes like eternity.

He returns, shouting orders. The first guard opens the gate.

We enter the dusty compound. The dirt seems more barren, more

286

forsaken than we left it. Men already in line for the spigot turn to stare. They're skinnier and dirtier than I remember—walking skeletons with skin sagging from their bones. Souls staring out from their human remains, waiting to be released.

I search for Billy along the perimeter of the fence as we're marched to headquarters but don't see him anywhere. I want to demand to know where he is. That he's alive.

But we got the Crate to deal with first. And if we don't do it carefully, all this will have been for nothing.

The Japanese flag sags overhead, the red meatball bleached nearly pink in the Philippine sun. A guard comes down the steps of the office building and gestures us to halt.

"Sir, we respectfully ask to see the commander, sir," Hank says.

The guard slaps Hank in the face. He points to the dirt and motions for us to stay like a pair of trained dogs.

We stand in the growing heat for what feels like an hour. Until I swear the skin on my face—still hot and angry from my day staked in the yard—feels like it's about to boil beneath the climbing sun, impatience crawling like fire ants along my tortured limbs.

We're desperate to see Billy.

But the Crate knows that. Of course he does.

"This is a bunch of bull," Hank murmurs, glaring beneath his brows. Fists balled tight at his sides.

When we're finally summoned, it's all I can do not to rush past the guard up the steps of the command building. The blast of the swamp cooler hits us as we're ushered down the hall and shoved into the room with the desk.

Hank drops the gunnysack on the floor.

It's already starting to smell.

And then we wait for the Crate to show up. In silence. Eyes on the clock, knees bouncing. With each passing minute, my anger flares. How was I fool enough to think they would speed things up a little, considering that a man's life was at stake?

"I'm goin' to find Billy," I say, crossing to the door.

Hank's on me in an instant. "Yeah, and what d'you think they'll do?" He drags me away. "They'll kill you and him!"

"He's dyin'!" I shout, trying to shake him off, the skin chafing raw inside my shirt.

The doorknob turns. Hank straightens and I shove away from him as the Crate comes in with two guards. Without acknowledging us, he moves behind the desk, pulls a handkerchief from his pocket, and takes his time dusting off the chair. When he finally sits, he stuffs the handkerchief into a pocket, produces a .45 automatic revolver, and sets it in front of him.

He leans back and regards us at last. Folds his hands. "I did not expect to see you here so soon," he says almost pleasantly. "I take it your journey was successful?"

"Hai," Hank says, an impatient muscle twitching in his temple. "The evidence you wanted is in the sack, sir."

The Crate makes no move to inspect it but sucks at a tooth as he regards us, all pleasantries gone.

"I handed you your freedom," the Crate says. "And you returned out of compassion for the weak. As I predicted. You had not even the pride to prove me wrong or the honor to defy me. And you wonder why I insult your country. Why I spit on your American flag. Tell me," he says, idly fingering the barrel of the .45, "do you know who Kit Carson was?"

"A frontiersman, sir," I say, eyes on the pistol.

"Yes." The Crate nods. "A frontiersman who forced the Navajo Indians to march two hundred and fifty miles from Fort Defiance to Fort Sumner. For twenty days, they marched. If a man got sick, he was killed by soldiers. If a pregnant woman stopped to have her baby, she was killed. You see"—he spreads his hands—"we are not unalike. No, you are worse."

Neither of us speaks.

He sighs and finally waves his hand at one of the guards. The guard walks over, unties the gunnysack, frowns, and hauls out the head. The Crate gestures it away and rises.

"We have removed your redheaded friend from the stake as promised. He is resting in Ward Z. You may see him for five minutes, after which you are to report to work detail for your betterment."

"Thank you, sir," I say with relief.

Outside, we hike across the compound as quickly as we can. When we reach the barracks, we run the rest of the way to the long hut known as Ward Z and duck inside. Glance frantically around as our eyes adjust to the dim interior.

An American medic tends to a man on one of twenty cots, a cup held to his mouth.

"Billy!" I say, rushing over. But the man lying there is older, and Filipino. Hank catches the medic by the arm when he straightens. The front of his shirt is covered with grime.

"We're looking for Private Crockett," Hank says. When the medic looks up at us, I can tell something ain't right with him. He's got a look in his eyes that's half caged and half gone. The cup in his hand is dry as a bone.

"Don't know him," he says.

"Private William Crockett. Redhead," I say. "He was staked outside."

"Oh. Him," the medic says, and points toward the last cot.

We pass by a row of men turned to skeletons by dysentery, malaria, and plain starvation. Others swollen with beriberi.

We reach the end of the row. A man lies naked on his stomach, head turned to one side, on the last cot. His back, arms, and legs are blistered and burned raw, skin sickly white. But I'd know that red hair anywhere.

"Billy," I whisper, squatting down near his head. He don't even twitch an eyelid.

"Doc!" Hank says, calling for the medic. "We need something for our friend!"

"Billy," I say, unsnapping my canteen. It's still got water in it.

The medic stops a few beds away, a bucket in one hand, rag in the other.

"Doc!" Hank says. "You gotta give him somethin'!"

The medic just shakes his head. "Nothing to give. This is Ward Z, buddy. Stands for Zero. It's where they bring men to die."

"Billy!" I say, more urgently this time. "We're back. We're here. Just gotta get some of this water into you." I fumble with the cap. "Help me, Hank . . ."

"C'mon, buddy. Gonna get you outta here," Hank says, shaking him gently by the shoulder. Struggling, finally, to turn him over.

Hank jerks back as Billy's arm flops off the cot. Billy's eyes stare up at the ceiling.

"Billy!" Hank says, in a terrible voice.

I drop the canteen. Gently slap Billy's cheeks, lean down to listen for his breath. Nothing at first.

The inhale, when it comes, is so shallow his chest don't even move.

It's followed by an even longer pause. The breath after it so slight I wonder if I imagined it.

We hold him in our arms and dab water on his lips. Whisper that we're back. That he's the best friend either of us could ever ask for.

That he don't need to wait for us anymore—we're here.

I don't know if he can hear us. If he can feel the wet cloth against his head.

We talk about Christmas mornings at home and fishing Three Mile Creek. Tell him we love him.

He's gone within an hour.

I turn away, hands on my head, as Hank buries his head against Billy's chest and weeps.

We bury Billy there, outside O'Donnell. I've dug hundreds of graves, but none as carefully as his.

34

I see him sometimes when I close my eyes.

Billy laughing as a little kid in whatever getup Claire dressed him in. Grinning when we poked blackberries in his mouth and crying when he grabbed a fistful of thorns.

How am I supposed to face his mama and sisters? What do I say to them—to Claire?

I can never go home.

35

JUNE 28, 1942
CAMP CABANATUAN, PHILIPPINES

At the end of June, we're transferred to Camp Cabanatuan fifty miles north of Manila. It's already filled with nearly six thousand men, and the conditions are no better than O'Donnell.

Some of the prisoners came from Corregidor, where they'd had more provisions, including quinine, sulfa, and antibiotics. You can tell which ones they are just by looking at them.

It's the rainy season, and water, at least, is in abundant supply. We collect it in rice bowls and rusty basins, wash ourselves in the downpour. My uniform is damp and musty, but it's the cleanest I've been in weeks.

A few mornings after our arrival, we receive actual Red Cross packages—the first since our surrender. There's chewing gum and cigarettes. Tins of corned beef and crackers. Coffee, powdered milk, dried fruit, liver paste, sugar, and soap.

The last item gets me. As the men laugh, light up, and eat like it's Christmas, I just sit and stare. The last time I touched soap like this, Billy was pouring a canteen of water on my head, washing death away.

I wipe my eyes and hide the soap in my meager pile of belongings. Stash the food. Light up a cigarette.

The last thing to arrive is even more unexpected than the Red Cross packages:

Mail.

I go up when they call Billy's name and retrieve two letters. One from his mama and a second from Claire at a Huntsville address I don't recognize.

I stare at that meticulous penmanship. Picture the way Claire's hand used to curve across the page as she wrote, left-handed, in school—despite every teacher who tried to break her of the preference. The tiny, determined crease in her forehead.

I hold it toward Hank.

He glances at it. "That ain't mine."

"It is now," I say.

"You keep it."

"You need to write her back and tell her what happened."

Hank chews the inside of his lip a second and then snatches it from my hand. A minute later, he holds it back out.

"I ain't the one she wants to hear from."

"You're writin' her back."

"Why d'you want me to do it?"

"Because I know, Hank!" I say, ripping the letter from his hand.

He squints. "You know what?"

Prisoners turn to stare.

"I saw you two together the night after the dance."

Hank looks away with a sigh. "Prop—"

I slap the letter against his chest and walk away.

That evening, Hank rakes his hands through his matted hair, shifts, and stares off at nothin'. He's procured a nub of pencil and a scrap of paper from someone and sits on the end of the bunk in the fading daylight, the page empty.

"I can't do this," he says at last.

I don't answer.

He pinches the bridge of his nose, exhales a long breath, and then shoves the entire mess toward me.

I shove it back.

"You like this, don't you?" he says. "Been waiting for it all this time."

I don't answer.

He gets up. "There's no guarantee a letter's gonna get home anyway!"

"You gotta do it."

"It ain't gonna matter. You know why?" Hank leans in and hisses, "Because we ain't makin' it back alive!"

"You're making it back alive if it's the last thing I see to," I say, low. "You're gonna do right by Claire."

He paces off, shakes his head, and spins back, "You're an idiot, Propper. You know that?"

Heads turn, a few other men in their bunks watching us with half-lidded eyes.

"All I know is that you ain't gonna do by her what you done by other girls," I grit out. "You're gonna make it right."

"So what. You want me to go back and *marry* her?"

"That's exactly what you're gonna do!"

"Prop, she don't want me!"

"I ain't talkin' 'bout who wants what. I'm talkin' 'bout what's right." I lunge for the letter on the bunk and tear it open, something about that Huntsville address bothering me. I read it near a section of thatch propped open beneath the eaves as the rain starts up again, pattering the muddy ground outside.

Dear Billy,

I hope this letter finds you well and celebrating the birth of our Savior in whatever way you can. I pray for you boys every night.

We're all in Huntsville at Aunt Judith's for the holidays. I'm thinking of staying on awhile. She could use help with the boys and I could use the change of scenery. The truth is, Billy, you're about to become an uncle . . .

I swallow hard and turn the letter toward him.

"You see this?" I say, holding the thin paper up in front of his face. I toss it away in disgust. "Congratulations. You're a father."

Hank blinks. Stoops and snatches up the letter and starts to read. "That ain't—that ain't poss . . ."

I don't stick around but storm out into the monsoon rain.

Footsteps sound behind me.

"Propfield!"

I spin on my heel to find Hank striding through the mud right for me. "You got a lot of nerve, judgin' me."

"*I* got nerve?" I say, stabbing a finger at my chest.

"This whole thing about Claire," he says, raindrops spraying from his lips like spittle. "It ain't about Claire. It's about you."

"Me?" I laugh, anger flaring.

"You're still followin' on my heels like you was in grade school. Tryin' to prove how much better than me you are, wishin' you were me the entire time. Talkin' down to me for havin' what you always wanted. Wishin' you were the one goin' back to make her an honest woman."

"I ain't goin' back to her!"

"That's right. You won't touch her now. 'Cause she's damaged goods. That it? I ruined her."

"She deserved better!"

"Better—like you?"

"That's right, like me!"

"Well guess what, Prop. Claire chose to do what she did. While you were tryin' to find a way to stand up to Daddy, she wasn't waiting around for you to become a man!"

My fist smashes across his cheek. Hank stumbles back, and then lunges at my midsection.

We go sprawling into the mud, fists flying. I pummel him for all I'm worth. He climbs over me and cracks me across the jaw.

The prisoners in the bunkhouse flood the doorway. The guards standing beneath the eaves of the next building shout and egg us on.

"You just can't figure it out, can you?" Hank says, breathing hard through his nose when we both come up for air.

"Figure what out?"

"Who you are without me."

"Without you we wouldn't be here!" I roar. "And Billy would still be alive!"

His face goes ashen and my fist plows into his nose. It explodes in a crimson spray.

A pistol goes off behind us, but I can't stop. I hit him again and again until they grab me by the arms and haul me off of him.

Hank pushes up from the mud with a grimace of a smile, his teeth bloody. The guards are yelling something, but I ain't listening as they drag me away.

I move to a different barracks that night.

36

December 18, 1942

Camp Cabanatuan, Philippines

They line us up in the morning, shove rice in our hands, and send us out to the fields to plant rice, eggplant, corn, and okra.

We chop knee-high anthills down with hoes. Hack at baby cobras. Keep count of the men around us. The guards shoot ten prisoners for every one man who escapes. And so we've become like crawfish, pulling one another back into the pot.

Today we've been sent to carry water from the river in five-gallon buckets to irrigate the field. It's dry and dusty, our faces coated with grime. I've just stopped to wipe the grit from my eyes when one of the prisoners—a gangly, towheaded kid who can't be a day older than nineteen—drops his pail and the water sloshes into the dirt. The guard some of the others call Big Weasel rushes over with a wooden hoe and starts yelling.

The kid picks up the broken bucket, but Big Weasel bats it out of his hands. When the kid scrambles after the bucket, Big Weasel wallops him over the shoulders.

Before I even know what I'm doing, I've closed the distance between us. The kid is too young for this. Something in his face maybe reminds me of another kid too young. The next time Big Weasel swings, I catch the handle of the hoe with both hands.

The guard's face registers shock—and then darkens.

Someone hollers in loud Japanese from behind him.

The commander.

I let go of the hoe and Big Weasel smashes the handle across the side of my head. My vision gets dotty and starts to blur, but I can see the hoe handle has busted in his hand.

The commander strides over to us with an angry shout.

Big Weasel greets him in swift Japanese and bows low. The commander's taller than our old enemy the Crate, his features sharper, the frown carved into his face. He takes a hard look at me, and just when I think that flinty gaze is the last thing I'm ever going to see, he turns to Big Weasel and barks at him, slapping him across the face. He yells in Japanese, spittle flying from his mouth, and slaps him again, shaming him real good—right in front of everyone.

"What're you doing?" the kid whispers, yanking me away. I don't know how to tell him that I got nothing to lose. Not my friends, not my integrity. Not my pride. If I don't get shot today, I will tomorrow. Ain't no difference to me now.

By the time Big Weasel hollers at us to get going—*Speedo! Speedo!*— his cheeks are crimson. He spins around looking for me, but by now I'm hustling to the river with a set of buckets. I can hear him yelling, the kid saying he don't know where I've gone.

That night in the barracks, I realize it's my birthday.

I am twenty years old.

I don't expect to see twenty-one.

37

DECEMBER 25, 1943
CAMP CABANATUAN, PHILIPPINES

There's a radio in the building next to our barracks. I can hear it tuned into the *Zero Hour* show, a broad who goes by "Orphan Ann" and speaks perfect English coming on the air to greet the GI boneheads listening to her. Sure enough, there's usually a crowd of prisoners squatting on their haunches listening each night, just for something to pass the time.

It's Christmas. I wonder what family my parents are eating dinner with after service today.

If they're gathering with the Crocketts.

If they know I'm still alive, living on rice and colored water they call soup, and sneaking bites of onions and okra before putting them back in the earth because the urge to eat has a funny way of outlasting the desire to live.

I wonder what Claire's baby looks like. If Hank's heard from her—gotten a picture, maybe. If he even knows if it's a boy or girl.

But if he has, he don't say.

I close my eyes as Orphan Ann closes out the show with Bing Crosby singing "I'll Be Home for Christmas."

That night I dream of corn-bread dressing and sweet-potato pie. Fresh bedsheets right off the clothesline. The soft *thwak* of the morning paper hitting the porch before dawn.

And I dream of Claire, her face so vivid that when I wake, I swear I can smell her perfume.

38

September 20, 1944

Camp Cabanatuan, Philippines

Asound rumbles from the far end of the field. No—from somewhere beyond. A drone, like a distant swarm of locusts. Not locusts . . . airplanes.

I drop to the ground.

The only planes I've seen over Luzon have always carried bombs.

But then a few of the fellas on my detail leap to their feet and start to cheer, waving at the sky. I look up, finally, and see American planes overhead.

The first ones I've seen since we surrendered.

My breath catches as one of the fighters peels off and circles over Cabanatuan, wagging his wings.

The guards call us in early that day, lock us in our huts, and cut our rations.

And I realize they're scared.

Hank sneaks into my barracks that afternoon. I'm drowsing in the afternoon heat, conserving energy, when he comes hurrying down the row of bunks until he gets to the one I share with a soldier from Little Rock named Lucky—which I think is a stupid name for anyone here.

"Propper," he says.

We ain't talked for more than two years.

From the look of him, Hank's down to maybe a hundred and twenty pounds. His arm has a bump in it. I heard it got busted by a guard.

"What d'you want?" I ask. Lucky, dozing against the end of the bunk, cracks open an eye.

"It's happenin'," Hank says. "Did you hear? Those planes dropped bombs the day we saw them. We're gettin' out of here."

I exhale a sigh. There's been so many rumors over the last two years, more men have died of optimism than dysentery.

"Listen," Hank says. "This is real. We're goin' home."

I close my eyes. "Lemme sleep."

"No. We been sleepin' too long. You ain't ready to give up like this."

"I been ready for years," I murmur.

"I know you snuck the tuna fish to me in Ward Z while I was laid up with my arm."

"Don't know what you're talkin' about." I pull a stale cigarette from my pocket and poke it between my lips. Hank snatches it, tosses it away.

"Hey!"

"What's it gonna take for you to fight like a man, Prop?" he says. "And I ain't talking about us going at it again."

I roll over, my face to the wall.

"Okay," he says. "Fine. Go ahead and die. But I'm gonna do some push-ups today."

"Have fun."

"No, on second thought, I'm gonna bang out these push-ups, and so are you."

I sputter out a laugh.

To my surprise, he smacks me on the side of the head. I shove up, riled.

"Don't wanna? Fine," Hank says. "Bet your friend Lucky will. Hey, Lucky, c'mon."

Hank slips onto the filthy floor and stretches out. Puts his hands in the push-up position, but his arm don't bend right where it broke and he can't lift his body up. Lucky gives me an apologetic glance and gets down beside him.

"Get outta my way," I say, kicking Hank aside and dropping down onto the floor with a grunt. "Count of three, you sissies."

I heave, not knowing how on earth I ever got this heavy while being this skinny.

We each grind out a single push-up.

I drop back to the floor and push back, dust my hands off, exhausted from that single act alone.

"There," I say. "Satisfied?"

"That was nothing," Hank says. "I got one more in me."

"All right then," I say, and go back onto my hands and heave myself up. This time a prisoner two bunks down joins us.

"One more!"

We bang out another.

"That wasn't hard," Hank says, sweating.

We do another. And another.

The sixth push-up takes so much out of me, I nearly pass out. By the seventh and eighth, we're both gasping for air. By the ninth, my heart's thudding in my ears and my shoulders are on fire.

We do a tenth and collapse on the dusty floor.

They keep us locked up for more than two weeks. Hank sneaks over a few nights later for push-ups, and again a few nights after that. More men join in each time.

As September rolls into October, I'm more rested than I've been in almost three years.

Five days later, they let us out.

They load us onto trucks like cattle. Pack us in train cars in San Fernando. Ours has a small hole near the door just like the one we held Billy up to so he could breathe, and I wonder if it's the same one we rode in on the final leg of our journey to O'Donnell.

We spend the next two months sitting in Bilibid Prison, listening to the Americans bomb Manila Bay.

39

DECEMBER 13, 1944
MANILA, PHILIPPINES

They line us up, march us through the streets of Manila tied in columns of four, half-hitch loops around our arms.

Locals stop to stare from both sides of the street. I lower my head, unable to meet their gazes. These are the same people who used to shake our hands. Who once saw prestige—and pesos—at the sight of our uniforms. Who fed and took pity on us on our way to O'Donnell.

We walk in disgrace past the old walled city. I wonder if our barracks survived. If the slop chute still has beer. We used to drill—there, outside the Spanish walls on the grassy lawn. Catch calesas to the Metropolitan and taxis into town as I dreamed about university classes and the officers' club.

Just down this boulevard we found the lieutenant in his idling car and drove him to Stotsenburg.

I tell myself that was three years ago, but it feels like twenty. Like it happened to someone else or like I saw it in a movie about three friends from Mobile—a place as far away and make-believe as Oz.

Beside me, Hank is silent as we approach Port Area. The place—once piled with crates of goods, booze, and food—stands scarred.

We stop at Pier 7, where Hank, Billy, and me arrived on the USAT Washington in August 1941. I remember hanging over the rail in wonder as the old city came into view, the scent of flowers wafting toward us on the water. How I'd stared at the bright Hudson taxis, military vehicles, trucks, and horse-drawn carts inching along the boulevard in the most leisurely traffic jam I'd ever seen.

Today, all that easy elegance is gone. I stare at the imposing Japanese freighter looming in front of us—the biggest ship I've ever seen. Within minutes a rumor comes down the line that the Red Cross is negotiating for our release. That it's first-class sailing all the way back to the States for us now.

I begin to believe that we're finally going home.

I glance at Hank, the image of him wavering through a lens of tears. It's all I can do not to start sobbing.

For Billy. For Yancy, Knox, Buggy, and the towheaded kid whose name I never knew. For all the ones we buried and are leaving behind.

For the mayor of Santa Rita.

Last of all, for the Private Jimmy Propfield I once was.

"C'mon, Prop," Hank whispers. "We're goin' home."

I wipe my eyes and move forward on wobbly knees.

The guards bark orders, and we move up the steel gangplank. But something feels very wrong as we're herded toward a big square hatch in the middle of the deck.

"Stick together!" Hank says. But his expression is grim.

Darkness falls across my shoulders as we climb down a rope ladder into the ship's hold. The inner walls are steel. The place is a metal box, maybe fifty feet square.

Broken straw and giant piles of crap are strewn across the wooden floor. The last people inside this compartment weren't people at all.

More men climb down behind us, pushing us toward the wall. Too much like the train car as others jostle for position. An old sergeant stakes out his area.

"Don't come any closer or I'm gonna start breaking jaws!" he says.

Hank and I sit on the floor two feet apart. Stick out our legs as wide as we can, claiming as much space as we dare. The hold can't fit more than a hundred men. Looking up at the ones climbing down and remembering all those in line behind us, I panic as the temperature rises, the sun baking the metal deck above. The old sergeant starts yelling and a fight breaks out. Hank and I get pressed closer to the wall. There's got to be two hundred men down here now, with more climbing down the ladder.

I fight down claustrophobia. Distract myself with a tally of heads. Three hundred. Four hundred. Four fifty. Four eighty.

Five hundred.

The rope ladder gets hauled up, a plank chucked across the hatch.

No sound of engines. The ship sits in the harbor without moving for what feels like hours. There had to be a couple thousand men on the dock. I wonder if they're getting packed into other holds.

In the darkness, a prisoner howls like a dog.

"Shut that guy up!" someone shouts. The howling continues.

"Water!" someone cries. "Who's got water?"

"Help," the man next to me croaks. "They're crawling up my throat!"

"What're you talkin' about?" Hank says.

"Hurry! It's the spiders. They want out!"

The man throws up. Sour rice splats my shoulder.

The man grabs my leg and I push him off. A minute later he upchucks on someone else. The fella on the other side of him clubs him with a fist but he don't go down. Instead, he leaps to his feet.

"HAIL MARY FULL OF GRACE OUR LORD IS WITH THEE!" he cries, toppling headlong onto someone else. "BLESSED ART THOU AMONG WOMEN AND—"

I hear them throw him off just to land on someone else. The poor man keeps bellowing, but there's nowhere for the next group of fellas to throw him except on someone else.

A *whump* silences him at last as someone's canteen connects with his skull.

"This place is goin' nuts," Hank says.

By now sweat's draining from every pore in my body, and all I can smell is puke. A chant breaks out: "Water! Water! Air! Water!"

A man starts screaming on the other end of the hold.

Finally, a guard sticks his head over the hatch.

"Quiet!" he shouts. "No quiet—close the hatch!"

The shouting gets louder. The guard throws another plank over the hatch, blocking out most of the light—and the air along with it.

Someone stands up near the back of the hold in the unnatural twilight. The chaplain.

"For the love of Christ, forebear," he shouts. "Please! If you all just settle down, I'll preach and calm our hearts. Now listen to the Gospel of—"

He collapses in a violent heap as someone kicks his legs out from under him.

"Water! Water! Air! Water!" Men pound the sides of the ship. "Water! Water! Air! Water!"

Hank's on his feet. A minute later he wades to the middle of the hold through a mass of prisoners, his shoulders back and head held high. He folds his arms and looks around, staring man after man in the eye.

The chanting slowly dies down.

"Men!" he calls out, his words echoing through the chamber. "Use your heads and think. Who are we? We're soldiers. The finest fighting men in the world!"

A smattering of cheers rises in the darkness. But Hank ain't done.

"Think of your mother! Your girl. Your wife. Your little brothers and sisters. Whoever you got to go home to. Whoever you got to be strong for. Do it for them and to make them proud to know you. Why? Because *you're* fighting for them. And who are we?" He thumps his chest. "We're the battling bastards of Bataan!"

Men get to their feet. They roar and shout and pound the hull. All I can think in the din is that I ain't felt such pride in anyone ever.

Or such shame for myself. Because everything Hank said about me is true. I've known that for quite a while now.

I've been jealous of him for as long as I've known him.

But in this moment, I've never been so in awe of him or grateful to call him friend. Not because of who I am with him, but for who he is.

The cheers go on a long time. Someone sings "America the Beautiful" and others join in. And then "Amazing Grace."

A few minutes later, the entire hull is swelling with sound. At the end of the last stanza, the engines start to churn.

A little air wafts down the hatch. It ain't much, but it stirs the heat.

Hank sits back against the wall, lets out a hot breath as men begin to talk again, jostling as they settle in.

"What d'you reckon now?" I say.

Hank shakes his head. "I reckon this ship ain't takin' us home."

Hank's speech works for a while. But as hours pass, prisoners start to beg for water and air again in the inky dark. A few feet away, a man rises. Warm liquid splashes onto my feet.

A few seconds later, I hear him lapping at the floor.

Hank seems to be asleep. Another man has taken the place of the prisoner next to me who went nuts. When dawn shows gray through the hatch at last, I see him licking condensation off the inside of the hull.

The planks scrape away from the opening and a blast of cold seawater cascades down onto those in the middle. A few minutes later a bucket of rice and fresh water get lowered into the hold.

The place turns into a mob.

The freighter churns throughout the day. Into night again. I try to sleep. Lose track of time.

Think of home.

I wonder if there was a jubilee this year and who won the Murphy High–McGill game.

What my parents are doing right now.

Every morning we gulp a handful of rice and water, if we can get to the pail. Each evening we scramble for another. When the boards stay open long enough, men hand up the bodies of the dead. Sometimes the guards even take them.

Twelve days later we're ordered up on deck. They hose us off with cold seawater and let us walk around for an hour before ordering us below. A few men refuse to go back. They're promptly shot.

A couple soldiers have a pair of dice and organize a game of craps. No one has anything valuable to bet—a shoe maybe, a picture of a girl from someone else's letters. An old dollar. The men with the dice acquire a decent amount of worthless goods until a high-rolling captain comes in with the game figured cold. He cleans the men out and lugs his pile of loot back to his corner and looks at it all afternoon.

Next morning the captain is dead.

The weather cools off. One of the men reckons we're in the South China Sea. Winds gust across the hatch and raindrops fall into the hold. We clamor to hold our canteens—boards, cups, hands—out, our mouths open and heads back.

The storm continues all night, the freighter rocking so hard no one can make it to the corners we've designated as latrines.

The days blend together. Twenty-five by my count, though Hank swears it's been twenty-six.

Then one morning the freighter gives a last chug and stops, dead in the water.

"Listen," someone says.

There's a drone outside, a *pow, pow, pow* and a swirling sound. I glance around me as a *rat-tat-tat* fills the air.

"That's a plane. An American plane!" someone shouts.

Cheers break out, but another man calls for quiet.

"Listen!" he says.

The *rat-tat-tat* comes again.

"They're shooting!" Hank says. "They're shooting the ship!"

They don't know it's full of prisoners.

We flatten out as activity erupts above. I hazard a glance to the square of sky through the hatch as a fighter strafes the deck. Bullets ping through the hull. A man in front of me takes one in the throat.

A blast shakes the ship. Dust rises in the air. Men shout and grab for anything to hold on to. Another bomb, and then another. One of the girders supporting the main deck starts to collapse with a sick, metallic groan, and then goes, raining beams down over half the hold.

Screams from those pinned beneath. Another blast rocks the hold as bullets swarm through the air.

Timbers collapse over the hatch, and all goes dark.

Moans all around me. Men gasping for air. The engines start again and then the freighter is moving. Scrape of boards high above. Light falls down on the wreckage and dead around me.

"Prop."

I find Hank against the hull cradling his arm. I push my way toward him. His mouth is tight. He's taken a bullet right over the elbow.

"Get it out," Hank says, and I can practically hear him sweating.

I roll up the tatters of his sleeve, find the burn hole oozing blood. Same arm the guard busted last year.

I look around for anything I can use.

"See that chunk of metal?" he says, nodding toward a busted beam. I turn, see it. I push my way over and grab it. It's a yard long, thin, rusty—and not nearly sharp enough.

I bandage him up with the sleeve of my shirt instead. Help lift beams off those trapped. But the few men we free are dead.

A week later Hank's arm is green and yellow and smells like moldy garbage. I give him water, feed him his rice and half of mine, but he's burning up.

"C'mon, Hank," I say, slapping his clammy cheeks as his eyelids droop. "You ain't gonna let a piece of crap metal take you down. Not now."

He gives a thin grunt and his head lolls to the side.

"You think a little gunshot's gettin' you off the hook 'bout Claire? Think again. You ain't allowed to die."

"Okay, Jiminy Cricket," he murmurs, his eyes closing. "By the way, remind me to tell you somethin' next time I wake up."

"Will do," I say, propping him up. "You sleep now."

An hour later they lower the rice. I grab a handful and return to Hank.

"Wake up, Hank. Chow time," I say, slapping at his cheek.

But this time, Hank don't move.

40

Your friend dead?" an officer next to me asks.

"No."

"His arm looks rotten."

"He took a bullet."

The man shifts, pulls something from his pocket. "I found this on one of the bodies yesterday," he says.

I flick a glance at the jackknife and look away.

"The blade's still good," he says.

"Won't do no good now."

"I don't mean to take the bullet out, son. Your friend's arm isn't going to heal. Best get it off. Get some salt water. Wrap it real tight."

"I can't," I say, unable to voice the thought stuck in my mind, knowing it don't make sense: I can't take Hank's throwing arm, which no one but me and Billy knew was as good as Cowboy's. Maybe better.

"Leaving him to rot won't be an easy way to go. You're better off slitting his throat."

I look down. Blink back helpless tears. "I ain't killin' my friend."

314

"The arm's the only chance he's got. He was strong before. I can see that. He might survive."

I know the officer's right. Worse yet, I know if it were me, Hank would've had my arm off yesterday.

But I ain't Hank.

Never have been.

I killed a man to save Billy. I tell myself taking Hank's arm can't be worse than that.

I glance up. "Show me what to do."

He nods. "Let's get some help."

When he comes back, he's got five fellas with him and a piece of board they pried up from the floor.

They spread around him, a man each for his legs and his healthy arm, another for his back. We yell up at the hatch. The guard up there sees what we're doing and surprises us by lowering a bucket of seawater and removing the boards from the opening to give us more light.

The officer washes his arm while I tear several strips from my shirt and twine them together. That's when Hank's eyes flutter open.

"I can hear what you're fixin' to do . . ." he rasps.

"You want something to bite down on, son?" the officer says.

" Try not to leave a scar." Hank laughs, the sound rattling through his lungs. He coughs and we climb on top of him. "Wait. Anyone got a cigarette?"

"Ain't got nothin' to smoke but horse manure," one of the men says. "Been wrapping it in the pages of the dead chaplain's Bible."

A few minutes later, the fella rolls a cigarette from a page in Matthew.

"Blessed are the poor in spirit," he says, lighting up. He pokes the cigarette between Hank's lips. Hank takes a deep drag and coughs.

I tie his arm off tight as I can, right below the shoulder. Snap the pocketknife open. The blades are shiny, at least.

I take a deep breath as the officer points round the skin and then just start cutting. Hank don't even flinch. I slice through muscle and sinew, all the way around the bone. At some point, Hank passes out, which I reckon is a mercy. Two of the others wedge the lower half of Hank's arm beneath the board, get up, and jump on it real fast.

The bone snaps. The arm is off.

We soak the stump in seawater, pack the wound with more strips, and tie it fast.

A few hours later Hank's skin is gray, but he's breathing. Heat radiates off his brow. He starts to come to, moans, and passes out again.

I watch him through the night. I need him to wake up so I can tell him it's all right if he don't go back to Claire. That it's all right, long as he comes back from wherever he's headed right now.

That night I pray for the first time in months.

American planes bomb us the next morning.

Our captors didn't mark the ship. The pilots don't know we're down here. Someone starts shouting, "We're here! We're Americans! C'mon, boys!"

A few others frantically bang on the hull as the ship shudders beneath us.

Water gushes through a fissure at the far end of the hold. Rushes cold across my feet.

We've been hit. I grab Hank and haul him as close to the corner as possible, stagger, and fall as we start to list.

Men scramble away from the water, trampling anyone underfoot.

Light and smoke from above. The planks that partially covered the hatch have been tossed aside. Shouting overhead.

"Prisoners out!" a guard yells. "Out!"

The rope ladder falls. Men scramble up like rats fleeing a flood.

"Son, you have to leave your friend!" someone says. The officer with the pocketknife. "You can't carry him up the ladder."

He shoves his way through the crowd to the rope and I see him reach the hatch thirty seconds later.

The water's up to my thighs, shocking my veins to life as it continues to pour in.

Hank's eyes crack open.

"Wha's happenin'?" he mumbles.

"We're about to take a swim, buddy," I say. "Hang tough."

"Been meaning to get out this hellhole," he murmurs just before his body goes limp, floating in my grasp.

Men struggle to stand, push against the onslaught of water toward the ladder, frantic to escape. I lose my footing in the rising flood and strike out for all I'm worth with my free arm. The ship's whistle shrieks and blows again. Someone kicks me in the ribs, grabs and shoves me back, trying to grapple their way toward the rope. I grab and try to pull past him. His shirt rips free in my hand.

An explosion overhead. Another bomb rocks the ship. The ship groans. The river of water turns into a surge.

I fumble with the sleeves of the shirt, shivering in the icy water as I bind them around Hank and lash him to my back.

"Take a lungful, Hank!" I yell, just before we go under.

I swim hard toward the hatch, find the edge of the rope ladder, and let it ride through my fist as seawater roils around us. The hull fills with a roar and we shoot up through the opening to the water's surface above the deck.

Men thrash all around us, Japanese and Americans alike. And it strikes me funny that at the end of a life, it don't matter what uniform we wore.

I wonder what all those others are fighting to get overboard for, grappling onto anything that floats as the stern tilts up in a final salute.

And then the wall of water comes and sucks us into the sea.

It hits us like the fist of God. Throws me backward in a riptide. Knocks the air from my lungs, tries to tear Hank from me.

And all I can think is, *You ain't getting him!* Though I don't know who I'm yelling at—God or the devil.

Salt fills my nose and mouth as the ship drags us under in a watery black hole.

I swim hard as I can. The ship groans beneath us, shuddering in the dark.

My arms are numb, fingers frozen. I can't feel my legs or my lips or my arms.

I close my eyes and push for the surface, lungs on fire. Just as I imagine we're about to break free of the ship's desperate gravity, I tear free of something else with it.

I wrench around in time to see Hank drifting away.

He's conscious again, trying to swim with his one arm. I lunge and grapple for him, fingers grazing the back of his collar.

My vision speckles, head pounding. I burst up into the air with a gasp, and then plunge back down as the ship sinks into the whirlpool of its own destruction.

I scramble beneath floating wreckage, swim up for air, dive down again, searching for any sight of him. Nothing. Resurface, gulping at air as the water churns beneath me.

"Hank!" I cry, searching around me. "Hank!" I plunge down as deep as I can and see the vortex of the sinking ship below, taking anything—and anyone—close enough with it.

I dive again and again, screaming his name beneath the water until all that's left is a watery howl.

But Hank . . .

Hank is gone.

41

cling to a wooden beam on the oily ocean and wonder why I don't
let go.

42

A second plank drifts by, trailing a frayed bit of rope. I lunge for the rope, pull it to me, and lash the second plank to the first with dumb hands.

I search for Hank for hours. Call his name until I'm hoarse.

The sun's begun to sink when I spot something shiny floating a little ways off. I paddle toward it and find a canteen bobbing on the surface. I unscrew the lid and it's a quarter full, but it's brackish inside, undrinkable.

Darkness comes and the wind picks up. I lay on the planks, shivering.

Sometime around dawn something bumps against my makeshift raft. A body.

The man's arms are spread over his head, his face in the water. But I can tell by his uniform he's Japanese.

I tug him closer and go through his pockets. Finding nothing, I help myself to his shirt and belt before pushing him away.

The sun rises, a bloody yolk on the horizon.

A bamboo mat drifts by. I pull it out of the water, hold it over my head on the narrow planks as the heat blazes, the Japanese shirt over my shoulders.

I shiver, teeth chattering, through another night. Doze into the morning.

When I wake, I think I've managed to sleep until twilight. Then I notice the graying sky. The bank of clouds in the distance.

The wind picks up with the current. A drop of rain hits my face. I open the canteen and tip back my head as the skies let loose.

I shout at the heavens with what little voice I got left. But no one cares if you're a raving lunatic when you're lost at sea.

Sometime later I float, belly bloated with water, beneath the thinning clouds. In the distance, a shadow has appeared on the horizon.

Land.

I roll over onto my belly, feet in the water, and kick. The land don't get closer. If anything, it slides further away.

I drift through the rest of the day and through the night . . . and another day and night after that.

The morning of the fifth day, I wake and see the shore.

White breakers separate me from the sand. I drift parallel to the beach for a while, then sling the canteen over my shoulder and tie it snug with my belt. I unlash the planks and set one of them adrift. Clinging to the second, I kick as hard as I can.

The first breaker hits and rolls me over. The plank knocks me on the head. I let go and another wave shoves me down.

I kick for the surface, lungs about to burst. Swim for land.

Ten strokes. Fifteen. Twenty. Fifty. Sand beneath my feet.

I drag myself to the beach and collapse.

For a long time all I can do is breathe, my skin shriveling beneath the sun, covered in salt. Eventually I drag myself to a thicket of palm trees. I drink deeply from the canteen, recap it, and close my eyes.

It's night by the time I wake. I'm surrounded by broken coconuts and am vividly aware that I haven't eaten for a week. I fail to bash one open and settle for dried seaweed. I chew and chew. It stays down. I gather more to make a bed, and it's the softest mattress I've had in years.

At first light I drink the rest of the water from the canteen, push up to stand on unsteady legs, and trudge inland. A mile on, I collapse beneath a tree.

How long were we on the freighter? A month? I don't even know what direction we were going—they never said. The storms, the bombings . . .

If we went north, I might have landed in the Ryukyu Islands. Formosa, maybe. East, any one of the tiny islands of Micronesia. Maybe Guam. If south, I could be somewhere on the coast of China.

Or worse yet, Okinawa.

I have no bearings. No weapon. No money, friends, or strength to go on.

I lay there for a while, eyes closed against the world.

Alone.

I try to imagine Hank and Billy yukking it up in heaven, feeling bad for my sorry self down here. Hank reunited with Cowboy. Telling me to hurry up already.

I was raised to look forward to leaving this life behind. And I never much feared death until lately . . .

After killing the mayor.

I'm pretty sure that changes things for me, and I'm scared. It's bad enough being without my best friends in this life.

I curl into a ball and sleep, on and off, all day.

Eventually, it ain't hunger or even the mosquitoes that get me up, but a frantic, desperate thirst.

Just before twilight, I prowl up the coast looking for water and find a stream. I drink deeply, then fill my canteen. Emboldened by the falling darkness, I follow the stream inland for about a mile . . . where I spy the glow of firelight.

I crouch in the shadows outside a village of three dozen thatched roofs. No Japanese flags. No weapons that I can see.

A cow lows in the distance. A stack of bananas still on the stalk is piled against the closest hut with several leafy pineapples.

My mouth waters at the thought of fresh fruit—a thing I never much cared about at home but will never take for granted again.

I can't take it any longer. I rush to the hut as quietly as I can. Break off two bananas and grab a pineapple.

A shout issues from inside. I run, pineapple cradled in my arm like a football, as I try to find my way back toward the beach. But it's dark by now, the sallow moon obscured by clouds.

I trip and slide down a shallow ravine, the pineapple tumbling from my hands. I search for it in the dark and grab it up, but before I can take off again, two forms skid down after me and grab me by the shoulders. I struggle and try to twist away, but I'm no match for a kid half my age, let alone two men.

One of them smacks me in the head, and next thing I know my ears are ringing as they drag me back to camp, yelling in Japanese.

43

I spend the night tied to a stake in the center of the village, guarded by an armed local old enough to be my papaw. He does not wear a military uniform. Neither is he interested in my attempts to communicate in Japanese.

Instead, he looks nervous. Everyone does. Wherever it is that I've landed, the locals do not want an American soldier discovered in their midst.

The next morning, two elderly men march me to a dock manned by Japanese soldiers who don't seem particularly surprised or concerned to see an American escapee. I am taken to a small supply ship and tied to a rail like a wayward dog. A little later, I'm given a ball of rice and some water.

The following day we arrive at a busy port where I'm loaded onto a truck with several other prisoners and driven to a banana plantation.

The next morning I begin work.

I work the plantation for a few months and fatten up on bananas before a bunch of us are taken back to the docks and loaded on another ship.

Some fella says we're bound for the Japanese mainland but I don't care anymore.

We dock, and once on shore I'm issued a bento-box mess kit, green burlap clothing, cloth boots, a pair of sandals, and a wool overcoat. It's the most clothing I've owned in years.

They shave my head and face and issue me a new number, which is sewn into my uniform.

14,360. My new name.

I'm loaded onto a train with real seats and fed rice and black tea. I never ask where we're headed. It don't matter.

The work camp is a collection of steel girders and sheds, pipes, and buildings. Dark mountains spike the horizon.

I'm given a bunk to myself and a blanket. The barracks has electric lights. They feed us rice and fish and ration me ten cigarettes.

I sleep better that night than I have in years.

The next morning, the Japanese interpreter for the man in charge tells us new arrivals that we have been given the privilege of replacing the Fukuoka Camp miners drafted to fight American dogs. The prisoners here are a varied mixture of Brits from Singapore, Javanese Dutch, Canadians, Australians, Koreans, and Americans.

In the mines, we ride down the tracks and hike through a jagged archway down into the mountain. The further we go, the hotter it gets.

We shovel coal and load the baskets into carts. One car before lunch and another after. There's a sick man on our crew with slime running out his nose. He moves slower than a growing turnip, and when we don't fill our cart in time, we all get clubbed by guards.

Slime Nose ain't there when we get back from lunch.

Ten weeks after my arrival, a cough settles in my lungs. I hack through each shift, and then through the night. The others give me anxious and then angry stares. I trade my next ration of cigarettes for tea, but nothing helps.

One afternoon the sergeant next to me slips on the wet stone and breaks his ankle. The guards don't believe his screams until one of them examines it and the sergeant passes out when his foot flops the wrong way. A skinny corporal and me get recruited to carry him up top.

The infirmary's a series of wooden buildings with dingy metal roofs and broken steps. A redheaded prisoner sweeps the floor but don't meet my eye when we come in, so we lug the sergeant down the hall to an empty cot.

"Who's the kid sweeping the floor?" I ask.

"Some goldbrick, claims he's too weak to work. They got a couple nutcases in here who work as orderlies. It's light duty if you can get it, but you've practically got to be in a wheelchair before you can pull it. Redheaded Kid never says nothing. I think his tongue was cut out in Davao. There's another guy works the night shift, some private. A real loony. They say he talks to ghosts."

"They got a doctor here?" I ask the corporal.

"Three." He nods. "One's a medic and dumb as a doornail. There's a Japanese doctor who comes in once a week, though if you ask me you're better off drinking cyanide. The other fella's okay, though. Heard he was a surgeon back in the States. Friday-Off Fournier's his name."

"Why d'they call him that?" I say, before falling into another coughing spasm.

He lowers his voice. "If a man wants a day off bad enough, he'll get someone to smash his hand with a shovel. Maybe drive a railcar over his foot."

"Fellas do that?"

"Where you been, kid? There's a Greek who stays a couple barracks over. Don't know his real name but they call him the Bone Breaker. For ten cigarettes he can give you any injury you want. Better'n you doing it yourself. The angles look better, see? The guards are quick to sniff out a self-inflicted wound."

"This Bone Breaker's good then?"

"Even if they don't believe the wound, a fella still has a chance if he can get to the infirmary. Captain Fournier knows how to get things. Bandages. Quinine. Novocain tablets. Even morphine. Shoot, some poor devil broke his back a while ago. True accident, that one. The camp doctor said the man would never walk again. But Captain Fournier built the man a rack to straighten his back out. Screamed for a week and a half straight. But a month later the fella was walking. That Captain Fournier is one of the good ones."

A few days later, my entire body shakes when I cough, and my back seizes up when I lift my shovel. Pretty soon I'm getting enough dirty looks, I think I'm probably in for it soon. But if I'm going to take a beating, I'd rather it be of my own choosing.

I spend several nights awake and coughing. Expecting to die.

But I don't.

Why? Why? I chant the question in my head.

Finally, right before dawn, a thought comes to me I hadn't had before. About the night that Hank and me learned Claire had a baby and Hank was a daddy.

The idea of her living away from home, trying to provide for a child, trying to protect it from the gossip and judgment I've seen happen even in my own high school and church, fills me with more pain than any beating.

Claire needs to hear that Billy held out like the champ he was. How

Hank lived and died—a hero. And so does her baby, who deserves to know what kind of man his or her daddy was.

A good one.

I'm the only one alive left to tell them.

44

July 7, 1945
Omuta, Japan

Ten cigarettes roll against my palm, spilling flakes of cheap tobacco out the end. I slip out to the Bone Breaker's barracks after the evening meal of rice and fish and stare around the dorm lit by a single electric bulb until a fella near the entry catches my eye and juts his chin toward the end of the line of cots.

I stifle a cough against my shoulder as I make my way down the line. The Bone Breaker lays on his back, smoking, one leg crossed on the other at the knee. A scar runs down the outside of his eye and into his beard like jagged lightning. He's a big man, his wrists the girth of my calves.

"You're the Greek," I say, standing at the end of his bed.

"What do you want?"

"I hear you have another name. That's what I'm here about."

He finally looks at me. Purses his lips. A full minute goes by and he never blinks.

"Ten up front," he finally says. "Plus your breakfast tomorrow."

"I heard ten flat."

"You heard wrong."

329

I nod, seized by another coughing fit.

"We do it near the end of tomorrow's shift," he says. "Guards will be less suspicious after you have worked a full day. Do not look for me. Do not ask for me. I will find you. You got the ten with you now?"

I hand him the cigarettes.

He sniffs them and feels along each seam to make sure they're full. I wait, coughing.

"Get away from me," he says. "You are sick."

The next morning the Greek appears at my side in the chow line. I hand him my bowl of rice. He sits down with it across the mess hall, not looking at me.

I cough on the train, lungs aching. I'm paired with a prisoner I've never met before. He don't talk, and I don't press him. I didn't speak for days when I first came here.

Toward the end of the shift, I'm shoveling with my back to the cart when the guy I'm working alongside stops and walks off.

I glance over to see the Greek standing in the torchlight, a shovel in his hand.

"Hold your hand against the wall," he says.

"Not my hand," I say. "My leg."

"I did a leg two days ago. It needs to be your hand."

"I don't want my hand broken. What else do you do?"

"Your hand or nothing. I do not have all day."

I put my hand against the wall, then yank it back. "Wait—how's this work?"

"Your thumb and index finger. You will not be able to hold a shovel. It will buy you a month. Maybe more. The blow will be quick. As soon as I do it, I will shovel some rocks on the floor. You will tell the guards the rocks fell on you. The man you worked with today will confirm your story. Mention me, we slice your neck. Understand?"

I nod, throat dry, and put my hand against the wall, last three fingers curled under.

The Greek rears back and smashes my fingers with the shovel. I stifle a scream, hold my wrist tight against me as he hauls several larger rocks over beside me.

The other prisoner returns as the Greek disappears into the shadows.

"Get down," he whispers.

I thrust my hand in the pile and a minute later, he shouts for a guard. When he comes round the corner I grimace, but it's the next bout of coughing that makes me groan as I pull free of the rocks and see my hand's a bloody mess. The guard nods and escorts me to the surface, where another examines my hand and records something in a notebook. I'm light-headed by then, and he orders me to sit before I topple over.

When we get back to camp, there's no line at the bathhouse like usual. A guard orders us out of the cart and points us in the direction of the main compound, where men are lined up in formation in front of the barracks, strained looks on their faces.

I suck the blood off my knuckles and look around, but when I start to ask about the infirmary, he clubs me in the back of the shoulders.

We stand in formation for half an hour. My hand drips blood and goes numb. I fight to stay standing. As it grows dark, we haven't moved.

Finally the civilian boss strides over and starts barking in Japanese.

"The rules have been broken," the interpreter says. "Guilty parties will be punished!"

We stand for another hour. Guards come with torches. My knees start to wobble.

A few minutes later, they drag someone out in front of the company, too badly beaten to walk on his own.

"Oh no," someone whispers. "It's Captain Fournier."

A chill marches down my spine as they dump him on the ground and order two prisoners forward. The guards thrust shovels into their hands and order them to dig. A few minutes later, a plank is set upright in the hole and the dirt filled in around it. The rope around Captain Fournier's wrists is looped over the top of the plank, pulled tight, tighter, until he's dangling in the air.

The guards beat him with short bamboo poles. Through it all, the surgeon is silent.

Finally, the boss holds up his hand. The guards stop as he addresses us through the interpreter.

"The work you do here must not stop! You are guests of the emperor. He treats you with fairness and care, yet we have learned that men injure themselves to avoid work. This man has been caught stealing medicines from the emperor to give to those who are lazy. We have a new commander in camp—and he is not happy."

My gaze falls to the ground in front of me. There ain't no going to the infirmary for me now—and that's if I'm lucky.

"You are ungrateful for the emperor's generosity and benevolence! Discipline from here on shall be severe. You will now learn from the example before you!"

The beating starts up again, though Captain Fournier has long since passed out, the flesh hanging off his back in bloody strips as he swings in the night.

Across the compound, the door to an administrative building opens and slams shut.

A shadow flanked by three guards strides toward the assembled company.

Someone curses. I flick a glance his way.

"It's the new camp commander. Look sharp."

He marches past us straight to the surgeon. Someone hands him a pistol, which he raises without hesitation. He blasts the surgeon point-blank in the head.

Captain Fournier twitches and twists on the rope, limp, as one of the guards sets something down in front of the compound.

A box.

The officer ascends it with a single step.

And I find myself staring at the Crate.

45

July 8, 1945
Omuta, Japan

The Crate lectures us for half an hour. The instant we're dismissed I slink away to wash and wrap my hand the best I can, but I know I won't be able to hold a shovel the next day. I don't think he saw me, at least. Ain't positive he'd recognize me if he did.

The next morning, men eye me with venom. Worse yet, my coughing kept them awake all night again.

Despite being put on basket duty, I only have one good hand to work with. By noon our cart is short. The guard clubs us all good. I pretend not to hear the mutters of the others as I force my lunch down.

I scramble all afternoon. Try to lug a coal car and end up pushing it from behind. My legs feel like rubber as sweat pours from my forehead. My gut aches from coughing.

I collapse on the cart that hauls us back to camp.

I wake the next morning beneath a blanket of dread. But there's something different going on in the barracks. Men talk with excitement and line up for chow with more energy than I seen since I got here.

"What's going on?" I say. "Today special or something?"

"Didn't you hear?" the guy ahead of me whispers.

"Hear what?"

"Nazis surrendered. Hitler's dead. We're winning the war!"

"What?"

"Keep your voice down!" he hisses. "They ain't exactly happy about it here."

"And this is good news?"

"We got them on the run, yes sir. We really got them on the run. The Allies'll turn all attention to the Pacific now."

But I've heard good news before. And every time I've ended up in a worse pickle.

That morning we're ordered to the center of the compound and made to stand at attention for an hour. The civilian boss comes out afterward, but at least there's no sign of the Crate.

"We have wiped out so many of your troops," the interpreter says. "You cannot possibly stand a chance of winning the war!"

We stand at attention the rest of the morning. But when we're released for lunch, we're each given a double portion of rice.

I stare at my bento box in disbelief.

"One of your officers demanded an increase in rations," one of the men, a Brit, says. "They complied."

And I finally believe we really might be winning.

Either that or Jesus is coming.

We stand in the yard the rest of the afternoon. My hand throbs, my head and my throat feel swollen, and my diaphragm twitches uncontrollably, but standing is easier than the mines.

"You got off lucky," one of my barracks-mates mutters when we're finally dismissed for the day.

That night my cough has just settled long enough for me to drift off when six guards come crashing into our barracks. They order us up and out of bed. We jump to attention and stand.

They spend the next fifteen minutes overturning mattresses, throwing shoes and clothing everywhere. Searching high and low. They club one prisoner to the floor. Knock another to his knees. And then they're gone, commotion coming from the next barracks over. They spend the next three hours shaking down the camp.

Next morning, it's work as usual. We ride to the mine on railcars. Hike down the shaft. My hand aches. My fingers are purple.

Thanks to me, we miss quota again and my group takes another clubbing.

If the guards don't kill me soon, the other prisoners will.

We're ordered out after lunch and stand in formation at the mouth of the shaft where we're dressed down by the boss and threatened with punishment if we don't work faster.

"That's the last beating I take on account of you," one of the prisoners growls after we're ordered back down.

I try. I'm expecting abuse, but instead I'm given some space. The other fellas are twenty feet away. A half hour later, they're even farther. The men with the shovels are nowhere to be seen. I scramble, trying to make quota, but it's quiet, and now I'm unsettled.

I stop for a breather and realize I can hear the water dripping from the rock beside me.

That I'm alone.

And I know what that means.

I drop what I'm doing, start to hightail it back up the shaft, coughing so hard I have to stop a moment, my hands on my knees. But I don't see anyone. My swift clip turns into a hacking run. I pass a couple guards, but when they shout at me to halt, I don't stop.

That's when I hear it—the shout, amplified by stone.

"Fire in the hole!"

The earth shudders and rattles. A second later the ground behind me explodes in a massive fireball. Flames shoot past me, propel me forward in a burning river of heat. Something sharp smacks me in the shoulder and I fall forward, my hands out in front of me.

Pain shoots through my bad hand like lightning, and I leap up and run for all I'm worth as rocks rain down over me. Not just rocks, but huge chunks of coal. Timbers, flying through the air.

I'm slammed to the ground, the breath knocked from my lungs. I roll and try to get up, but my legs won't work. I'm pinned down as a cloud of smoke and debris blasts by me, filling up my lungs and blacking out the world.

46

JULY 11, 1945

OMUTA, JAPAN

He still alive? Look at his eye!"

Pain shoots through my legs. Someone screams, loud inside my head.

Rough hands grab my shoulders. Carry me toward daylight.

I try to talk, but it comes out as a groan.

"You've been in an accident," someone says.

"How many guards you think we got?" another man asks.

"Enough to make me happy. Get the kid to the infirmary."

I feel more than hear the rail cart beneath me. Struggle to breathe and then cough—which hurts so much I hope to God I never cough again.

Blinding daylight gives way to the dimness of indoors. Only one of my eyes works anymore.

They stretch me out on a cot.

My head burns. A little while later someone swabs my forehead. I open one eye—can't open the other—to see the redheaded kid.

Sometime later, I lay beneath a lamp. Someone leans over me and the light eclipses his head. The Japanese surgeon. He's got a scalpel right in

338

front of my face. Too close to my eye. If they've given me something for pain, it ain't enough. I try to scream as the narrow blade comes closer.

They have to hold me down.

Someone's sweeping.

A figure bends over me. A night orderly, but this one's hair ain't red.

His hand's on my face and he pinches my mouth open. Shoves something inside it.

The room spins around me, and I stand in a field of light. It's late summer and humid, and the scent of ripe blackberries hangs in the air.

Claire and me are walking along the ditch, swinging our buckets. She's wearing a calico sundress and her arms are tan.

I never told her I thought she had pretty shoulders.

"This one's for you, Jimmy," she says, a fat berry in her fingers. I open my mouth and she pushes it past my lips. It's juicy and ripe and I take her hand like I used to do when we was kids.

I try to tell her that this time I'm never letting go, but the words don't come out.

"Sleep now," she says. "Rest up and get better. It won't be long now. It won't be long."

Everything aches. My hand. My legs. My head. I reach up to touch my eye, find the socket bandaged tight. My arm is so heavy it falls off the cot when I drop it back to my side.

It's dark and quiet in the ward.

Except for the sweeping.

Someone comes and mumbles over me. Lays my arm back at my

side. I try to talk when he opens my mouth and then thrash as he pours something inside it.

I choke and then swallow as the room swirls around me.

I hear Claire singing before she comes over the hill. She's doing the dance from *The Wizard of Oz*—the yellow brick road one—kicking her foot out and skipping just like Judy Garland. When she gets close enough, she scoops my arm in hers and keeps going, laughing as I try to keep up.

"James Propfield!" she says. "I swear you have two left feet. How are you ever going to dance with me at prom? You *are* takin' me to the prom, aren't you?"

I reach over and take her hand, try to twirl her around. It's all backward and she has to duck under my arm. We end up tangled instead.

I hold her tight. Ask her what kind of corsage she wants and talk about anything that makes her happy. Because if the size of my world is no wider than her smile, that's big enough for me.

The room is dark again when I wake. No sound of sweeping. But I'm not alone, I know that much. A minute later someone checks my bandages. This time I grab that wrist before he can push the pill between my lips.

"My eye . . ."

"Gone, I'm sorry," he whispers.

My head is hazy. My words slurred even to my own ear.

"My legs?"

"Both broken, but you'll walk again. You just need to rest. C'mon now." This time I give no resistance. A few minutes later I fade away.

I notice the cicadas first and think that it's dusk. But when a couple birds start in, I realize it's just before dawn.

My good eye's crusty and hard to open, but when it does it's clearer than it's ever been.

A figure stands at the foot of my cot, a pole—no, a broom—in his hand. I strain to make out the silhouette in the darkness.

"Is the war over?" I croak.

"Shh," he whispers. "You just worry 'bout getting better."

He's thin. Thin as any man in a war camp.

"How come I never see you in the light?"

"Don't want to shock your system."

I nod, getting it. "Face injury?" I ask, having seen enough of them to last a lifetime.

"I been prettier, no thanks to you," he says. He sets aside his broom with his only arm and sits down on the edge of my cot with a grin.

In an instant I'm bawling like a baby.

"'Bout time you came back from the dead, Prop," Hank says and grabs me tight.

47

JULY 14, 1945
OMUTA, JAPAN

Y ou realize," he says, "when we get back, folks are gonna think
we spent this whole time layin' around some tropical island,
drinkin' from coconuts, being waited on by native girls. Which
is why the official story's got to be we was attacked by sharks."

This time when he smiles, I see the lines on his face. The hollows in
his cheeks. He looks like he's thirty.

A couple of his front teeth are broken.

"Hold on," he says. He gets up, grabs the broom, and disappears. I
hear him sweeping in the outside ward. A few minutes later, he's back.

It's nearly time for breakfast. I hear dirt crunching under boots from
the direction of the yard. A cup clanking against a mess kit from those
first in line to eat.

"Guards are up, but they don't bother much with the infirmary."

"You drowned," I manage to say, my nose stuffy and good eye swollen. I still can't believe it's him. That he ain't a ghost.

He slides a wooden stool close and sits down.

"After you cut off my arm, I was all kinds of not seeing straight,"
he says. "The sting of that salt water probably kept me alive. Took

everything I had to get to the surface. By the time I did, you were gone. I hung on to some debris for a while, floating along with the current. Soon as night hit, I figured I was a goner. But there I still was the next morning. Well, the mist cleared and the sun came out and here comes this Japanese trawler. It must've been hiding in the fog 'cause all of a sudden, it's right on top of me. My first thought is there's no way I'm bein' taken alive again. But then I remember my papaw. We used to play poker and I got pretty good but he'd always win. One day I ask him what his secret is, and he says sometimes you gotta let the deck give you a hand. And boy did I need an extra hand right then." He glances toward his missing arm and grins.

I shake my head.

"It didn't *feel* like layin' down my rifle," he adds. "Not this time. More like sayin' yes to the ride that saved my life. Like I got something left to do in this world."

"You mean . . . the baby."

He nods. "Turns out they got orders to look for survivors swimmin' in the wreck, and they got an American doctor on board who got wind of it and weaseled his way onto the trawler." He gets up and goes out to sweep, making sure he looks busy, holding his broom tight against his waist with his one arm, and comes back a few minutes later.

"So then what?" I ask, wondering if I'm still out of it and dreaming all this.

"They only found three survivors and the doc treated me real good. He bandaged me up, gave me some drugs he had stowed way. I ask his name and he says it's Fournier."

"Captain Fournier," I say. The man who was beaten and shot before the explosion.

Hank nods somberly. "The trawler takes us to Japan and the captain brings me here to the infirmary. When I start to heal up, doc gets me this job as an orderly." He leans back out to look down the ward. "The redheaded kid's on duty in two minutes. I'll be back when it gets dark. Man, I'm glad you're alive."

He has no idea.

I wait until he's gone and start blubbering all over again.

That day I sleep the best I have in weeks.

But Claire don't come back neither.

The next night I ask Hank what he's been giving me. He tells me about the pills he stole from the Crate's quarters, the cocktail he whipped up for the IV he rigged up one-handed. The one that kept me alive, still hooked to my arm.

"I'm mighty glad for your new doctoring skills," I say, honest-to-goodness impressed.

"I'm thinkin' I might just go into medicine when we get home. It ain't like I'm gonna be much help at the mill. You ever seen a one-armed doc, Prop?" He grins.

"I think that's real good," I say.

Hank hesitates, looking down at his hand. "D'you think Claire might . . ."

"I don't think Claire'll care one whit if you have one hand or two."

"Actually, I was wondering if you thought she'd like the idea of bein' a doctor's wife?" He glances up.

I hesitate. "I think you'll have to ask her that," I say at last.

"Jimmy . . ."

"No, it's okay. I'm so happy you're alive, and I ain't jealous. Not anymore. She's gonna need you." I give a crooked smile. "An' you're gonna need her to keep your head from gettin' too big when you're a doctor."

"Yeah, well, there's somethin' I need to tell you." Hank lowers his

344

head. Scratches the back of his neck. When he looks back up, his expression is somber. "That baby ain't mine."

"Hank—"

He lifts his palm. "I ain't sayin' I'm innocent. But what didn't happen is—we didn't. She was grievin' and not thinkin' straight. I was too upset. Too drunk. And before things went too far, she came to her senses and told me to go home."

"But the baby . . ."

Hank narrows his eyes. "I figured you never got farther than that part in the letter—where she said Billy was gonna be an uncle."

"No, I suppose not." My head's still fuzzy, but now that I think about it, I never did read the rest.

"She explained farther down that she and Cowboy got married in secret before he shipped out. They didn't want to wait but still wanted to do right by each other."

I blink and try to make sense of what he's saying. Remember the days following their prom engagement, when Claire was gone so often.

She believed in waiting. It tortured us both.

"Why didn't you tell me?" I ask, staring at him.

Two years. Two years we spent hating each other.

That I spent hating him.

"Every man's got a confession," Hank whispers, looking at me. And I think back to the priest who said that the day I pulled the trigger on the mayor. The life I took that didn't even buy Billy back his own.

"You've always been good, Prop." Hank shakes his head. "And I could never compete with that. After a while, I guess I just got tired of tryin'."

I lower my head.

"Hank . . ."

But what can I say?

I've been out of stones to throw for a while.

"I'm still gonna ask, Prop. To marry her," Hank says. "I want—" he pauses and looks away. Swipes at an eye. "I want to be the daddy my brother couldn't be. I'll never be Cowboy. But if I can be there for his little girl or boy, and Claire . . ."

He don't need to explain it. That child is all he's got left of Cowboy.

He also don't need to explain what I've known for years: that he's loved Claire nearly all his life.

We all did.

"Then do it," I say, lifting my gaze to his with a nod. "She's your family now."

I can't fathom what the last three years have been like for Claire— mourning a husband no one knew she had. Moving away to have a baby on her own. I can only imagine the stares and the talk at the dinner table after church, where gossip gets ladled like gravy.

"Maybe you should just write to her and ask her," I say.

He lowers his head. Shakes it. "Naw, not 'til she gets a chance to see—" he gestures to the stump of his shoulder.

"No one'll love her better," I say quietly, and mean it. Not because Hank's the baby's uncle, and not because it don't hurt—I know for sure that's one ache that will never fade. But because Hank's always done everything better than anyone else.

And I want the best for Claire.

The next night I sit up for the first time in months—and promptly vomit. I try again the next day. And two nights after that, Hank's got me standing up, if only for a few minutes.

"What d'you think you'll do when you get back?" Hank asks when I'm huffing and puffing after struggling a few painful steps. I know he must be wondering how it'll work, me and him both being home.

Especially if he marries Claire.

I ain't sure of the answers. I just know he won't have to worry.

"You really think we're goin' home?"

Home.

The word is as distant and exotic to me as the Philippines was once.

"War's gonna be over soon. We better get you back on your feet if you plan to kick anyone in the head on your way out."

Within a week I'm walking across the infirmary floor on crutches. I sleep by day, hide my progress from the guards. But by night I'm starting to walk by myself as Hank sneaks me extra food and the latest rumors. Namely, that Greta Garbo's died and that Henry Ford's going to give each soldier a brand-new car soon as we get back.

Hank also heard someone say there's probably no chance we'll ever have kids after being so malnutritioned.

By the first week of August, I pull off five full push-ups. Hank does them with me, one-armed.

"That's real good, son. But I still got you beat," he says with a grin.

And that's just fine with me.

Two nights later, Hank hurries in earlier than usual.

"Saw somethin' I ain't ever seen today," he says.

"A rescue mission?"

"Some kind of bomb," he says, not smiling.

I close my eye, still tired. "You've seen bombs before."

"Not like this, I ain't. There was a big cloud like a white balloon that hung over the edge of the mountains, all blue 'n' gray around the edges." I crack my eye open as he gestures with his hand. "It just kept goin' higher and higher. Never seen anything like it. No one here has. When I asked one of the guards, all he said was '*Boom*.'"

I lift my brows. I don't know what Hank's described, but if it's scaring the Japanese, ain't that a good thing?

That night I jog around the ward for a full half hour, pull off fifteen push-ups. Wolf down dinner with my best friend.

Just before I doze off that morning, Hank hurries over to my cot.

"The Japanese doc assigned to this camp just arrived, mighty upset." Hank grins.

"About what?"

"He says the Americans dropped a bomb that wiped out a whole city. Says he's scared he's gonna get killed now that they've lost the war."

Lost the war.

Hank slaps me on the shoulder as my eye goes wide, and then covers my mouth before I can let out a loud whoop.

"It's happenin'!" he whispers. "Not long now."

We're going home.

48

'**ve finally dozed off when a crash startles me awake.**

Commotion, from the outer ward. It's early—before the start of day shift. I can see Hank from the corner of my eye gesturing me to silence as guards burst into the room.

I push up onto my elbow as guards pull out drawers, toppling tables and metal bedpans with a crash, shouting patients to their feet—*Speedo! Speedo!* They overturn the beds of those strong enough to rise, and a few with the patients still in them. A crutch launches through the eaves beneath the thatch. Instruments clatter from shelves. Bandages roll across the floor.

I get to my feet as one of them upturns my cot. Another orders us outside.

"What d'you figure this is all about?" I murmur as we join the formation in the yard. The rest of the camp is already there: seventeen hundred skinny prisoners arrayed like a forest of toothpicks.

"Them showin' their true colors," he whispers.

The guards comb through one barracks after another, throwing clothing, shoes, mess kits—anything they find—out onto the ground. Getting their last jabs in while they can.

349

The sun rises, hot and dry. I'm thirsty and wouldn't mind a little chow, though I'm sure the rest of the guys around me are just happy to be standing here and not working the mines below.

The racket finally dies down an hour later. A door slams from across camp. I know that building, and the man who lives in it, though I haven't set eyes on him since the day I got my hand broke.

The Crate strides across the compound with two guards, ribbons fluttering on his chest. They look a little faded, the Crate himself thinner than before. Am I seeing things, or does the civilian boss at his flank seem to glance anxiously around?

But of course he does. They've seen the white cloud from that bomb. If it's as bad as Hank says, they've got to be terrified about what's going to happen to them.

The Crate paces for a full fifteen minutes, the corners of his mouth turned down all the way to his chin.

He's got to sense the same thing we do: that the tide has changed and his grip on us is slipping.

Who's the dog now?

The Crate stops, arms at his sides.

"What wise men you are!" he shouts. "So filled with intelligence!"

"Well, that's a turn," I murmur to Hank.

"Brewer's yeast!" he says, pacing off to the side. "Who knew? The answer: One of you. You, in your cunning."

Brewer's yeast? I glance up, wondering if the Crate's gone whacka-doodle at last.

"A wise man knows there is enough vitamin B in one tablet of brewer's yeast to turn a bad case of dysentery. But a wise man is also a fool to give cowards the coward's path, and no mercy shall be shown to such a wise fool." He says something in clipped Japanese, and a man steps forward.

The Japanese surgeon. The one Hank said was afraid now that they'd lost the war. The same one who cut out my eye. He bows his head, gets down on his knees, and pulls open his shirt.

One of the guards hands a knife to the Crate. He, in turn, hands it to the surgeon.

The surgeon unsheathes it, sun glinting on its blade as his chest rises and falls in a succession of quick breaths. And then he plunges the knife into his own gut, blanches, and rips the knife to the side.

I tell myself to look away but I can't. The surgeon gurgles, his face twisted as he collapses forward, shoulders heaving.

The Crate steps forward with a grunt.

"What you have seen is an honorable death for a man who served his emperor. An honorable atonement for his traitorous act," the Crate says, though the surgeon isn't dead—he's still writhing on the ground. "But he was not the only traitor in this camp."

I glance around. If the Crate wants to knock off a few more of his comrades, I figure I can stand the heat a little while longer.

This time no one steps forward except the guards—right into our ranks. They make their way through the rows of men in front, glancing from one man to the next. Searching for someone specific . . .

Until they get to Hank. The first guard grabs him by his arm. The other fumbles with the nub of his shoulder and settles for a wad of his shirt as they jerk him out of line beside me.

"Hank!"

He glances back at me.

"Everything's fine," he says as they shove him forward. "Just keep your mouth shut."

A guard steps into my line of sight as another yanks my arms behind my back and pulls me from formation.

My heart pounds as they push us through the lines of men in front of us. The Crate lifts his chin in my direction.

"The traitor who tended that man's wounds died after allowing theft within the domain of his charge! There is the thief"—he swings his outstretched finger toward Hank—"who stole the brewer's yeast and shall now atone for his crime in far less honorable fashion."

One of the guards kicks me in the back of the knees and I go sprawling in front of the assembly. I plant my hands in the dirt, ready to leap up and shout that they've lost the war and we all know it.

But the dirt is wet and red. And when I turn my head I find myself face-to-face with the surgeon. His dull gaze meets mine. A shallow breath rattles through his lips.

The guard hauls me to my feet and pushes a shovel into my hands.

"Dig!" the Crate commands, pointing to the ground. "Three feet deep! Six inches wide!" And now I see where two Xs have been scratched in the soil.

I don't move.

The Crate pulls his .45, cocks and levels it—not at me, but Hank. Hank's eyes meet mine.

My hands shake on the handle. I drive the spade into the dirt. Several feet away from me, a guard throws a shovel at Hank's feet. Yells at him to pick it up.

I glance up at the Crate as I toss another scoop of dirt aside.

I'm gonna kill you.

I thrust the shovel into the earth, winded.

The next scoop, I straighten, wipe the sweat from my forehead. Glance back at Hank struggling to dig with one arm. That's when I see the furrows around his mouth. The tight line of his lips.

I lean over to suck in a breath, forearm resting on the handle of the shovel.

One of the guards moves toward me. I straighten to my full height, which is a good foot taller than him. The guard pulls out his gun.

"Don't, Prop," Hank says.

I jam the shovel back into the earth, finish the hole, and then go help Hank.

The Crate gives an order in Japanese and the guards march us across the compound, guns at our backs. At the lumber pile, one of them gestures. "Pick up!"

The timbers are about fifteen feet long. I heft one up by the end, hold it for Hank as he gets his arm around it. Lug up another as Hank starts off toward the holes, and drag it after him.

"Stand them in the holes!" the Crate shouts. "Pack the dirt around them!"

I maneuver the timber around, drop the end into the hole. Stand it upright. Struggle to shovel the dirt in beside it, and tamp it hard around the base.

By now I'm breathing hard and sweating harder, and it takes Hank and me even longer to set up the other pole.

"What's he playin' at?" I whisper, bent over to pack the dirt with the flat of the spade.

"Just do what they say," he murmurs, low.

I start to respond but after a quick glance at the dying surgeon, keep my mouth shut.

Two guards bring a third beam, and another arrives with two folding ladders. He sets up the ladders and the guards climb up with the beam, where they nail it atop the first two like a giant goalpost.

I glance at Hank. He shakes his head faintly.

Now one of the guards trots out with a wooden box like the one we first named the Crate for. He steps up on it a little more slowly than I remember, but his expression is harder.

"These two traitors not only defy the goodwill of the emperor in an effort to save their own wretched skin," he announces. "But they pretend to care for the welfare of their countrymen even as they endanger them with their treachery—first at Camp O'Donnell, where their attempted escape resulted in the death of their so-called friend."

Hot anger floods my face. Across from me, Hank's expression goes flat, pulled down into something feral and dark.

"This one purposefully injured himself to avoid work," he says, pointing at me. "But as you can see, he is healthy enough to dig. And yet he has lain in the infirmary for months, leaving the rest of you to bear the burden of his laziness. But no honor shall be afforded thieves and miscreants for the dishonor they heap on their own heads!"

My heart pounds in my chest. Because now I understand. This ain't just a punishment for Hank giving brewer's yeast to the sick, or my finagling to get out of the mining detail that would have killed me—and then surviving the explosion set by my fellow prisoners that nearly did. This is the Crate covering his tracks now that the end is near, making sure we never live to tell about the mayor of Santa Rita.

One of the guards tosses a short rope over the crossbar. An end dangles on each side.

Like the two loose ends we are.

"As with our benevolent emperor, I am not without mercy," the Crate says. "Unlike you Americans with your philosophy of cowardice, we do not cater to the weak. Here"—he gestures to the structure—"as in life, the strongest shall survive.

"The rules of the contest are simple," the Crate says lightly. "The cowards shall each grasp the end of the rope. The ladders will be removed. Let go of the rope first, and you die. Let go at the same time, and both die—along with ten others. Only the man who falls to the ground with the rope in his hand will live."

No. I look around frantically. We're about to go home!

The guards nudge us up the ladders with their bayonets.

I look wild-eyed at Hank.

"I ain't doin' this," I say.

"Grab the rope, Prop," he says.

"I ain't grabbin' it!"

"Grab the stinkin' rope!" he says, reaching up to wind his end tight around his wrist.

I grab the end of the rope. Twine it tight.

Hank nods. "Both hands," he says.

"No way."

The ladders get kicked out from beneath us.

We drop with a jerk and crash into one another, dangling mere feet from the earth.

I wonder if I've ever heard the camp so quiet. Even the rattling breaths of the dying surgeon seem to fade away. Do I imagine it, or does a breeze riffle through my hair as we twist, my shoulder bumping his where his arm used to be?

Hank and I used to play a game like this on the school playground. We'd dangle from the high bar and kick and try to tie the other up with our feet. Drag them down until they had no choice but to fall.

War, we called it.

"Hang on, buddy," Hank says, too low for the Crate to hear. "Let's just you and I talk a bit, two old friends."

"You hang on," I say. We dangle and twist as the sun beats down. Waiting for something to happen, trying hard to think of a way out. Because it can't end like this.

"How long did you say it'd be 'til this war's over?" I say, pretending to check my watch.

"Can't be long now," Hank says. "Why? You worried 'bout missin' chow?"

"Heard there's extra maggots in the rice today."

"Little somethin' to look forward to."

I swing like one of my mama's wind chimes, twisting in the breeze. And I look out over the assembled company, their eyes averted, cast down.

I know what they're thinking: *Don't*. They're *this* close to going home. Just like Hank and me.

My wrist burns, rope biting into the skin. I can't feel my fingers.

"Listen, Hank," I say. "I need you to tell Claire somethin' for me."

"Sorry, no can do," Hank says. Sweat beads on his forehead.

"Tell her I'm sorry. For everything."

"No." Hank shakes his head. "You got nothin' to be sorry for. Ever. In all my life, you ain't been nothin' but perfect. A perfect friend. A perfect son. A perfect man. All this time, Prop, I spent it wishin' I was like you."

"No," I say. "That ain't right."

"It is." Hank's mouth tightens with a grimace and sweat rolls down his cheek.

"I got you," I say, trying to hold him up with my free arm.

"She's a good girl, Prop. She deserves a good man."

"She's gettin' one," I say, unwinding the rope from my hand.

"Yeah. She is," he says.

And lets go.

49

AUGUST 15, 1945
OMUTA, JAPAN

The shot that kills Hank reverberates through my body.

I barely register being hauled away. Staked to the ground by the same rope I thought I let go of before him.

A fist knocks me flat. The blows—from heels and cudgels and boot toes—crack my ribs, cave in my shoulders, and deafen my ears. I pray. Not that it'll end, but that this time it'll be enough.

I spy the surgeon in glimpses through their legs. He stares back, his gaze vacant. But his lips are still moving with each faint breath.

I feel bad knowing I'm leaving before him.

The ringing in my head gets fainter, and the surgeon fades from view as my eye swells shut. The next kick sends me rolling onto my back, shadows and sunlight jostling above.

I wait for Hank to lean down over me. Am looking forward to Billy's grin.

Almost there.

Just one final blow.

"Halt!" someone says.

The shadows abandon me to the sunlight, bright red through my eyelid. Hot on my sticky face.

No . . .

"Wait," I rasp.

I struggle to lift my hand. To pry my eye open with my fingers. Across from me the surgeon lies dead.

"Come back," I grind out, and try to shove up from the ground. Toss a weak handful of dirt with an arm that don't work right. "Finish me!"

But the guards are gone.

They're lined up behind the Crate, who's still standing on his box. He looks pale and waxy, a paper held between two fingers of each hand like it might detonate.

"I have just received—" he begins, hoarse. He clears his throat. "I have just received new orders. I am informed that His Imperial Majesty, the emperor, has ordered all hostilities to cease immediately. I am instructed to surrender this compound to the highest-ranking American officer present. Will that man come forward immediately? This is not an order . . . but a request. The war is over." He lowers the paper. "You have won."

Bedlam breaks out in the yard. A few men take up "The Star-Spangled Banner," and soon the crowd of seventeen hundred newly liberated prisoners are cheering with all their might.

50

I can hear them in the yard, snoring beneath the stars. A lot of the men have opted to sleep outside in the open air.

A medic tells me that Lieutenant Colonel John Davidson stepped forward to assume command, accepting the Crate's .45 and his sword, which the lieutenant colonel offered back in case the Crate wanted to commit suicide.

The Crate declined, saying he was too old.

The medic tells me about the bombs that leveled Hiroshima and Nagasaki.

And he tells me I'm going to be fine.

But I know that ain't true.

Earlier, he read me a letter he swiped from the main building.

I am pleased to inform you that we received military orders for stop of warfare. Since you were entered in this camp you have doubt-less had to go through much trouble and agony due to the extension of your stay here . . .

By order, we the camp staff have done all in our power towards

your management and protection but owing to the disturbed exter-
nal conditions here we regret that we were unable to do half of what
we wanted to do for you. But I trust in your great understanding
in this point.

Sig. Fukohara Tai Dona

I lay in the infirmary for days while the other former prisoners go
scavenging in the city. They come back with everything from booze and
Red Cross medical supplies marked 1943 that the Japanese have hoarded
while we've been starving and dying of disease, to a cow they slaughter
and cook up. The orderly brings me a plate and I make myself eat it
in tiny bites. Even then, it makes me nauseous, my stomach unused to
anything but wormy gruel.

Navy planes fly overhead. Some of the men here have painted POW
in bright letters on the roofs of the buildings. The pilots wag their wings
and drop supplies: corned beef and K rations. Flour, salt, and strawberry
jam. Issues of *Coronet* and *Reader's Digest*. Cigarettes and movies. The
boys hang a sheet for a screen and run them all afternoon—newsreels
about the war, *Popeye*, *For Whom the Bell Tolls*, *Shadow of a Doubt*,
Arsenic and Old Lace. An orderly wheels me out for an hour or two to
listen, my eye too swollen to see.

The boxes they dropped landed with red, white, and blue parachutes.
By the time I'm well enough to stand in the doorway of the infirmary,
they've been sewn into an American flag. Old Glory flies over the camp
now.

First thing I do the day I leave the infirmary is visit Hank's grave. The
redheaded kid who worked the day shift after Hank goes with me.

I know the place. The men who buried him carried me on a stretcher so I could accompany his body.

Hank rests on a small rise beneath a couple trees, which is about as picturesque as it gets out here near the mines.

I hate that he lies in the soil—not just here, so far from home, but anywhere.

He don't belong in the ground.

The minute I'm within ten feet of his grave, I pause. Wonder if my eye ain't working right.

The mound is covered in cigarettes.

"There's one for every man he saved," the kid says.

I stagger to the site and drop to my knees. Count the rolled tobacco—some of them in better condition than others, some of them broken, which seems just about fitting to me.

Forty-three.

His grave is marked by a simple wooden cross. I look around for a rock or anything sharp, and finally ask the kid if he's got anything. He hands me a pocketknife but as soon as I flip it open, I hesitate.

I could carve up and down that entire cross and still not have enough room for all I want to say.

Hank Wright.

Friend.

Brother.

Unapologetic heathen and ladies' man.

God's favorite prodigal.

I can practically hear Hank's voice in my head as I falter.

Ain't you carved on me enough, son?

I drop down to my knees and etch two simple words:

"The Best."

51

SEPTEMBER 21, 1945

OMUTA, JAPAN

The rescue team that arrived three days ago let each man dictate a ten-word message to his parents. But when it was my turn, I didn't know what to say. How to sum up the last four years. The loss of Billy and Hank.

I ain't the son who left that night in July.

That boy is dead.

I don't even know if my daddy wants to hear from me, given the way we left things. But I figured I owed it to my mama to let her know.

So I dictated only "I am alive."

On board the train, the Japanese porter serves rice, vegetable soup, roast chicken, and wine. I eat the food, drink the wine. It don't take more than a glass to get me drunk and I sleep most of the trip, waking just long enough to stare out at a barren hellscape of ash and twisted steel. Of women and children trudging along the road with their possessions on their backs.

The next time we stop, I look out at the old men, women, and children huddled near the depot. There's a little kid on his mama's hip, sucking his fist the way Billy used to when he was hungry. Next thing

I know I'm pushing off the train and digging the roll I brought from camp out of my pocket. His mama shrinks back as I limp toward her, but the kid reaches for the bread. I give it to him and he mashes it to his mouth. Tears fill his mama's eyes. They fill mine too. I search my other pocket for the chocolate I saved from one of the drops. Even after food became abundant, the urge to hide it hasn't left me.

I give her the chocolate, hurry back onto the train, and sit down in time to see her waving the little boy's hand as we roll away.

"What're you doin' feedin' the enemy?" a fella sitting across from me demands.

"They ain't my enemy," I say.

Just before nightfall, we board the gangplank of an American Navy ship in Tokyo Bay. The big fellas there take one look at us and usher us straight into the mess hall, telling us to order anything we want. I chew my way through a steak and mound of mashed potatoes covered in gravy. But it's the chocolate ice cream that gets me. I stare at a double scoop like Mama used to buy me on special occasions at Woolworth's— minus the whipped cream, but served on a clean mess tray with a real spoon—and have to swallow the lump in my throat before I can even eat it.

I learn from a few other men that MacArthur returned to the Philippines almost exactly a year ago. That Wainwright was rumored to have been held prisoner in China—and he actually saved a ton of lives by surrendering. That Greta Garbo is alive and well.

We're deloused, given hot showers and new uniforms. They line us up to see the surgeon, who wants to ask about conditions in the labor camps. How much we ate. What kind of work we did. When I tell him about the mines and Camp Cabanatuan and O'Donnell before that, about drifting at sea for days after the hell ship, he puts down his pen and takes off his glasses.

"Son, you and I both know there's no way any man could have gone through all that on so little for so long and survived. You're about one more lie away from a court-martial."

I get up and walk out. Slam the door behind me.

We put ashore in the Philippines, where we get trucked to Clark Field. I can't believe this is the same place Billy, Hank, and me first witnessed hell; the sprawling base has been transformed with a dozen new runways and hundreds of buildings. They feed us burgers and French fries, Coca-Cola and fresh pineapple.

I think of Marisol and wonder if she and her father survived. If Andres made it back to his family, and what Felipa's been doing since the Japanese surrendered. If she's even still alive.

We wait three weeks for the next ship, during which time I collect my back pay in cash. There was a time when I would have gawked at so much money. Would have planned how to spend each dollar. Now I just stuff it in my barracks bag.

Early morning before I ship out, I roam the streets of Manila's old city. Stare at the ruin of the old Spanish walls, the burnt shell of Santo Domingo Church. The barracks I briefly called home and took so much pride in is gone, as though Billy and me never slept by the breezy bay windows up on the second floor or ate our fill of roast beef and creamed corn in the mess hall. The guardhouse is gone, along with the slop chute.

But as I pick my way through the ruins, I notice fresh, new tendrils of bougainvillea climbing their way through the rubble and remember how fast the cuttings Daddy brought home to Mama took root and climbed all over. I wonder what Mama's back fence looks like now. The backyard Claire, Billy, and me used to play in as toddlers seems more like a dream than a memory.

A leather-skinned woman comes over to me. She's the lone hawker here, at what was the main sally port where I used to see her every time I left the old city.

"Joe? Joe!" she cries with a toothless smile and grabs my arm with

364

her bony hand. She peers up at my face, and I know she's taking in my eye patch and sizing up how thin I've become. She's got an armful of garlands made out of the same flower that Marisol pressed into my hand on our march to O'Donnell.

"You remember me?" I ask with a smile.

"Yes! Yes! I remember!"

"I look a little different, don't I?"

She pats my cheek. "Same Joe. You going home?" she asks, with a nod toward the ocean liner towering over the pier.

"Looks that way," I say, unable to quite believe it—or bring myself to say it out loud. I've grown superstitious about getting my hopes up.

She lifts a garland from her arm, holds it up with both hands.

"For you, Joe."

I bend down and she lowers it over my head.

"Thank you," I say, my vision wavering. "How much for the rest?"

"All?" she asks, her brows lifting.

"All," I say.

I pay her twice her price and leave with a kiss on my cheek.

On board the ship, I pass my days sleeping—whenever the nightmares ain't too bad. Drink whatever I get my hands on when they are. Eat whenever I can. Despite the fact that I don't know what I'm going home to—if I even got a home to go home to—the excitement on the ship is contagious the closer we get to the States.

Arriving in San Francisco, I make my way to the rail with the rest of the fellas. There's more seagulls than people to greet us. No band, no mayor, no key to the city. And definitely no brand-new Ford.

But that's just fine with me.

52

I stare out the window as the train rolls into Mobile, the poplars and maples I've known all my life familiar and foreign to me at once. Stately and staid compared to the wild bougainvillea and roses of Manila, the jungle of Bataan.

A couple older fellas across the aisle are talking about the Crimson Tide's perfect season and the Mississippi State game this weekend in Tuscaloosa. It's weird, realizing football's been going on here like normal. I remember how I used to read about the games in the paper, my heart surging with pride every time I saw Cowboy's name. How I carefully tore out the page to give to Hank and his daddy each time.

The thought of Hank stabs me in the chest. It's followed by a surge of anxiety.

Claire doesn't know about Hank. I wonder if she even knows about Billy.

The train pulls into the big white station I used to think was a giant church when I was a kid. As I get off the train, I scan the platform for familiar faces, even though I ain't told anyone when I'm coming home.

That I'm coming home at all.

I head through the terminal to the street and glance back at the big, columned arches all along the first level. For a minute I ain't looking at the station at all, but the Manila Hotel with its white columned porticos decked out in garland for Christmas.

My reverie is broken by a passing car. The driver honks and I nearly jump out of my skin. I spin around in time to see a kid in the back seat waving. Takes me a minute to realize he's waving at me. That the kid's grin has turned to a stare.

I lower my chin and head up Beauregard Street to Spring Hill Avenue. When I reach the Dew Drop Inn, I'm winded—I ain't walked this far since before the explosion—my legs ache, and my stomach's growling.

But even though I've dreamed of their burgers and franks for years, I keep walking. Because no hot dog on earth is going to make the flutter in my belly feel any better.

I start to limp, but keep going, picking up speed past the high school, the last half mile as long as a hundred.

I turn up my street and finally slow, breathing hard. Stagger the last block, heart jackhammering in my chest.

Until I'm staring at my front porch.

It never seemed like much to look at before, but I swear I ain't never seen anything so perfectly unchanged in my life.

I hesitate, mouth dry, and move up the walk. Just as I reach the steps, the side door opens with a creak as familiar to me as my own voice.

The door falls shut with a slap. Someone calls from inside.

Mama.

Pulse pounding in my ears, I limp toward the corner of the house and stop at the sight of the figure lifting the lid off the old galvanized garbage can I dented the first week I learned how to drive.

He looks older, his salt-and-pepper hair nearly gray. He's thinner, I note, as he leans the lid against the side of the house and bends to lift the kitchen waste bin.

"Need a hand with that?" I hear myself say, my voice hoarse.

He gives a slight wave. "All good, thank you," he calls. He lifts the bin . . . and then goes still. Turning slowly, he looks directly at me for the first time, his expression stricken.

"Jimmy?" he rasps as though he ain't sure what he's seeing is real. The bin falls from his hands, clatters to the ground.

My father takes a step toward me and then breaks into a run, closing the distance between us in an instant. He grabs and pulls me into his arms with a broken cry.

"Jimmy! My Jimmy—my boy!"

He clasps me so hard I can barely breathe, saying only, "My boy, my boy . . ." over and over, shaking so hard I don't know which one of us is sobbing as he rocks me side to side.

"Hi, Daddy," I manage, holding on for dear life.

"You're alive," he sputters against my neck and then lifts his head. "Evelyn! Evelyn!" He pulls me toward the screen door he emerged from just a moment before.

Footsteps cross the kitchen floor inside. An instant later, my mother appears in the doorframe. She halts on seeing me, her eyes widening as her hand flutters up to flatten against the wire mesh. She mouths my name and then bursts from the house and throws her arms around me.

Mama fixes a mess of biscuits, swiping at her eyes so often I finally tease her that she won't need to add any salt.

"You just look so thin!" she says, biting back tears as she starts the gravy. "And your eye . . ."

"It's all right, Mama," I say.

Daddy calls in to the church and says he won't be going in today—that his son is home.

He don't leave my side through the entire morning as I protest that I'm too full for another bite and Mama asks over and over what I want for dinner. I say it don't matter at all.

"About a year ago, the Crocketts received a telegram from the War Department that Billy died," Mama finally says quietly.

And I don't know if I'm relieved or not that Mrs. Crockett knows, because that means Claire does too.

And I wonder if she hates me.

"Three," I say, shame constricting my throat. "He died three years ago."

He was seventeen.

For a moment, no one speaks. Daddy rests a hand on my shoulder.

"How's Claire?" I ask finally.

"Ah, well . . ." Mama says, shifting on her seat and glancing at Daddy and back to me.

"It's okay, Mama. I know."

She exhales, visibly relieved.

"Claire moved to Huntsville not long after you boys left. I suppose she was tired of having to explain herself. Can't say I blame her. It got so bad that her mama and the girls started attending the Presbyterian church."

"And her baby?"

"She had a little boy. He'll be four next month." She chuckles softly. "He's quite the charmer."

I can't help a wry smile. "I can only imagine."

"Did Hank Wright come back with you?" Daddy asks. This time, there's only curiosity in his voice at the mention of Hank's name.

I lower my head, shaking it. Try to school my expression, the tremor of my chin. And then hitch a breath, my mouth twisting.

Mama reaches for my hand.

"No," I manage. "Hank died savin' me."

I've never cried so hard as I do the rest of that day. And I can't remember ever crying on my daddy's shoulder before.

He holds me as I tell him everything, sputtering snot and tears. Not because he asked, but because I need to say it. Because I am empty even with so much taking up space inside me.

Because every man has a confession.

I tell him about the war. About the march to O'Donnell. How Billy died.

And about the mayor.

I expect him to push me away like poison.

But he don't let go.

53

Each night I get taken prisoner again. Sometimes the mayor visits me. Sometimes he turns into the Crate. Once or twice, I see Felipa in the swimming hole.

Every night I grapple for Hank as he lets go of the rope. Sprint to save Billy.

Wake up in a pool of my own sweat.

I help my daddy repair the back fence and build a new lattice for Mama's sweet peas. Wash up afterward and change into a clean shirt—and then realize my barracks bag is missing from its place beside my bed. I search my room with rising panic but can't find it anywhere.

"Mama?" I shout. "Mama!"

She comes hurrying down the hall. "Jimmy, what's wrong?"

"My bag. I can't find my bag," I say, my chest tightening.

"Why, I took the dirty clothes out and put it in the closet," she says. "Jimmy Propfield, what's gotten into you?"

I rush past her to the hallway closet, find and retrieve the duffel. Pull out the Bible the ship chaplain gave me, its pages perfumed by the white flowers pressed between them. Feeling for the inside pocket, I nearly collapse in relief.

Back in my room, I sit down hard on my bed with the duffel and empty the inside pocket's contents.

Two dog tags.

All I got left of Billy and Hank.

Sunday morning, I try on my old trousers and shirt Mama took in for me last night. As I turn sideways in the bathroom mirror to check the fit, I remember a time four years ago that I did the exact same thing in a freshly cut uniform when I was thirty pounds heavier with far fewer scars . . .

And one more eye.

I'd promised to get Billy's uniform cut down for him for his birthday.

I knot my tie and comb my hair. But when it's time to leave for church, I start shaking at the thought of all those people staring and asking me questions.

"Jimmy?" Mama says, laying a hand on my shoulder. "James, something's wrong!"

"It's all right, son. It's all right," Daddy says, steering me toward the sofa. "Evelyn, why don't you just stay here with Jimmy this morning—"

"I just need a minute," I say, waiting for him to tell me to get it together. That I need to make a showing.

"Trust me, son, you've heard today's sermon before," he says, patting my shoulder.

"But—what about dinner at the Boyingtons'?" I'd noticed the name on the wall calendar hanging over the Philco radio my parents acquired during my absence.

"I'll go just long enough to be polite and bring home dessert," he says, putting on his coat.

I look at him then, trying to reconcile the father I knew with the man he's become.

Mama takes off her gloves and sits down on the sofa beside me. As the truck pulls out of the driveway, I reach over and take her hand. That's when I notice the little pearl pendant hanging around her neck. It looks just like the tiny pearl I sent her what seems a lifetime ago.

"Is that—"

She smiles and reaches up to finger it. "Your father had it set for my birthday two years ago."

I try to imagine him going to the jewelry store, the pearl in his pocket. Picking out the thin gold chain.

"What happened while I was gone?" I ask.

She sighs and squeezes my fingers before letting them go. "A lot. You have to understand, your father loves you. He was devastated when you left. It may not have seemed like it, but he was. After Pearl Harbor . . ." she shakes her head. "The morning he saw the headline about the attack on the Philippines . . . I have never seen such a look on his face—such a terrible look on any man's face. He got on his knees and we spent the entire day praying. Our only consolation was that we knew you weren't at Clark Field."

I nod, seeing no reason to correct her.

"It got worse from there—for him, and for us. Pastors are not perfect. Neither are pastors' wives. It was difficult for both of us. I think we realized we had more differences than things in common. About a year ago, I considered leaving him."

My jaw drops.

She waves her hand in the air. "Obviously I didn't. But we did find out just how wounded we were. Your daddy stepped back from preaching for six months. He called it an unpaid sabbatical so the church would understand, but it was more than that."

"*What?*"

"He had something of a crisis of faith," she says. "Certain things just didn't seem to add up anymore."

"What happened? What did you do?"

"He took out some of our savings, and we left Alabama and just drove wherever the road took us. We went up north, and we went to Appalachia, and we talked, and we prayed, and we listened. I saw your daddy cry for the first time. I'd never seen him so lost. In a way, his being lost helped me find my place again."

"But he's . . . doing better now," I say carefully.

She gives a small shrug. "Only he can tell you that." She gets up. "Now. While you get changed, I'll make dinner."

That afternoon, I borrow the truck and drive to the Crocketts'. The gas station looks the same, though the paint on the sign has faded some. The "AND CAR REPAIR" line at the bottom has been covered by a board. Starting toward the side door I've gone in and out of all my life, I think better of it and make my way up the front porch. But before I can even lift my hand to rap on the door, a figure from inside yanks it open.

Betty, Claire's younger sister, stares at me, taking in the patch over my eye. For a minute I don't even recognize her but think I'm staring at Claire the year I first asked her to the school dance.

"Jimmy—is that you?" Before I can even answer, she's thrown her arms around my neck.

I hug her as her twin, Margaret, appears in the foyer. After blinking at me for an instant, she comes bounding out, yelling, "Mama! It's Jimmy!"

They talk excitedly, asking when I got back, Margaret swatting Betty's arm when she asks what happened to my eye, as Dorothy Jean appears on the stairs.

"What's all this ruckus?" Mrs. Crockett demands, coming from the direction of the kitchen, wiping her hands on her apron. On seeing me, she halts. Stares as though at a ghost. I worry she'll tell me to leave and never come back. To say her son is dead because of me.

Instead, she rushes toward me with a cry, sobbing as she folds me in her arms.

I stay there all afternoon, Dorothy Jean leaning against my shoulder and staring up at my eye patch as I tell them how Billy kept the men in good humor even during the worst of the war, how he saved me the night he brought me the soap and poured water over my head, washing the stink of death away. That he lived and died a hero.

When Mrs. Crockett tells the twins to take Dorothy Jean upstairs "so the adults can talk," I know she's about to ask me questions I'm not sure I want to answer.

But I do, telling her how he recovered from his wound on the march. How the Crate singled him out to ensure Hank and me would return from our mission. That Billy told us not to come back, ready to give his life for us. I break down in her living room as I ask her to forgive me for not being able to save him. She absolves me through her tears.

I reach into my pocket and hand her Billy's dog tag. The other is with his body. She covers her eyes and weeps, and I just sit in silence and let her as she dabs and dabs at her cheeks with her handkerchief. She's always been fair-skinned. I'm shocked at how translucent it's become, the shadows beneath her eyes like bruises.

"I reported the exact spot he's buried during interrogation on the hospital ship," I say. "I promise I'll do all I can—go anywhere, and testify anytime—to make sure the camp commander responsible for Billy's death is tried for his crimes."

Mrs. Crockett asks me to stay for supper, but I say I should get going.

"Your mama said you know about Claire and Roy," she says.

I nod. "Claire wrote a letter to Billy. We got it after he . . . We found out from the letter."

"You need to understand that I knew, but it wasn't my secret to tell," she says, sniffing and lifting her chin slightly. "The first person I told after Cowboy died was your mama."

I glance down at my hands. "Hank was fixin' to ask Claire to marry him right before he died."

"That boy always loved my Claire," she says.

"Yes, he did."

I rise to leave, then hesitate. "Ma'am, what happened to the garage? Did Billy's uncle shut it down?"

"Maurice died of pneumonia a couple years ago. I run the station—the girls help when they're not in school. But there's been no one to run the garage during the war."

"I'm sorry, ma'am."

"Thank you. It's been hard. And this town's changed. It's bigger now, and there's been violence. It's not the same place you boys left. Servicemen come by—it's hard for them, finding jobs. But I can't have just anybody around my girls." She hesitates. "Unless you need a job?"

"Just so happens I do," I say. "It would be good to get my hands greasy again."

She shakes her head slightly. "I couldn't pay you much, I'm afraid."

"I need the work more than the pay. If you'd send anything you want to pay me to Claire without mentioning my name, I'd be grateful."

"You sure? Because I'll take you up on the help. And be glad to send some extra Claire's way."

"Yes, ma'am," I say, as she walks me to the door. "Night, Mrs. Crockett."

I take the porch steps carefully, trying to hide my limp, and am halfway to the truck when Mrs. Crockett calls after me, "She's coming back for Christmas."

I turn back and nod.

My heart hammers the entire drive home.

The next morning, I gather up the small stack of Hank's effects and drive to the sawmill.

Few things in Mobile look the same since I got back, but the mill ain't changed a bit.

I can't say the same for Hank's daddy.

His thickset shoulders look frail, the lines of his face turned to furrows.

"I got a telegram a few days ago." He glances at the package of things in my hands. "I suppose you're here to tell me how my Hank died."

"I am. But maybe I oughta tell you how he lived first."

He sits down on a rough-hewn bench and pulls out a pack of cigarettes and offers me one. Lucky Strikes. We light up together.

I tell him about O'Donnell. How Hank smuggled food for Billy and me. About the hell ship and how Hank lost his arm and showed up in the infirmary.

About the last day of the war.

"Your son saved my life. And not just mine; he saved lots of lives with that brewer's yeast and whatever medicines he could find. That's how he lived—savin' others. And that's how he died . . . savin' me."

Mr. Wright's lips are trembling, and his jaw has clenched up repeatedly throughout my story. I hand him the package that includes Hank's dog tag and a hand-drawn map marked with his gravesite.

Finally, he says, "You make sure to do something good with your life." His voice cracks on the last word.

"I'll try, sir," I say.

"My Hank always was full of piss and vinegar—"

I sputter a laugh.

"But he was a good boy. He was *my* good boy. And you're welcome here anytime. You ever need anything, you let me know."

"Thank you." I choke the words out and get up to take my leave. At the door, I wipe my eye on my sleeve and turn back. "You should know, he wanted to be a doctor. He was fixin' to go to medical school."

"A doctor," he says faintly, and then nods. "Hank would've been a great physician."

"Sir, he was."

54

MOBILE, ALABAMA
DECEMBER 4, 1945

pull the board off the Crocketts' gas-and-repair-shop sign. Sweep
out the garage and take inventory. And find myself staring at Billy's
old Model T.

That afternoon I drive to the auto parts store. With my back pay, I
pick out a flathead V-8 and new set of tires, some long chrome headers,
and a couple new car seats. I borrow a welding torch and a spray-paint
machine.

I spend nights and weekends working on the car.

Sometimes Billy's mama comes out to see the progress. The day I
drop the engine in, she pulls me aside.

"When this car's ready, James Propfield, you take it out on the highway."

"Beggin' your pardon, ma'am, but I can't." I don't know how to
tell her that this was always Billy's baby. It ain't right to drive another
man's car.

"My Billy isn't here," she says. "But you are."

Three days before Christmas, I paint "The Ginger Streak" on the
side, complete with fiery flames the same color as his hair. The next
day, after it's dry, I take Billy's hot rod out on the highway, roll down the
windows, and holler and whoop into the wind, shouting Billy's name.

55

MOBILE, ALABAMA
DECEMBER 24, 1945

Every time I grab a broom, I think of Hank. I've even taken a stab at sweeping one-handed in his honor—only to wonder how he did it and give up.

It's Christmas Eve and Mama's cooking dinner. My aunt Betty and uncle John and at least five of my cousins are already there, having come in last night from Tuscaloosa. And here I am sweeping the cleanest shop floor in Mobile and stocking shelves that are already full. Waiting for Claire to arrive home.

Trying to summon my courage.

I don't know what to expect, which is why I'm prepared to say what I need to as fast as possible.

I just ain't sure what that is yet.

I'm so deep in my sweeping that I don't hear the car pull up at the pump. And I resent the intrusion as the bell above the front door jingles. I thought I locked that already.

"We close in five minutes," I say, looking up.

And there she is.

Her hair's shorter. And though I'd recognize her anywhere, standing there in her high heels and red lipstick, hat tilted on top of her head, she clearly ain't the seventeen-year-old girl I left behind, but a woman with sorrow and joy vying in her eyes, turning the corner of her mouth.

And no woman has ever been more beautiful.

"James Propfield," she says, lifting her chin. "I heard I might find you here."

My heart pounds in my ears.

"Claire," I whisper.

And for a moment, it's as though both a lifetime and no time at all have passed between us. Because even though I have no idea what the last four years have been like for her, I could sketch the cant of that gaze beneath those lashes, trace the bow of her upper lip, from memory.

I watch her take me in—from my missing eye to the fresh scars above my brow and my awkward stance on a leg that never healed quite right. If anyone ever considered me handsome before, I know they certainly would not now.

I wait for her anger. For her to rail at me in grief. For her to say I never should've made it back alone. Because I know I'm the last man who ought to be standing here right now.

Instead, she crosses the floor between us and clasps me with a cry.

I drop the broom. Close my arms around her. And realize they're trembling. That hers are too.

She smells like jasmine.

"I love you, Claire," I say, vision blurring. "I'm so sorry. I'm sorry . . ."

And then I'm crying, and I ain't sure who's holding who as her shoulders hitch with her breath, arms tightening around my neck.

"I missed you so much. I worried—I prayed for all three of you. I'm so sorry, Jimmy . . ."

"You kept me alive," I say, voice thick.

She pulls away, her mascara smeared, expression quizzical, as her eyes search mine.

"When I thought I was dying and would never come home . . . Claire, I know there's so much about the last four years that don't make sense, but one thing I know clear as day: I love you. I always have, but I was a coward. And I can't say I'm any better of a man today. But I do know that you could turn and walk out that door forever, and I would still love you the rest of my life."

"You were my best friend, Jimmy Propfield. My best friend and my first love. I was wrong to ever let you go." She shakes her head with a sniffle. "I hope one day you'll forgive me for that."

"I know your heart, Claire Crockett. I knew it then, and I know it now. There ain't nothin' to forgive. And if you still want me to, I'll be that best friend for you, Claire, with everything I am. For as long and as much as you need, for the rest of your life. And I will love you in any way you want, with all I got, whether you're with me or not. And I will love your son and do everything I can for him—anything you want. I may have only one eye left, but I see everything now. And I can say that, with all surety, for as long as I live, I will love and fight for you."

A fresh tear streaks down her cheek. She swipes at her eyes, clears her throat, and lifts her chin.

"Come by after church tomorrow, Jimmy. You hear?"

"Yes, ma'am," I say, as she takes my hand.

She smiles, her lashes wet. "I reckon there's someone you ought to meet."

56

Four-year-old Roy William Wright runs out the front door the minute I arrive and stares at the fishing pole I hold out toward him.

"For me?" he says, eyes wide. I have to force myself not to chuckle at the expression on his face because I know it so well. It was his uncle Billy's.

"Sure is," I say, a coffee can of worms in the crook of my arm. "Happy birthday, buddy. You ready to go?"

Claire comes out and hands me her old lunch pail, a napkin tucked on top. "He was so excited, he couldn't be bothered to eat," she says.

"That's all right," I say. "We've got all day."

"No, you don't," Claire says. "Your folks and Mr. Wright will be here at five o'clock for supper and birthday cake."

I turn to Roy. "Guess we better get to fishin'!"

I hand him the pole and we pose so Claire can get a photograph with her mama's camera before Roy takes off down the porch steps like a madman.

"You better hurry," Claire says, one brow arched slightly higher than the other, and I swear she's prettier than Vivien Leigh and Hedy Lamarr combined. "Or he'll disappear on you."

I stare at her for an instant longer, and then grab the lunch pail and take off after little Roy with a grin. I'll never be able to run like I used to before I broke both my legs. But a four-year-old's no match for me yet, at least.

We spend the morning fishing Three Mile Creek, eating cookies, as the sun climbs up over the water. At some point, I notice Roy staring out at it like he ain't here, but somewhere else.

"What're you thinkin' about, buddy?" I ask.

"I wonder if my daddy can see me," he says. "Him and my uncle Billy and uncle Hank."

I consider the wild ginger of his hair. The laughter in his eyes. The daring in his dimples—all of which have caused me to think I've seen Hank, Billy, or Cowboy out of the corner of my eye more than once today.

"Yes," I say, smiling at him. "I know they're all here."

AUTHORS' NOTE

Hours after crippling Pearl Harbor on December 7, 1941, the Imperial Japanese Army attacked the Philippines.

For the next four and a half months, Filipino and American troops fought back with fury. But without the support of a Navy, and with their backs against the sea, the Allied forces had no choice but to fight without reinforcements or fresh supplies. Sick, hungry, outgunned, and outmanned Allied troops fought a delaying action to hold the Bataan Peninsula.

At last the unthinkable order came. On April 9, 1942, approximately ten thousand American and sixty-two thousand Filipino soldiers laid down their arms on Bataan and became prisoners of war. It was the largest surrender of American troops in history. For some, the order to surrender came as a relief. But for most, their horrors were only beginning.

Allied troops were rounded up and marched sixty miles up the Bataan Peninsula en route to prison camps. Having underestimated the number of Allied prisoners and overestimated their condition, the Japanese were not prepared for the vast number of POWs in sick and emaciated condition. Although the exact death count is difficult to determine, historians estimate some six to ten thousand men died on the Bataan Death March alone.

Imperial soldiers had been indoctrinated not to show mercy for enemy soldiers, particularly those who surrendered. The prison camps became places of starvation, beatings, disease, and death. There was no art to staying alive—only luck.

In his book *Death March*, Donald Knox writes,

These Bataan men—most in their late teens or early twenties when the war began—entered a wilderness that had no rules. What a prisoner did to stay alive one day might cause his death the next. There were no maps to show a prisoner how to get from sunup to sundown alive. Every emotional and physical path had to be explored afresh each day. Men who did so successfully lived; those who didn't died.[1]

After enduring the prison camps of Bataan, some prisoners were shipped to the Japanese mainland and forced into additional hard work details. During the crossing, some men went insane in the bowels of the "hell ships," as they were called. Some men drowned.

Lt. Colonel Ovid O. Wilson writes,

Many men lost their minds and crashed about in the absolute darkness armed with knives, attempting to kill people in order to drink their blood or armed with canteens filled with urine and swinging them in the dark. The hold was so crowded and everyone so interlocked with one another that the only movement possible was over the heads and bodies of the others.

. . . A man's arm was removed with nothing to soothe his pain.[2]

1. Donald Knox, *Death March: The Survivors of Bataan* (New York: Harcourt Brace Jovanovich, 1981), xii.
2. From the deposition of Lt. Colonel Ovid O. Wilson, contributed by Jane Charmelo,

The Japanese ship *Arisan Maru*, among others, was sunk by an American submarine and took down with her more American prisoners than those who died at Camp O'Donnell. A rough count suggests that more than five thousand Americans died when Allied forces unwittingly bombed or torpedoed ships loaded with POWs.

Japan announced its surrender August 15, 1945. For the soldiers who surrendered on Bataan and survived, the entire war consisted of forty-one months of hell.

Regarding the mayor of Santa Rita: History has recorded how two American soldiers, Private First Class Blair Robinett and Private Leon Beck, escaped from Japanese imprisonment during World War II and freelanced for various guerilla squads in the Bataan outback.

The mayor of Santa Rita's exact role in having a young boy executed was never determined, but townspeople blamed him for the murder. Robinett and Beck decided the mayor was harmful to the resistance movement and went to the mayor's house late one night intent on executing him. When they knocked on the door, a woman who appeared to be his housekeeper answered and the mayor started yelling loudly from inside. With the Japanese garrison headquartered across the street, Beck and Robinett fled in the noise and confusion and split up to avoid being captured.

Later when Beck and Robinett reunited, they compared notes. They had learned the mayor had indeed been taken down to the railroad bridge and executed by an unknown killer. But both Beck and Robinett vehemently denied doing the killing.[3]

To this day, no one knows who killed the mayor of Santa Rita.

Oryoku Maru Online, accessed June 14, 2016, http://www.oryokumaruonline.org/lt_colonel_ovid_o_wilson_deposition.html.

3. Knox, *Death March*, 324–25.

Regarding Felipa Culala: The powerful female commander led a group of Filipino and American guerilla forces on Bataan in the region of East Pampanga.

Her unit was part of the Hukbo ng Bayan Laban sa Hapon (People's Army against the Japanese), popularly known as the Hukbalahap, or simply the Huks. She was sometimes known by the nickname Dayang-Dayang—a title that means "princess of the first degree."

U.S. guerilla Doyle Decker, who met her during the war, described her as "a gray-haired Filipina wearing two .45 pistols around her ample waist and carrying a Thompson submachine gun." She greeted them with a "stern but pleasant smile," and spoke to them in fluent English.[4]

The commander was known to roam her occupied homeland freely and wage her war in various clandestine ways. "She moved confidently through the forest, despite a high bounty placed on her head by the Japanese forces."[5]

She was executed by fellow guerillas in 1943 following accusations of financial impropriety.[6]

In May 2009, seventy-three survivors of the Bataan Death March met in San Antonio, Texas. This was the final time the American Defenders of Bataan and Corregidor met as a group before disbanding due to age.

---

4. Malcolm Decker, *From Bataan to Safety: The Rescue of 104 American Soldiers in the Philippines* (Jefferson, NC: McFarland Publishing, 2008), 118.

5. Kallie Szczepanski, "Felipa Culala, Guerrilla Leader in the Philippines," Asian History, accessed June 14, 2016, http://asianhistory.about.com/od/philippines/fl/Felepa-Culala-Guerrilla-Leader-in-the-Philippines.htm.

6. Teresita Gimenez Maceda, "Amazons of the Huk Rebellion: Gender, Sex, and Revolution in the Philippines (review)," *Philippine Studies: Historical and Ethnographic Viewpoints* 60, no. 4 (December 2012): 559–62, https://doi.org/10.1353/phs.2012.0032.

At the gathering, Japanese ambassador to the U.S., Ichiro Fujisaki, formally apologized on behalf of his country for "having caused tremendous damage and suffering to many people, including prisoners of war, those who have undergone tragic experiences in the Bataan peninsula."

Fujisaki closed with these words: "Today Japan and U.S. are the closest friends, best allies. But we should always keep in our minds . . . this status of past experience and efforts."[7]

The Bataan Memorial Death March takes place annually at White Sands Missile Range, New Mexico.

To learn more about the Defenders of Bataan, the Death March, and subsequent imprisonments of Allied soldiers, the following nonfiction books are recommended as a start:

Death March by Donald Knox. An oral history project done with sixty-eight of the Defenders of Bataan and Corregidor, published in 1981, when the veterans were in their early sixties.

Some Survived by Manny Lawton—a South Carolina native, college graduate, and U.S. Army captain imprisoned in the Philippines during World War II. As noted historian John Toland wrote in the introduction to Lawton's book, Manny is "a sensitive, objective man with a remarkable sense of recall."

Tears in the Darkness by Elizabeth Norman and Michael Norman. An authoritative narrative that chronicles the story of Ben Steele, a Montana cowboy and aspiring artist, who sketched many images from his imprisonment.

7. Vija Udenans, "Japan Apologizes for Bataan Death March," ABC News, May 30, 2009, http://abcnews.go.com/International/story?id=7717227&page=1.

In 2013, a World War II veteran told an interviewer, "We know a lot about Pearl Harbor and other things [today], but nobody knows about Bataan, unfortunately."[8]

We aim to help remedy that.

8. Lester Tenney, Voices of the Manhattan Project, interview by Cindy Kelly, president of the Atomic Heritage Foundation, December 3, 2013, http://www.manhattanprojectvoices .org/oral-histories/lester-tenneys-interview.

ACKNOWLEDGMENTS

Thanks to Kelsey Bowen, Michele Misiak, Andrea Doering, Karen Steele, Kristin Adkinson, Brianne Dekker, Laura Klynstra, Erin Bartels, Nathan Henrion, Mark Rice, Molly Nagelkirk, Hannah Hohman, Dwight Baker, and the entire team at Revell. Greg Johnson at WordServe Literary. Donald Caldwell. Erin Healy. Christina Boys. Stephen Parolini. Sherrie Saint and Sue Evans. Early readers H. C. Jones, Dorothy Brotherton, David Kopp, Robert Craddock, Becky Kimball, Bill Hamilton, Chantel Gardner, Cindy Schmit, Dave Smith, Paul Woodadge, Russell Humphrey, Tracy Compton, Maja Katinic, Jmar Gambol, Ton Aalbersde Jong, Ken Brehm, Gregory Wentworth, Kate Russell Wentworth, Tony Hughes, Scott Santos, Boy Eysbroek, Mick Reynolds, Steve Wallace, Laura Moncrief, Susan Jaskolka, and Peter Sheldrup.

Thank you to our spouses, Mary Margaret Brotherton and Bryan Ritthaler, and to our families. We are grateful for you every day.

DISCUSSION QUESTIONS

1. Before reading this book, how much did you know about the Pacific theater of World War II, and specifically the battles in the Philippines and for Bataan?

2. The story centers around four best friends: Jimmy, Claire, Billy, and Hank. How would you describe the personality of each character? Who do you identify with most?

3. How does Jimmy, Claire, Billy, and Hank's friendship as children differ from their friendship as young adults? Do their adventures remind you of any favorite times with friends during your childhood?

4. Discuss the intricate relationship between Jimmy and Claire. As boyfriend and girlfriend, what works between them? What doesn't?

5. Describe Jimmy's relationship with his mother and father. How does Jimmy's father embody—or not—the values he teaches in his role as pastor?

6. Do you think Claire is justified in breaking up with Jimmy? Discuss her choice to let him go—and Jimmy's efforts to win her back.

7. What surprised you most about the war in the Philippines and the battle for Bataan—or about the Allied surrender of 1942?

8. At the start of their incarceration at Camp O'Donnell, Jimmy is put on the grisly work detail of burying dead bodies. He is

saved by the gift of soap and fresh water from his friends. What do you believe to be the symbolism in this scene?

9. Hank and Jimmy are sent on a mission by the Crate during which time Jimmy, who prides himself on always doing what's right, is faced with a decision in which right and wrong aren't easily discernible. Would you take an innocent life to save a friend? When was the last time you faced a "gray" decision—and what did you do?

10. Female guerilla commander Felipa Culala existed in real life. What did you admire—or not—about her, and what would you be curious to learn more about as it relates to her life?

11. Before the mayor's time is up, he asks to see a priest so he can confess. The priest offers to hear Jimmy's confession, but Jimmy refuses. Why might someone like Jimmy, with his faith so affected by his father's religion, refuse the concept of grace?

12. While the boys endure the horror of Bataan, Claire goes through her own difficult time at home. What might it have been like in that era to be unwed and pregnant?

13. Chapter 41 is one of the most unique in the book in that it contains only one sentence. What does this chapter mean to the story overall, and what was your reaction when you read it?

14. The identity of the one-armed, broom-sweeping medic is revealed late in the book. How is this version of Hank different from the one you described in questions 2 and 3?

15. Discuss the changes in Jimmy, his mother, and his father after Jimmy returns from war. How does Jimmy eventually find grace/redemption—or does he? In what ways has he changed the most?

16. How does the friendship of these four friends come full circle by the book's end?

ABOUT THE AUTHORS

Marcus Brotherton is a *New York Times* bestselling author and coauthor dedicated to writing books that inspire heroics, promote empathy, and encourage noble living. Notable works include *A Bright and Blinding Sun*, *Shifty's War*, *A Company of Heroes*, *We Who Are Alive and Remain*, and *Blaze of Light*.

Born in 1968 in Canada, Marcus earned a bachelor's degree from Multnomah University in Portland, Oregon, and a master's degree from Biola University in Los Angeles, where he graduated with high honors. He and his wife have three children and live in the Pacific Northwest. For more information, please visit MarcusBrotherton.com.

Tosca Lee is a *New York Times* bestselling author of eleven novels, including *The Line Between*, *The Legend of Sheba*, and *Iscariot*. Her work has been translated into seventeen languages and has won two International Book Awards, Killer Nashville's Silver Falchion, and ECPA Fiction Book of the Year.

Born in 1969 in Virginia, Lee earned her bachelor's degree in English from Smith College. She also studied at Oxford University. A former first runner-up to Mrs. United States, she lives in Nebraska with her husband and three of four children still at home. For more information, please visit ToscaLee.com.

CONNECT WITH
MARCUS

marcusbrotherton.com

CONNECT WITH
TOSCA

toscalee.com